THE POTTERY MAKER

MAKER

A story for the people of the world

By

KARL BOHANAN

For my daughter Sophie.

CONTENTS

ACKNOWLEDGMENTS

My thanks go to Adam and Michelle for their utmost encouragement and inspiration.

To the Chicagoans who I encountered at the Art Institute, and to the people at the Cahokian ancient city -hospitality unbounded.

Thank you to the wonderful cultures of the world, for the richness you bring to this good Earth.

PART ONE

PEOPLE OF THE WILD ONION

Prelude I

The blackened, wrought iron door of the earthen kiln opened slowly. A brilliant light shone into the dark, web infested room, revealing the cracks and mould on the damp walls. Lines of dust and rot on the floor became exaggerated as the light transcended all points of this hidden place. Next to the kiln was an old tri-legged round table made out of cotton wood; placed upon it a stone tablet, perfectly square in shape bearing the chequered markings of a game board. Golden hieroglyph symbols adorned each of the board edges, shimmering in the incandescent light, as if they were chattering, and coercing.

Earthen clay figurines stood on the tablet in rows – facing each other, militaristically, their intricate facial and bodily detail making them appear to dance and jostle in the emerging shadows. The Pottery Maker looked down upon them, hardly daring to keep eye contact because of their sinister and morose presence, it was as if the figurines were morphing into miniature marionettes about to come to life.

The Pottery Maker stared at the ancient instruction, marveling at its significance, expectantly fearful of its transcending revelation. Next was the task of inserting the stone board and the life like figurines into the kiln. The figurines were on the board as instructed, now in this ancient hearth they would dance - they would dance to a tune of spiritual misdemeanour, a dance of precedent.

Scorching heat was to forge them, rejuvenation was to envelope them. A transformation would take place that would define the spiritual balance of the world, a destiny that the Pottery Maker had no control of, for he was merely forsaken to help forge the ancient prophecies.

He braced his body, wincing at the prospect of seeing the latest creation, now only time would tell; time a concept barely understood by humankind, but one the Pottery Maker had endured above all others.

The definable clunk of the locking mechanism ensured that the door of the kiln was shut tight…and then the Pottery Maker stood back, head bowed, waiting for the moment of truth. Nothing could alter the prophecy now, the transformation was set in motion…time knows no bounds.

Chapter 1

The News Breaks

It wasn't that Sam was overly annoyed about returning home early from vacation, nor the fact that he had woken an hour before his alarm was due to sound; it was more the self-regret at the petulance he had offered his Bureau Chief, Carl Walters, during the time of that dreaded phone call. A phone call that had dragged Sam away from an important visit, a visit that had somehow unsettled his soul, and one which had revealed more questions than answers. It was now 4.30 am on Friday, the day after his return from Cuba.

Cuba - how exciting it had been – initially at least; it was the culmination of a hectic tour of the West Indies, re-discovering some of his family roots, visiting relatives he had never encountered before. His last stop, which had been cut painfully short, had been in the capital, Havana. He had been enjoying a

3

resplendent open top bus tour of the City's refinery, basking in the heat, marveling at the old colonial and baroque buildings whilst watching the ancient automobiles parading along the streets. He had been witness to a carnival atmosphere within the central Plaza Vieja, 'The Old Square' - situated in Old Havana – a Plaza adorned with four centuries of colonial architecture enveloping the grey brick cobbled expanse. People were enjoying a new found freedom it seemed – the locals mingling together with invigorated American and European tourists, soaking up the splendour. Sam had visited, as was his custom for such things, the 'Museo de la Revolucion', expanding his knowledge on the complex recent history of such a small isle. He had been engrossed in the contradiction of the Museum Palace, whose interior design by Tiffany's of New York, had been left intact by Fidel Castro as testament to his overthrowing of the American backed Fulgencio Batista.

It was at that moment - when delving into the rituals of the former dictator, Batista - Sam received the fateful telephone call from his Chief, telling him to come home from his holiday. The telephone call had shattered Sam's indulgence and he rued the fact his phone had been switched on – yet the call must have been urgent for Carl Walters to have even dared contact him on vacation.

Events explained to him in such a way by Walters had made Sam depart from Cuba early, leaving him unfulfilled. An empty space filled his heart, one he couldn't really fathom but one he knew was born from, at times, the frosty reception he had received from his mother's relatives whilst staying just to the west of Havana in a small residential town called Bauta. His mother's family were generational farmers, growing fruit and vegetables in the surrounding Bauta countryside – and were renowned musicians with a penchant for living life to the full. Having pre-conceived ideas of this, Sam had been perturbed at the reaction from his Bauta relatives. It was there for the first time he had met some of his maternal aunts and uncles along with a string of cousins he never knew existed. Although initially welcoming, they had looked upon him cautiously and with some suspicion; he couldn't quite figure out why.

Sight-seeing in the wonderful city of Havana was helping him deal with those estranged emotions from people whose reaction had also ignited the sadness of the death of his mother, Georgia, so many years ago. Any deliberation about the odd reception Sam had received from his mother's relatives would be a question for his father, James, upon Sam's return.

Now, back home in his apartment, Sam transcended his thoughts to real time. It seemed that a precarious situation had arisen in Chicago, one that Sam had not rationalised properly through his initial distemper. He climbed out of bed, stretching his tired, jet lagged body out of slumber and stared at the clock, cursing its presence, before walking into the open plan living room; black coffee was needed, his dry mouth beckoned for liquid.

Lucid thoughts returned and a brutal reality took shape. A number of his fellow police officers had been mercilessly attacked in somewhat bizarre circumstances, four of them in a serious condition, two of the four extremely critical – not expected to survive. The nature of the attack was undeniably disturbing, as was the curious fact that Carl Walters had been explicit in the need, at this point anyway, for restricting the level of detail offered to Sam. Walters, had made the hasty telephone call eighteen hours ago, informing Sam that he must report home for a live television broadcast with Chicago WGN9 News Group on Friday morning - this very morning.

Coffee in hand, Sam stood by his living room window, looking across the Chicago City skyline, the Willis Tower in the distance just starting to catch the emerging sunrise. His natural inquisitive mind searched for some reasoning to the perplexing events, before the radio alarm in his bedroom sounded with a nauseous 'Good morning Chicago', reverberating around the whole apartment. He cursed the clock again, and cursed himself for forgetting to switch the alarm off.

He meandered back into his bedroom and removed his Police Commander's uniform from the wardrobe, checking that the gold coloured name badge was in the right place, just above the top left pocket of his tunic. The dark blue uniform, with its gold maple leaf lapels, was pristine - and the name badge stood out, ensuring any onlooker would not mistake the owner's full name; Samuel Campbell.

Once dressed, Sam stood in front of the large bedroom mirror, staring at his dark brown complexion, habitually pinching the skin on the back of his hand to test its pliability and see how long it would take to settle; at 45 years of age, he was beginning to see a hint of change.

The intense, arcing sunlight poured into his apartment from the south facing bedroom window making him squint as the light caught the edge of the mirror, soon to consume the whole object. He continued to stare at his reflection, noticing the lines in his brow, his flat perfectly shaped nose and the hint of grey in his tight, neatly trimmed, black hair - cut just long enough so that he could look and feel every part of his African American heritage.

His thoughts transcended again as his mind swayed back and forth from the task he had been given, and the events in Cuba. Samuel Campbell was a man of profound thoughts, having a deeper sense, which he would sometimes find difficult to contain. It was inherent within him, part of his complex character and he would find himself continually questioning everything; even his own intuition, which at times seemed all consuming.

He walked out of his fifth floor apartment and into the communal elevator, still scoping his experience in Cuba – it had made him reflect on who he was and where he had come from. He knew that the name Campbell must be a 'slave' name, a name that had perhaps travelled from England to the New Territories in the seventeenth and eighteenth centuries; perhaps a name for the owners of a cotton or tobacco plantation in the 'New World'. His thoughts elaborated on his name and ancestry, picking up on what his father had once told him - that a long time ago modern humans had descended from one place…Africa. The prospect of whether a great human migration (a procession of homo-sapiens out of the vast African continent) had actually occurred tens of thousands of years ago, for Sam, was an enduring question.

The walk from the apartment block to the famous Tribune Offices in North Michigan Avenue was a brisk one, his contemplation of all things never far from his mind. Cuba, Africa and the impending interview seemed to compound in his thoughts as he struggled for sense.

The Tribune Centre stood opposite the junction with Illinois Street, across from the Chicago River, and still had the old Chicago Tribune newspaper sign adorning the right hand side of the Neo Gothic building, reaching out its 1920's prowess to a modern audience. The policeman stared at his surroundings, noticing the pleasure boats already running their engines for a day's work ahead – and early tourists with their cameras pointing up and down the river sections, snapping at the Tribune complex, then turning their heads in the opposite direction towards the tall Donald Trump skyscraper, its ground floor facing right onto the river front.

Heading for the Tower section, Sam walked across the small plaza in front of the Tribune offices, making a beeline for the WGN 9 News Group. He stopped and peered through the reflective windows of the entrance lobby and pondered again. He was perplexed as to why he had been pushed into giving a live television interview on something he had very little information about. Although desperate to know and willing to get involved in any way he could, he felt vulnerable and unprepared – not something he was used to. Carl Walters had given him enough to get by, but Sam knew that he was going to have to use all of his remaining guile if he was to convince the Chicago public of the police story.

An impressive black and white tiled floor dominated the entrance lobby, and a plush mahogany reception desk immediately caught the eye of persons entering the famous media centre, the surround of the lobby not shy of the latest hi-tech TV screens adorning the walls.

'Commander Sam Campbell, Chicago Police Department, I am here to see the morning news crew,' said Sam, sounding a little nervous.

An unexpected reply came from the receptionist.

'I remember your father,' the man said, staring directly at Sam. 'He was a reporter at the Chicago Tribune, I know…I used to work with him at the paper'.

Taken aback by the comments, trying to process the information, Sam noticed the receptionist was an aging man, dark skinned with long grey hair, not balding, but very thick, tied in a smart pony tail. The man looked very much Native American - a man, Sam thought a little naively, who would not have looked out of place riding bare horseback across the plains.

The retort by the receptionist was not unusual, many people in the media business seemed to know or had worked with Sam's father; nevertheless, Sam was slightly bemused by the comment.

'My name is Mike,' said the receptionist. 'Mike Tremble…your father will remember me, if you see him soon, please mention my name and give him my regards if you will, I'll leave you my details.'

Sam paused, reflecting again on the direct comments. 'Mike, it is a pleasure to meet you and my instinct would be to indulge further about my father, yet I am curious...did we ever meet?'

'I saw you as a child, but only briefly – I doubt you would remember. I moved away and lost touch with your father for a while. I remember you at your father's house out in the suburbs, but that seems a long time ago. Forgive me... I'll show you the way to the interview prep room.'

The Native American man busily shuffled some paper and handed Sam a visitor's pass before taking him to the prep room just a few metres along the main corridor. Sam looked at Mike Tremble, and although struggling to remember him as one of his father's acquaintances, there was an element of pride realising just how well known and revered his father was.

'How is retirement for your father Sam?' Mike queried as he ushered Sam through a heavy duty red door into the prep room. 'I remember him being one of the most respected reporters and columnists of his time, he took the Chicago Tribune into a new era...as I recall he broke many racial barriers, one of the very first African American reporters to work on international stories.'

'He is fine... and yes I will be seeing him over the weekend...I'll be sure to let him know about you.'

Dry powder adorned Sam's brow after the makeup team had encrusted his face, and at one point he thought the stuff would glue his eyes together as he prepared himself to be on air. A famed newscaster by the name of David Wilmshurst walked into the prep room; he was a short, rounded, middle aged man with a ruddy complexion, dressed in a smart grey suit, white shirt and a red tie with gold coloured initials 'DW' emblazoned on it. The brief dialogue with Sam left the Police Commander with no uncertainty - the conversation, live on air, was not going to be easy.

'David and Commander Campbell…we go on 5,4,3…,' the last two digits displayed in silence as the woman with the clip-board gave the two men the prompt. Sam was now live on television, facing the hardened expression of his renowned interviewer.

The TV cameras were menacingly honed towards Sam's chair as he fought to concentrate through his tiredness, nerves and the searing heat of the TV lights cooking him inside his police uniform, all of which seemed to make his heart pound through his chest.

'Good morning ladies and gentleman and welcome to a special live broadcast from Chicago WGN9 news room. The breaking news yesterday of the vicious robbery at the Chicago Art Institute has caused a sensation, not least of which we now know has revealed the theft of an expensive piece of art – but perhaps despairingly, we have discovered that the painting was in the hands of the Chicago Police Department at the time of the violent attack. Police officers have been seriously hurt.'

Heartbeat tripping, hearing the beat through his eardrums, Sam's attention was drawn to the hard stare of the newscaster. The policeman took a deep breath, composing himself, ready to make the most deliberate comment he could muster.

Wilmshurst interrupted and fired the first awkward question.

'Commander, as you can imagine the Chicago public requires an explanation to the events yesterday and you have a chance here to explain the circumstances. I am intrigued, what on Earth happened with your colleagues at the Institute?'

'David, I do not want to make any excuses on live TV as to why the painting has been stolen, and I would hate to think the public may suspect any foul play on the part of the police. But we do know that the painting is very valuable, and I have a number of police officers injured…,' said Sam, stumbling.

Wilmshurst maintained the pressure, 'Yes, yes I accept the concern about the police officers and we all hope that they recover, but I hear the painting is believed to be worth ten million dollars, and we need to know why the police fouled up by having it stolen from them - you can understand the public's speculation, surely?'

A further barrage of questions came as Sam looked visibly perplexed on air, and Wilmshurst became more and more animated.

'I think we want to know how the City is going to solve this Commander, and I am sure we would all like to know who owns the painting and why the police got involved in the first place? And who are the culprits - and where are they now?' Wilmshurst retorted, making Sam squirm.

'I believe it is a valuable, somewhat mysterious painting, and yes it was in police possession for protection,' said Sam. 'Officers have been badly injured and we are treating this matter very seriously, the painting is one thing, but the way my police officers were attacked is another…'

'Commander, forgive my intrusion but everyone, I am sure, wants to try and understand what the Chicago Police Department were doing to make such a mess of this. If someone is prepared to attack the police in such a violent way, what chance have the rest of us?'

'I appreciate the concern and I know how it looks, but the high value of the painting, which I have to say has only very recently been found out, determined that it needed to be moved – and quickly,' explained Sam, frantically trying to sound genuine.

'The Art Institute of Chicago is full of valuable things – why not put it in the museum vaults? I heard it's like Fort Knox,' drilled Wilmshurst.

'Well…what we know is that the painting had been exhibited in the lobby area of the Institute, not that noticeable to anyone really. No-one knew of its true value until a couple of days ago.'

'I heard it was an Egyptian lady, a Benefactor of some kind…she was the one, I have been told, who pointed out the painting?' said Wilmshurst, interrupting again.

'Look David, there is a lot we need to do and I will be speaking to many people connected to the Institute.'

'So are you the main investigator for the enquiry?' queried Wilmhurst, quickly.

Damn! Sam thought; whilst under the spot light his mind had raced away from him. Walters had hinted previously that he should take the lead with the investigation due to the potential escalation of events, but he hadn't wished to reveal that part on air.

'I will be working with many of my colleagues to try and get to the bottom of this theft and vicious attack on my officers,' replied Sam, unable to think of anything else to say.

Wilmshurst didn't press any further, there was not enough air time, and the interview concluded. Sam wiped the sweat and congealed makeup from his brow, he nodded to Wilmshurst with a nervous smile and walked off set. He was furious with himself, cringing with embarrassment. Much of what he wanted to say did not come out, he hated being on the back foot, Carl Walters had to be spoken to.

So far, all Sam had been told was that a 'mysterious' Benefactor for the Art Institute had deemed the painting in question, valuable - and had wanted it removed for authentication. The Benefactor had visited the Art Institute on Wednesday, the police got involved on Thursday and the rest was now all over the news.

Walters had told Sam that the initial accounts from the Art Institute staff revealed how the Institute Benefactor had become intrigued by the painting. The Benefactor's name was Anippe Khu, a lady from Egypt. Sam had been told nothing more, other than Walters explaining to him that Anippe Khu had supposedly set the value of the painting herself. Whether she was trying to gain attention to it, no one knew at this stage. Walters had gone on to tell Sam that the lady had offered to purchase the painting at the very price she had set...*a very odd set of circumstances*, Sam thought.

Sam had been asked by Walters to appear on TV, in an attempt to explain the police perspective. The intention was for Sam to be humble, honest and apologetic, perhaps gaining sympathy for the plight of the injured police officers. This didn't happen, although it had not yet been revealed how critically injured his fellow police officers were. In any event the public focus was now on the mysterious valuable painting and the daring heist against the police. Everyone did indeed want to know who the culprits were.

The Police Commander returned to his apartment and quickly changed into his every day, dark grey, two-piece, pinstriped suit – a mark of his detective status. At the point of preparing to contact Carl Walters, the apartment phone rang - uncannily in anticipation.

Instinctively, Sam recognized the bellowing tone of his Chief, a fellow African American police officer who was a formidable, principled character with a strong moralistic approach to life, perhaps (as Sam perceived) endured through indignation and prejudices suffered by Walters early on in his career.

'Sam, I thought I would take a chance and catch you at home, a difficult job you just had, and I appreciate what you did.'

'I wouldn't ask you to presume that I would thank you for it, although I did flounder if that is what you mean,' said Sam, slightly annoyed.

'You did what I asked and forgive me, I just needed a face on the TV, you came over honest in the least.'

'Perhaps, but joking apart Carl, we need to get a grip of this and I certainly need more answers.'

'Sam, there is quite some mystery to this painting, I will admit – but I was keen to engage the media as soon as I could, it makes them move onto the next thing sometimes. The trouble is we have injured officers and the media don't know the extent of that yet. Families of those men and women want to know what went wrong and I can't reveal any more information to them just now.'

A little perplexed at Walters' comments, Sam wasn't sure whether Walters was hiding something because of genuine concerns or whether his Bureau Chief was being steered from elsewhere. Sam's honesty was always matched by Walters' diplomacy in these circumstances – *a true politician if ever there was one,* Sam thought; however, the public face of Carl Walters was something different than the hard-nosed policeman in reality.

'How did the painting get into and then out of our hands, and can you tell me what the plan is now?' said Sam, pushing for answers.

'Come and see me in the morning, I'll be in my office first thing, we'll put our minds to the task, you will need to take the lead on this inquiry, I will get some people to work with you.'

Sam was puzzled.

'I would like to start right now, we seem to be off the pace, this thing was stolen from our grasp yesterday, surely?'

'Not quite off the pace, I've got some people working on it, forensics and such like. There is a meeting later tomorrow with the Art Institute staff, together with the insurance team, you could link into them.'

The last comment was a directive; Sam being loath to argue the point. As usual, his thoughts were perplexed – this was indeed quite a mystery and much background work was needed. He was not going into any kind of meeting cold. It was now 2:30 in the afternoon - Friday; the Art Institute of Chicago would not shut until 5pm, time for him to get there and conduct some meaningful investigation.

Chapter 2

Oddities

The Art Institute of Chicago was a place Sam had visited many times. It was a wonderful building, with a symmetrical design showing off its nineteenth century architectural prowess through an elaborate angled central roof section. It had a grand presence set against the other, rather plain buildings existing in South Michigan Avenue, and the splendour of the two magnificent bronze lions guarding the steps to the entrance was all enticing to any onlooker.

Taking a moment to look up towards the roof line, Sam caught a glimpse of famous names that had been carved on the upper tier wall adjacent to the roof itself; names of people that he revered, such as Michael Angelo and Da Vinci, ones that inspired his curiosity with all manner of things. With anachronism, Sam would often ponder what it would have been like to meet such people. To be able to watch Michael Angelo paint the Sistine Chapel in Rome during the sixteenth century was a frequent day dream.

Walking up the steps, in between the bronze statuesque lions, the policeman passed through the arched entrance into the main hall of the building. He stood in the lobby, noticing the tourists busying themselves trying to get tickets, and the Art Institute staff standing either side of the central reception desk, hurriedly trying to cope with the influx, as excited people rushed into the heart of the building, eager to see the wonderful artifacts. Leading from the lobby was a huge central stairway, designed in a concave X shape, impressing any observer – daring people to visit every annex of the spectacular surround. Within its famous rooms, the Institute housed one of the finest African and Native American pottery collections in the United States.

'The Curator please,' said Sam, showing his police badge as he approached the reception desk.

'The head Curator is not here, I can get one of the deputy curators for you, replied the young woman behind the desk, taking a closer look at Sam's badge.

'Okay, that's fine, can you give me a name please?'

'The lady available today is Joyce Marsh, I'll make contact with her. She is actually the Archive Manager but represents the Curator's office. If you would like to take a seat, I'll phone her.'

Sam politely declined to be seated, he was too keen to look around the grand Institute foyer, ambling around the pottery figures and paintings that seemed to tease prospective onlookers as to what lay beyond. He mused at his surroundings, reflecting on the times that his father, James, had brought him here. They would both be as giddy as school children every time they entered, excited to see something new, never having time to see it all. The record and collection of American arts along with detailed African artefacts was to be beholden. Sam was convinced that his incessant curiosity to learn all manner of things was due to his regular visits here.

'I'll take you to her office,' said the receptionist. 'It's on the basement floor.'

Sam followed, continually eying up the contents of this fascinating place. Before reaching the steps to the basement section he stopped and stared at a new artifact, the likes of which he had not seen in the Institute before. It was a rectangular block of stone, over two metres high, engraved with a system of people scenes, depicting a historical event. It was an ancient, magnificent Buddhist 'Votive Stele' – a Stele devoted to the people of religion; a vow of dedication. He fathomed that the scenes were a form of sacred text, perhaps handed down from one generation to the next, which for him was a fascinating insight into another world.

'Sir, this way please,' motioned the young woman, Sam begrudgingly turning his attention away from the Stele.

The steps led to a more enclosed system of corridors, each adorned with encased artifacts and paintings from Europe. Sam was further distracted by the ornate miniature 'English Rooms' - a combination of intricately detailed Georgian and Victorian stately rooms, modelled behind small glass cases. It was as if they were actually real and he fully expected miniature people to be sitting at the dining table or climbing out of one of the tiny four poster beds.

The Deputy Curator's office was adjacent to these wonderful models. The receptionist opened the door, leaving Sam to sit on the guest's leather sofa and to await the arrival of the occupier. There was an elaborate dark oak desk, centre piece to the room, upon which was a standard decorative green lamp with its light on. Each of the four walls had spectacular photographs and paintings of animals from all corners of the globe. Lions, tigers, elephants, sea creatures and creatures of the arctic such as the magnificent polar bear – all engrossing, all eye catching and perhaps a testament to the adventures of the person who occupied this office.

Waiting patiently, Sam heard the loud tannoy ring out, calling for Ms. Marsh to attend her office. A woman rushed in, slightly out of breath, peering at the policeman who seemed to be staring at the pictures with intrigue.

'Hello, I am Joyce Marsh, the Deputy Curator – well, actually, I am the Archive Manager in my real job, but as you can imagine, extenuating circumstances have put me in this position…I am sure you understand. How can I help you?'

Sam smiled, her attractiveness hit him instantly, and perhaps biasedly, he thought the English accent seemed to befit her pale skin and full bodied auburn hair.

'Please take a seat at the coffee table, I'll get some coffee, or would you prefer tea?' she said.

'Black coffee please,' said Sam.

'I don't like to sit behind desks talking to people…I noticed you were looking at the photograph of the Tiger? My father took that picture in India...I must have been about ten years old, I was with him when he took it...a bit scary, but we knew the beast had eaten and was probably ready for a nap after a full belly,' said Joyce, nonchalantly. 'Impressive don't you think?'

'Yes, indeed,' said Sam, immediately intrigued by this woman before him.

Despite her bravado, he detected a little nervousness about her, which was probably understandable with the events unfolding as they were. He also noticed that she had natural warmth, with a friendly attractive smile and a distinct feminine poise. Joyce Marsh was slim but quite athletic in stature. Looking no older than her 35 years, she had refined, distinctive facial features, including a slightly long, symmetrical nose, blending with her attractive face. Sam noticed her high cheek bones and distinctive jaw line, her well-kept teeth and looked again at her striking shoulder length, wavy auburn hair. She wore a smart, blue pinstriped suit and white blouse, impressing Sam with her attire and countenance.

'You must be here to talk about the painting. Of course, I never knew how important it was, it has come as a bit of shock to us all, if only we had known. We would have taken our own precautions. Have you any news? Has it been recovered? Is there anything you would like me to do?'

Sam nodded in acknowledgement to the torrent of questions, trying to relax himself as they sat on the easy chairs around a small pine coffee table. He also had a heavy load of questions on his mind but he knew he would have to temper it a little, he didn't want to make a fool of himself like he did earlier during the live TV broadcast.

'Can I take you back a step and talk about the type of painting it was. And can you give me some information on the Benefactor - her name was Anippe Khu I believe? Additionally, can you let me know why the police had been asked to transport the painting?'

Joyce smiled, the last question was a little odd she thought, *surely he should know that or was such a question just a ploy?*

Her nerves subsided a little as she answered. 'Mr. Campbell, please excuse me, I know you are a policeman, I just didn't expect you to sound like one so readily.'

'Excuse me?' replied Sam.

'I am sorry that you couldn't speak to the Curator, my actual job is to manage all of the requisitions and archives. I am actually the second in command, if you pardon the expression. I try to keep a handle on all that we have here.'

Sam nodded, feeling a little humbled.

'I apologise Ms. Marsh, It's been a frantic day and in my haste I have been trying to piece things together, I am slightly confused like everyone else, even with some of my own colleagues.'

'I am sorry too,' said Joyce. 'The absence of the Curator has thrown the staff off balance here.'

'I see – perhaps we could just start with what the painting looks like?'

Joyce went on to explain that she couldn't recall

what the picture actually portrayed, but she did know it had been displayed with a small group of other paintings depicting art and craft through history. It had been displayed in a corridor leading from the main lobby, just underneath the grand staircase. She described that the Curator, Mr. Krell, had been contacted a week ago by one of the main benefactors of the Art Institute. Her name was confirmed to Sam as Anippe Khu, a Director at the Cairo Museum in Egypt.

'I don't know what conversations Ms. Khu and Mr. Krell had had on the phone, but she arrived at the Institute here in Chicago on Wednesday afternoon, this week,' Joyce explained.

'Did you see or speak to her?'

'Only briefly…she explained to a group of us that she had flown into Chicago to examine various artifacts and paintings here in the Institute. She said she wanted to cross reference and match items she had got at the Cairo Museum.'

'But you said she was a Benefactor here?'

'Yes she is, but I hadn't realised to what extent. I have found out since, that she is extremely wealthy in her own right, acting as a patron to us as well. She links in to our Board of Directors quite frequently I am told.'

'Interesting,' said Sam. 'How did she focus on the painting?'

'This is the confusing bit. Having had a look around the building for a couple of hours she signalled to Mr. Krell for a private chat in his office. None of us were in the room, so I have no idea what was said. After about half an hour, Ms. Khu came out and went straight to where the craft paintings were situated in the corridor, leading from the lobby. She asked for one in particular, pointing out that Mr. Krell had given her authority to remove it.'

'Did you see this?'

'Not particularly, although generally aware, I had enough of my own work to do - so I left them to it.'

Explaining further, Joyce stated that Ms. Khu had considered the painting extremely valuable and that she needed to take it back to Egypt to have it properly examined and authenticated. The painting had no individual name and its suggested value seemed extortionate; in the millions of dollars.

'Ms. Khu had it removed from the wall, packaged and placed with the security guards - their office situated at the back of reception. The police arrived early yesterday morning to collect it from the guards and transport it to the airport. They never got there; after being handed the painting, the police were attacked in the Institute basement car park…surely you know this Mr., Campbell?'

Sam didn't dare reveal how little he actually knew at present.

'I guess the police bit is for me,' said Sam. 'So I presume Anippe Khu left for Egypt on her pre-arranged flight - obviously now without the painting. Why didn't she stay? Or perhaps she did stay?'

'I have no idea. I don't know how contactable she is. You don't think she set this whole thing up?'

'Maybe…but it doesn't make any sense,' said Sam.

'What was Mr. Krell doing all this time, I mean from the point after his conversation with Ms. Khu?'

'I don't know. No-one has seen him since Wednesday night. I need to do some digging to get to the bottom of this, including re-checking the systems for the original sale of the painting – unless it was donated. I need to know Mr. Campbell, whether any money has already been exchanged…and if so, who has got it?'

'What I can't understand is why the painting was released so quickly?' said Sam. 'Surely there should have been a referral to the Institute Directors with something so valuable. The authentication and value could have been checked here. Why didn't the Institute put it in a bank vault or something - and contact your lawyers?'

'I can't argue with that, yet Anippe Khu seems to hold a lot of sway. She must have convinced Mr. Krell to release the painting…although I have no idea what authority *he* may have operated under. I only know the Board of Directors would normally authorise that sort of thing…perhaps Anippe Khu has direct contact with them or the City offices, or even the Mayor?'

'Who put the value on the painting?' said Sam.

'Ms. Khu herself…on the Wednesday, after her tour around the Institute and her conversation with Mr. Krell. As soon as the value was revealed, he had it removed and placed with the security guards.'

'So Krell brokered the deal then?'

'I suppose so…perhaps he was due for some of the money, or am I too far ahead in my thinking?'

'It's a possibility,' said Sam.

Not wanting to respond any further just yet, Sam sat forward, drinking the last part of his coffee, wincing a little at the taste, not coffee he was used to. He contemplated the odd situation. Joyce continued talking, but his mind started to drift a little, it had been a strained last twenty-four hours.

'I do apologise Mr. Campbell I must sound vague, I have so many unanswered questions myself. I am going to re-check everything from the acquisition inventories to the archives and back again to see if I can shed any additional light on the painting…my worry is whether I might find any of the records having been erased,' said Joyce, trying to gain a response.

Sam was already imagining the scope of the investigation. The Institute, City Hall, The Banks, the Egyptian connection, the painting, Mr. Krell and the Chicago Police Department - they would all need scrutiny. His mind focused on what was probably the primary objective and that was to recover the painting as quickly as possible and find those responsible, notwithstanding that 'in the eyes of the public' the police were inextricably involved.

Key people within his own organisation needed to be seen - he certainly wanted to get more out of Carl Walters. What did Walters really know? And how would the meeting at the Institute unfold tomorrow?

'I'll be needing a number of things - the age of the painting, the name of the artist, the original bill of sale, when it arrived at the Institute and why was it here in the first place? And anything else you can think of Ms. Marsh.'

At the point of finishing his list, they both heard the final call for the public to leave the building; it was near to 5 pm, time had passed so quickly.

'I'll contact you tomorrow as soonest,' said Sam, his mind still whirring with questions.

So little had he known before he went on air this morning. He would ring Walters tonight, things could not wait, there was too much of the story unexplained.

At the exit to the Institute, Sam stopped abruptly, deciding to focus on the man named Krell, firing a further barrage of questions towards Joyce to get an understanding of the person who was deemed as the Curator.

'He is a brute of a man – with cropped blond hair, a towering figure, generally polite, but a bit moody,' said Joyce. 'He seems to have all the credentials, but he looks more like a giant rugby forward than a museum curator, I don't think I have ever seen a man so tall and so thick set, very imposing. He has a strange look too, as if he is up to something, can't quite work that bit out with him.'

'Where does he hail from?' said Sam.

'Same as me...England, at least I think,' said Joyce, slightly embarrassed. 'Although he has a German father I believe, hence the name Krell...that's all I really know.'

Desperate to get on and contact Carl Walters, Sam gave his farewell and rushed down the last section of steps leading to South Michigan Avenue. He stared to the right and winced at the sight of the Michigan

Avenue Bridge over the Chicago River, knowing that the Tribune headquarters was nearby, *not a good recent memory*, he thought. He looked left and caught the sight of tourists milling around the mirror bubble, an iconic Chicago attraction situated in a small park. The people were smiling and shouting towards one another, amusing themselves by taking pictures and pulling faces in the contortion of the reflection. Heading south, away from the Institute, the Chicago Police Department Headquarters was on the same street and although he thought the walk would do him good, it would take too much time to cover the five kilometres. Instead he would contact Walters and put pressure on him to meet him somewhere close by.

Sam walked passed the mirror bubble plaza, noticing some street musicians gathering in the nearby park and out onto the Avenue pavement. His ear tuned in particular towards an older gentleman who had already engrossed a crowd of passers-by with his eloquent playing of the clarinet, sending out a wonderful hypnotic jazz sound that was hard to resist listening to.

The neo-nineteenth century street lights started to shimmer with their soft orange light flickering into life, hailing the start of the evening. The sight of the street lamps, accompanied with the sound of the clarinet, had a temporary soothing effect on Sam's hectic mind. The Cuba experience hit him for a while and he put it down to the sound of the clarinet – the essence of the lively Havana streets momentarily swirled around in his head as the music played out – reminding him also that there was unfinished business there.

It took a number times for Sam to get through to Walters' cell phone, but finally, after what he counted as the third tune from the old man's clarinet, Sam got an answer. He knew Walters would still be at work in his office, he never left early – not even on a Friday evening.

'Carl, we need to talk, I am convinced matters cannot wait, I am just too far off the pace and I would appreciate a frank, honest discussion,' said Sam, determination in his voice.

'I am busy and we are meeting tomorrow morning are we not?' said Walters.

'Appreciated, but I thought we could meet somewhere close to the Institute, I have been to see a member of staff there and I have left them with a few tasks…'

'I haven't really got time, although I was going to call you…I have a little information on the man called Krell, but like I said, it may be better discussed when we meet tomorrow…'

'Sir, no…curiosity is getting the better of me, if we meet now we'll be better prepared, I am sorry to press on the matter.'

A moment of silence.

'There is an out of the way place at the back of the Chicago Hilton Hotel, along South Wabash Avenue. I know the people there who run the place…It's called Harold's Chicken Shack, excellent food there, and it's not far from the Institute. I'll meet you there in fifteen minutes,' said Walters, reluctantly.

In a short space of time, Sam found himself

around the back of the Hilton Hotel, walking underneath the famed Chicago monorail, before reaching the entrance to Harold's Chicken Shack. He pushed at the squeaky revolving door to the eating house, making his way to one of the empty red plastic seating booths facing the window front. The place was small, yet busy with students from the nearby musical colleges lining up to get their boxes of take away chicken and fries. Sam felt a little out of place in his suit, so removed his tie and jacket and fumbled around with his cell phone as a distraction. The shop TV was on in the far corner, bellowing out a profile of The Chicago Bears Football team, ahead of Saturday night's game against the Green Bay Packers – the Bears incessant rivals.

Ten minutes passed and the larger than life Walters strolled in, a huge smile across his rugged dark skinned face. As tall as Sam but much thicker set, Walters was like an old bear, as strong as an ox in his looks with shoulders and a back beyond normal size. His skin was very dark, accentuating the wrinkles in his brow and the crow's feet adorning his broad smile.

At the behest of Walters, food and beverage arrived very quickly, but Sam could hardly think about eating, he was far too eager to get to the truth.

'I went to see Joyce Marsh at the Institute, she helped, but was a little vague. Through her own volition she is going to try and find out more for me…'

'I am sorry to cut you short Sam, although I should have guessed that you would start to inquire…but I thought we were going to cover this tomorrow, I have to tell you it is very tricky at the moment.'

'But why? If I am now the appointed investigator, surely I need to know what I am dealing with...please tell me more of what you know.'

'The Curator, Krell, has gone missing, no-one can trace him,' said Walters.

Sam remained silent for a few seconds, pondering over the last comment.

'I have not long come from the Institute, Joyce Marsh said Krell had gone off somewhere...again you seem to have knowledge of this, who has spoken to you?'

'I told you it is difficult. I have been in contact with Mayor Johnson, he is on the Board of Directors for the Institute. The Board have not long had an urgent meeting, undoubtedly they assumed that Krell must have gone missing. I know for a fact that there is no reply to his phones or any sign of him at his apartment, the checks have been made.'

Sam was now confused and wondered if Joyce had tried to initiate contact with Krell. *Or did someone on the Board contact her?* he thought – in any case none of which she had revealed earlier.

'What about getting a team around to his last known abode with a warrant? We have more than enough to suspect him,' said Sam, desperate for action.

'I have ordered that already. I had a young lieutenant get on to it, she went with a SWAT team to try and locate him.'

'How can all of this be unfolding without me knowing?' remarked Sam.

'I should have told you, but when you are getting orders barked at you from the Mayor, you have to react, albeit I acknowledge that sometimes two angles on the investigation are better than one, you know how it goes.'

The realisation that Walters had allowed Sam to carry on using his own initiative was still infuriating – and was perhaps a typical ploy adopted by the Bureau Chief, even though Walters himself would carry on with his own investigation.

'Mayor Johnson spoke to Anippe Khu directly over this,' said Walters further. 'She contacted him and that's how the police got involved. There wasn't time to organise a security firm, so the Mayor directed the police – he called me and I agreed. When it all went wrong, and with you out of town, I had to get some things done. I needed you, that's why I called you back from leave – I thought I'd get you to pick up some of the pieces when you got back, but I couldn't not be involved…'

Sam interrupted. 'From what you are now telling me, you arranged for the officers to go to the Institute?'

'Yes, but on the Mayor's orders. I am guessing that the Mayor and Anippe Khu must know each other pretty well, he is a Board member for the Institute like I said.'

'And she is a Benefactor and a patron as we know,' said Sam. 'Why didn't you tell me this last night when you rang?'

'Like I explained, you needed to look honest and not know too much. What has happened, has happened – I never expected this to go so wrong, and I don't think anyone else did,' said Walters, his face forming a deep frown.

'The list of people to be seen keeps growing…what a caper? I keep getting different aspects, including from you, we must consolidate, there is too much at stake,' said Sam, utterly frustrated.

A text came through to Sam's cell phone.

Just to tell you – I have been contacted by one of your lieutenants - a police team entered Krell's apartment – no sign of him, no painting found – possible information on flight details to England. Can you call me? Joyce.'

Sam read it over to Walters, merely receiving a nod. He then changed tack.

'How are our people from the attack?' said the younger man.

Walters' demeanor changed rapidly. 'It is worrying me. Two out of the four officers are critically ill in hospital, they will be there for a while – One of them I don't think will survive, and I am not sure about the other critical officer either. The other two non-critical officers have been released, one with a broken arm and the other badly bruised. I have been trying to keep the seriousness of the other cases under wraps. I have not revealed the extent of their injuries, nor will I if I can help it.'

'What do you mean?'

'The squad cars arrived at the Institute and picked up the painting as ordered, this was about 8 am yesterday. The plan was to take the painting straight to the airport on the instructions of Ms. Khu, her flight was due back out to Cairo that evening. The police cars parked in the basement car park under the Art Institute, the painting was placed into one of the cars, but the officers got attacked before they set off.'

'The spotlight is therefore on us or someone from the Institute. Krell remains our number one suspect then, that part is obvious. What of the injuries?'

'This is the most terrifying part,' Walters said slowly and quietly, his furrowed brow deepening. 'The officers who have been released from hospital have stated that all four of them got attacked by one man, an unarmed man. He went through them like a dose of salts, before they even had time to draw a firearm. You know one of the seriously injured officers is Dave Gregg, a huge man himself?' stated Walters.

'Yes I had heard… he is an enormous, cropped haired white fellow, six feet four inches, 280 lbs., a power lifter I believe…there should be no one who could get through him…why?' asked Sam.

'He is the one I really don't expect to survive. He is in a coma, in a very serious condition. Like I mentioned, a male and female officer have been released; they have given their account.'

Walters drew breath and quietened his speech even further, drawing Sam closer to him.

'They said that the attacker was an enormous man of unbelievable strength, even making the powerful Dave Gregg seem like a child. Gregg was dragged out of the driver's seat of one of the squad cars and picked up by his belt and neck, then thrown across the underground car park landing on his back. Before the others had time to react, they were beaten almost senseless by this brute. One of them managed to stay semi-conscious, just about making out what happened next. Gregg tried to draw his firearm whilst he was lying on the ground – but the brute got to him before he had chance to shoot. This beast picked him up again, this time with only one hand, throwing him against one of the supporting pillars, smashing Gregg's shoulder bones. The attacker then went back for the painting, snatching it out from the back of a squad car.'

'It is difficult to comprehend what you are saying,' said Sam, stunned.

'Just a moment…then came the worst part, Gregg was still trying to get up and feel for his gun, so the brute returned to him. He grabbed hold of Gregg, pushing him down with one hand on Gregg's chest. Gregg couldn't move. With his bare hand, this beast of a man grabbed hold of Gregg's left collar bone and tore it through his upper chest, ripping the bone through his flesh. So I have been told, the scream was akin to something out of a horror movie…so piercing…can you imagine?'

Sam was reeling. 'I can't believe what I am hearing.'

'When help eventually came, the attacker was long gone. The scene was carnage, the brute had even smashed in most of the panels to the squad cars and had destroyed most of the weapons.'

The usually calm exterior of the Police Chief was now waning. Sam was starting to make sense of why Walters had been acting a little strange, it was obvious that the Bureau Chief had become inextricably involved, and certainly at least believed himself partly to blame for what had happened. Perhaps now Carl Walters was trying to mend his own perceived wrong.

'Joyce Marsh said Krell, the Curator, is a huge, monstrous man. It's beginning to fit, it's got to be him, but you must have guessed that, hence you ordering the warrant on his address, and that's why you sent the Tactical team?'

'I received the news just before I got here Sam. The Tactical team cleared Krell's apartment, we can assume he has fled the country.'

'You think?' said Sam, sarcastically.

It was all too odd for Sam. He was still trying to comprehend the horrific attack on his fellow colleagues, fathom out why Carl Walters was behaving out of character and wondering what line of enquiry he should go onto next. Joyce sent him another text.

'Please call there is more information on Krell.'

'Ring her Sam, I will contact Lieutenant Craddock, she is still at Krell's address…then at some point we will compare notes,' said Walters slightly relieved.

Joyce described the evening events and apologised for not contacting Sam sooner. She explained that shortly after they had parted at the Institute, she was contacted by Lieutenant Craddock. The Lieutenant wanted to know where Krell's apartment was. Joyce mentioned that she had found Krell's file. Krell hadn't been employed long at the Institute but had arrived with an impressive CV, of course upon reflection this could not have been genuine and needed to be tested. Checks had started to be made on his previous employment and one by one, the Personnel team had found discrepancies. Although the detail appeared legitimate at first, with more digging the team found most of the references to be inaccurate.

'Sam, you are right, we must sort this one, and quickly. Please forgive me, I am relieved you are on board. This debacle is my fault,' said Walters, remorsefully.

'The pieces will come together. Krell is the main suspect and I'll get after him, and Anippe Khu for that matter – she will have to be seen. Perhaps you can speak to the Mayor about that, I will need to get to Egypt at some point, that I am sure of…and I need your help in maintaining the impetus. I will get Krell and I will find that damn painting!' said Sam, assertively.

Walters seemed humbled – but this didn't puzzle Sam – it was the occasional look of fear in his Chief's craggy face that did, in all the years he had known him, he had never seen such an expression.

Sam said his goodbye's, continuing to deliberate over the day's events, trying to search for logic in this most odd of circumstances. He knew that before him, lay a very difficult task. His objective was to find the painting and get Krell, still assuming he was the perpetrator – but what was behind it all, and who, if anybody, was behind Krell?

And why was Walters afraid? That aspect troubled Sam the most. He needed answers and he needed wisdom, tomorrow he would search for both with his one true oracle – his father, James Campbell.

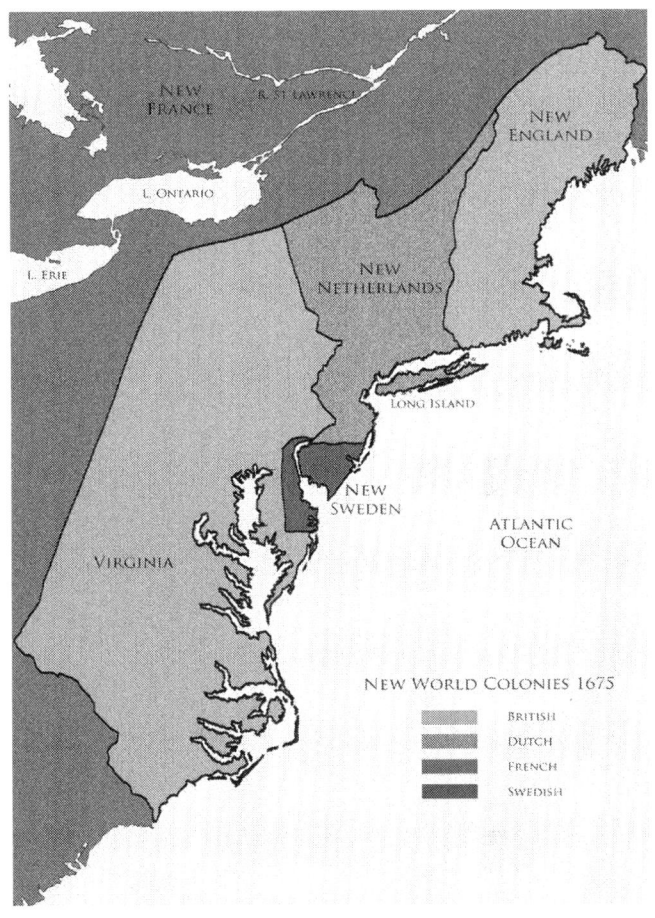

NEW FRANCE

R. ST LAWRENCE

NEW ENGLAND

L. ONTARIO

L. ERIE

NEW NETHERLANDS

LONG ISLAND

NEW SWEDEN

ATLANTIC OCEAN

VIRGINIA

NEW WORLD COLONIES 1675

BRITISH
DUTCH
FRENCH
SWEDISH

Chapter 3

The Slave

1675 A.D.

The slave hit the stony ground hard, as if it seemed he had been hit by a bear. His face crunched into the dust and small rocks, breaking the gristle of his nose and almost gouging his left eye, tearing the skin of his eye lid. The pain in his knees and hands was even worse as he had tried to stop falling on the rocky trail before him. He wore no shoes, the shredded trousers he wore were but knee height, his cotton shirt was torn - he had been running for hours, now utterly exhausted, dry with thirst and almost delirious, his fall was inevitable.

His body screamed for rest but his mind told him to press on. The trail ahead lurched towards a dense thicket, flanked by an ever increasing number of pine trees, beginning to shut out the light of the sun. The rushing sound of the nearby river seemed to get louder as he strove towards it.

Flashes of his initial escape from the tobacco plantation came to him, his father's voice ringing in his ears as he continued to run bare foot through the woodland. The pain in his body started to go numb, too much fear and adrenalin seared through his veins for him to notice. In any case, he was used to pain - as a slave on the plantation, he had been used to beatings and whippings.

Through the thicket, the ground along the trail became softer under foot; the foliage and line of trees becoming ever denser as the river neared. The slave looked back from whence he came, glad now for the softer ground. But he knew behind him, chasing him down hard, were evil men, men who would kill him without a moment's hesitation. He had escaped their clutches and he was running for his life.

'You are born a slave but you will not die a slave, as God is my witness,' his father had said, the words repeating in the slave's mind. The slave had made a promise to his father that he would never relinquish – or he would die trying.

The trail rose and fell to the contour of the river valley until the slave reached a marker that his father had described. The marker was a small cliff that had a sharp descent to the river down below – this was to be where he crossed to reach the north side of the river bank. Stepping off the trail, the slave hung onto branches and thicket as he slid down a steep embankment approaching the edge of the small cliff. Intrepidity would have to be absolute, for he knew this is where he would have to jump.

He reached the edge and stood still for a moment, holding his breath, trying to listen as acutely as possible. He turned his head back towards the trail, sure that he may have heard the sound of dogs. Unenviable fear gripped his stomach, the horror of the sound of the barking dogs was almost too much to bear. He regained his composure and stepped right onto the cliff face knowing it was now or never. The current below was fast flowing, and once in the water, he knew it would be treacherous and he would have to use all his strength to get to the other side.

The slave jumped, screaming inside as he braced for the impact of the cold water, ten metres below. He had managed to clear the overhanging branches and jutting rocks, but hitting the water hurt, the pain from his fall returning. As he plummeted under water, he felt the gristle of his broken nose crack again under the pressure.

He surfaced quickly, coughing and spluttering, trying to gain breath and brace his body for the swim. He remembered his father telling him to get out of the dangerous waters as quickly as he could.

The slave thought his heart was going to burst through his chest as he imagined the black dogs catching up with him, snarling and snatching; saliva dripping from their gnarling mouths ready to tear chunks of flesh from him. He swam hard, being carried by the current, focusing on getting to the other side. His frantic swimming left his body drained of oxygen, and his limbs became numb with the cascading cold water. He could hear his father's voice once again.

'Run fast, make for the large river, head for the

north side.'

'How do I know where to go father?' he had asked.

'Asemota,' his father had said. 'Row the small boat which you will find along the small river and it will take you to a path by the big river, then turn north but stay out of the water until you reach the crossing, you will move more quickly, stick to what I say and you will be free to join your mother. Now tell me your name boy?'

'Asemota, my name is Asemota father.'

For a moment the river became calmer, and now was his chance to surge for the river bank. A root from a large Cypress tree extended out into the water, Asemota the slave fixed on it and before long he was scrambling along it, crawling over the silt of the bank and reaching for the dry foliage of the forest. He wrenched himself upright then stepped onto the soil, noticing another forest trail extending in front of him. His father's voice returned again.

Stories his father would tell, of the Native men and women in the forests of the Northwest, many miles from where they were both enslaved. The Natives were tribal people just like the tribe his father had come from in the land of Africa. Asemota heard tell that many of the Natives or Indians as they were known, had also become slaves – working for the white men, as such white men commandeered the tribal lands.

Driven by his father's wish for his son to be free, Asemota ran and ran, praying that soon he would come across the Native people his father spoke of.

He recalled the emotion in his father's eyes as he had said farewell in the dead of the night. *They would have killed him by now*, Asemota thought, what sacrifice for his son's freedom. Knowing his father's plight, this drove Asemota on, and he would make his lungs collapse if he had to.

*

It was spring in the year 1675 in the New World. Slavery had become prevalent and now legalised in the new American colonies. Asemota had escaped from a tobacco plantation built on the banks of the King James River, near the town of Richmond in a claimed English territory called Virginia. It was a time of chaotic interaction between the peoples of many cultures, Asemota having been born from the union of an enslaved couple, an African Prince and a Native American 'Indian' Princess. Asemota's mother had escaped slavery when he was just a small child, leaving his father to fend for him at the plantation.

The British, French and Spanish were fighting a bitter feud over territories, claiming rights to the Native American lands. Slaves were mainly people from the West Coast of Africa, but there were many Native slaves too. African peoples and Native American peoples would be shackled together in camps working as chattel slaves, having labour forced upon them to grow tobacco, cotton and other crops. Many of the Native men had become interned as trackers for the white men.

Asemota's mother and father had been slaves at the very tobacco plantation in Richmond that Asemota was now running away from. His father was indeed a Prince, a royal subject from a tribe living along the West African coast. His mother was a Native Indian Princess from the ancient Cahokian tribe, living in the Northwest American tribal lands.

Falling to the mercy of the white slave traders, Asemota's father had been taken from the land of Benin, relinquished by his own father, Asemota's grandfather, who was the Benin King. The troubled King traded with the white slavers, selling his own people for profit whilst trying to protect others. Some saw his acts as despicable, for which he had become loathed.

One day, the acts of the King came to a head. In an effort to show his impartiality, the King chose two of his four sons to be enslaved, throwing them to the white traders to be shackled. Asemota's father was one of those taken prisoner - but at the last minute, the King tried to stop his sons from leaving, wanting to exchange them with other male members from the tribe. A terrible fight began between the tribal warriors and the white men, resulting in the death of the King and one of his sons.

*

Asemota's recollection of the story about his father and the King was vivid, helping him to strive for freedom. He clutched his pocket, remembering what his father had given him. He had sewn a piece of cloth to the inside of one of his trouser legs, a memento given to his father by Asemota's mother. Asemota had to protect it and reveal it at the right time, he would know when, he had been told – the day of his coming of age, this very day upon which he was running for his life.

Asemota drove on, still clutching his pocket, sure that the sound of the dogs was drawing ever nearer, he could hear their barking above the sound of the rustling trees and twittering of birds, and the noise of the river dissipated now as he ran deeper into the forest.

Sure enough, the bellow of the men from the plantation could also be heard, urging their dogs on as the barking of the dogs became even louder and fiercer. Perhaps they could sense that Asemota was near. Instinctively the men and their dogs must have crossed the river earlier on, they must have known somehow which direction he would take.

His heart pounded ever faster, his limbs stretching ever further to plough a way through the forest path. He knew that the dogs would be released upon him at any moment and the thought of his limbs being torn apart by them made him violently sick.

The slave trackers from the plantation, five men led by a thug named Jackson, had second guessed what Asemota might do and had managed to cross the river further upstream along some natural stepping stones before the river dropped. Jackson was the leader, shouting commands at the other men with their dogs. The thuggish Englishman was a mercenary, a tall, fat, ginger bearded man in his thirties, employed by the plantation to catch slaves. He was a man of no mercy, a seditious man who pleasured in the pain of others. Asemota had recognised Jackson's bellow, petrified at the prospect of confronting him.

'Move your backsides, you filthy scum, release the Bloodhounds along the forest trail, they'll sniff him out now!' shouted Jackson, at the top of his voice.

Asemota was in a quandary, but he had to keep moving. Did he move deeper into the forest? Should he try and climb a tree? Or should he stick to his plan and stay on the trail, praying for safety? Confused, he just ran harder, beset with profuse fear, lactic acid building in his muscles, air in his lungs stinging; his heart was beating so fast he thought it was going to come out of his mouth.

Two German Rottweiler dogs had been released along with the two English Bloodhounds. The Bloodhounds, with their long snouts and lumbering gait, were notorious for their scent and had captured Asemota in their sights very quickly. Soon the rampaging Rottweilers would charge past the Bloodhounds, scampering more quickly along the trail, ready to strike the running man with a killer instinct, bred in them since the time of the Romans.

'We have him men,' snarled the mercenary, adjusting his brown leather britches and his sweaty, dirty white cotton shirt. His thick ginger beard was laced with dust and perspiration, forced upon him by the chase over the last eighteen hours. He would have his prize though, at any cost.

Asemota had run further into the forest away from the river, picking the easiest route to gain speed. Pure instinct now drove him on to save his own life. Jackson and his men were encouraged by the actions of their dogs, feeling pleasured at the impending capture. The men ran as fast as they could to see the spectacle.

The two Rottweilers pounded along the ground,

incensed by the scent of human flesh, ready to pounce. The track widened a little and Asemota found himself in a small clearing. Up ahead he could see the outline of a building, a broken down wooden shack – not unlike the shacks and stalls built on the plantation. With a further burst of speed, in the hope of finding something or even someone, he pelted for the shack. Turning his head back towards the chasers, he could see the outline of the Rottweilers.

Extreme fear, to the point of collapse, came upon him as he entered the shack through an open doorway. The wood was rotten due to lack of repair and use. Green mould wrapped itself around the base of the frame, whilst the roof had lost many of its wooden slats. Desperately searching inside, Asemota noticed the shack had two small rooms. There were tables and chairs overturned, shredded and dilapidated woven baskets on the floor and filth everywhere.

'God help me, what can I use?!' he shouted at the top of his voice. Asemota grabbed a chair leg and wrenched it from its seat; it broke off easily, crumbling in his hand. The dogs approached the door way, snarling furiously, hot breath exploding from their mouths and saliva spitting across the ground. Asemota threw away the useless chair leg and scrambled into the second room shutting the one interior gated door as hard and as fast as he could. The door was off its top hinge, but he was able to shut it and use all of his strength to press his shoulder against the frame, stopping the dogs from lurching towards him. Looking through the slits in the door panels, Asemota saw the gnashing, salivating teeth of the dogs as they clawed at the door. He quickly looked around, observing broken bunkbeds against the back wall and an old pine table still upright placed against a small window opening to the front of the shack. The window shutter had long since collapsed and was lying forlornly on the rotting wooden floor. He gasped as he recognised that the small opening was big enough for one or two of the dogs to force their way through if need be. Then the men arrived, the sound of their voices making him despair even more.

On the table was a small knife with a bone handle. The blade was rusted right through but the knife looked long enough and intact enough to be able to inflict some damage.

Asemota just managed to keep one foot against the interior door and grab the knife with his left hand. He pressed back hard against the door and switched the blade to his right hand. Left foot and shoulder now forcing the door, he prepared to strike through the gaps.

'I'll get your eyes…I'll stab your eyes you damned dogs!' he shouted, at which he thrust top down, aiming for a point which would hit any one of the dogs' faces.

At the point of his first strike, he was shocked to see the dogs suddenly back away and rush out of the shack. Thinking that they would immediately bear down upon him through the small open window, he rushed to place the table up against the space.

Confronting him, he saw the five men staring back at him through the opening, the four dogs now tethered once again – and there was Jackson. Jackson had no dog with him but was, obtusely, pointing a long black flintlock pistol towards Asemota's position. The men were all but ten metres away, grinning, goading, and relishing the thought of the dogs once again being set upon the young slave. Asemota stared through the window and froze; all sense of capability leaving him. All he could do now was respond to the whims of the vile Jackson.

'Your choice slave, the dogs or the bullet?!' roared Jackson, callously.

Asemota knew that the only other alternative would be shackles, a whipping and then a certain putrid death back at the plantation, he was doomed either way.

Jackson had no intention of shooting Asemota, but would gladly let the dogs loose on him if Asemota did not conform. Asemota stepped through the small window and stood in front of the shack, facing the men and their barking, rabid dogs.

'Take me back to the plantation, let me have a chance,' cried Asemota. 'I can work, I will work harder…just give me a chance,' came the plea.

'Your chance ended the moment you ran slave – but believe me if I don't let the dogs have you, you will be going back. I will make an example out of you, you filthy scum.'

Asemota knew what that meant, imagining the horrors of what would become of him – no runaway slave from the Richmond Plantation had ever survived when eventually caught. The usual treatment was to be attacked by dogs or stabbed repeatedly until the blood drained out of your body. The carcass would then be put on parade for all the other slaves to see.

'Step forward, you heathen animal,' said Jackson. 'Get your hybrid sniveling hide here to me right now.'

There seemed to be no other choice for the young Asemota – but he thought he would be able to buy some time and plead with Jackson, perhaps later biding his time to try and escape again. He had placed the knife behind him, tucked into the rear of his shredded trousers. *This may be foolish*, he thought, but at any given moment from now, he would be fighting for his life.

Two small stocky white men, ragged in appearance, had hold of the Bloodhounds, these dogs were slightly calmer than the gnarling Rottweilers. Of the two men holding the thrashing German dogs, Asemota noticed that one of them was a Native man – an interned slave taken from one of the Native 'Indian' tribes; the other man looked rather like Jackson only younger and less portly.

Jackson maintained his stance by pointing the pistol at Asemota, who had inadvertently placed his hands above his head showing a face riddled with a desperate plea.

Waiting for the onslaught, Asemota stared at the dogs but noticed that they had become more agitated, perhaps distracted in some way. The snarling dogs started to pull violently away from their bemused handlers. All the men shouted at their respective canines telling them to be calm and settle, but all four dogs continued, seemingly oblivious to their masters' wishes.

'Ha! The dogs want to tear you apart slave, no mercy for you it seems!' shouted Jackson. 'Should I let them upon you – you slithering rat?'

Jackson looked at the dogs and began to wonder himself why they seemed more infuriated than usual. By now they were forcibly pulling with all their might against their handlers, certainly not focusing on Asemota anymore. The strength of the dogs exerted on the men was causing the men to lose their footing as they desperately tried to regain control. One of the white men lost his ground and thudded into a fir tree, still hanging on tightly to one of the Rottweilers as it wrenched his arms.

'Control your dogs men, what in God's name has got into them?'

'Boss!' said the Native man. 'They are in fear, something has spooked them.'

'Fear of what?!' said Jackson. 'What on Earth should they fear? I see or hear no sign of any animal!'

The man who fell by the tree, made one last effort to regain control of his Rottweiler. He pulled at the leather dog lead with all his might, but in so doing, enabled the dog to lurch at him and tear at his right leg. Seething pain jolted through his body as he punched frenziedly towards the dog's head. The Rottweiler let go of its grip, free now from the lead, and the dog bolted, charging away from the men, back along the original forest trail from which it came.

Asemota stood in silence, by now his hands were back by his side as he watched the unfolding drama before him, not believing his eyes. Jackson continued to shout at the men and the dogs, trying to fathom out what was going on. He had almost forgotten his focus on Asemota, but then momentarily caught the young man's eye.

'Is this your doing slave?! What voodoo magic is this?!' he remonstrated, stepping forward and pointing the pistol right in Asemota's face.

The pointing of the pistol was only temporary. One of the Bloodhounds also bolted, tearing itself away from the Native man, clawing and biting at his hands before the pain made him let go of the lead. In an instinctive frenzy, this second dog searched for an escape route, before running full pelt towards the direction of the river. The remaining two dogs were seconds behind, gnarling their handlers in the same way before charging off into the forest. With all four handlers blooded and incapacitated, one of them unable to walk, Jackson started to quiver and panic.

The gruesome slave tracker was trembling, trying to point the gun at Asemota, whilst furtively looking around for signs of danger. The other men were crying out in pain, attempting to stem the flow of blood to their wounds.

'Boss, boss – let's get out of here, shoot the cursed slave and let's be gone!' they all cried repeatedly.

Jackson's perpetual trembling could hardly control the weapon as he attempted to put it close to Asemota's face once again. Asemota thought now might be his chance and decided he must lunge for Jackson with the knife. There was no need.

Within a split second of his thought, he witnessed the thud of a feather tailed wooden arrow, piercing into Jackson's chest, followed quickly by a second arrow slicing into Jackson's stomach. Jackson reeled, his pistol flying out of his hand and falling to the ground as he himself crashed heavily into the foliage, smashing his head against a tree stump. He lay motionless.

Asemota stood still in utter disbelief, mouth wide open – staring at Jackson's blood soaked body. The other four trackers screamed in abject fear and as they tried to stand up and move away, they too met the same fate. Almost simultaneously like a hail of stones, more wooden arrows thudded into their bodies, killing them all instantly.

With the sight of the contorted, blood stained bodies strewn across the ground, Asemota fell to his knees, clutching the cloth in his trouser pocket, the cloth that his father had given him. He bowed his head, closed his eyes and prayed, muttering under his breath, expecting arrows to pierce his heart at any moment. Nothing happened.

Still kneeling, Asemota dared only to open his eyes after reciting his little prayer. He looked all around him, through the forest and back towards the river - nothing. An eerie silence had enveloped the forest - his fate, he thought, was still in the hands of someone else…or something.

Movement.

He had his back to the wooden shack and was peering to his left, deep into the forest. The undergrowth between the densely packed trees was very thick and tall, but he could see the top of it moving, as if a wave was being parted. Asemota rubbed his eyes, trying to clear the dust and the gunge sticking to his eyelids. He caught sight of a giant, silver fur coated animal, the top of its head scything seamlessly through the bushes and the thicket. He thought he must be hallucinating – if it was a creature it would be too large, perhaps even too large to be a bear.

'Who are you?!' Asemota shouted.

He wanted to move, but couldn't. He turned to look at the disheveled shack, trying to force his body to move towards it for some sort of cover, but it was no use. He remained knelt and transfixed on the movement coming out of the forest. The creature was now more defined, stepping out of the dense bush, moving slowly and deliberately towards him. What he saw emerging was beyond his comprehension, beyond all reasoning – nothing that he could have ever imagined.

He stared at the silver furred creature - as it stared back at him. It was not growling nor did it make any attempt to move directly towards him. It stopped twenty metres from his position, standing upright, breathing calmly and rhythmically, trance like. Asemota forced his body up, never removing his eyes from the creature's gaze. Counter intuitively, the creature appeared to be smiling, the lip of its long snout turned up at the edges. The creature's intelligent looking, deep blue eyes were captivating, mesmerising Asemota into believing they looked almost human.

The creature stepped a little closer, but not in a threatening way; by now Asemota gained a true measure of its size. Its head was over twice the height of Asemota's, and he knew he was tall boy, having been measured two or three inches over, what the white English men at the plantation called 'six feet'. He thought he would be able to walk under the creature's chest. Its glorious thick silver fur graced its whole body, save darker patches towards the base of its legs and tail.

Asemota tried to clear his mind, continuing to stare at the gigantic wolf like being. Moments later the animal turned its head behind, then moved its head back towards Asemota as if signaling something. Before the creature stopped its movement, a tall, elegant, dark haired woman stepped from the creature's side. She was a Native woman, a so called 'Indian' from the wild country.

Mouth now open in utter disbelief, Asemota strained to accept what he was seeing. The woman was beautiful, dressed in what seemed to be light skinned animal hide garments, top and bottom. A huge wooden bow was strapped to her back with a pouch full of arrows fixed to her side. She strode towards Asemota, her eyes glistening with emotion… and she was smiling.

As she approached, Asemota pulled out the cloth that his father had given him. He stared at the embroidered appearance on the material, gasping at the image and the woman's face as she came closer. She smiled inexorably, tears welling in her eyes. He dropped to his knees once again, staring at the cloth then looking back at the woman's face, barely hearing her words as she spoke. He was finally succumbing to the copious anguish he had so bravely endured.

'My child you have been through so much,' said the woman. 'I hoped beyond all reason that this day would come.'

The young man passed out before the woman spoke her last sentence, her face fading and her voice diminishing as he fell to the ground.

*

Asemota woke to the sound of water being splashed by men holding long wooden poles as they pushed the tree hollowed canoe along the river. He tried to clear his head, but the pain and fatigue in his body had consumed him, the events of the last two days taking their toll. He lay still, covered in what he thought was a bear skin, wrapped around him, keeping his body warm from the elements and the cold bottom of the canoe. Gazing across the length of the boat, he could make out at least eight native men in standing positions, six of them pushing the poles into the water, two of them keeping watch – arrows poised in their thick wooden bows.

And then there was the woman, it wasn't a dream after all. Asemota clutched at his right leg, desperately trying to find the woven cloth his father had given him – but then, albeit still hazily, he started to remember what had happened. He tried to sit up, but his body would not let him. Thirst tore at his throat as he furtively looked around for drinking water. One of the lookouts at the rear of the canoe caught his eye, shouting incomprehensible words towards the front of the boat where the tall woman was standing. She turned and faced Asemota, her beautiful radiant smile even more noticeable, with the sun glistening across the river waters, catching her face. She walked gracefully over to him and sat gently beside him.

'Do not fear young Asemota, I can speak your tongue…rest easy,' she remarked.

'I need some water,' he said, trying to think coherently and fathom his surroundings.

The woman fetched a small rounded clay pot, full of fresh water, from the rear of the canoe, close to where Asemota was lying. She dipped a wooden ladle and brought the water to Asemota's mouth, calmly ensuring he took only small sips.

'My cloth?' asked Asemota of the woman.

'Don't worry, I have it safe.'

'You are the woman in the image?' Asemota muttered, feeling drowsy, trying to suppress the chronic desire to sleep again.

'Are you my mother?' he said, feeling his heart thump through his chest, hoping for the right response.

The woman cupped her hands around his jaw and smiled, a smile so wide and true there could only be one answer.

'Yes…yes I am my beautiful Asemota.'

He could hardly breathe, tears welling in his eyes. Their embrace was long and tight, Asemota was so overcome with emotion he started to cry uncontrollably, before the woman placed her hands on his face again, reassuring him that all would be good now. He calmed, feeling a little embarrassed in front of the men, but he saw the smiles on their faces. Only warrior pride prevented them from showing any further sign of emotion, although inside they shared the glorious moment.

Asemota had so many questions but his mother told him that he should rest more, his body must repair, there was a long journey ahead.

'How long?' he asked.

'Many many weeks,' she replied, a look of discomfort falling across her face as she pondered what lay before them.

'We are of the Illini tribe and our lands are far to the west from here, near to the famous lands of Cahokia. We are descended from the old Cahokian tribes, something you will learn more of in time. I will tell you of my ancestors and talk to you of the glorious Native City of Cahokia, with its thousands of inhabitants who lived freely for hundreds of years, making good of the land and its creatures. You will see this land and you will learn our ways Asemota.'

Hairs on the back of Asemota's neck stood up as he listened. Some of what his mother said made sense, recalling what his father had told him of her people. He would listen intently to more he felt sure, for now he was just happy to be in her presence.

'Where are we at present? Are we safe?'

'The white men call it the James River, after their King, or so I hear. Your slave masters would have used this name. We know this land as the Powhatan land and these waters are the Powhatan waters…it is their river,' said the woman, sternly. 'We will be safe, although we must be prepared, the Powhatans rule this part of the world and we are merely their guests.'

The woman's comments were processed but only for a fleeting moment; in recalling his experiences of the so called 'James River', Asemota's recent vivid memory of such a waterway would never be a fond one, nor would be the memory of the nauseating smell of the plantation, with the washing and drying of tobacco leaves along the river estuaries. From birth that was all he knew, the only work he had ever been given – day and night, the pungent smell filled his nose every time he thought of the tobacco sheds. This was not helped by him noticing a large pile of dried tobacco in the canoe.

'For trade,' his mother remarked seeing him scorn at the sight of it. 'We will need food and shelter along the way, this is fine tobacco and will prove very useful to trade with.'

The canoe was packed with trade items and food for the journey. The voyage would be long, lasting months and they would most probably encounter hostility along the way, much bartering and peacemaking would therefore be needed.

A war of attrition existed between the British, the French, the Spanish and the native tribes. Back and forth lands were being possessed and re-possessed in what seemed an eternal battle for supremacy across the whole of the American Northeast and other eastern frontiers.

Asemota's mother feared for these troubles, knowing that, inevitably, wars would come to her land. For now, she had to suppress her anxieties for the immediate tasks at hand and simply concentrate on getting Asemota to safety.

With strength now to stand, Asemota scanned the canoe, and took more note of the cargo, seeing the plethora of provisions; with stone axes, timber poles, fur skins, squash and pumpkin, corn seeds and an array of copper trinkets, not to mention the tobacco that had made him squirm.

The canoe itself was huge, made of an oak tree, hollowed out, at least six metres long and nearly a metre wide, and it would be mightily heavy he thought.

The hair style of the native men, and to a lesser extent his mother, fascinated the young man. The men had their hair shaved high above the ears, but it was kept long elsewhere, tied in plats to rest in front of their bodies. Only his mother kept her hair free. Animal hide loin cloths adorned their bodies, somewhat sparsely as a matter of fact, much to Asemota's concern.

'You will dress the same as the other men now Asemota, you are Illini and you will learn our ways. Here are your clothes. Next you will check the provisions with me…then your most important job comes after that.'

'What will that be?'

'Lookout with me. Very soon I will need all eight men to work the canoe, there are some difficult waters ahead.'

Asemota had sensed that the canoe was working harder against the current. The Powhatan waters had their source in the Appalachian Mountains and as they got closer to the mountain range, they would feel the bite of the river torrent even more, forcing them to hug the river shoreline.

Throughout the journey, Asemota began to dwell on the Giant Wolf, something he had dared not speak of, for fear that the men would think him senseless. He would wait for a quiet moment with his mother, perhaps when they struck camp further on.

*

Days passed as the party headed further up river towards the mountainous ranges. Native tribes would be encountered and trade would take place, in the main for extra food, using the trinkets they had, or in the least permission to hunt for food on tribal land.

At a point where the main Powhatan waters split, was a spring fall, a landmark that Asemota's mother recognised, one which she knew marked the end of this first part of the river journey. They had arrived when dusk was upon them.

'We have arrived at what the local tribes call 'Falling Spring Falls', we need to rest here for a few days and gather food.'

The men brought the canoe further inland, dragging it out of the water with all their might to place it away from the shore line. Once ashore the men quickly struck camp, scurrying to find dead leaves and foliage, along with fallen branches to make a fire. Food was prepared, cooking a previously caught brace of hare over an open spittle. The men were chatting exuberantly, excited that they would have the opportunity to stay on land for a few days. Tobacco would be smoked, hunting and gathering would take place, a shelter would be made and stories would be told.

Asemota watched them intently, learning how to make shelter and hunt small game with a bow and arrow. He would learn, tentatively at first, about how to fell trees with base fire and how to carve canoes from the tree trunk. As much as he could he would start to converse in their language, the Illiniweck tongue, something he would learn was spoken by many tribes in the valleys beyond the Appalachian Mountains.

He got to know the men, the oldest of whom was called Etchemin, meaning "canoe man". Asemota thought that he looked as old as his father, perhaps forty years of age, yet Etchemin seemed so tough, and all of the other men looked up to him, doing as he commanded. Etchemin was not very tall but had wiry muscles with many tattoos that must have been etched onto his skin over many years. Like all the men his head was shaved high at the sides, with a great length of grey-black hair flowing from the top of his head, beaded tight to rest on his chest. The tallest of the men, as tall as Asemota, was Askuwheteau, so named because "he always kept watch". Askuwheteau had a very stern face and was always on guard; it was if he never slept. He was Etchemin's son.

The other men would tease Etchemin for having such tall offspring, much to his constant annoyance, but he was very proud of his son; Askuwheteau had proved to be a great warrior. Asemota's favourite was Aharu, so named as "the boy who laughs". He wasn't much older than Asemota, perhaps nineteen years, but was a gifted archer and woodcutter, so enthusiastic and always smiling. He liked Asemota and wanted to be his friend, going out of his way to teach Asemota all that he could. Although smaller than Asemota, Aharu was incredibly strong and would take great pleasure in wrestling Asemota to the ground, showing off his prowess.

For ten days and nights the party rested and prepared, and on the evening of the tenth night a good feast was prepared to mark the beginning of the next stage of the journey. A fire was lit and all were seated around it, gorging on generous portions of meat and fresh Squash. The air was still and warm.

'Mother?' said Asemota tentatively.

'Use the tribe name for mother Asemota,' she replied.

'Anna, we have travelled many days and you have not yet revealed your name?'

The men fell silent from their buoyant chatter, intrigued as to how she would answer. To them she was their leader, their Princess, her name was revered. She looked around at them, raised her hand and smiled.

'I have many names my Son. Some call me Hurit, which means "beautiful woman", although I am not too sure of using such a name. Others know me as Nadie, which means "wise woman", most I sense will use this name and I have to respect that.'

Nadie watched Asemota process in his mind what she had said, his expressions reminding her of his father, *so handsome* she thought.

Asemota's inquisitiveness remained.

'How long is the rest of the journey from here Anna?'

'Many more days than we have already travelled,' she said. 'Tomorrow we go on foot and follow the

Great Indian Trail, it is called the *Mishimayaget,* and we will see more of our kind, and we shall trade some more and go in peace. Then after many days we will find water again and build another canoe to take us on the great river towards home.'

Nadie translated her words to Etchemin and the rest of the men; they all looked a little pensive, knowing that the trail would perhaps have war parties foraging along the route.

'There could be trouble along the route, we are only eight warriors and could be against many,' said Etchemin.

'Trouble will not be with us I hope,' said Nadie. 'But we must work hard and travel fast.'

'Including Asemota!' chortled Aharu.

Asemota could guess what Aharu was saying, he knew that the Native men were going to have to work harder than ever. He would show them that he was strong.

Their last evening at Falling Spring Falls was drawing to a close as the party of nine men and one woman chatted, laughed and told stories, Asemota only understanding some of the conversation after brief translations by his mother.

Later on he saw that his mother was becoming pensive, perhaps worried about the days ahead. At one point she returned to her makeshift shelter and started to check the provisions in the camp, counting off the animal hides, clay pots and the copper trinkets, all so desperately needed for good trade along the route. But something else was troubling her, Asemota could see it in her eyes.

He left the men to their stories and their tobacco smoking around the fire, and went to her.

'I am glad you came to me, my Asemota, I was hoping that I could get your attention.'

'What is it Anna?'

'I want you to come and walk with me, there is something I must do.'

'Into the dark, away from the light of the fire?'

'There is enough moonlight, let your eyes adjust – it will not be a long walk.'

Asemota felt obliged to do what his mother said but he couldn't help wishing that two or three of the men should accompany them.

As they set off, Nadie caught Asemota looking back at the men still laughing and smoking around the fire.

'We will be safe young Asemota, we do not need the men.'

A shallow climb, nearly half a kilometre from the riverside camp, left Asemota a little tired. He followed his mother along a well-trodden path, forged by forest animals, a trail surrounded by a mixture of trees and bushes, densely packed either side. He looked back repeatedly, occasionally catching a glimpse of the camp fire and the moonlight shining on the river waters down below. Through his observations, Asemota fell behind his mother and at one point he had to run hard to catch her up, her purposeful stride catching him out.

A short while later, they came upon a ragged rocky face, extending above the height of the surrounding trees. A spring fall from an outlet at the top of its crest, cascaded over the rocks and misaligned stones around the edges. Concealed behind the gentle waterfall was a large opening, broad at the base and rising to a point just beneath the overflow.

There was an unusual symmetrical line of oak trees either side of the cave entrance, bracing themselves against the stones, as if on guard to the opening. Any breeze catching their leaves had now ceased, in fact Asemota was aware that everything else in the woodland had become silent and still. He had experienced this before, feeling a terrible chill in his veins, wishing now that he had spoken to his mother earlier about such things.

'Wait here Asemota,' said Nadie as she climbed up the fallen rock debris and through the falling water. 'I will return, do not venture.'

The only sound Asemota could hear was the blood swishing through his ears as his heart started to beat faster and faster, even the water fall seemed silent. Although it would be only minutes in reality, the wait for his mother's return seemed interminable and he was not sure whether he should enter the water clad cave himself.

Suddenly, to his astonishment, the same incomprehensible sight of the creature he had seen once before, greeted him; his mother leading the way as the creature slowly morphed through the cascade of water. Its shape seemed to fill the entire entrance to the cave, before it stepped robustly down the rocks and onto the moonlit trail. The creature's majesty transfixed the young man's gaze, its blue eyes penetrating, once again, the very essence of Asemota's soul.

'*Manitou Mahweewa*, my Spirit Wolf, say hello to my son,' Nadie said calmly. 'He is frightened, show him you mean him no harm, show him who you are my beautiful Protector.'

The great animal walked a little closer and bowed its head towards Asemota in a form of greeting. The wolf like creature smiled again, just as Asemota remembered, and he felt its human like eyes reading his every thought. Asemota was determined not to appear frightened, forcing himself not to tremble or fall into a nullifying trance. Nadie stroked the Spirit Wolf's chest and thighs, having to raise her hands to do so. Her smiles were reciprocated by the wolf, the grin on its face getting broader with every comment and gesture Nadie gave.

Asemota had not dreamt about the Giant Wolf after all, and no awkward questions needed to be asked of his mother now.

'Come Asemota, come and be with my Protector, she is the *Manitou Mahweewa*, the great Spirit Wolf of the Illini – isn't she beautiful?'

The young man very carefully stepped against the wolf's fur coat near to its chest and leg; he could easily walk under the body of the huge beast without touching his head. The wolf stood up proud, stretching her head and pushing her front legs against the ground. Asemota came away a little and saw that the wolf's head must have been at least five metres high. Her legs were enormous, with a muscular stature far more defined than an ordinary wolf, more the definition of a lion, and her striking, brilliant silver fur practically glowed in the moonlight.

'My Spirit Wolf, we must continue our long journey tomorrow along the Great Indian War Path before we reach the home rivers again and we need your protection,' said Nadie with a resolute plea.

Again, to Asemota's astonishment, the Great Wolf bowed its head, scratching the ground twice with one of its front paws in acknowledgment. This truly was a spiritual beast he thought, a wonder of the world, a Godly creature – and she was real.

'I did not dream of the creature then Anna, how can she be among us?'

'She is truly a blessing to our people and the Earth, I cannot answer your question just now Asemota, you will have to be patient and wait for the right moment when we are home.'

Nadie stood away from the beast sensing an unease, the wolf had dropped its tale and her eyes had narrowed, she looked furtive.

'What is it that troubles you my Protector, what do you see?' said Nadie.

The wolf turned to point at the mountain ridge on the opposite side of the river valley, lifting its head as high as possible, nodding its snout as if in warning. She then turned abruptly to face Nadie, before sitting on the ground in a prone position, closing her eyes and lowering her head as if to mimic something.

Nadie appeared startled, worrying Asemota a little as he saw his mother ponder on how to react to the mimicking creature, desperate for his mother to respond.

'The time is near my Spirit; you have told me

so…then we must make haste. But we are so far away from home,' said Nadie in despair. 'Come Asemota we must go.'

'What does the wolf see Anna, are we in danger?'

'You must not worry my Son; Spirit Wolf will protect us on our journey.'

Asemota was not convinced with her sentiment but turned to follow his mother back along the trail to the camp, traversing at a speed Asemota found hard to keep up with. It seemed like only minutes before they arrived, Nadie hardly out of breath as she approached Etchemin and the warriors, who were still smoking their pipes around the fire.

Etchemin stood up, quickly noticing Nadie's poise, concerned that he should draw her away from the others.

'You have been spoken to by the spirits my Princess?'

'Yes Etchemin… we must strike the camp now, then rest a little before moving off at dawn. Every day is precious now, how long to our home?' said Nadie

'Nearly three full moons…and that is if we move each day…all day,' said Etchemin.

'I fear for our village Etchemin, and we are so far away with eight of my finest warriors here with me on my quest,' said Nadie, forlornly.

'Your quest is a worthy one,' said Etchemin. 'We will move as quick as we can across the mountain ridge tomorrow, reaching the Great Trail the following day. The next river point is many days away and is to be reached through the Warpath Trail and the *Haudenosaunee* country, but that will lead us to the special *Kanawha* waters, the waters that will take us home.'

The men busied and struck camp on Etchemin's command, not knowing why but not questioning their orders. Asemota did what he could but was too concerned about his mother.

'Please tell me Anna, what troubles you?'

'You and I have a destiny Asemota, but I cannot predict what may happen. It is unfair to keep things from you, yet I cannot tell you at present, for I have no idea how our destiny will be revealed.'

'And the Spirit Wolf, what does she sense, she was mimicking something wasn't she?'

Nadie remained silent for a moment, looking at the full moon casting its cold looking light on the mountain ridge, which they would have to climb at the break of day. She gave out a long sigh.

'I fear there is a bad spirit heading toward us, and it will be near our village in the Illini when we arrive home.'

'How will we know?' said Asemota.

'I will not be sure until we are at the village. Spirit Wolf will travel ahead of us, guarding our trail. When she senses it, she will warn me of how close the evil will be.'

'But Anna, why does she not carry some of us back home, it would take days not weeks.'

'She cannot be revealed to the men Asemota, I have told you, she is a revered spirit not to be seen, only her presence felt. Rest now Asemota, we will be on our journey very soon.'

Wooden trestles prepared a few days before, had animal skin sacks lashed to the frames to hold the trade goods and provisions. The trestles would have to be hauled, like stretchers, over the mountainous terrain, in the very least for the next seven days before they reached the Great Indian Trail. The trusty canoe, which had been built by the men on the very site they were now leaving, was now abandoned, a new one would have to be built once they reached the waters of the *Kanawha* – at the end of the Trail.

. The warriors carried loads on their backs that were only just bearable, not to mention the four large trestles, one between each pair. Determined to be one of them, Asemota placed as much weight on his shoulders that he could, whilst Nadie remained fleet of foot, preferring only to carry her enormous cotton wood bow and sachet of arrows.

It would not be until the next full moon that they would reach the *Kanawha* waters where the 'Place of the White Stone' lay, marking the start of the traversable river beds once more. Before such time was reached, they crossed the Southern Appalachian Mountains, travelling along the Great Indian Trail, famed for its history of battles and ignominious trade between rival tribes. Already there were signs of the colonial French peoples, with their hamlets and chapels gracing the banks of the Great Trail River, a river the French had already named The Greenbrier.

Seeing the colonial settlements had put fear into Nadie's heart, she knew that the French had traversed towards the Illiniweck lands of her forefathers, plying for trade and building their own villages or 'forts' as she had heard them so called.

And then there was talk of the Jesuits.

Etchemin and the warriors built their new canoe at the *Kanawha* waters. It would be a further two full moons before they would reach home. They travelled through the *Haudenosaunee* country, making trade with the Matriarchal tribes of the *Cherokee* and *Tuscaroras* before the waters turned westward into the colossal waters of the O-Y-O River - their beautiful river - with a current running free in their favour to take them home to their treasured lands.

*

The last night of camp, before they entered the waters of their home village, was a buoyant one for the men, they had not seen their wives or children for over six months. When they left home it was spring, now it was autumn and the leaves of the trees were turning yellow.

Nadie spoke to the group around the ritual fire, sharing her concerns about the colonial white peoples. But Asemota knew this was only a deflection to hide her true fears, she would not reveal those fears to the tribe – not yet in any event.

The warriors learned that the French had travelled down from the great lakes of the north and along the very river the party were now on, the O-Y-O River. The French had named the river 'Ohio', pinching the phrase from the Native tongue. The colonials had already passed through the ancient lands of Cahokia, where now the tribes of the Illini had settled.

The camp fire burned brightly, adorning their faces with a golden embrace and flickering shadows, their conversation lively and debating while they chewed heartily on their roasted meat.

'I have heard that the French peoples have sent men of spirit and they have visited our lands. I hear that they wear crosses to emulate their God,' Nadie recounted.

'Who must they be to curse our land with such treachery,' said Etchemin. 'They have no right to bring their spiritual misdemeanor to our lands. Our gods and our spirits are sacred!'

'They call themselves Jesuits,' Nadie replied, trying to explain the term.

Asemota leapt to speak, 'I saw such people at the plantation, and they would wear long woolen robes and always bear a chain with a cross around their necks. They would preach and pray in wooden prayer houses near to the farm buildings. All of us were forced to do the same, to pray to their Christian God.'

Further cursing and cries of treachery could be heard amongst the warriors, some of them chanting briefly to their spirits, before Nadie asked them to be silent and pray for the fact that they had survived their long and arduous journey.

Nadie watched them, proud that they had helped her and proud that they had stayed so loyal, working so hard for her and her new found son, Asemota.

She sensed her Spirit Wolf, the *Manitou Mahweewa*, nearby, knowing that the great beast would have always been near to them along their journey. The giant creature had been carefully and stealthily keeping watch over the party, keeping extra vigilance as familiar home territory neared.

Nadie turned her thoughts to the night at the Falling Spring Falls where the *Manitou Mahweewa* mimicked in front of her and Asemota. Nadie knew what this meant. A terrible presence was coming near, an adversary so powerful that the destiny of her people would truly be in the hands of the spirits.

Matchitehew – the one with the evil heart was coming - and he was after 'The Maker'.

Chapter 4

Wise Head

The old white house could be seen through the birch trees as Sam drove along the winding gravel drive towards his father's abode. Recently renovated, the house had a white stone build replacing the old timber frame, something which James Campbell, although a little sad of the change, thought was wise for the building's longevity. A timber frame veranda, painted white, had been kept and still surrounded the entire house, maintaining part of the traditional nineteenth century façade.

The front of the house was south facing and had a circular gravel track turning back on itself, encircling a large, immaculately kept lawn. In the centre of the front lawn lay a beautifully arranged flower bed, with all manner of colours, ranging from yellow and red tulips, purple pansies, white crocuses and a smattering of blue bells. To the right of the house frontage, blending into the forest of birch trees, was a small Japanese garden. With small streams, little bridges and a collection of bonsai trees; it was like a miniature far off land, one which Sam revelled in. He always reminisced the miniature garden from his childhood days, where he would sit for an age on the west part of the veranda, overlooking the little garden, admiring its intricacy.

The house was set in a picturesque tree filled parkland near to the Will County Forest Preserve, practically an enclave within the huge expanding conurbation of Chicago. One could get to the house from the roads near Spring Creek, just a few kilometres from the City centre, being quick and easy to get to, depending on the time of day. It was a true sanctuary.

At the rear of the white house was a huge expanse of lawn, some two hundred metres long, leading to a dense tree line which marked the boundary of the land. Most magnificent of all, set on a raised part of the lawn, was a solidly built pine log cabin, perhaps fifty metres or so from the main house. The cabin was almost square in shape, but appeared oddly tall with an out of proportion brick chimney stack rising through the centre of the structure.

The policeman stopped his car, crunching the wheels to an abrupt halt on the gravel; Sam was always excited to be home and childhood memories, as would happen every time he arrived, flooded his mind.

He sat for a moment, marveling at the log cabin, remembering as a small child when his father first constructed the large square frame. It seemed to fit perfectly on a purpose built mound, all sides of the raised earth evenly spaced around the base wood paneling. The large brick-stacked chimney came years later, adding a central column nearly five metres tall. The original wooden slatted pitched roof had been altered to a steeper angle to accommodate the chimney. The four sides formed a perfect box shape, with the embossed pine trunks constructed in neat horizontal rows as if subservient to the chimney stack.

Sam could see a small plume of grey-white smoke billowing gently out of the cabin chimney, indicating where his father might be, probably busying himself with chores whilst stoking the cabin fire.

This was Sam's family home. He had such fond childhood memories growing up with his parents, and with the circle of friends they all had, there was never a dull moment, always doing, always learning – that was the environment his father preferred and it was to be relished.

Sadly, each time he arrived home, Sam couldn't help but reminisce over the passing of his mother, Georgia, who died some years ago. She had lived long enough to see Sam progress through his early years in the CPD, and see him married to his College sweetheart. Georgia died before Sam's marriage broke down and in some ways he was glad she never saw the turmoil. For fifteen years, James had been on his own, yet as each day passed, Sam knew his father would not miss Georgia any less.

Doors to the white house and the log cabin were open everywhere; there was a half empty glass of lemonade on a rickety old table near to the Japanese garden, and the smoke coming from the cabin seemed to get thicker – *he is busy and content*, Sam thought.

As he stepped out of his car, Sam caught the familiar gate of his father bounding across the rear lawn, coming from the direction of the cabin. A lanky rangy man, more than 80 years old, James Campbell was extremely fit for his age. The old man strolled down the tiered lawn with a great big beaming smile, always so pleased to see his son. Father and son embraced with a warm hug, they hadn't seen each other for a few days, since before Sam left for Cuba, and now James was anxious to catch up with the younger man – especially keen to hear about the exploits of Sam's vacation.

The old man was covered in wood chippings mixed with black dust, masking his brown hessian lumberjack shirt; his favourite old desert boots, looking tired and worn after decades of use, were also covered in dust. *Such an endearing quality*, Sam thought, his father's pride in those boots, boots of which Sam could not remember a day when his father was without them. In fact, James always joked about his boots and insisted that when the time came he should be buried with them on.

'You look troubled Sam, I have food and wine ready, it's been a hectic few days I can see, and no doubt you need to talk. To the cabin we shall retreat,' said James, calming Sam as he spoke.

Further childhood memories continued to fill Sam's senses, remembering the smells of the wood chip, the smoke billowing and the smell of the grease and oil from the old tools placed in a store at the back of the cabin. As long as he could remember his father always liked to keep all of the old 'gear' - cramming the store until hardly a glimmer of room was left.

'Busy couple of days Sam, I have read the news on your story – very curious events, they caught my interest that's for sure.'

'It would be nice to talk over it, see what you think, I've got a lot to do.'

'Seems that way Son, but we'll get to that, first tell me about Cuba?' said James.

Daily newspapers were strewn over a small lattice table on the cabin porch, distracting Sam from answering, his anxiousness was hard to hide.

'Relax Sam, stop reading the story for a minute – how did you get on with your Uncle Ermano?'

'He was the one that welcomed me – and I told him that I remembered him from Mom's funeral fifteen years ago…but there was quite a bit of indifference with the family, especially as time went by. After a couple of days, I felt he, and certainly the others, had had enough of me.'

'Who else did you meet?'

'Mom's youngest sister, Andria – she would not talk to me and shunned me completely when she came around to Uncle Ermano's farm house. Her reaction was unnerving, and that made me leave early for Havana.'

'Many of the Bauta people are simple farmers, I wouldn't worry about her ways, I never knew many of them that well, but she was never one to socialise, so I hear.'

'No it was more than that Dad. She looked straight through me with dark eyes and an aging scowl that I shall never forget. It was almost hatred, a deep resolute dislike that I could not fathom. I asked Uncle Ermano and he just brushed it off.'

Perhaps they blame me, and indirectly you, for keeping Georgia over here in the States.'

'But she loved it here, did she not?'

'She loved us Sam, that's for sure…dearly…and that's where her heart lay, no matter what her longing was for her family and her roots in Bauta.'

Sam was slightly choked and had to compose himself a little, a tear started to roll down his left cheek. He quickly wiped it away, trying to avoid his father's gaze, and James too was keen to avoid such emotion.

'I see my old paper's got the exclusive on the Art Institute Benefactor,' James remarked, as he picked up the Saturday edition of the Chicago Tribune.

Together they gazed at the pictures and text on the front page of the iconic newspaper, Sam's commentary emblazoned, it seemed, in bold letters at the start of the first column.

'You get quite a mention Sam, says you looked nervous on TV…also says Wilmshurst made you feel uncomfortable?' James recounted, spotting the anguish on Sam's face. 'I never did like the man anyway, pompous old creature – he takes great delight in unnerving people.'

'I'm on the back foot and I need more information. It wouldn't be so bad if Walters had got a grip of this with me, but he seems all over the place…I've never seen it in him before,' said Sam.

James laughed a little sarcastically at the dilemma,

then strode back to the house kitchen to fetch extra food that he had forgotten. He returned with bread, cheese and some wild onions, together with a bottle of his favourite Chardonnay red wine – already opened to warm in the midday air.

Both men settled and were now sat on the edge of the cabin porch, legs dangling over the porch frontage, just able to scrape their feet on the tiered lawn below. From their vantage point they had an open plan view of the expanse of the white house and intricate Japanese garden, mesmerising Sam for a moment.

'It's all looking very lush and peaceful father,' remarked Sam.

'I try my best, it keeps me fit,' said the eighty-two year old. 'Come on, tell me what's on your mind – what do you think has happened? Tell me more? Then I'll tell you what I think.'

Sam reeled off what he knew so far, trying to keep the facts simple before getting to the point.

'My main lead has got to be Krell – there is so much unexplained about him. Joyce Marsh at the Institute mentioned that he has gone missing and we know now that he is probably back in England as you and I talk. As for the Benefactor, Anippe Khu, she is back in Egypt – at least the flight manifesto says she should be,' explained Sam.

'You are smiling again Sam, seems Joyce Marsh may have had an effect on you,' said James, cheekily.

'Are you listening Dad?'

'Mmm...I went to Egypt once,' mentioned James. 'It was during the Suez Crisis – so long ago, I was one of the first black reporters ever to get such an assignment.'

Sam was thrown a little, he knew of his father's reputation and had figured he was a well-travelled, worldly man; but he had never heard him speak much of his endeavours.

'Can we stick to the story? I need to work out which way to go next.'

'Seems like Egypt or England - take your pick…perhaps it is all an elaborate ruse. You don't think Krell and Anippe Khu are in cahoots?'

'At the moment I feel as though anyone and all could be involved, I don't know who to trust. Both Khu and Krell need tracing that's for sure.'

'Well then keep it simple,' said James assuredly. 'Follow your hunch, you usually find by sticking to the simple leads something will crop up. Just out of interest who actually owns the painting?'

A good question, Sam thought. What he did know was that Anippe Khu had stopped the payment transaction at the bank the moment she knew the painting had gone missing, so he supposed that the Chicago Art Institute and the State itself were the true victims, not that anyone knew how valuable the painting was originally. It would have been like lottery money for the Institute treasury if the transaction had gone through. The painting would now have a 'commercial value' of over ten million dollars, but this did not detract from the fact that, if everything was to be believed, the City of Chicago had lost a potential historical find.

'I am about as confused as I can be,' said Sam.

'What we do have is everyone running around like headless chickens – no painting, no exchange of money, but the City jumping up and down wanting it found and the culprits bought to bear. One important point is being forgotten, police officers have been injured – two of them very seriously with one of those expected to die very soon and the other perhaps unlikely to make it.'

'Then go and trace the painting, perhaps start in Egypt with Anippe Khu...that's just a feeling I have of course,' said James nonchalantly, forever remaining cool and objective.

Sam calmed a little and stopped shuffling his feet on the tiered lawn. He contemplated and hatched a plan; then he remembered what his father had said earlier.

'Egypt...Suez Crisis, what happened over there?'

'I never thought you would ask, it just struck me when you mentioned the Benefactor. But before I go on, why was Anippe Khu curious about the painting...I mean what was the picture of anyway?'

'I don't rightly know, Joyce Marsh said that it was some kind of craft painting, in a group of paintings depicting ceramic arts, she can't recall exactly. There seemed to be a protracted conversation between Krell and Anippe Khu and thereafter the painting was removed quickly, not many other people took much notice, including Joyce.'

'Well there is plenty of notice now; everyone will want to know what the picture is and for certain where it has gone,' said James.

James switched tack again, recalling his time in

Egypt, wanting to tell Sam of his adventure there.

'Go to Egypt, I found it fascinating all those years ago – and I came across a very strange story, I would say. I remember going on a bit of a trek to Cairo along dusty roads, catching a lift here and there. I was already in Egypt covering the Suez…well there is no point in me beating around the bush…I'll tell you the whole story.'

Sam's mind was reeling, and now that he had hatched a plan, he was too keen to get on with it. His father's story would have to wait – even though he had prompted a response from him.

'Sorry, I know I asked, but I just haven't time now, I think I know what I am going to do, I would love to hear your story with all the detail - but I have got to make arrangements. You make sure you tell me when I get back.'

'Have you decided on Egypt then?'

'Yes, well - there is a good bet I can find Anippe Khu at the Cairo Museum in Egypt, your hunch has become my hunch and I am grateful to you. Krell could be in England or anywhere, I'll get after him when I know more about his connections.'

'Don't forget with these things, the more time goes by, the less chance you will have of recovering the painting.'

'Perhaps,' said Sam.

James looked at Sam affectionately, fatherly instinct overwhelming him.

'Be safe Son, perhaps take someone with you, two minds and all that…'

The younger Campbell stood up, pushing his body off the cabin porch with a leap onto the lawn. He grabbed his father and gave him an extended hug, promising he would keep in touch as much as he could. They walked back to Sam's car, James taking his time, putting a slight delay on his son's departure.

The vehicle eventually started to move off, but then Sam remembered something, winding his window down to shout back at his father, who was now strolling back to the cabin.

'I take it you miss me already Sam,' said James with a beaming smile.

'I nearly forgot – I met an old friend of yours yesterday at the TV studio, said his name was Mike Tremble. He looked like an old Native American fellow, a strong looking proud man, must be in his seventies.'

'Well I never…Mike Tremble, I haven't seen him for a good while. He used to call around here when you were a young boy, but you may not remember him. I saw him years later in Chicago doing a few odd jobs for the media companies. He was a good front-man…a good guy to have around. I bet he was on reception?'

'Good guess, he looked like some old Native American Chief, people seemed to be drawn to him.'

'My goodness, he is a *real* Chief,' said James. 'He is a very proud but humble man. His tribe hails from around these parts, not sure where though, but certainly from Illinois that much I am certain. "Chicagoans – People of the Wild Onion", he always used to remind me. You see the wild onions we have been eating – they are called *shikaakwa*, translated by the French into the name 'Chicago' – well never mind…I had better get in touch with him again.'

The car moved off as James finished his last sentence, and the old man was reluctant to move for a second even when the vehicle passed out of sight.

He sauntered back into the log cabin, hands on his head, brushing his tight grey and black curls away from his furrowed brow. Worry enveloped his mind – Egypt was a volatile place again, and certainly had been whilst he was there so many years ago. Now his only child was about to embark on a potentially dangerous enquiry, journeying to a foreign country. His own memories of Egypt came flooding back and he decided to look for a particular diary he had hidden in the cabin.

In a little annex area, away from the main cabin space, James kept articles and journals that he had prepared throughout his career – these were items of his most treasured possession. As he stood in the little room, contemplating, the wood burning smell reached his nostrils making him twitch his nose whilst he removed the marked floorboard, revealing his hideaway. Carefully lifting out a faded orange coloured leather bound diary, blowing off the dust, he opened it up on the first page.

'A curious story indeed,' he said out loud.

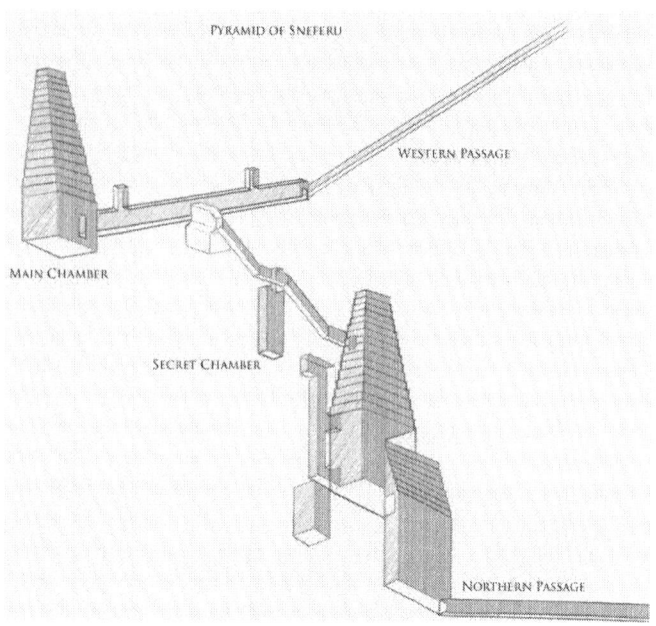

The Chambers of the Snefru Pyramid.
Dahshur, Egypt.

Chapter 5

The Parchment

1956 A.D.

'Get your bloody head down Yank!' bellowed the British Army Tank Commander.

The tall moustached soldier stared down at the young James Campbell, who was pressing himself against the desert fighting Centurion tank, desperately trying to see over the embankment wall towards the Egyptian Army position, on the opposite side of the Suez Canal.

The Commander had half of his torso above the turret line, some three metres above where James was crouched. The soldier, with his fearsome glare, turned away from James and out towards the Egyptian armoured column. Pressing desert binoculars closer to his eyes, the Commander then banged hard on the tank turret, signaling to his gunner.

'Fire!'

The 105mm gun thundered an armoured piecing shell across the waterway, taking a split second to hit a concrete rampart, narrowly missing its target.

'Damn!' shouted the Commander. 'Reload!'

By now the Russian built SU100 Egyptian Army tank destroyer, which had been the focus of attention, was starting to move and point its gun towards the British position. James peered over the wall again, desperately clicking off photographs with his brand new state of the art, Canon 35mm single lens reflex camera. The black and silver camera had become a trusty companion during the last few months, now it would have to prove its worth in the heat of a desert battle.

As the dust and smoke cleared, James managed to capture photographs of the flurry across the water. Abject fear struck him and he could barely hold the camera as he saw the enemy gun start to train on the British tank. Without warning this time, the Centurion tank fired its huge gun once more, hurtling its killer shell with pinpoint accuracy towards the target. The SU100 tank destroyer was obliterated, killing all within and around it.

'Got what you needed? Now get the hell out of here,' bellowed the Army Commander once more.

No argument from James as he saw the fearsome grimace once again, *time to depart* he thought. The British Army tank fired up its engines, a sure sign for James to alight his position. He searched around and saw, fifty metres to the rear of the tank, a collapsed sandbag barricade, enough for him to get his head down and compose himself before making an attempt to return to the Army depot.

He dashed for the sandbag refuge only to be met by a troop of British Royal Marines running to reach moving cover behind the Centurion tank. He narrowly avoided colliding with the leader, a small stocky, hard faced sergeant, before diving into the sandbag enclave. James turned his head and peered back at the soldiers, still having the presence of mind to take photographs of the unfolding scene. Then he took breath.

He lay still for a while, waiting until his breathing returned to somewhere near normal. Dust covered his khaki trousers and his torn press corps brown leather jacket. One thing he was grateful for, was the pair of robust British Army desert boots he had purloined from a Naval auxiliary, on his journey aboard a British Navy minesweeper from Malta to Port Said. They were a life line for his tired legs and feet.

A moment of reflection for him, not that this perturbed him from his overall excitement nor suppressed the adrenalin surging through his body – it was as if the pieces of the unfolding drama had suddenly been fitted together. With his trusty orange coloured, leather bound notebook, faded at the edges, he took it in hand and made some relevant notes.

November 7, 1956…Front line…Suez Canal, British and French forces strike Egyptian Army positions…All around me I see rubble, broken buildings, death…soldiers and tanks from the British Army and Marines press forward.

Photographs of Russian built SU100 destroyed by British

Centurion tank...and Marines from 45 Commando [with tank]. Photos of deserted streets and stricken bodies [Egyptian civilians].'

James lost concentration at the sound of more troops and vehicles moving towards his barricaded position. He stared along the military column, knowing that he needed to head towards from whence they came – the military depot at the El Gamil Airfield. There was no suppressing his intent as he boldly climbed out of the barricade, fastening his camera and notebook inside the camera pouch, then raising his hands towards the soldiers. One young lieutenant pointed his pistol towards the nervous reporter, but soon lowered it once hearing James' voice and seeing the USA press corps badge on James' jacket.

'Move along as fast as you can Sir,' said the soldier.

'You bet' said James, picking up his pace as he passed the line of sweat ridden, dusty clothed military men.

Half a mile to the depot, James had guessed, and he was desperate to get there. Now under relative safety, he still observed his surroundings despite his anxieties. He knew he was perhaps fortunate and privileged to be a young black reporter given such a prominent task, but he thought of himself as a pioneer following in the footsteps of his mentor, Vernon Jarrett, a popular columnist for the Chicago Defender and the African Negro Press, a man who James saw was set for stardom. James modelled his photographs on the inspiration of another of his heroes, Gordon Parkes who was one of the first black men to take photographs of the black experience in America and have his work published in the Life magazine. James had visions of making contact with Parkes and sharing experiences with him. For now, both Jarret and Parkes would remain an inspiration for the young reporter, and he wanted to make them proud.

Before long James stumbled into the El Gamil Airfield depot and strode quickly towards the press enclosure. The military had secured the airfield two days ago, encountering very little resistance – now it was a hive of activity as resources poured in.

Tired, with muscles aching, and using every ounce of energy just to breathe, James flopped onto his makeshift Army bunkbed, one of a number crammed together in the press tent. The green canvas British Army square tent had two rows of wooden framed beds, a row pressed against each edge of the tent. In the middle, squeezed into the gap, was a row of small trestle tables adorned with field typewriters. *No sleep just yet*, James thought, as he stared ominously at the typing machines.

He wrenched his aching body out of his bunk, grabbing his note pad from the sand filled camera pouch. As he sat at the tables, and with some reluctance at first, James pulled one of the olive green Hermes typewriters closer to his chest.

'Let the story begin,' he mumbled to himself.

He started to tap the keys, becoming invigorated slightly, recognising that he had so much to say in so little time.

Note to Editor – Chicago Defender [and transition to Chicago Tribune as desired]

November 7th 1956 – British, French and Israelis have pushed Egyptian forces to the banks of the Suez Canal. Ceasefire called at midnight on 6th. [Pockets of fighting still exist, as I witnessed].

Word is, Russians have threatened nuclear conflict and President Dwight Eisenhower has threatened everybody. British military seem furious – there is an imperialistic attitude out here – but they are not welcome – the last permanent garrison [of the Empire?] left only months ago, now they are the aggressor once again. The Egyptian President Nasser has declared the nationalization of the Suez Canal.

Sending my eye witness account with this telegram [Have photographs of British attack on Egyptian positions].

James peeled off the typed report, nearly ripping the bottom edge in his haste. He ran to the Army telephony post and asked for it to be wired by telegram as soon as possible. Luckily he was one of the first of the press corps to have his story sent, the telephony post was starting to become very busy with Army press staff already fraught with nerves trying to interpret the unfolding events. The message transmission would take only seconds to reach the night duty editor at the Chicago Defender, and James was eager to wait for any acknowledgement.

Excited at the prospect that his news would also reach the Chicago Tribune, James remained at the post. Within minutes a reply came, yet the middle part of the return message recorded something entirely unexpected – and that part was a direct response from the night editor of the Tribune. James tried to fathom the context of the message.

His tiredness didn't help, his aching body desperately needed rest as he struggled to read the message for the second and the third time, it was bemusing, leaving James slightly befuddled. The middle and last paragraph, although short, seemed so incongruous, so out of context - it read;

"Leave Port Said, head to Cairo - meet with a Dr. Bektamun Ayoubi [eminent archeologist]. You will be taken to the ancient Pyramid site at Dahshur…

Historic find…very significant…we are interested…[Tribune]

We have enough on Suez to run what we need…President Eisenhower is going to give a statement.

Can you make plans for Dahshur right away…? [Have a contact number in Cairo]."

Adrenalin surged through his body, helping to clear his head from any residue tiredness, and having absorbed the detail, James' first thoughts were on how to plan and accomplish such a mission.

Despite trying to work out how to get there, he needed to understand what was in store and who might be waiting for him. He had heard of the ancient site at Dahshur and knew it was pretty close to some of the famous pyramids, but his real knowledge was confined to childhood curiosities, reading manuscripts in the Chicago Museum. James also knew that the Dahshur site was a militarised zone, and it wouldn't be easy getting to Cairo through a war torn country, let alone to Dahshur.

From the frying pan into the fire, he thought, enthused at what the historic find may be – perhaps it was a tomb of an ancient Pharaoh, or a significant historical religious find - whatever it was, he felt captivated. It also meant that he could spend a little while longer in Egypt, a place of deep fascination for him, particularly with him being a writer and knowing that this was the place which saw the birth of such sophisticated writing techniques – like the hieroglyphs. The re-discovery of the hieroglyphs through the famous Rosetta Stone was undeniably poignant to him and perhaps this new discovery was related somehow. In any event he couldn't help wondering about the irony, that here he was in Egypt, amongst the French and the British, the very two nations that literally fought over possession of the Rosetta Stone at the turn of the eighteenth and nineteenth centuries.

The erstwhile reporter ran back to the press tent and fetched his purloined Army issue duffle bag, crammed full with his camera, note pads and other belongings, before making his way to the hectic vehicle depot in search of an Army field telephone.

Barging his way through the mounting number of reporters and military personnel, James eventually caught the attention of a portly, harassed looking British Army Quartermaster who reluctantly gestured James into a side annex of the depot pre-fab building, hastily constructed as a check point. The Army field phone was hanging precariously on a temporary wall and James wondered if he would ever get through to his contact with such forlorn looking equipment.

The call was placed through an operator, James desperately hoping to hear English.

'Do you speak English?' James said shouting down the phone.

'Yes,' came the reply.

'Where have I been put through to?'

'The Museum of Cairo,' said the voice.

'I am after Doctor…erm…let me get this right…Bektamun Ayoubi.'

'I'll put you through to her.'

'Dr. Ayoubi?' shouted James over the turmoil of the vehicle depot.

'Yes,' said the deliberate female voice.

'My name is James Campbell, from the Chicago Defender, I've been asked to contact you…actually by the Chicago Tribune.'

'Yes of course Mr. Campbell – I have been waiting for your call – can you make it to Cairo?'

'Where to in Cairo?'

'The Museum of Antiquities, right in the centre, I'll give you directions.'

At the time of the call, and much to James' concern, a British Army Bedford truck hurriedly pulled up alongside the depot building and started to load reporters and soldiers, intent on travelling across to the other side of the Canal - the very place where James had been informed earlier that he needed to get to if he wanted a lift to Cairo.

Anxiously scribbling in his notepad, James

recorded the directions given to him by Dr. Ayoubi, shouting the pleasantry goodbyes to the Professor over the phone as he quickly turned his attention to jumping onto the back of the Army wagon.

The Bedford lorry started to set off before he could reach it, and he ran in desperation to catch up with the vehicle, using all his speed and strength to grab hold of the rails at the rear, before he and his kit bag were hauled ignominiously by his fellow reporters into the bodies of other personnel crammed into the bay.

The truck sped off, struggling with the weight, full to the brim with supplies, soldiers, and reporters with their respective kit bags. James clutched his bag tight to his body, trying to remain seated as the truck drove south along the dusty, potholed Alexandria Port Said road, heading directly for the main conurbation. The vehicle travelled under the press banner, making its way through the war torn streets of the southwest point of the town; there was an uneasy peace, made more real when the onboard soldiers cocked their rifles, keeping an eye out for potential guerilla tactics from a remnant Egyptian army.

Dispatched near to an armada of supply wagons, waiting to move off to deliver much needed cargo to the city of Cairo, James flashed what cash he could muster to entice one of the Egyptian drivers to give him a lift. It wasn't long before one of them caught his eye and having parted with what seemed a lot of money he managed to hitch a ride on a rickety old grain wagon - its open top storage bay full to the brim of ground corn.

'I going straight Cairo, through Ismailia Desert Road,' said the wiry, dark haired truck driver in broken English. James could only hope that the driver would stick to his word.

*

Surprisingly, the 160 kilometre journey only took five hours, even with the seemingly endless road checks being conducted by the Egyptian Army. Much to the driver's amusement en-route, James had perpetually examined and re-examined the directions given to him by Dr. Ayoubi, trying to match them with a shoddy map he had commandeered from a fellow reporter. Luckily the truck driver gleaned a sense of where James was headed and took him as far as he could into the busy, bustling, yet tense streets of Cairo City.

'Carry on to walk by Mereit Basha Road, you will see museum,' shouted the driver as he waived his hand in the general direction.

James raised his hand, returning a friendly gesture, listening to the churning of the gears as the driver tried to find the right gear to move off. The young reporter stared in all directions, eventually catching a glimpse of the Museum through the Tahrir Square Plaza. He headed off, walking through the array of palm trees, and found himself outside the main entrance of the famous Cairo Museum of Egyptian Antiquities. He stopped for a while, feeling bewildered, amusing himself at the thought of how people in the City were just trying to get on with life, even in the middle of a war - ignoring the occasional dropping of bombs and propaganda leaflets by the British.

The large entrance of the Museum was dominated by a huge white archway, sunken into the red brick surround, rather like an old Victorian fire place. Two large pillars on either side of the archway led the eye to statuettes of Egyptian Princesses, placed high above either side of the huge doorway. As he walked through into the Museum lobby, James noticed the light shining from rows of small circular windows placed neatly at the top of the archway. The effect was stunning as the sun light poured through, creating individual beams of light. The hall way was galleried with rows of pillars giving rise to a wide stair case, its central surround dominated by giant marble and stone carvings of Egyptian Pharaohs. The marble floor covering, littered with neatly placed tombs and caskets, appeared grand; giving rise to the knowledge that this was one of the first concept museums of its kind in the world.

James walked wearily up to the main reception desk, catching the eye of an attractive, neatly dressed woman standing against the public side of the desk. She smiled at him – beautifully, he thought.

'Please tell me you are Dr. Ayoubi, or should I say Professor?' James said, returning an infectious smile.

'I am, and please call me Bektamun,' said the woman. 'You are undoubtedly James, you look so American,' she laughed.

'I thought I was blending in,' said James, continuing to smile.

The woman reached out her left hand, placing it gently onto his shoulders, guiding him away from the main hall.

'Let me get you some refreshment and explain to you why I put the call in to your paper.'

'That would be a good start,' said James.

She was a striking woman, he thought, not much older than himself, with a beautiful strong face. The English she spoke was near perfect, *very 'Westernised'*, he thought, determined to find out why. As the pair walked along one of the immense corridors, feeding from the main hall, James became implored.

'If you don't mind, but where did you learn to speak English so well?'

'Mainly in England and a little in your country, I studied abroad for a few years, I like to follow Western history as well as the work I do here. I have a fascination for world antiquities and how everything came about. The West's perspective is very important you know, especially when it comes to the past.'

'I guess, but how did you get on being…?'

'An Egyptian woman?' she pre-empted. 'Well, England wasn't so bad, my father is well connected through the Cairo Museum and he pulled a few strings for me to stay at King's College in London. It meant I could research one of the largest collections of Egyptian artifacts outside of my country. England has the…'

'Rosetta Stone?' James interrupted.

'Touché, Mr. Campbell, we interrupt each other quite cleverly,' said the Professor, smiling outwardly.

Inwardly she was smiling too; she had taken an immediate liking to her new found friend, Mr. James Campbell.

'What about America?' said James, curiously.

'I spent two semesters at the University of

Chicago, studying American cultures, I gained an affinity for the place.'

'Ah, am I perhaps detecting the connection, your call to the Tribune?' said James.

'I put a call into quite a few papers, yours was the first to respond with some interest, and you happened to be here!' she smiled broadly again.

James reciprocated, not wishing to correct her and explain again that he actually worked for the Chicago Defender.

From a central corridor, they entered a room through towering three-metre high, glass double doors. It was a room the like of which James had never seen, he was overwhelmed. It was laden with gilded edge books wall to wall, immaculately kept in tidy rows right up to the ceiling which extended another metre or so beyond the height of the doors. An office desk made of oak wood, sporting a brown leather top, sat central within the room - so that the person seated could look all around, no doubt as James imagined, being embraced and consumed by the collection. From the labelling etched into the wooden shelves, James spotted the conglomerate book themes, a mesmerising multi-national book collection of historical artifacts.

'You can see James I have been working on a project, hence the papers all over the desk,' said Bektamun. 'I am excited to tell you what I have planned - but not here.'

James was still transfixed on the book collection, 'I've never seen anything like it, the books are bound beautifully, there must be thousands of dollars' worth here.'

'Mostly my father's work, it's his collection really, I just look after it for him and use it for research. Come on, I have what I need,' she said retrieving some papers from the desk. 'I've got you booked into the Semiramis Hotel on the Nile River bank.'

'Impressive' said James. 'No expense spared! I have heard of it but never stayed there of course, I take it the Tribune approved?'

'Well of course!' said Bektamun, laughing. 'It's not far from here and it is a pleasant walk through Tahrir Square.'

The duo left the Museum in a chatty mood, taking a slow walk towards the Grand Semiramis Hotel. Opened in 1907, James recalled that it was the first hotel of its kind to be constructed by the Nile River side, its design influenced by European imperialistic architecture of the time. As they both glanced around, Bektamun pointed out the nearby Palace of Kasr Al Nil, which, poignantly, had housed the British Army of occupation over the years Egypt had been part of the British Empire. *Yet another strange irony for my notes*, thought the young reporter.

Walking through Tahrir Square, James more readily noticed the lush palm trees and vegetation. His foremost desire was to talk to the illustrious Professor about the current political situation, notwithstanding the plethora of contradictions he perceived, but perhaps now was not the right time. He would enjoy the walk, absorb the exotic sights and sounds along the riverside, and revere Bektamun's company; she hadn't called the newspaper to talk about war.

Near to Tahrir Square, The Semiramis Hotel was indeed a grand building with its exuberant baroque six story structure and extravagant internal decor, undoubtedly influenced by colonial imperialistic architecture and design – both British and European.

'There is so much to this hotel James. You are aware of the 'platonic' roof garden we have here?' said Bektamun cheekily.

'Legendary, Professor Ayoubi.' James expressed, as if he had anticipated the comment. 'I read somewhere about a famous event here last year, quite a celebration no doubt - pray tell, was it a sordid affair upon the roof garden?'

It was boisterous, but it had such meaning, especially for me, one of my heroes had a celebration,' said Bektamun. 'It was the Imamate of Agha Khan III, a recognition of his leadership in the Islamic world.'

'An interesting character, although I had heard he has not been too well lately. Why so poignant for you Professor?'

Bektamun looked at James and beckoned him to sit down in the lobby chairs near to a large window facing the Nile River bank, she was fascinated by the prowess of his knowledge, and she responded accordingly.

'Well his actual name is Sir Sultan Mohammed Shah - and, of course, he is highly decorated. For me, he is such an influential man in the Islamic world, bearing in mind James - he is the Imam to the Shia Ismaili Muslims. He was one of the founders of the All-India Muslim League'.

'Yes, I believe he was born in Karachi, now part of the new country... Pakistan, He must have had a hand in its formation I would think?'

'Correct,' said the Professor, pausing for a moment. 'You are so well informed James...for such a young man,' Bektamun laughed. 'I believe in him wholeheartedly, he is a peacemaker and the world needs men like him - and I need to know that there are people like him.'

'You are a follower then?' said James.

'I am a Muslim and I believe in his work, he is an Imamat and he is committed to helping the world solve its problems; he is a humanitarian, a protector. Last year he celebrated his platinum Imamate here at the hotel.'

'I guess you were there at the party?'

'Yes, I was privileged to be an invited guest with my father. We admired him, took strength from him for our work.'

Despite the scintillating talk with the endearing Professor, she had yet to reveal why she had convinced the Chicago Tribune to divert one of its freelance reporters into her midst. Normally, there would have to be an incomparable scoop on a particular story for the Tribune to run anything, especially in such circumstance. *The editors must have been beguiled by the Professor's charm*, James thought, charming as indeed she was.

'Listen, I know we could talk all night about so much - my beliefs, what I stand for, what I am trying to achieve and the fact that I, like my father, wish someday to emulate the Agha Khan's work. But there is something important I need to tell you. Of course it's the reason why I have dragged you here…it is about a discovery,' said Bektamun, excitedly.

'I understand your passion Professor and I am sure whatever your work is, a man such as the Agha Khan would have noted your enthusiasm. Please tell me of your discovery.'

'You may have heard of the region of Dahshur, which is south of here. There are pyramids there that have some renewed interest - a new dig is taking place and we have found something,' said Bektamun, continuing enthusiastically.

'I don't know whether you know about the famous pyramids of Dahshur – but it is the site of the Red and Bent Snefru Pyramids, the first of their kind to be built four and a half thousand years ago by King Snefru and his followers.'

'The first King of the fourth Egyptian Dynasty, he became King through marriage,' said James.

'Yes, yes…you know this! But now I need to show you. Unfortunately, the whole pyramidal site is a militarised zone, although of course the archeology team have got access. It has been so difficult working there over the years, particularly with all of the conflict…but we think we have made a significant break-through.'

'I have read of the two Snefru Pyramids,' said James. 'The Bent Pyramid actually looks bent, whilst I think the Red Pyramid takes the name from the red brick.'

'Yes James, but the interesting fact is that we think the Bent Pyramid may be the first non-step pyramid ever attempted to be built. There must have been a problem with their original techniques, hence the reason why it looks bent,' said Bektamun, revelling in the fact that she had James' attention.

'Can you imagine something nearly four and a half thousand years old and what secrets it may have? I believe its design is the founding father for the great pyramids of Giza, which everyone recognises.'

'The discovery?' said James.

'I am getting to it,' she smiled. 'The unusual circumstance to the Bent Pyramid is that there are two different entrances leading to two separate chambers – well at least that was the original design.'

'What do you mean?'

'Someone - sometime later - created a passageway, a link between the two burial chambers, we don't know who and we don't know why. Anyway we think we have discovered a secret vault beneath the link – we think this will give us a clue.'

'Hang on, you are losing me a little - what vault? And what clue?'

'We have found some unusual looking stones in the layout of the connecting passageway. The Pyramid is normally made of all limestone, but there are granite stones right in the centre against a wall; initial observations tell us there is something hollow underneath, if it is a vault, then we will have more of an understanding of the passageway.'

'James pondered. 'So I guess tomorrow will be the day you open the vault, and you want me there to cover the story, however that pans out?'

'Yes…yes my dear young reporter.'

The broad infectious smile from Bektamun captivated James ever more, and he couldn't help noticing her deep brown eyes sparkling as she embellished her excitement. Compliments and farewells were exchanged as James climbed the grand stairs, watching the intriguing Professor leave the hotel. Entering his room, being so exhausted, he practically fell asleep before his head even reached the bed pillow.

*

The road to the Necropolis of Dahshur was dry and dusty, made more uncomfortable by the slightly precarious driving of Professor Ayoubi in the commandeered open top Jeep. James hung on to the passenger door and the dashboard as Bektamun sped along the sand and the grit, desperate to reach her destination. The erstwhile reporter spotted the distinctive kinked shape of the King Snefru Bent Pyramid a few kilometres before they were due to arrive, and this had the effect, for a short while at least, of distracting him from his fear of landing in a ditch somewhere. The Pyramid was indeed peculiarly 'bent', purporting to be very steep throughout the base wall before giving rise to a less steep angular cone commencing half way up its overall height.

Bektamun eyed James' curiosity once again, shouting above the noise of the Jeep. 'Magnificent sight is it not? We are only a kilometre away now. Did you know that it's one of the most intact pyramids in Egypt? If you look, it still has some of its outer casing.'

'Why does it have the kink?' said James.

'We think that it was constructed at a steeper angle before being rectified to prevent a structural collapse…this must have influenced the builders for the later pyramids…' Bektamun stopped talking as they reached the military checkpoint, bringing the Jeep to a halt in front of two very tall Egyptian soldiers dressed in desert uniform and green berets.

The Professor did all the talking, diverting any suspicion away from James. The barrier lifted, affording much relief for the American and broadening the smile on Bektamun's face. Within minutes Bektamun drove the Jeep right up to the huge Pyramid, parking the vehicle abruptly near to one of the large walls.

Bektamun leapt out of the Jeep like a giddy school child, removing her goggles and orange headscarf - dragging James with her, imploring him to wipe the dust out of his eyes and follow her quickly. They passed the sight of a small temple dedicated to King Snefru, and towards the north wall of the Bent Pyramid, where they would have to climb into one of the entrances.

James was startled at the size of the pyramid stretching up before him, it seemed skyward bound, and the limestone casing higher up on the structure was totally unexpected; it was truly remarkable that the casing had survived for so many thousands of years.

Following Bektamun's instructions, James climbed a purpose built wooden scaffold ladder leading to a small opening some ten metres from the ground. His heart started to pound with anticipation. At the misshapen limestone entrance, he saw the beginning of a passageway, which descended into darkness only a few metres from where he was standing. The passageway was more symmetrical than the entrance, the oblong structure having neatly placed limestones angled for the descent, allowing any newcomer to marvel at the design.

The couple descended slowly into the bowels of this extraordinary pyramid, and there was a sense of awe and expectancy as they felt transported to an ancient time and place.

A dark antechamber was the first room they came to, a place where King Snefru's subjects would have placed all of his belongings at the time of his death. Next the reporter and the Professor hurriedly scaled a tall vertical ladder, at least fifteen metres high, leading from the antechamber and ascending towards a connecting tunnel - deep within the centre of the main structure. Voices could be heard, stemming from the tunnel.

'My team are here,' said Bektamun excitedly.

The climb was hard, James having to concentrate on not falling, whilst Bektamun sped up the wooden slats like a cat. There was a dim light at the top of the climb and it was something for James to focus on. At the top of the ladder, James scrambled over the final wooden rung to face a stepped limestone tunnel ascending to his left as he peered out. The tunnel had been built in large square segments, making it easy to walk through, and there, further along, he could just about make out the outline of bodies, a team of Egyptian archeologists chattering away, standing over a hole in the middle of the tunnel floor.

'Ahmed…Ahmed are you there?' shouted Bektamun.

'We are at the spot,' cried a male voice.

'Come on James, this is it, time to see our secret.'

An Egyptian man, slightly portly in stature, being at least 50 years of age, greeted the duo. The man groomed his black and grey beard, and smiled broadly with such excitement in his eyes. A strong hand clasped James' hand as pleasantries were exchanged.

'I am Professor Ahmed Khalil, Mr. Campbell, I welcome the Chicago Tribune to our humble surroundings,' said the man in strong accented English.

'We have removed the granite block stone from the tunnel floor already Bektamun, sorry for not waiting, but it seemed the natural thing to do, we have not descended yet.'

'That's fine Ahmed, let's take a look.'

Two other Egyptian men formed part of the archeology team, one of them very short and wiry whilst the other was tall, and both were equally as excited, smiling eagerly in anticipation. The atmosphere was electric and James too was absorbed with the overwhelming feeling of potential discovery.

Everyone stared at the gaping hole in the tunnel floor, the unusual out of place granite stone having been lifted to reveal a secret stairway.

'It seems to be in the right position,' said Bektamun. 'It seems to be right above the blind chamber we have suspected.'

'What do you mean?' said James, unable to refrain from asking.

'We thought there was another small chamber hiding behind the main chamber where you have just climbed out of, but it must have been blocked at some point, maybe thousands of years ago. We never thought anything of it until Ahmed and his team discovered the single granite block in this tunnel, the one that has been removed as you can see. The granite stone was obviously a marker for the opening to the secret chamber. Well here it is gentlemen; heaven knows what we will find but we'll know soon enough,' said Bektamun.

'There is just enough room for a person to squeeze through the gap,' said Ahmed. 'I will go first, if I can get through, anyone can!'

Bektamun laughed nervously, and followed the dim light of the torch Ahmed was holding. James was last in, turning his body to walk down backwards on all fours, squeezing his tall frame through the gap between the exposed stones.

The secret ante-chamber was small, cold and ghostly, the effect accentuated by Ahmed shining the dim torch light around the room. No more than three metres square, with a low ceiling, the room could hardly contain five excited people struggling to step around each other as they tried to fathom what they were seeing. Ahmed barked some orders to one of the other men to fetch more lighting as he and Bektamun focused on something in the far corner of the chamber.

'Look, here Ahmed,' said Bektamun pointing along

the back wall.

Two stone stelae were braced against the wall supported by larger stones on the floor. A third stone, perfectly rectangular shaped, not of the same composition as the other two, was propped up at an angle in the far corner opposite the chamber steps. It was this particular stele that the two Professors became engrossed with.

'Extraordinary, this particular Stele is made out of granite, like the tunnel stone we removed. The other two are what we would expect - limestone, with usual inscriptions about King Snefru…but this one…' Ahmed's voice tailed off as he stared closer at the unusual dark coloured tablet.

'Remove the dust and it looks like the Stele was made and inscribed yesterday,' said Bektamun.

James couldn't hope to imagine what the archeologists were actually feeling; he thought moments like this for such people must allow for the arduous years of meticulous exploration to be infinitely worthwhile, yet he too was caught up and enthralled by the excitement.

Bektamun turned to James, her own excitement hardly containable.

'It's thousands of years since anyone has stepped inside this chamber James. These stelae haven't been seen by human eye for maybe three or four millennia…it is quite unbelievable,' said Bektamun.

'You are focused on the tablet in the corner, why is it so different than the others?' said James.

Before he had finished his question Bektamun had

turned once again to look at the granite Stele, she and Ahmed scanning the hieroglyphs, chattering in their native tongue. James started to make notes in his journal, painting the scene within the chamber, recording the events moment by moment, desperate for Bektamun to reveal more.

After five minutes of frenzied conversation between Ahmed and Bektamun, the chamber fell deathly silent, as if the Professors' voices had suddenly been extracted from their bodies.

Trance like, Bektamun and Ahmed were completely transfixed. The silence became uncomfortable; James' instinct as a reporter made him intervene.

'Professors, perhaps you could share with us what you have found - I am sorry for asking.'

There was no response initially, save Bektamun placing her hands on her head and momentarily looking at James. Ahmed started to tremble, continuing to read the inscription at an increasingly rapid rate. Bektamun at last stepped back from the tablet, placing her hand on James' shoulder.

'The two stelae to your left, James, are normal, as normal as we have ever seen. They talk about King Snefru's life and death, including everyday activities in the Royal household, even down to what goods they would have purchased for banquets,' she said, gathering breath. 'This perfectly rectangular shaped one is on a completely different level, almost Godforsaken…a bit like the lost 'Arc of the Covenant'. I, or rather we, have never seen such a Stele as this before, it is incomprehensible.'

All James could do was listen, and he was in awe with her endearing commentary - further revelations he fully expected, notebook in hand.

'Ahmed has read through many of the words...what I can tell you is that the writings are entirely prophetic, almost supernaturally so, I mean in the sense that it reveals something, something that could not possibly have been known thousands of years ago.'

'In what way, how do you know this?' quizzed James.

'It is very detailed. Small intricate hieroglyphs adorn the Stele front and back, and the detail and uniqueness of the writing is incredulous, nothing like this exists.'

Ahmed, stepped back from the granite Stele, wheezing a little, his round belly moving up and down rapidly as he tried to formulate some words.

'How can it record such insight?' said Ahmed. 'The edges of the tablet reveal a remarkable journey of human history, mulling over thousands of years, starting well before the Egyptian civilization – an unbelievable prophecy...'

'What prophecy?' asked James, slightly frustrated.

Bektamun took over the recital.

"That mankind will spring forth from the central lands where the desert plains and the forest jungles lie, and spread across the good Earth throughout all of its far lands. Across wide rivers and great seas, men and women will travel...creed and tribe will grow apart, living within and making these far

lands their own…"

She stopped reciting, turning back to look at James and Ahmed, bewilderment contorting her face.

'How can it propose this?' she said. 'If it is referring to the migration of humankind, then judging by our normal estimate for the age of this Stele, say three to four thousand years, the extended migration throughout the world would have already happened. It cannot be a prediction on something that had already taken place?'

'Not necessarily,' said Ahmed. 'It may be proposing what was already happening at the time of King Snefru. The Egyptians and Mesopotamians were starting to decipher intricate knowledge of the Mediterranean cultures, finding elaborate pictorial stelae from ancient peoples. Perhaps the Mediterranean could be the great sea our newly found Stele refers to?'

'No Ahmed, let me read on, you know what we thought!' said Bektamun, somewhat annoyed.

"The greatest of all the earthly seas will be given to cross, a sea so great that only by the hand of Mother Nature will humankind walk the ice bridge to the pastures of tall forests and deep river valleys…"

Ahmed responded before Bektamun finished her recital.

'The Ancient Egyptians would have no concept, thought or rational perspective on the phenomenon of such history, including, what I think you are thinking, the impact of the last ice age and the transit across the Bering Strait. Only modern history records this, not ancient scripts such as this,' he said with certainty in his voice.

Bektamun read on, mumbling to herself whilst trying to interpret and decipher the hieroglyphs. 'This is the part where Ahmed and I think that the prophecy really starts, we are struggling to put the hieroglyphs into modern phraseology, perhaps you could help Ahmed.'

"*Humankind will transcend to have power over all earthly creatures, bearing testament to the Gods for their own forbearance, heed to the knowledge that presides over him that holds the key…*"

'Whatever that is supposed to mean? The next bit is really tricky, we can only state the literal meaning,' said Ahmed.

"*For he that shall be anointed to have sight of the sacred image…on the skin of the animal…shall endure the task set before him...*"

'I shall come back to that,' said Bektamun. 'There is something else, something we can't see properly, it's on the rear of the Stele facing the wall. It looks like some kind of embossed circle - we need to put the tablet upright.'

James and the other men grabbed hold of the Stele

and moved the granite object to an upright position, allowing Bektamun to crouch down between the Stele and the wall, shining a torch on the round object protruding slightly from its base. She carefully and deliberately brushed away the dust and cobwebs from the heavily embossed circular carving, whilst Ahmed and James were able to look on from their side.

'Good Lord, it looks like a globe, it can't be!' shouted James.

Nobody said a word. Bektamun painstakingly continued to remove the dust, controlling her exasperation as much as she could.

'It is a globe,' said Bektamun quietly. 'Look at it, you can see the outline of the oceans and the continents.'

The globe was embossed within the Stele, protruding the normal face by a few centimetres. James guessed that overall, the globe could be no more than twenty centimetres in diameter, but it clearly marked the recognisable modern day outline of the coast of Australasia, China, the Japans and the Bering Strait from Russia to Alaska. It incorporated the coast line of North and South America with prominence given to the vast Pacific Ocean.

After what seemed an eternal silence, Ahmed spoke.

'We must rationalise this…remember the Greeks presumed that the earth was a globe. Maybe the Stele is much younger than we think and this is their representation, perhaps this is their doing?'

'Then how do you explain the hieroglyphs?' said Bektamun. 'And the Earth model is unexplainable –

no one three or four thousand years ago should have had this knowledge.'

'Remember Bektamun…the Rosetta Stone was written in Greek as well as hieroglyphs, you know this - there may lie your answer.'

'There is no Greek on this Stele and I know this was made before the Greeks came to Mesopotamia – come on Ahmed!'

Ahmed was desperately searching for a logical answer in his mind. 'Four thousand years ago, man was well established in India, China, The Americas and in Australia, this could simply be a missing piece of recorded human history, one that gives knowledge of prior exploration.'

'Search your soul Ahmed, you know that can't be.'

'Then it must be a hoax,' he replied. 'Someone put this here but a few years ago.'

'This vault has not been opened for over 4,000 years, I know it in my heart,' said Bektamun. 'Look at the text before the globe, it reads on in the same vain…it keeps repeating a prophecy.'

"Heed to the knowledge that presides over him that holds the key for he is The Maker that shall prophesize with the sacred image on the skin of the dead animal and he shall endure the task set before him…."

'Now its referring to *"a Maker"* – and it repeats the text about the *"image on the skin of a dead animal"* many times. A better translation would be 'parchment', I think – that is our modern day equivalent,' said

Bektamun.

'Yes,' said Ahmed. 'Drawings, images or writing on animal skins or hides are called parchments, but the first parchments have only been thought to emerge in Egypt about 2,500 years ago. Ones that old would be corrupted and very hard to distinguish now.'

'But from what I have gleaned, this Stele is perhaps much older than 2,500 years, so it could redefine our thinking about when parchments first emerged and were used for writing or imagery,' said James, by now far too curious to keep his point of view to himself.

'We have a lot more to translate James,' said Bektamun. 'It will take a while, although it does tend to repeat itself - can you see the symmetry? Egyptians love symmetry – you see the writing in the vertical columns? There are symmetrical reversals on the opposite edges. It seems to be a progressive prophecy, one that repeats and adds a little more information each time.'

The Stele was gently placed back to its original position.

Exiting the chamber and making their way back into the connecting tunnel, Ahmed issued orders for the granite tunnel block to be replaced over the hole. They all agreed that each of them must remain silent until a rational decision could be made about the future of the Stele and the information it contained.

James understood the predicament and started to wonder whether any story would in fact seem a little far-fetched. This worked in Bektamun's favour; she had assumed James was a logical, thoughtful individual and she implored him not to reveal what had been seen – not just yet in any case. She suggested a cover story, one that simply articulated the ongoing work at the 'Bent' Pyramid where more stelae artifacts had been found, and perhaps elaborating the stories of King Snefru to stretch the public's imagination.

James agreed.

*

The young American reporter was relieved to be at the hotel again and was now very anxious to make plans for home and meet with his colleagues at the Chicago Defender, although his experience with Bektamun was one he had enjoyed immensely, fascinated by her presence and enthusiasm as much as he had found with the mystery of the ancient Stele.

Bektamun stayed with James in the hotel lobby for a while, wanting desperately to talk frankly with him and reveal more of what she had seen and understood, yet her pressing thought was how to protect the Stele. On the back of the Stele, she had caught a glimpse of a detailed prophecy that could never be revealed, at least not until the right time, whenever that may be.

'What shall you do with the Stele?' James asked.

'I don't quite know what to do with it in the long run, but for now, it will have to remain at the Bent Pyramid. No-one knows it is there, save ourselves and Ahmed's team,' said Bektamun, pondering.

'Can you trust them?'

'Ahmed? Yes of course…implicitly, and he can vouch for his men, I will have to trust him for that. The Pyramid is under military guard and so it will remain, I have good contacts there.'

'What of "The Parchment" described in the prophecy? Do you think it truly exists?'

Bektamun thought that was a very intuitive question, one she didn't expect.

'I don't know. I believe the Stele is real and tells a real story. One would presume "The Parchment" should be real in some form,' she said, stopping a little short for James' liking.

'And "The Maker", who or what is that?'

'Impossible to say, I would presume it refers to someone or something that has a grave or burdensome undertaking, it's hard to tell, I will need to read and decipher more.'

Again the answer seemed vague, and James wondered if Bektamun was fearful of giving away too much information.

'Time to say farewell James?'

'Yes my dear Professor Ayoubi. It has been quite an adventure and I will not press you for more even though my intuition is telling me otherwise,' he said smiling with her.

She laughed. 'You are indeed an intuitive young man, but as you may have guessed I desperately need to protect the Stele and get to the bottom of it all, you must see that. Your story must protect my interests, as we agreed, if you please.'

'I will protect your interests,' said James, charmed

by her plea. 'The story will centre around the King Snefru Stelae...will you put them in the Cairo Museum?'

'Yes,' she said, smiling very broadly now, her eyes filming a little, she was very happy that she had made James' acquaintance, an honourable, wonderful man she thought.

'Let's say our goodbyes now James, you have a lot of travelling to do tomorrow and I wish I could offer you a flight out of here, but as you know that's impossible at the moment. I will have someone get you to Port Said, then you will have to find your way on a ship from there.'

'That would be fine, if they can be in the lobby at 6.30 in the morning, I would be grateful. Farewell Bektamun, I shan't forget this, nor you...thank you for inviting me here.'

Bektamun stood to leave, placing her scarf over her head, not able to look him in the eye too much. 'Bye James, I shall look forward to reading the Chicago Tribune at some point...put us in a good light,' she chuckled nervously.

They hugged and kissed before the Professor walked away through the Hotel main entrance. James found himself staring at her, watching her elegant poise before she reached the entrance doorway. She turned back to look at him with a broad smile - he reciprocated, waiting for her to disappear before bowing his head, deep in thought and wonder.

Bektamun walked slowly back to the Museum, excited about her little adventure, thinking fondly of James. But she was also troubled.

The Prophetic Stele tablet had been found and it would have to be protected at all cost. How to do this would be all consuming, and there was much she had not told James. She did not mention what she had read of *"The Maker"* and the prophecy of *"The Parchment"* which had befallen in time to the people of the 'New World.'

Chapter 6

Book of Prophecies

Krell sat staring at the painting. He had been planning to commit such an act for a long time, but considered that the opportunity recently bestowed upon him at the Art Institute of Chicago, was too good to be true. He had been guided to the whereabouts of the painting by his endeavours, and had used his effective disguise as the Museum Curator in order to retrieve it. However, he never thought that the artifact would present itself so readily, and through such easy dialogue with the Benefactor, Anippe Khu, he was able to manipulate the prospect of its capture; the only question was – would he be bold enough to carry out the act and get possession of the painting? He would be.

Krell was now home, in comfortable surroundings, staying in a rented 'roundhouse' in the middle of rural England. Its brick kiln features were complemented by a stone cork like object placed concentric to the dome shaped roof, giving the house an appearance of a very large bottle. Inside it had two rooms, one down, one up; with an iron spiral staircase elevating out of the ground floor living room. The staircase led to the only bedroom, a room which wrapped itself around the central pillar of the house. The downstairs living room was dominated by a central fireplace embedded in the pillar, and huge beech tree logs provided for a roaring fire, which spread a flickering golden light to all nooks and crannies of this obscure building. Around the circular wall of the ground floor room stood rows and rows of books, each section categorised meticulously in alphabetical order, giving rise to topics such as Voodoo magic, pagan rituals, spiritual artifacts and the study of Tarot Cards through occult teachings.

A large mahogany writing desk, featuring a green leather top, was prominent in the space opposite the front door, its accompanying black leather chair enabling any person who sat upon it, to look right through the fire place and towards the only door to the outside.

Krell sat his enormous two hundred and ten-centimeter frame in the large chair, peering at a faded brown, leather bound book, placed in the middle of the desk. The book was entitled "The Book of Prophecies", so named by the scholars who had written articles within it. He had recently acquired the book through false means, convincing his father's friends in the Jesuit Order to loan him the book for scholarly work. The unblemished reputation of his father within the Jesuit Order, together with Krell's position as the Curator of the Art Institute, had allowed for the entrusted privilege.

The stolen painting from the Art Institute lay rolled up on a wooden shelf positioned on the circular wall, just to the right of the desk. Krell had studied the painting in detail, referring to notes in the leather bound book, trying to match the recorded transcripts against what he was seeing in the picture. But what of the painting? Where should he put it? He would be traceable here and would have to move out of the house pretty quickly, should he take the painting with him? If so, how would he ever conceal it?

For now, there was work to do. Examining the painting more closely, he noticed the intricate depiction of a chequered board, the familiar eight by eight black and white squares holding court to figurines not unlike chess pieces. Tentative knowledge of the board's design and its surrounding hieroglyphs, was hinted at within the leather bound book, and this had given Krell the partial clue he needed to identify the picture.

Krell was able to convince his Mentor - an obtuse, illusive man named Taraka from India - to confide in the potential whereabouts of the painting, or as it was hinted at in the book, 'The Parchment.'

An hour passed and he closed the Book of Prophecies for a moment. He stood up out of the chair aggressively and strode over to the mellowing fire, grabbing the woven log basket to place more beech wood chunks onto the fire's embers. Soon the large iron fire grate was full again, flames raging up the central pillar of bricks like crackling thunderbolts.

Krell stoked the fire further, creating an aura of shadows and movement that seemed to please him in an odd sort of way. He stood gazing into the red and orange flame, mesmerised by its mystique and its trance like features. Deeper thoughts came to him, ones he frequently succumbed to, and ones which were both frightening and exhilarating at the same time.

A raging instinct burned within him, one that he had identified at an early age, frequently pondering through his childhood why he felt so different from other children. He would often delve into an obscure world of fantasy and horror, testing his own intellect to decide whether he was inherently evil or not, or whether it was mere psychopathy – a genetic trait perhaps that had passed through generations. What he did know, was that it was becoming harder to control.

Was he supposed to suppress or release such tendencies? Will the quest he had embarked on provide him with that answer? As he continued to stare intently at the flame, his mind raged, and he ground his teeth, murmuring deeply in the process.

Moments later, Krell snapped out of his trance, pressing his huge muscular arms behind his enormous chest, stretching his limbs and drawing in an inordinate amount of air to fill his gigantic lungs.

'I have work to do,' he cried out loud. 'I will read this Book of Prophecies again and again until I understand this cursed painting and *its* prophecy!'

The flames in the fire seemed to flicker and shimmy in purported agreement. He settled back down at the bureau, once more opening the book.

It was a book that looked ancient, its brown leather cover was cracked in many parts, and the edges of the sleeve were frayed. The spine crinkled effortlessly as the reader turned the cover, only to observe that the first few pages were unfathomable due to the fading ink on the browning book leaves. It was old, very old. Krell had estimated that the first writings would have been placed in the leather binder over four hundred years ago; writings from Jesuit priests who had travelled far and wide across the globe. Within some of the first few pages, he could make out small amounts of text, but mostly he couldn't, so gave up, frustrated by the fading French handwriting that seemed to sprawl and merge into an undecipherable mess. It wasn't until he reached writings further on in the book that he could fully understand the entries, significantly at the point that he was most interested.

Eminent French scholars from the nineteenth century gave accounts of their adventures and discoveries, one in particular was an archeologist - a man by the name of Jean-Paul Ballard - who had worked with the much famed Jean-Francois Champollion in deciphering and publishing the Rosetta Stone interpretations. Ballard though, had made another discovery of which he had written in this particular Book of Prophecies with some detail.

Ballard's entry commented on another ancient stele, which had been found next to the Rosetta Stone. The entry hinted that the other stele, thereafter named in the book as Ballard's Stone, was merely an indicator – a sign post to point archeologists towards another inscription on a stone or tablet buried somewhere in the bowels of one of the ancient pyramids of Egypt. There was no hint as to which Pyramid.

Ballard had transcribed some of the important texts from his stone into the Book of Prophecies, most notably in general about the unfound inscription, but there was something else peculiar to such an inscription. Ballard had written notes relating to a parchment, and that the prophecy of such a parchment could only to be seen on this unfound inscription, something Ballard named the Prophecy Stone or Prophecy Stele.

Muttering to himself in an effort to gain clarity, Krell read on, trying to piece Ballard's commentary together. Before closing the book to rest his eyes and curb his growing frustration, Krell regained focus on something that he had skipped over previously, something that perhaps might provide a further clue. He noticed that Ballard had made a short note against a tiny drawing at the bottom of one of the pages. Krell had missed it before because it was so small, one could have easily mistaken the drawing for a smudge of ink, although a smudge symmetrical in shape.

Squinting at the indiscernible mark, Krell reached for a magnifying glass from the top drawer of his bureau, enabling him with much greater clarity to make out the drawing and associated words, words which he recognised as being in Ballard's hand writing. The miniature drawing depicted a human face as if woven into a cloth, with very thin lines crisscrossing the image vertically and horizontally. The picture could be that of any human face, it bore no resemblance to any particular man, woman from any race or creed. How Ballard inscribed it so small, Krell could not ascertain, and the words set against the drawing were even smaller – stating; *"Find the Vedas"*.

Krell closed the book again, his pattern of thought strained with the repetitive reading and deciphering. Matching the painting features in conjunction with book entries was cumbersome, nothing seemed to make sense, nothing seemed to align very well. The chequered board was the dominant feature in the picture and, having been agreed by Taraka, that was what had steered Krell into discovering the painting in Chicago. Any further detailed reference to the chequered board and its use, otherwise written in the Book of Prophecies, Krell could not find.

Confused and infuriated, Krell decided to make a bold step and contact Taraka in India, despite the five-hour time difference. The phone answered, Taraka's booming eerie voice seemed to fill the room, as if he was present in the house somewhere. Taraka spoke slowly and deliberately, being the only person on Earth to put Krell ill at ease, the only person he was truly in fear of.

'I answer only because I expect you to have good considerations from your findings and of course you are going to tell me, Jeremiah, that you have the painting?'

'I have it and it has the depiction of the chequered board just as we had discussed.'

'Have you studied the Book of Prophecies which you have so cleverly acquired?'

'Yes, parts of it I have read many times since this morning. Written over two hundred years ago, the archeologist named Ballard provides clues, but he did not find the Prophecy Stone, he found only the accompanying stone to the Rosetta Stone, both the

Ballard and the Rosetta Stones are housed in the British Museum. Nowhere do Ballard's texts elude to where the Prophecy Stone is.'

'It would never be that easy, the Prophecy Stone will be concealed somewhere…you know this!' bellowed Taraka. 'What else is there?'

'A facial image, barely to be seen…and the words – *"Find the Vedas",* said Krell.

'Vedas? An intriguing clue Jeremiah, a word that permeates through time, work of Indian scholars for three millennia. We have spoken of The Vedas, you know that it is a collection of ancient texts, they are the oldest scriptures of Hinduism. They are written in the Vedic Sanskrit…'

'Yes I do know this,' Krell interrupted. 'But how could the Vedas be connected to an Egyptian prophecy stone, they are worlds apart, separated by a thousand years?'

'You assume so narrow of mind Jeremiah, so biased is your view. Egyptian scripts may well refer to the Hindu Vedas and vice versa, how do you know there would not be contact between the Indian and the Egyptian peoples?'

'Forgive me my Mentor. Perhaps better interpretations can be made when I arrive in India,' said Krell, nervousness in his voice.

They parted company, rather abruptly it seemed, with Krell still reeling from Taraka's uneasy belittling demeanor. The Vedas they had spoken of before, and the mention of it by Ballard in the Book of Prophecies, had only confirmed their suspicions. Undoubtedly The Vedas was a distinctive clue from

Ballard's work, but why was the word next to the tiny image. The answers would lie with Taraka in India, Krell thought.

Taraka's endeavours had been, so Krell was lead to believe, to understand the Vedas through its ancient texts, or Mantras as they were known. Krell had understood from his Mentor that one particular part of the Vedas described the Hindu Mantras of ancient spells, charms and mysticism. Taraka had called it the Atharva-Veda. The Atharva-Veda and its sub-texts were believed to reveal the secrets of ancient prophecies, and perhaps this was the Vedas which Ballard had eluded to. An exciting thought if the Atharva-Veda would reveal the secrets of the Prophecy Stone and therefore the knowledge of 'The Parchment' – then this would give rise to the significance of the chequered board within the painting now in Krell's hands.

India beckoned.

*

Sam Campbell arrived early Monday morning at the home of the Chicago Police Department Headquarters, 3510 South Michigan Avenue. He strolled through the grand lobby, always humbled by the rows of silver stars representing fallen officers, each placed meticulously in the pristine glass cabinets which adorned practically every wall. The Commander smiled at the security staff who were busily looking at the CCTV monitors, routinely checking and re-checking the perimeter camera images. Sam's eye was customarily drawn to the magnificent murals, which dominated the lobby from the west facing wall, stretching twenty metres in overall length and reflecting a superb and fascinating depiction of Chicago life. The tall blindfolded 'Lady of Justice' dominated the centre mural as she stood proud on Lake Michigan surrounded by ordinary Chicagoans going about their daily business – workmen, police officers, scientists and teachers, etched into an intricate scenic portrayal of city life in a most humbling and just way.

Arriving on the top floor Sam sat and waited patiently to see Carl Walters, this time in a much more formal setting. Through a glass panel, Walters could be seen swiveling from one way and then to the next on his pristine, cherry red leather chair, barking orders at his police subordinates as they sat around the neatly placed conference table, nervous looks on their faces. Sam could not hear what was being said, but he had a good sense of the general conversational tone, somewhat confirmed by the ashen faces and silence of his fellow colleagues as they eventually filed disconsolately out of the room.

A nervous countenance came over Sam as he walked pensively into the room, quite concerned on two counts; first, that of ensuring Walters would approve of his decision to travel abroad immediately and secondly – to impress upon him that he should take someone with him. Sam needed support and Joyce Marsh was an obvious choice because of her skills in the world of artefacts, and because of her linguistic prowess.

For a moment there was silence and Sam found himself staring at the two stars on each of Carl Walters' shirt lapels, not knowing whether to open the conversation.

'Dave Gregg is about to die and there is nothing I can do for him, the machine is about to be switched off and I have just had to brief his commanding officers and colleagues. Not good,' said Walters, with much melancholy.

'Well then I need to get on and find out where Krell is, for the sake of Dave and the others,' said Sam.

'Yes you do Sam, I can see that. Have you decided where you are going? And who with?' questioned Walters intuitively.

'Yes Egypt will be my first port of call; I need to see Anippe Khu. Krell could be anywhere and I don't want to go on a wild goose chase until I get something more concrete, so Ms. Khu will be the safest bet I think.'

'If you get wind of where Krell is, then you will need to react, you know that, and the same goes for me if I find anything out. What do you think Anippe Khu will offer?'

'She is either a suspect or a direct witness, she has the knowledge of the painting and she appears to have had a conversation with Krell. That conversation prompted Krell to act. Joyce Marsh saw their interaction and we can only surmise that Anippe Khu may be an instigator.'

'Joyce Marsh will be your companion I presume, a clever move I would say, she will have to be aware of our protocols though,' said Walters, sternly.

'Agreed.'

'All approved then – when will you go?'

'Thank you Carl, it is appreciated...I took the liberty of booking two flights this evening.'

'I thought you possibly might,' said Walters. 'Sam, you do know it's very unusual sending a Detective Bureau Commander on such a mission, you are a high ranking officer and a key player here. You can imagine the interest this has sparked and there seems no abatement. The press are still baying at my door and I have one officer about to die and another I am not hopeful for; she is in a very serious condition. You were right, we don't need a wild goose chase – you have got to get this right. Don't forget it is Krell we need, if the finding of the painting leads to him, then I don't really give a damn about anything else.'

The message was clear.

Walters smiled and bid Sam farewell, the frown on his face returning once Sam had left. A potentially dangerous time lay ahead for his understudy and for Carl Walters, the prospect of Sam being seriously injured or killed had never been a considered one.

*

Joyce didn't need much persuading to join Sam on the 6 pm British Airways flight out of Chicago O'Hare International Airport - destination Cairo, Egypt - via London Heathrow. An exciting prospect lay ahead for both of them, neither of them being able to hide their exhilaration, with Sam trying to make himself comfortable for the long haul and Joyce anxious to continue her research at the earliest opportunity. She had news for Sam; a recent discovery which she was keen to show him once they were airborne.

'Long flight ahead,' said Sam as he started to relax a little. 'Nineteen hours on a plane all told, with a six-hour gap waiting at Heathrow, we can get through a lot…or we will get on each other's nerves,' he said, chuckling.

Joyce smiled, feeling comfortable being sat next to the Police Commander yet again. She was beginning to like him, he had a friendly manner, despite his utter determination to get on with the task, and she would look forward enthusiastically to the next few days with him.

'I have checked and re-checked the Art Institute inventory for the paintings and keep coming up with the same result. The stolen painting was part of a batch acquired just recently, from an anonymous contributor,' said Joyce, showing Sam the detail on her laptop computer.

'It seems that the painting was a donation, I am sure of it. If you look at the description of the others in the batch, they are all similar - depicting arts and crafts, quite befitting of course for the Art Institute. The bit I can't figure out is that there is no name recorded as to who the donor was.'

'Surely you must get anonymous donors all the time,' said Sam.

'We get plenty of items sent without any kind of reference, including many generous anonymous donations, but normally, all paintings of this ilk, which are then displayed, we insist on having the name of a source, confidentially recorded or otherwise…, you know, for theft and fraud reasons…'

'I still can't visualise what this painting really looks

like, do you have photographs of it in the inventory?'

'You must have guessed that I have tried to find it. I have found the others, but it seems that any reference beyond its arrival date has been erased.'

'Krell?'

'Probably,' said Joyce. 'I can't recall what it looked like in detail myself. No-one would have taken that much notice of the painting, it was in the lobby just for decorative effect, really. When Anippe Khu and Krell had their dealings, I kept out of the way.

'Clearly Krell did not want anyone studying the painting once he had decided to steal it, he must have erased the reference and photographs in the inventory beforehand?' said Sam.

'Assuming he had planned the robbery on his own. We do not know the full extent of who was involved,' said Joyce.

'Anippe?' questioned Sam. 'A curious intervention from her it would seem, we will soon find out I hope.'

*

Shortly before the flight from Chicago was about to land at London Heathrow, Krell had already set off on his journey to the airport. He had carefully hidden the thirty by thirty centimetre canvas oil painting inside a picture frame, concealed behind another painting, the whole item packed into a small black travel bag. The train journey from his home in the English Midlands would take nearly two hours, time for him to think more of the impending conversation he would have with his curious Mentor, the iniquitous Taraka.

Krell was in fear of no person or beast, save Taraka, for he was indeed fearsome - both in his physical appearance and his mental disposition. Shear dread filled Krell's stomach at the thought of confronting him again, but provided he was subservient in his presence, he would survive his Mentor's onslaught – besides which, there was much for them both to do, and time was pressing.

The train journey to Euston Railway Station, London, was on time, as was the rail link out westward to Heathrow Airport, at least giving Krell some satisfaction that his prior planning was going well. The next phase of getting onto the plane would be an anxious period.

*

At the airport, people ignorantly avoided the tall, very hunched old looking man dressed in traditional Orthodox Jewish clothing. He wore a large rimmed black hat, a long black three quarter coat and black trousers. His hair was shaved at the back, and protruding from the base of the hat rim one could see his long grey sidelocks, which seemed to merge with his proud grey beard. He had a small black travelling case, the contents of which he could provide a receipt of purchase for – if he therefore needed to do so.

On the other side of the airport lounge Sam and Joyce prepared to gather their belongings and make their way to the boarding gate, chatting nervously, oblivious to the tall, traditionally dressed Jewish man making way to his plane.

At 2 pm the Air India flight from London to Delhi taxied along the number one Heathrow runway. Krell was sat on board, thankful that his black suited disguise and grey wig had worked; along with his false German passport and ruse about the painting.

At 2.02 pm the British Airways flight from London to Cairo taxied along the same runway, queueing in line behind the Air India flight, anxious passengers waiting and watching as the plane in front readied its take off. Sam and Joyce braced themselves, and hearing the roar of the first plane, made themselves ready for the final leg, Egypt and Anippe Khu awaited.

Chapter 7

Coincidences

Sam would not have known that he was standing in the same public hall of the Cairo Museum of Antiquities, as his father had so many years before. Tired from the disjointed flight, he and Joyce had managed to find temporary comfort at the refurbished Grand Semiramis Hotel, before attending the Museum. It was Wednesday morning.

Joyce looked around, marveling at the Pyramidal art; the sphynxes, the stelae and the array of golden objects glistening behind bullet proof glass cabinets. Sam paced up and down, near to the central seating area, focusing on the young Egyptian man from reception whom they had spoken to earlier, and who was now scurrying along an adjacent corridor attempting to find Anippe Khu in one of the offices nearby.

Even though tired, the Police Commander was eager to press on, listing the questions he had for Ms.

Khu in his mind, sequencing a preferred order before she arrived. Instinct told him that he should actually arrest her, but he knew that was impossible without an international arrest warrant, besides which he had become too curious about her.

'This is all too easy,' said Sam. 'She is either very clever or very stupid, either way I wonder if she has received us all too readily.'

'Calm down Sam, we have no idea of her motives, just stick with your plan…I think this is her,' said Joyce.'

Joyce's voice was still ringing in Sam's ear as he caught sight of a female figure walking purposefully towards them from the far end of the main hall, having gracefully traversed the steps leading from the second tier gallery. The woman was wearing elegant black high heeled shoes, and dressed in a pristine beige suit with a smart brown leather band around her midriff. Surrounding her striking face was a brilliant white hijab that seemed to unfurl loosely around her jet black hair. As she stepped closer, Sam was immediately drawn to her charming poise, noticing at once, her beautiful dark brown eyes and her deep rich brown skin. His prior muttering and chatting to himself about what questions he should ask, seemed now suspended in mid-air, as he watched the woman shake hands with Joyce, whilst effortlessly at the same time glance over to him with a wonderful broad smile.

Sam readied himself for the customary greeting but was thrown a little when he noticed some scarring on the woman's face, mainly to her right cheek and near to her right eye socket. This made it a little difficult to judge her age, which Sam put at about fifty-five, and it took away a little of her beauty, but not significantly. He found her persona captivating, a face of grace and wisdom he could not recall having seen very often before.

'Hello Mr. Campbell, I am Anippe Khu – if you hadn't already have guessed,' said the woman, smiling infectiously.

Sam reciprocated, but was now off guard, beguiled by the woman's charm. Joyce chuckled to herself as she noticed Sam blushing in Anippe's presence, something she had not supposed would happen with him.

'Ms. Khu, I am glad to meet you at last, I am desperate for some answers as you can imagine, Joyce and I were wondering…'

'Please don't be nervous Mr. Campbell,' interrupted Anippe. 'I won't bite and I know we have a lot to talk about. Shall we have some drinks and relax, I would dearly like to know something about the both of you, and how we are going to retrieve the painting.'

Thrown off guard again, Sam reeled at Anippe's perfect English, hardly a hint of any accent, and almost hypnotically (although slightly frustratingly) she continued to embrace the couple with her charm.

The threesome walked away from the main hall into a long wide corridor, adorned either side with statues of Egyptian Pharaohs and Queens, the glass roof of the corridor permeating light onto their intricately carved faces. Half way along the corridor was a taped barrier, marking the start of the private business section of the Museum.

'Follow me through here,' Anippe said, turning around to face them, walking backwards as she spoke. 'Shall we call each other by our first names?' She said, the broad smile never leaving her face.

Sam and Joyce looked at each other and smiled, nodding back to Anippe in agreement, the policeman still looking a little embarrassed at the fact that he knew Joyce had seen him disarmed just moments ago. He did indeed find Anippe engrossing, not that he had any physical attraction for her, rather this was something else – more an innate reverence that he couldn't fathom.

Anippe lifted the barrier tape and beckoned the pair through into the private section. Sam stepped through the tape; but immediately to his right, his attention was drawn to a set of very tall double glass doors - marked with the words 'Artifacts and Historical Records.' Behind the glass doors was an immaculate looking room full of gold leaf edged books; such was the effect, it was as if the walls of the room were gilded with gold. The books were all of similar appearance reaching from the floor to the ceiling on all four sides within neatly placed wooden shelves. In the centre of the room was a rich looking oak desk accompanied by a studded, high backed red leather chair, neatly placed behind it. The room was so striking, Sam's curiosity got the better of him and he instinctively tried to open one of the glass doors, only to find it locked.

'Sam, I'm afraid that room is out of bounds, very sorry,' said Anippe.

Joyce gently grabbed Sam's arm to guide him away, but she too became curious, finding herself gaping into the room.

'Those books look incredible, what *is* that room…. and who would make such a collection?' said Sam.

No answer came, instead Anippe merely signaled the visitors to walk further on – passing through an administrative centre, with staff busily typing on their computers – to a secluded narrow corridor which appeared to run parallel with the large corridor they had just walked along.

Anippe's office was well away from the busy clerical staff, and was a complete contrast to the 'room of books' witnessed just a moment ago. Papers strewn everywhere, books piled in corners, and cabinets filling every space along the walls, making the room feel claustrophobic. Anippe was a little embarrassed as she saw the pair scan the room with some disdain.

'You two stay here for a moment, if you don't mind, I just need to fetch something,' said Anippe, somewhat nervously.

She returned with a book, not just any book, it was obvious from its cover that it belonged in the magnificent collection, sparking an instant fascination. It was bound in rich, deep brown leather, with gold leaf writing on the spine, and it looked heavy, being nearly eight centimetres thick and thirty centimetres square. Silence permeated the room as Anippe opened the ornate book at the first page.

'Before I get onto the painting from the Art Institute in Chicago I want to describe something, so you will have to bear with me,' said Anippe deliberately. 'Within this book is an account of a person who worked here decades ago, and as you may have noticed from the room of books, we make a point of referencing everything in this way here. These books are used for a sole purpose, to record the accounts of historical finds, especially finds relating to ancient artefacts.'

For a moment, intrigue overcame Sam's impatience and desire to start questioning Anippe immediately; he thought he would listen to her for a while.

'This is a record of a significant historical find, something which was found at the Dahshur Pyramids nearly sixty years ago. Much of the detail I cannot reveal to you because of the Museum rules, but there is something I must mention to you.' Anippe turned the leaves of the book a few pages on. 'Buried within its contents, a prophecy is revealed,' she announced. 'I know that sounds far-fetched, but hear me out. I shan't bore you with the actual detail of the prophecy, but in the writings, there is reference to a picture or literally, as it states, a Parchment – it is a Parchment which unfortunately bears no name…'

'I am slightly intrigued, but I will have to ask you some questions at some point,' said Sam, still trying to listen.

'Please stay with me Sam, I know you are eager to interrogate me, but you see, I have an account here in this book about a Parchment which bears an uncanny resemblance to the description of the stolen painting.'

'Forgive me Anippe, I need to ask, and I appreciate your sentiments – but I need to be direct with you – now you mention it, what do you really know about the painting? And where do you think it could have gone? Surely you must understand that I need those questions answered?' said Sam, abruptly.

'What?' said Joyce, turning to Anippe. 'What description?'

'I thought you had seen the painting Joyce?' said Anippe.

'Only briefly, I never paid much attention to it, the only thing I can remember distinctly is the chequered board resting on a tri-legged wooden table, and strange figurines placed in rows on the board, rather like chess pieces.'

'Yes and that is described here. The book makes reference to such a chequered board embodied within the Parchment, as part of the prophecy.'

'Why were you at the Art Institute...and what about the conversation you had with Krell?' said Sam, interrupting and forcing Anippe to change tack.

'I had an inkling that the painting had been given to the Art Institute, I am a Benefactor and I quite often see what new items have arrived. I saw the photograph of the painting on the website and got curious, I had to see it for myself...and from the work I have done researching the findings in this book, it seemed too coincidental.'

'You have not mentioned your conversation with Krell,' said Joyce. 'And by the way, there is no record or photograph of the painting left in the archive records.'

'I saw it and needed it protecting, I was willing to pay a large sum of money for it, I asked Krell to organise the painting going into safe custody before I planned to bring it here and conduct further research,' said Anippe.

'I am not convinced at the moment,' said Sam.

'Let me tell you about the connection with the painting…please,' said Anippe, desperately trying to get to the point. 'This book replicates the text discovered on an ancient Egyptian Stele, or stone tablet, whichever is your preference. The notes, written by the original author, refer to the Stele giving an account of a Parchment. The Parchment is believed to have magical powers, hence the reference to a prophecy. The detail about the chequered board rears its head constantly within this 'Book of the Stele'. Again, the picture at the Chicago Art Institute showed a chequered board…'

'There could be hundreds of paintings depicting the same thing,' interrupted Sam.

Anippe started to feel a little uncomfortable, she didn't know whether much of what she was saying was sinking in with Sam, and she was trying desperately to explain without giving too much away.

Getting at the truth was becoming even more frustrating for Sam; he looked to Joyce for support but her fascination and innate intrigue was taking a different course.

'Anippe, please tell us, what is the secret to all this? You know we are perhaps a trifle suspicious, and I for one am curious. Recordings of parchments and chequered boards etched on an ancient Stele? This is highly unlikely for the time, such things are unlikely to have existed in the manner you describe…and why are you so clear with the link from the information in your book to the painting which has been taken from the Institute?' said Joyce, inquisitively.

Anippe stood up out of her chair and gently closed the leather bound book - 'The Book of the Snefru Stele' as it was so named. Her dilemma had not faded, revealing much more at this stage would have exasperated the situation, and it simply wasn't part of the plan. *And what of Krell's whereabouts?* she thought. There were too many concerns and not enough time - a phone call was needed to her contact.

'Look, the painting has considerable significance to me and I have to admit, I was willing to pay an extortionate amount of money for it. I truly believe there is a link to the work I am doing here. But if you ask me honestly, I believe Krell has taken it and he is responsible for the attack on the police officers. I rue the day I said anything to him, it is so regretful…even to the point that I have tried desperately to find out something about him,' said Anippe.

'So you think he's got it then?' said Sam.

'Yes, but I think he'll probably move it on soon. He'll get away from his base and take the painting with him, perhaps trying to find someone who is interested in it'.

*

The twelve-hour flight from London to New Delhi was uncomfortable for Krell, his front row seat did not make the wearing of his disguise any easier. He had not slept, practically having to keep one eye open; he did not trust anyone or anything, such was his disposition. With a vice like grip, he had clutched his black holdall throughout the entire journey, noticing people on the plane staring at him with such preconception, and air-stewards greeting him with unease.

A mixture of tension and relief went through his mind as the plane landed early morning at the Delhi 'Indira Gandhi' International Airport. Relief that the plane had actually landed and that he would be able to get out of his disguise - but tension at the thought of confronting the detestable Taraka, and the isolation he would feel in Taraka's presence.

He walked through the passport gate and out into the airport lounge, picking the first opportunity (in a public toilet) to remove the Jewish Orthodox disguise. He placed the clothes in a garbage bin near to the main entrance and made his way to the taxi rank, thankful for his ordinary every day clothes – a grey super-sized T-shirt, blue cotton trousers and black walking shoes. He was also grateful to feel the air on his newly shaven head, sodden with perspiration after wearing such a dreadful, claustrophobic wig.

Sat in the rear of a black and yellow Ambassador taxi, watching the driver fighting with the car through the impossibly busy streets to the railway station, Krell had time to go over the instructions given to him by Taraka. He was to travel out of the Delhi region to the Balrampur district in the Northern Indian State of Uttar Pradesh. He would then find his way to the small religious town of Tulsipur, not far from the border with Nepal - within sight of the vast Himalayan Mountain range. Tulsipur, Krell had noted, was the home of a very famous Hindu worship temple called the Devi Patan, and it was there at the temple he had been told he would have to wait.

Delhi Railway Station was hectic and once dropped off, Krell had to wade his giant frame through the masses of yellow and green auto rickshaws, parked in ad hoc rows with their owners beside them, furiously plying for trade. He was relieved to see that all about, signs were written in English as well as the traditional Sanskrit; if this was common, he thought, it would help him navigate his way through the long hot journey ahead. He joined the unending crowd of people on the open platforms, all clamoring for a place on one of the eastbound trains, with every conceivable object waiting to be transported, from motorbikes to bedding, boxes full of home items and countless goods for selling in shops.

As he boarded, the second class compartments were already becoming crammed with items and full of people struggling to find a seat. He barged his way through the crowd, finding a seat towards the front of the train, placing his huge body once again into cramped, unsettling surroundings.

The train was the eastbound Shaheed Express, destined for the town of Gonda, a place revered for its role in Indian Independence. A journey of six hundred kilometres, the train would take as long to get there as the flight Krell had endured from England. There would be a long wait for the connecting train at Gonda, extending his journey to the following day, before finally reaching his destination at Tulsipur.

The large man tried to settle on the train, the curiosity of the local people making him uncomfortable, exasperating the heat surrounding his body even more. He clung onto his belongings, never letting go for one moment the black holdall containing the painting and the Book of Prophecies he had now placed in one of its pockets.

The long exasperating journey unfolded before him, passing through many towns and villages, through countless fields and farm land, and crossing the huge Ganga and Ghaghra rivers in the Northern Indian districts. Throughout, Krell concentrated on how the interaction with Taraka would unfold, perpetually running through the detail of the painting and meanings described in the Book of Prophecies. His worst fear was being off guard in any way, and at all costs he knew that he would have to hold firm with his informed dialogue, save any derision from the wicked Taraka.

The change at the town of Gonda went on time, before finally, the slow rickety old train to Tulsipur arrived at the town's single platform station; it was 10 am on the Wednesday, the third day of Krell's journey. Having had barely any sleep during his travels, he strained his eyes to look at the signs on the railway platform, searching for the direction towards the Devi Patan Temple, where ultimately he would find Taraka - he hoped.

Carrying his luggage was becoming uncomfortable, the shoulder bag for his personal items and the holdall were an agitation as he walked along the main street of Tulsipur, fighting to concentrate in the searing heat and humidity. The road ahead was lined with shops and stalls for the market day, with masses of people already milling around to see what was on offer. Rickshaws and animals filled nearly every other gap, before Krell eventually mustered a way through the crowd to reach the famous Temple of the Devi Patan.

The Devi Patan, was a 'Siddha Peeth' Temple, a place of reverence established by a twelfth century Hindu Guru named Gorakshnath. Krell was uncomfortable near such a holy place, yet he found the curious building quite fascinating and he would attempt to suffer its presence, until Taraka arrived.

Its red and white stone facing walls formed the base of an ornate symmetrical design, with casted small conical stones positioned along the wall sides and on each of the corners of the roof. It had a distinctive ten-metre-high semi-ovoid tower, dominating the rear of the building and four white stone pillars to the front, inviting onlookers to peer through the open plan spacing towards the centre of the temple.

After a further two hours of waiting Krell could examine the structure of the temple no further, Taraka was nowhere to be seen, and Krell was angry - wondering whether his Mentor had done this on purpose and was further testing his protégé's initiative.

Taraka would certainly be nearby, perhaps at his hiding place, manipulating his protracted disguise. For it was said, and Krell believed it, that Taraka lived in these parts, hiding on the pretence that he was part of a religious sect that had been founded by the Guru Gorakshnath. The Guru was a master of meditation and Yoga, and had founded the Nath cult - an order which had endured, and one which Taraka purported to belong. The Nath cult had a subsect called the

Sadhu and it was this subsect that Taraka falsely endeared himself under, pretending to be a devout follower of Hinduism and living as a 'naked Sadhu' amongst the caves and tunnels of the Tulsipur region.

Annoyed, the giant Krell decided to move on, following the befuddled directions given to him in the event of Taraka not showing; a walk to a secluded hide, no more than a kilometre from the Temple, heading north along the partially dry banks of the Surya River out of Tulsipur.

At the nape of a long river bend, Krell came across a small rectangular sign, bolted onto a wooden post, recently painted white. The wording on the sign was in Sanskrit, which he didn't understand, yet he knew this was probably the marker for him to turn east away from the river and find Taraka's hide. A short time further on, he found himself scrambling through a clump of trees and dry foliage, soon arriving at a rocky face that stretched nearly ten metres high to another tree line. The small trees and bushes seemed to envelope the rocky surround, making it difficult to see what lay immediately behind. Scanning the upper part of the rocks, just below the higher tree line, Krell could make out a large, circular rock, standing upright - resting neatly on a rocky ledge. As he climbed towards the circular rock he got close enough to see that it had two iron prongs protruding slightly from its surface; the prongs were cleverly camouflaged within the grain of the rock itself.

Standing on the ledge, Krell could see that the rock had been moved several times, forming a heavy groove to the right hand side. He pulled at the two-metre-wide rock using the iron prongs, noticing straight away that it would take all of his mighty strength to move it. He was eventually able to roll it along the ledge, leaving enough space for him to squeeze through the exposed opening. Once through the opening, Krell stared into what appeared to be an entrance to a cave. Straining his body again, he carefully replaced the circular rock to its original position, moving it so that it closed the gap and fastened itself to two interior giant prongs embedded into an adjacent stone wall.

Peering further into the chasm, he was surprised by the small, dim electric lights on each side of the cave walls. The light was enough for him to see his passage, observing a sharp inclined cobbled slope descending ten metres or so to a small flat concrete platform, beyond which all he could see was a void.

The cave was suitably cool, giving Krell instant relief from the overbearing humidity outside. Yet he found himself in an eerie place; a disused mine perhaps, mined for some sort of ore, although he couldn't be sure. Fixing his travel bags over his enormous shoulders, he slowly moved down the steep, brick-cobbled slope, relieved when he eventually placed his feet on the level concrete platform. From there he saw the apparent void for what it actually was, a straight drop descending at least fifty metres, or maybe more, he couldn't quite tell.

His eyes started to adjust more to the dim light, seeing that on the opposite side of the void, there was a slatted wooden ladder which would take him down to the base, or so he hoped. He stepped from the safety of the concrete platform, over the metre-wide gap of the void, and grabbed the top slat of the ladder, slowly lowering himself completely onto the fixing, praying that it was robust enough to take his weight.

The concentration needed to descend the precarious wooden ladder was but a momentary distraction from the nervousness he was starting to feel at the prospect of meeting Taraka. At one point, as he neared the basement floor at the foot of the ladder, his nerves intensified so much, he thought his wrenching stomach would not recover from its tight unassailable knot.

Krell stepped off the ladder onto a flat cobbled stone floor and immediately faced a solid, three-metre high, wrought iron gate, which reached the rock ceiling of what he presumed to be the start of another tunnel situated behind. The iron gate had supporting fastenings to each side of the tunnel walls, but he could not fathom how to open it. He did not have to wait long, for at the point of searching for clues, he gulped at the sound of Taraka's redoubtable booming voice emanating from the other side.

'You are late Jeremiah, I waited for you near to the Devi Patan Temple, but you did not appear, I am not in the habit of waiting for a subservient being such as you!'

The gate opened inwardly from where Krell was standing and there stood the towering, gigantic, ungodly figure of Taraka. There was no smile or greeting, just a motioning for Krell to enter. Taraka was dressed in elaborate green coloured robes, which had embroidered gold sequins adorning the edges, the robes partly draping over his enormous open leather sandals. Around his neck was a gold chain, two centimetres thick, with a triangular pendant attached to the chain resting on Taraka's sternum. He had a round pot belly, bare to see showing his dirty oily skin, his belly protruding through his robe and hanging over his green silk trousers. His jet black hair was tied in layers on top of his head, whilst his long black straggly beard looked like a tightly woven spider's web reaching from ear to ear. Such a guise was befitting to the traditional style of the cave dwelling sect, the Nath Sadhu.

Krell stepped into his Mentor's domain, feeling child-like as he passed the gigantic frame of the only person in the world he felt physically intimidated by. Taraka was indeed a giant, standing over fifty centimetres taller than Krell and seemingly twice as wide. Krell avoided shaking Taraka's hand, knowing that his own hand would be completely, and feebly, consumed in his Mentor's vice grip.

Ominously, Taraka closed the heavy iron gate behind them, moving ahead of his nervous understudy, who was waiting to be guided further into the lair. Krell was sure that Taraka was able to read his thoughts, and he tried to compose his mind, focusing on what he needed to do, attempting to pre-empt Taraka's forthcoming inquisition. The interior tunnel leading to the lair seemed long, judging by the ten minutes or so it took to get to the second gate. This time the gate was smaller in the form of double oak doors coated with thick black tar, the height of which just allowed Taraka to pass through without stooping.

Behind the oak doors, Krell stepped straight into a large furnished room, dim with light, but a more familiar surrounding. Patterned Indian carpet lay in the centre of the room leaving a perimeter of observable stone flooring around the edge. At the far end of the room, opposite to the doorway, stood a large oak writing desk, its presence dominated by a gigantic red leather chair adjacent to it. To the left of the entrance, centre piece to the room, was a huge open fireplace, ornately ingratiated with indecipherable wooden carvings threaded through a copper back plate, which seemed to wrap itself supernaturally around the burning logs.

Krell scanned the room for other openings, curious as to where his quarters may be.

'Look in the far corner to the right of the desk Jeremiah, you see the outline of a door way merging into the wall?'

'Yes, barely,' said Krell, unnerved by Taraka's mind reading comment.

'Go to it and you will see a lever by the small metal table – then pull.'

The humbled traveller did as he was duly told, approaching the far right hand corner of the room, noticing the feint outline of a doorway camouflaged into the many colours of the stone walls. As he pulled the lever, the door hissed open, moving outward - towards another passage way.

'Your room is to the right, you will find everything you need, including an iron bath, although I am afraid you will find that the water is not too warm,' bellowed Taraka, who was now standing by the fireplace, looking decidedly menacing.

Hairs on the back of Krell's neck stood on end as

he turned his gaze away from Taraka and walked into the narrow passage way to unlock the small wooden door to his room.

'Be quick Jeremiah, I want to talk with you right away,' snarled Taraka, his deep resonant voice piercing Krell's tired body.

A nod was all Krell could muster as he stepped inside his room. The bedroom was similar in style to the main room, with dim lighting, and a red and blue Indian carpet smothering the higgled stone floor. An elaborate wooden four poster bed dominated the room, with the large iron bath placed near to the bed against the far wall. The bed beckoned and the temptation to lie down was all consuming, yet Krell knew he couldn't, he had barely enough time to wash himself, before he would have to re-engage with Taraka in the main room.

'Place the Book of Prophecies and the painting on my desk and let us observe,' said Taraka.

Krell removed the backing from the picture frame and pulled out the painting behind the false picture cover. He opened the 'Book of Prophecies' at the page where he had last read the notes.

'The chequered board on the table is prominent and you can see the hieroglyph markings on each of the visible board edges,' said Krell. 'The figure in the picture, I presume represents…'

'The Maker!' interrupted Taraka.

Krell remained silent for a moment, continuing to look at the painting, desperate to find inspiration to impress his Mentor.

'There is something missing,' barked Taraka. 'The painting is oil based and seems real enough, but whether it is a true depiction of the ancient Parchment, I would not know - your research may have the answers Jeremiah. Open the Book of Prophecies and show me the tiny drawing of the woven face you had mentioned.'

Krell did as he was ordered, showing Taraka the book, which thankfully he had already opened at the right page.

'You'll need a magnifying glass my Mentor,' said Krell.

Taraka did not reply, instead he fixed a deep, dark stare on the tiny picture, it was as if his eyes were sinking further into his eye sockets, the white parts becoming indistinguishable.

'It is The Cloth,' announced Taraka

'The Cloth?' questioned Krell.

'You said it yourself, it looks like a woven cloth in miniature detail. The Cloth is part of the prophecy, that much I know. But there is no cloth in the painting, there is no reference point…I feel sure that if it was the true Parchment or a representation of the real Parchment, there would be a clue as to how The Cloth would work.'

'Forgive me, I do not follow. The Cloth is another clue then?'

'The Cloth is integral to what we need to discover. The painting has the chequered board, it has the depiction of 'The Maker' we presume, but I cannot fathom the function of The Cloth without a representation,' said Taraka.

'Then the drawing by Ballard in the Book of Prophecies has meaning? He was onto something?' said Krell.

'In my findings here in Tulsipur, I have discovered that The Vedas Hindu writings in the Atharva-Veda should describe what is written upon the Prophecy Stone, which is the stone hinted at by Ballard. I am convinced that the Prophecy Stone will identify how 'The Maker', or should I say 'The Pottery Maker' is ordained, yet I see no clue in this painting as I thought we should do. The miniature cloth portrayed in the Book of Prophecies must mean something, Ballard was perhaps fortuitous with his discoveries,' said Taraka, sounding impatient.

Krell felt uneasy, it was perhaps not his place to challenge, not here – he was totally isolated, there would be no compromise with Taraka if he said the wrong thing.

'Does not the Mantra in the Atharva-Veda give verse to The Cloth and its link with 'The Maker', surely such a Vedic script would do so?' said Krell, tentatively.

'No, No, No,' said Taraka. 'The Vedas, I would say, gives verse to the legacy of The Prophecy Stone, which in turn, I believe, will talk of a Parchment and of the chequered board hinted at in the Book of Prophecies – The Parchment and the board will be the functions of the Pottery Maker, that much I am convinced.'

'Perhaps *The Cloth* is *The Parchment*,' said Krell, slightly unwittingly.

'Are you an imbecile? The Cloth has its place but it cannot be The Parchment. The Parchment is much more; I had thought that this painting would give us the conjecture…what did Anippe Khu say to you?'

Taken aback, Krell had not expected that question. In his mind, the task had mostly been fulfilled, he had captured the painting and they were now merely deliberating as to how they would eventually move towards the next phase, a phase which would indubitably seal their fate.

'I have not mentioned her presence before, but now that you ask my Mentor.'

'I do ask!' shouted Taraka, the stone walls of the room appearing to shake as he spoke.

Krell became overwrought, feeling belittled as he sought to physically distance himself further away from the beast in his lair. His brain whirred as he tried to figure out Taraka's concerns, merely wanting desperately to be given another task.

It appeared that Taraka had more knowledge than he was prepared to reveal and now Krell fell short of asking his Mentor to talk more of the Mantra in the Atharva-Veda scriptures, for fear of insulting him. He would not dare to question his authority on such matters, even though he knew Taraka's embrace of Hinduism was undoubtedly pretentious.

'Perhaps I would be better to wait for my next task?' said Krell.

'I want you to think. If the prophecy reveals itself to us, then you must be in a position to act, and act quickly – we must understand who The Pottery Maker is and how they operate. This is for you

Jeremiah, it is you that shall embrace the power, it will be your job!' shouted Taraka.

Evil, disconcerting eyes followed Krell, as he moved tentatively toward the roaring fireplace, trying to think as he did so, much to the increasing annoyance of his observer. Taraka followed him, getting closer to him, clearly in an oppressive manner, wickedly gauging his protégé's response. Krell became agitated, not knowing whether to feel anger or fear at Taraka's poise, although he knew at all cost he must never show any rage - the outcome would not be favourable.

'I do not like your silence Jeremiah.'

'Forgive me, but you do not seem to reveal all you know my Mentor, I apologise if…'

Krell was stopped short as Taraka lurched towards him and grabbed him by his chest with both hands. It was impossible to back off and Krell found himself pressed against the edge of the oak fireplace surround. Taraka bore down on him squeezing his chest ever tighter, pinching the shirt on his torso, to a point where Krell could hardly breathe. It was a vice like grip and he could not move, despite his own great strength. To his horror, Taraka then lifted him up off the ground, the shirt fabric giving way and tearing off his back. He fell to the ground, but before he could react, Taraka grabbed him by the throat and jaw, once again lifting him high off the floor.

Powerless and dangling like a rag doll, Krell could do nothing as Taraka held his full weight with one hand, walking him across the patterned Indian carpet towards the main oak doors. Krell went into a rage and started to pound Taraka's arm, hitting the elbow, clawing at his hand, punching with all his might but it was to no avail. Taraka did not flinch; he stared at Krell, displaying a wry, evil grin as his protégé started to lose consciousness trying to break free. Taraka threw him mid-air towards the wooden entrance doors, smashing Krell's whole body against the frame before he tumbled onto the ground.

Lying on the floor, Krell tried to regain his composure, watching Taraka walk back to his desk to look at the painting, as if nothing had happened. Krell struggled for breath, although he was anxious to speak, and forced himself up trying to cover his torso with the torn clothing.

'If I have offended you my Mentor, then forgive me, I will endeavour to serve you better.'

There was no response; the pretend Nath marched fervently out of the room and into the rear passageway towards his chambers, leaving Krell to step unsteadily back towards his bedroom, completely in disarray with his thoughts. He was petrified, yet at the same time in awe at the pure evil he had just witnessed – the gruesome, unbridled Taraka had undoubtedly revealed himself.

Seeking solace and comfort in his room, Krell reflected on one thing – he had not had chance to answer the question from Taraka about the conversation with Anippe Khu, he was loath to answer it, and he was embarrassed, beginning to think that the discovery of the painting was perhaps nothing but a ruse.

*

'Sam, Joyce…I think I need a break from this for a short while, I feel a little under pressure from you both, but no matter, let's have some refreshment and I can re-charge my batteries' said Anippe, standing up from behind her desk. 'In any case, I need to check on my staff,' she said.

The pair stood up and stepped over the plethora of paperwork on the office floor, walking out into the narrow corridor to stretch their legs. Joyce headed off to the rest room and Sam thought he would explore the narrow corridor a little further, wondering curiously if he would be quite near to the room of books.

Anippe was hopeful that the guise of wanting to speak to her staff appeared convincing, the real reason for sloping off was for something else; a private phone call was needed and she made her way to a small office nearby.

'It is difficult, they are both very bright and quite forthright, I am trying to put the focus on Krell, but I am sure they smell a rat with the painting,' said Anippe.

The voice on the phone bellowed through, 'You know that Krell is the culprit is he not? Your work has engineered that, but they cannot know what you have done, not yet anyway you must hold your nerve lady.'

'What of Taraka? They need to be warned, surely?' said Anippe.

'We don't know what he is capable of yet, they will have to trace Krell first and confront Taraka when the need arises. There is no guarantee that Taraka and Krell will be together at any point,' said the voice.

'What now then?' questioned Anippe.

'Move them on, but hint at meeting them again…there is much work to do, your path with them will inevitably cross again, you know that.'

'Ok, better go,' said Anippe, placing the handset down quickly before making her way to one of the staff offices.

The narrow corridor was, at first, a little difficult to judge and Sam had trouble maintaining his bearings before at last he came to an unmarked door, notably scuffed at the base as if frequently used. To his surprise the door opened, the turning of the worn handle being quite loose, allowing him to enter the tiny room with relative ease. The room was no more than two metres in length and one-metre-wide, with a small worktop against one wall, allowing only for a single person to sidle through the space.

Two steps in and Sam was immediately confronted by an outline of another door with a small peephole in the centre. There was no door handle and he couldn't fathom how it would open. He stared through the peephole and smiled; the room of books was there as he had surmised. He could see the glass doors at the opposite end of the bright room and was able to make out the cherry red leather chair close to his position. *Oh to be able to indulge in those books,* he thought.

He decided for a moment to focus on the small ante room where he had found himself, realising that there was a small computer screen placed next to an old traditional telephone handset, both situated on the work top, tucked in behind the open door. He dared himself to look at the screen, pressing the spacebar on the key board and finding, to his amazement, that it was not timed out. A search program appeared to be running, against an index system with artifact references flitting past the screen in a seemingly endless fashion.

A concerned Anippe did not stay with her staff long, realising to her horror that she had probably left open the small ante room adjacent to the room of books. She feared that Sam's inquisitiveness and his investigative passion would lead him to it and this would not be in her plan. She rushed passed her office only to be followed by a perplexed Joyce who had been sat waiting patiently for both her and Sam to return.

Together they approached the small room and sure enough saw him there, staring at a computer screen. The computer had stopped its search.

'Sam, what are you doing?' Anippe shouted.

He continued to stare, not saying a word, trying to process what he was looking at. Joyce shared Anippe's concern, feeling equally frustrated with Sam, yet clearly he was onto something.

Anippe walked into the room, pressing herself against Sam to look at the computer screen, her efforts to distract him being futile. The picture on the computer was clear, it was a photographic image of the stolen painting. At the bottom of the image, the words - 'The Pottery Maker' – were ominously clear.

Chapter 8

The Pottery Maker

1675 A.D.

Nadie knelt by the water's edge, watching the other women from the village gather clay from the natural deposits in the river, and then place them into woven baskets to take home and make ready for pots and trinkets. She filled a large sandy coloured earthen pot to the brim with water before making her way back through the long meadow grass towards the village houses. Nadie looked around her as she strolled, soaking up the beauty of the land and its people. Other women and older children were busy working near the village centre, sat in groups by their houses, making clothing and sacks out of bison hair, then pinning the garments to wooden A-frames for stretching and drying. The people chatted and laughed as the yarn was spun on the crude wooden spindles, younger children playing around them, fascinated at the spinning implements.

Up ahead, near to her own house, she could see Asemota cradling a pile of logs which looked almost too much to bear as he neared the stock pile. As usual, young Aharu was with him, both of them laughing and fooling around as one tried to trip the other and cause the logs to fall. Nadie gazed proudly at her son and wondered what was to come, having contemplated their recent return to the village, not more than a week ago. It was Spring when she had set off with Etchemin and the other warriors to find her son, now it was Autumn – disbelieving that her journey had taken seven full moons.

'Teekwaakiki…it is Autumn,' Nadie said to herself, she and the others in the village now embroiled in the gathering and stockpiling of provisions for the winter months ahead. As she neared her house, she stopped and looked around the entire circumference of her village. It really was so beautiful, set in a lush meadow with a life giving river running from west to east along the southern perimeter, and an extended rocky knoll to the north side, which had a ridge running from the base of one forest area right through to the base of another forest. The ridge itself was bare of trees, in part due to purposeful felling and the subsequent quarrying of chert, used as a crystalline quartz mix for making knives and crop tools. Despite the advantage of the quarrying, the top of the ridge served as another good purpose - by allowing the tribal warriors to have a panoramic view of the landscape, helping them to patrol and keep watch from the highest vantage point.

In the forests to the west and east of the village,

men were busily chopping down large cotton-wood trees, using base fires to fell them before they carved out the trunks for new canoes and timber frames for the village longhouses. Some men were cutting and carving the strongest of the tree branches to make bows for hunting, although a good stock of bows would always be made in readiness to defend the village. Thinner stems of wood were being lashed to finely chiseled stone arrow heads, making lethal arrows to kill prey and, when necessary, their enemies.

The village longhouses were set nearer to the East Forest than the West Forest, the East Forest starting at the top of the knoll and working its way down behind the village before expanding out across the river and along the south ridge of the valley in which the village lay. A small lake featured in the East Forest, not far from the village, where children and youths would often play, and communal gatherings would take place to celebrate festivities for the change of the seasons. The lake was considered a spiritual place, a place that Nadie revered.

Nadie and Asemota's longhouse stood on a small mound on the outer edge of the village, closer to the lake than the others. Like all longhouses, her house was built from a remnant ancient style - akin to those of the old Cahokian tribes, with an extended wooden frame mounted on risen earth, the frame itself covered with a dense thatch of reed mats. These same mats the villagers would use to place on the floor, providing warmth and comfort to the families who lived within them. The wooden posts for the frame were sunk into small pits, filled with stones to secure the house against the elements. Nadie's house had a basement room below the line of the small wooden entrance door, a room she would use as the sleeping quarters for extra warmth in the winter months, making sure the bunkbeds had ample woven blankets and animal skins for comfort.

The most prominent longhouse, on the highest mound, was that of the village Chief, situated in a dominant central position towards the north end of the village, overlooking the small village Plaza, close to the base of the knoll. Next to the Chief's house was the village stockade, made of square and round wooden bastions to protect the maize crop and the stores of nuts and berries. The Chief lived in his grand longhouse with his extended family, often gathering the tribal elders for talks and celebrations. It was a place where the Chief would frequently ask for Nadie's counsel.

It was all too easy to be consumed by this idyllic place and Nadie had to wrench out of her absorption, she had to be prepared, she was sure that the evil she had so prophesised would soon reveal itself. She called Asemota to stop fetching the logs and asked him to prepare some food with the water she had fetched from the river, her attention was drawn elsewhere.

A lone figure stood at the top of the knoll ridge, standing on ground at its most central point. Nadie could see that it was a tall muscular man in warrior clothing, his torso bare and his bow being held in one hand. The man was waving in Nadie's direction, she felt sure it was the village Chief, the 'Akima', any doubt subsiding when she heard his familiar powerful voice.

'Nadie! Nadie! *Pyaahkani…pyaahkani!*' said the Chief, waving his arms frantically, pointing to the other side of the knoll ridge towards the small valley out of sight from the village. Asemota joined his mother, looking up to the knoll, where by now two other warriors had climbed the well-worn track to join the Akima.

'What does the Chief want Anna?'

'He said "Nadie you must come", he seems frantic, he must have seen something that needs my attention. Here is the water, start the food Asemota, I will climb the knoll and go to him.'

Asemota did as he was told; fetching the fruits and the corn from the store at the back of their longhouse, and readying the fire to cook the wild turkey caught some days before. Proudly, Nadie watched her son for a few moments before she turned and ran quickly across the busy village Plaza, to the base of the knoll before joining the track and climbing up to the ridge where the Chief and his warriors were standing. Some of the villagers had turned to watch what was going on, fixated on Nadie as she ran to meet Akima. At the top, Nadie greeted the Chief and paid her respects a little nervously, fearful of what he had seen.

Looking out from the ridge, towards the base of the shallow valley, Nadie could see two men walking; they were crossing a narrow stream with laden pack horses trailing behind them. The men were dressed in dark coloured robes, both sporting bushy beards, one of the men average in height with the other enormous in size. She could see that they both wore metal chains around their necks, with a trinket in the shape of a cross resting on their chests; the trinkets were sporadically catching the sunlight as the two men walked up the valley side to where Nadie and Akima were standing.

Akima ordered his two warriors to draw their bows and point arrows towards the two strangers. The two robed men saw the threat and waved furiously at the at the party of warriors, clasping their hands and shouting at the top of their voices in an incomprehensible language. The action caused Nadie to step in front of the warriors and plead with Akima.

'*Pyaawaace...pyaawaace Akima*...let them come my Chief...I will speak with them - I believe they are the white man priests I told you about. If they are, they should mean no harm, we can perhaps do trade and learn about their customs. I have heard that many villages have found such men peaceful, it is their way,' said Nadie, hiding her reticence, feeling a sense of unease as the two men got closer.

'You had better be right Nadie,' said Akima. 'You said yourself when you returned home that you feared evil would come, and you have not been settled. I do not like it when you are not settled. These strangers had better not send harm our way.'

'We should perhaps be wise and learn from them, they may give us some answers as to what more is to come from the white peoples.'

'So be it, but I will keep careful watch and I will seek counsel,' said Akima as he barked at his warriors to withdraw their bows and step back to the ridge.

The two priests had been anxious, standing with hands in the air in the face of the fearsome warriors, only now they could breathe a sigh of relief with the threat diminished. The shorter of the two men permeated a broad friendly smile through his thick black beard, and shouted towards Nadie.

'Mon Dieu, merci, merci beaucoup.'

Nadie was unsure of the words but knew they were not English. Surely they were the French Jesuit Priests she had heard of, and contemplated speaking English to them - assuming that if they were well travelled and educated enough, they would know the language.

'The English tongue I can speak with you,' she shouted back.

The shorter man, who appeared to be the leader, turned to his colleague and after a brief discussion with him, turned back to face Nadie and the Chief.

'Not that I want to speak the tongue of our sworn enemy, but if we can talk this way, then it is a blessing,' said the short man, his big expressive grin never leaving his face.

Nadie tentatively smiled back as the priests reached her position. Akima gave orders to his men to help with the three horses, but their reluctance to hold the strange animals was all too plain to see and the priests beckoned the warriors away with a friendly gesture.

Most of the village had gathered in the Plaza as the party descended the knoll track, all eyes on the priests, particularly the larger man. Nadie was the tallest person in the tribe, man or woman, but the large priest seemed much taller than her and certainly, he was of such large build that no-one in the village could ever recall seeing someone so big. Despite his humble demeanor, the giant blond haired, blond bearded priest appeared to have a mightily powerful frame beneath his robed attire.

Akima allowed his people to make a fuss of the strangers and their curious animals for a short time before he ordered business. The pleasantries ended and people dispersed, Akima directing the priests to his own house, demanding Nadie's presence along with Asemota if she so wished.

Akima's wife, Kauti, a small wiry, good looking woman, so named as the lady 'who sings' prepared extra reed mats in the house communal area for people to sit on. Nuttah, the Chief's mother, was an elderly woman, round in stature with a rugged face and grey hair but still fit and strong – she prepared the food for the guests. The gathering of people was added to by the Chief's most trusted aids, Etchemin and his son, Askuwheteau. They all sat in a circle on the floor as the two strangers introduced themselves through Nadie. The Chief and his entourage grew even more curious at the mode of dress adorning the new arrivals, scanning their heavy duty dark woolen robes, leather sandals and a distinctive silver cross and chain around their necks. Tied around their midriffs was a piece of cord and placed through the chord was an ornamental dagger, the handle also in the shape of a cross. Feeling a little uncomfortable at being watched, the smaller of the priests spoke first, a nervous disposition in his voice.

'My name is Louis, Father Louis Bertrand and this is Francois, Brother Francois Martel, he is not yet a priest, but he is my understudy – only priests are called Father. We are of the Jesuit Order, we are French missionaries, carrying the word of our Christian God to the Illiniweck people, or as we French call them, the Illinois...'

Nadie interrupted and asked the Chief for permission to speak, but he silenced her in readiness for his own authoritative speech, pointing to his own chest, he directed his words to Father Bertrand.

'*Akima, Akima. Inoka-Illini... waapamikaanke... tipeelimihsoohkaanke.*'

'He is giving his title, Akima – the Chief - and he is correcting you from your term Illinois. We are of the Inoka peoples and the Chief is expressing himself as the Illini which means what he actually is, a mature man. He then said that you must look at us but you must not control us, meaning be free to observe us but do not tell us what to do,' said Nadie, mindful of ensuring that Father Bertrand knew of the Chief's standing.

'I would never wish to offend,' said Father Bertrand. 'Myself and Brother Francois Martel merely wish to get to know your people and study your language, we have visited many villages and we have started to understand some of the words.'

'But you wish to spread the word of your God?' said Nadie. 'That is the part where you must be careful, we have many customs and deities and the Chief would not take kindly to any interference.'

'What are you talking about Nadie?' shouted the Chief in frustration, not knowing what was being said.

'Forgive me Akima, we were talking about their deity, their belief in the one God.'

'May I say something?' queried Father Bertrand. 'I follow the teachings and writings of my Master, Father Jacques Marquette, who unfortunately died in these lands during the Spring of this year. It is his peaceful word that I would wish to spread, we mean no harm and we are very accommodating, I for one like to remain happy and jovial, perhaps unlike Brother Martel here who can be a bit serious,' laughed Father Bertrand, his beaming smile once again shining through his big bushy beard.

Nadie thought his demeanor was quite infectious and his audience also started to smile with him, although not a word was understood save Nadie's translation.

'He is like Aharu,' said Kauti, the Chief's wife. 'They could make a pair with their smile and their jolliness. Akima, the food is nearly ready, do you wish to stop the talking for a moment?'

General conversation followed but Nadie could not relax, she was concerned with these men and wanted to know more about their religion, how it came about and what their intentions were. Kauti and Akima conversed, organising accommodation and provisions for the priests, calling upon Etchemin and Askuwheteau, together with their wives, to ready a vacant longhouse for the visitors.

Asemota, didn't say much and was intent on listening, curious about the strangers. He found himself gawping at Brother Martel, he had never seen such a large human being and could not find the courage to find conversation with the introvert giant. Father Bertrand was clearly the inquisitive one, trying to get as much out of Nadie and Asemota as he could.

The relaxed atmosphere changed into a more formal one once again.

'Nadie, ask the small one how long he and his companion will be staying,' said the Chief.

'Father Bertrand mentions that "perhaps when the hospitality runs out, or you stop giving us food", he jokes I think,' said Nadie, and they all laughed, even the Chief breaking into a momentary smile.

'And what of the fighting between the white tribes, I know of the Spanish peoples, and I now hear of the French? The English, Nadie has spoken of, but you all fight each other for our lands - how can I trust you?' said Akima, assertively.

'We are not men of war, only peace. My blessed leader Jacques Marquette, God rest his soul, only wanted to bring the word of God to these lands, I am merely carrying out his work – even in the face of the enemies to the French,' said Father Bertrand.

'You preach peace but I see your face is passionate against the other white tribes,' said Akima. 'I will not have trouble here, I have enough to do negotiating peace with people of my own kind, any sign of mistrust then I will banish you.'

Father Bertrand was clear with that comment, a nod from Nadie was enough to indicate he should take heed. Brother Martel looked up from his normal rounded posture, pumping out his enormous chest, not saying anything but looking stern in Nadie's direction. She became uncomfortable, shifting her gaze towards Akima. Asemota caught the interaction, growing ever the more curious and suspicious of the giant fair haired Jesuit.

The conversation drew to a close with Akima formally welcoming the Jesuits to his village, despite his reservations. He informed the white men of his plan with the accommodation, making them aware that he would expect them to work for their stay. The priests acknowledged this and were grateful.

Once inside her longhouse, Nadie sat down and wrapped herself in a thick brown shawl, which had been meticulously spun from bison hair. She was feeling a little cold and uneasy. Asemota stoked a fire he had prepared near to the entrance of the house; he could see that his mother was troubled.

'There is an unease now, these men have made me unsettled, even more so than before,' said Nadie.

'I don't like the look of Brother Martel, he looks like a brooding giant,' said Asemota moving to sit by his mother. 'Is he to be trusted?'

'I do not know, I will call Spirit Wolf, she may sense things,' said Nadie looking pensively at Asemota. 'I will need to talk to you as well my Son, before it may be too late.'

'Yes Anna, is it about the secrets of the Spirit Wolf?'

'You are here for a reason, I brought you here for a reason, I made a promise to your father...' Nadie stopped short, wrapping the shawl even tighter around her shoulders and staring at the glowing fire.

'But I am your son,' said Asemota, emotion welling in his voice. 'Why shouldn't I be here, you saved me, my father knew you would save me. Anna, he loved you dearly, I am here because of him and because of you.'

'The light fades,' said Nadie. 'Perhaps we should wait till dawn.'

'I will not rest now - you must talk to me Anna.'

'I am ashamed Asemota. I am ashamed that I have put you in danger, you are my son and I don't know whether I can protect you.'

'If we are in such great danger then you must share your thoughts, how can I help without knowing what you should reveal?'

After a moments silence, Nadie spoke softly, 'I made you for a reason, your father and I made you because I asked him. I became a slave just like him and by chance we were thrown together in the same camp. I knew he was the one...he was the one I should mate with, he was so strong, so powerful, so honest - it had to be him.'

Asemota was stunned, trying to register what his mother was saying. He got back on his feet and went to the entrance of the house to stoke the fire, moving the circular stone surround to accommodate more wood. He prodded the embers angrily, fighting the feelings of confusion and isolation, as if all of a sudden he was just a mere by-product of some pre-organised union.

Nadie stood up and wrapped the shawl around her midriff, she walked to him by the fire.

'Let the village settle for a while and I will show you what I mean. You have a destiny Asemota that, at present, will be unimaginable to you. You are on this Earth for a reason and that is my doing. I met your father and I knew, I just knew...'

'Knew what?' said Asemota, annoyed. 'You were both slaves, surely you fell in love - you had a child, I am that child.'

'I loved your father as I love you, and yes we did fall in love, but I knew when I first saw him he was the one that I needed. A strong powerful, beautiful looking Prince from the Africa lands, a man so proud and so just that I knew I would never find an equal to match him...it had to be him.'

'Had to be him for what?' said Ascmota.

Nadie stared at the fire, which had now gathered flame again. It was dusk. To the east and to the west she looked up, seeing the shadows of the forests forming, obscured a little by her eyes trying to adjust from the firelight. She saw the outline of two warriors on the top of the knoll, walking slowly, purposefully, guarding the village. *Time to act*, Nadie thought. She had shown weakness and needed to redeem herself, she needed to show strength.

'There is a place I must show you, there we will see *Manitou Mahweewa,* we shall go and see the Spirit Wolf again,' said Nadie, resolutely.

*

Father Bertrand looked around his temporary accommodation and noticed how warm it seemed, the sunken pit where the bed quarters lay had an extraordinary warmth. Reed mats were everywhere and offered a further layer of comfort and insulation. It was clear that the wives of Etchemin and Askuwhetau had prepared the house lavishly, with new reed mats laid on the floor, fresh food in the form of squash fruit, nuts and corn, and bedding supplements provided in the form of bison furs and deer hides. Brother Martel started to open the leather horse packs that had been brought to the house for them, bringing out their personal belongings, including the all-important bibles. A small silver altar cross was taken from one of the side pockets and placed on a wooden box that had the mark of a crucifix emblazoned on it. Spare robes, footwear and writing material were placed on a wooden framed hammock.

As he continued to unpack, Brother Martel waited for an opportunity to see whether Father Bertrand would be distracted, only to notice that his Mentor already seemed to be in a world of his own, preparing the beds and sampling the food as he muttered to himself by recounting the afternoon events with the Akima.

Sat on his bunk, Martel turned his enormous frame away from Father Bertrand, hoping that he would not be seen removing the next item from his leather pack – his study diary. Martel was behind with his scholastic writings and therefore his training. Father Bertrand knew this and was becoming furious with Martel's complacency, reminding Martel that he would increase the length of his novitiate if he did not complete the disciplines and virtues he had been assigned.

Father Bertrand was professed and by definition a fully-fledged priest having recently acquired the making of his fourth vow. This vow had been confirmed by his Master, Jacques Marquette who had informed The Pope himself about Father Bertrand's commitment to the Holy Mission in the Americas.

Unfortunately, Marquette had died before he could see Father Bertrand finally inaugurated into priesthood. Father Bertrand was devout and completely committed to the Jesuit Order; however, his reservations about Brother Martel were acute. He had grave concerns about Martel's commitment to the Order, at times thinking that Martel may not even be committed to God.

The understudy priest loathed the thought of looking at his study diary, convulsing at the prospect of having to write in it and explain himself to Father Bertrand. To Martel, the missionary had become a clever guise, an affront, a way for him to embark on a different more sinister mission. He left the diary in his pack and turned his attention to another book, one that he had disguised as a bible. It was a book of prophecies, a book that he had been given by another priest who had resided in the Vatican, and it was this very priest who had unveiled a prophecy so powerful that Martel had been seduced over the past years, consumed by its legacy, yearning to consolidate a destiny for which he believed would be revealed for him.

Martel was sure that he had arrived at the right place and that 'The Maker' would show themselves. The time was now right to call upon his protector, the very powerful and evil *Machk Matchitehew*.

*

Nadie and Asemota stepped out into the dark, letting their eyes adjust to the near full moon light, which was only slightly hindered by the sparse clouds whisking across the sky. Disbelief would soon consume her son if Nadie could not make him understand the nature of the events about to unfold; her strength would be key, yet he would have to learn quickly and heed her knowledge to find such resolve without fear.

She carried a sack made out of white tailed deer hide, having fetched it from a hiding place beneath her bunkbed. Having let their eyes adjust, they hastened their walk into a steady run, turning into the East Forest, passing the lake not far from the village before reaching an extremely dense thicket of oak trees. Asemota guessed they must have travelled nearly a kilometre from their house and that the eerie clump of oak trees rested at the very end of the knoll ridge incline. The trees looked old and ghostly as if at any moment they would peer down at him and grapple him in their thick black branches to carry him away. The air seemed all too familiarly still, predicting an event which Asemota was becoming accustomed to.

At the centre of the cluster, Nadie appeared to be counting the trees. The natural light from the moon had all but vanished and she had to use her intricate knowledge of the surroundings to find her way.

'I have found it,' said Nadie. 'I wasn't too sure because of the dark, I haven't been here since we got back, although I should have been. Come close to me if you can and stoop down as I do.'

Asemota was astonished to see Nadie lift a camouflaged covering, made out of a wooden lattice frame and a reed mat smothered with branches, dirt and leaves. There was a small wooden marker in the shape of a tree branch, which gave the position of the handle to lift the frame. Nadie lifted the frame to head height and braced it with a wooden pole, taken from under the lattice. They both peered inside, and even though there was only a withering light, Asemota was surprised at how deep he could see the Pit was, at least half a metre above his height. He stepped down and perused the scene as best he could, trying to fathom his surroundings.

At the far end, opposite to the Pit opening, he saw a brick and stone built hearth covered in soil and grass, not unlike the ones in the village used to bake the clay collected from the river banks. Next to the hearth was a wooden palate, the top covered with an animal hide. Most curious of all, was the batch of small clay figurines that lay on the animal hide, intricate figures that he had never seen the likes of before. He knew of the clay pots, trinkets and spirit dolls that had been made in the village, but none so detailed as those he could see now - a range of humanoid and animal figurines which appeared so meticulously carved.

'The moon light fades through the trees and the clouds Anna.'

'Yes, I can see. Pull the pole away quickly and lower the frame, I will light a fire torch.'

As soon as the task was completed, Asemota watched his mother remove a small square base, no more than twenty centimetres square, from the sack she had been carrying. The base was weighty, being made of stone, perfect in shape with pigmented black and white symmetrical squares covering the one side. Strange symbols, gold in colour, were engraved on the four outer edges, sparkling in the fire torch light. Nadie carefully removed the figurines from the wooden pallet and placed them with precision on the stone board. Asemota looked closely at the hearth, seeing how the stone bricks were pyramidically knitted together - creating a kiln one metre across and at least half a metre deep. A large mound of earth stretched from the ground of the Pit and covered the entire top layer of bricks. The kiln had two openings, one at the base where Asemota assumed that the fire would be lit, and one nearer the top where the pottery figurines would be placed.

An anxious but curious Asemota remained silent as he watched his mother work, placing the stone board and the figurines into the opening in the top of the kiln; she packed the opening with more earth ensuring that the board and the figures were completely encased. Then something astonishing happened.

Nadie knelt down and placed her head next to the bottom opening of the kiln and she blew gently into the gap. A fiery glow started to emerge, slowly filling the Pit with light.

'How can this be?' Asemota shouted, breaking his silence. 'The embers cannot last that long and you have placed no fresh fire wood to warm the stones!'

Nadie did not respond, she would only speak when everything was in place. She opened the deer hide sack and part removed what looked like a scroll, reading some of the inscription. Asemota could not see what his mother was actually doing; she shielded the scroll from him and then quickly replaced it fully into the sack.

The light from the kiln grew more intense, like daylight, filling every corner of the Pit. Asemota could not look at the light source directly, shielding the brightness with his hands. Nadie placed a free standing stone against the opening which had the effect of dissipating the light, making it more bearable.

'In my father's name Anna, please tell me what is happening?' said Asemota, utterly perplexed.

'We must wait Asemota, we must wait to see what is revealed on the stone board, the prophecy will show itself and Spirt Wolf will be guided - she is near to us now.'

'I am lost and you are frightening me, you must tell me what will be revealed?' said Asemota.

'The clay figures will dance and they will fall into place according to what I have seen, we must prepare my Son.'

Asemota stepped closer to his mother and placed his hand on her shoulder turning her gently to look deep into her eyes. His own eyes welled up with emotion, desperate to understand what was going on, knowing that his mother was conflicted and distraught as to what she could tell him.

'Who are you Anna?' said Asemota deliberately and slowly.

Nadie paused and reflected upon whether or not she should tell him, time was pressing, and as she feared, the occasion may become all too much for him to bear. Yet this is why she had brought him home, never mind that they had hardly spent any time together, she could not have foreseen how quickly the circumstance would change – she would have to tell him and he would have to see what the prophecy revealed.

'I am the guardian, a guardian of a sacred prophecy…I am what is known as The Maker, so called as The Pottery Maker, being born to serve and born to protect.'

Nadie placed her hands on Asemota's face.

'There is so much I have to tell you and I have no time, you must bear with me, please just work with my conscience and my actions,' she said, rather forlornly.

'*Manitou Mahweewa* is here,' shouted Asemota.

'Yes, you feel her presence now, that is a good sign,' said Nadie.

They climbed out of the Pit into the darkness, searching, waiting, looking furtively into the surrounding forest, listening intently for any signs of the Great Wolf. The air became still, the trees and the thicket stopped rustling to any degree and out of the shadows came the Spirit Wolf, her magnificence to be beholden, filling Asemota with awe. He was proud to have felt her presence and the Spirit Wolf could sense this, her smile was broad and her deep blue human like eyes shone hypnotically once again as she bowed her head to mother and son.

'My beautiful Protector, the time has drawn close I fear, we must prepare for the dangers ahead, I know not what lies in store for us, or for you great beast.'

Spirit Wolf answered with a further bow, her smile disappearing to be replaced by a sterner look and a low growl. The wolf walked over to the Pit cover and scratched at it, looking knowingly at Nadie.

'She knows of the Pit?' queried Asemota.

'Of course, she is my Protector, the Protector of The Pottery Maker, foresworn to guard me for all time and to the death. She is anxious to see what prophecy will be revealed and what adversary she will have to do battle with.'

The configuration on the stone chequered board was all too conspicuous, where two of the clay pottery pieces had moved of their own accord to the centre of the board, one from each side of the rear rows, now in open play facing each other, no spaces between them. One figure was in the shape of a hideous black bear, the other in the shape of a magnificent silver haired wolf, both creatures standing on their hind legs with their mouths open, and teeth gnarling towards each other.

'How can this be Anna? How could they have moved in the kiln by themselves?' asked Asemota.

'This is the prophecy Asemota. I barely have time to explain properly, you must learn quickly as I talk. On each side of the board, the clay figures represent deities, the guardians of the deities, and their foot soldiers. The deities and guardians stand on the back rows, and they depict sacred gods and demons from all manner of beliefs in this world. The guardians you see on the board are the true protectors, they are the ones whom the deities choose to complete their bidding on this Earth, whilst the soldiers you see on the front rows are, as legend would have it, only to be used in the time of all-out war.'

'Therefore one side is evil and one side is good?' said Asemota.

'Yes, generally, but it is not quite that simple. The

189

deities you see behind the black bear are inherently evil, but sometimes the good deities become angry. In all my time as the Maker I have only ever seen the Guardians move, or as I prefer to call them - the Protectors. Never have I seen the deities move position, nor the soldiers on the front rows. The anger or will of the deities is only ever expressed through the movement I have described.'

'I don't think I have been any more afraid,' said Asemota. 'But what of the soldiers, you must have more knowledge?'

'The soldiers are powerful demigods and will only reveal themselves in times of great anguish. It is said that they can only be conjured if one of the deities shows its physical presence here on Earth...I pray that this never happens because if this becomes so, the pure evil of the monstrous deity called The Piasa will be unleashed, a great beast of the underworld who would wreak havoc across all lands.'

'Demigods, The Piasa - what sorcery is all of this?' said Asemota, concern in his voice.

As Nadie spoke, Spirit Wolf glared through the Pit opening, viewing the board, her eyes narrowed and fixed on the two pottery figures in the centre. Her low growl turned into a deep snarl, rumbling and shaking the Pit walls, and the frown on her face became more pronounced. Conversation between mother and son ceased at the wolf's activity, dawning upon Asemota that one of the figurines must be a representation of the great Spirit Wolf – and the black bear undoubtedly her forthcoming adversary.

Terrified, Asemota's cognizance with this strange

circumstance was somewhat array; he had been thrust into a strange world of spirit animals, prophecies and demigods – not to mention the unfathomable concept of an evil deity, a vile, dark creature from the underworld named as 'The Piasa'. The quest to advance his knowledge on such matters was imposing. Soon, he supposed, he and his mother would be embroiled in supernatural events that neither of them could predict – and it all seemed so imminent.

Observing the chequered board and its figurines was seductive and Asemota had to prize himself away from its grasp when hearing the shout of his mother. Nadie had scrambled out of the Pit and was trying to calm the Great Wolf, following the creature wherever she paced, stroking her and trying to make her still for a moment.

'The *Machk Matchitehew* is upon us and Spirit Wolf must do battle!' shouted Nadie.

'The bear with the evil heart, so this is the evil heart you mentioned on our last night before entering the village?'

'Yes,' said Nadie. 'Now we know it is Spirit Wolf's adversary, a mighty beast equal to her in strength and size, revealed so by the prophecy on the chequered board.'

The wolf settled for a short while, responding to Nadie's charms as she gently stroked the enormous chest of this most magnificent beast.

'We must stay calm, the battle will come soon enough my Protector... where is he, where will he come from? Where is the *Machk Matchitehew*?'

Spirit Wolf pointed her head towards the village

and then lifted her nose in the air repeatedly before Nadie spoke again.

'Stay settled my *Manitou Mahweewa*. He will come from the West Forest?'

The wolf scratched her right paw, twice into the dirt, confirming Nadie's suspicions. The *Machk Matchitehew*, Nadie explained, would take many forms, and this time the prophecy had revealed that it would indeed be a bear, a giant evil bear who would be prepared to fight Spirit Wolf to the death to gain dominance for its Master, whomever that should be – a master who would dare to become the Pottery Maker, only this time a Maker with evil intent, whose only desire would be to plunge the world into darkness.

Asemota was bewildered with such a concept.

'She is calmer now Asemota. We shall return tomorrow evening and then the next evening, and we shall read the inscriptions and place the board into the earthen kiln to see if more prophecies are revealed. We know now that very soon the evil bear will emerge from the West Forest; of an exact time, I do not know….it could only be a matter of days. In the mean time we must discover who the Master of *Machk Matchitehew* is and we have to do it quickly.'

'I am frightened for us Anna, and I am confused – why should I be the one chosen for this path?'

'Please stay strong Asemota, there is more I will tell you over the coming hours, for now you must concentrate on helping me prepare…I need you to work by my side. The village must be warned; I must speak with Akima right away.'

*

Martel sat on his wooden framed bunkbed, staring at the small fire blazing in the centre of the longhouse, smoke billowing through a central hole purposely created in the roof. He was reading the book of historical prophecies, one which Father Bertrand despised. Perpetually gripped with his forbidding, malevolent quest, Martel read repeatedly through the scant knowledge he had acquired of the legacy surrounding the so called Pottery Maker, trying to decipher the Latin conjecture in the text, some of which appeared to have been derived from an ancient Hindu scripture. According to Martel's true Mentor, a mysterious pagan priest from his homelands in Brittany, the relevance to the Hindu scripture from the Latin copy hinted at a prophecy within one of the old Vedic scripts, which one of those scripts, no one knew.

He had been given the knowledge of the book by his true Mentor years before, and since that time he had charmed his way into the Jesuit Order to retrieve the book from a priest in Rome, before seeking his way to the new lands in The Colonies. Martel had learned so much from the reclusive pagan and now through his acute senses he was sure he had found the village where the Pottery Maker resided.

The most sinister thing of all, his pagan Mentor had surmised, was the prophecy of the evil spirit beast. Legend had it that for every spirit beast born to protect the Pottery Maker, an evil spirit beast of equal size and strength would arrive and be destined to roam the earth like a jackal until it found its Master.

On his travels in the New World, Martel had sensed the evil bear, until finally, one evening in a secret hideaway, he confronted the great evil beast, bonding with it and gaining acceptance as its Master.

His concentration was broken by the voice of Father Bertrand, who was busy placing more wood on the fire.

'You have been reading that cursed black book again, don't think I don't know, I have seen you with it before. You should be studying the bible - why do you defy me so?'

'Surely as Jesuits we should know all that may possibly oppose us, which is why I read this book of ancient prophecies and customs. To know what is written and understood by other beliefs is to know how other people of the world behave,' said Martel, manipulating the conversation. 'Our interpretation of these good people and their customs would bode well in such a book, don't you think?'

'It is evil, and as far as I am concerned it reveals evil sentiment, and it challenges God, how on Earth do you not see that?' said Father Bertrand.

Martel did not reply, in any event he had no real faith in the Christian God, he would only read the bible out of curiosity and lie to Father Bertrand about the piousness he shared with him. Soon he would discard such notions and reveal his true self.

'We must discuss this more tomorrow. I implore you Brother Martel, we must talk about these issues, but I am too tired now, let us rest.'

Father Bertrand slowly climbed into his bunkbed, pulling the thick bison fur over his body, unable to think or move anymore due to his profuse tiredness – the day had been long and mentally arduous, he fell asleep immediately.

Martel carried on reading for a while; thoughts of sleeping were not foremost in his mind. Two nights from now he would lie in wait for the Pottery Maker, he had his suspicions as to who it might be now, and if he was right, together with the *Machk Matchitehew* they would destroy her and her deplorable spirit beast.

Chapter 9

Battle the First

Unusually, a strike for winter camp was ordered, away from the village; Akima not hesitating once he had heard the news from Nadie the night before last. Older women and the children would start to move out of the village, seeking temporary refuge on the far side of the West Forest where the younger members of the tribe had been working furiously to accommodate them.

Under Akima's impeccable authority and direction, three war parties had been organised, a mixture of men and women – one to protect the edge of the West Forest nearest the village, one to protect the older people and children of the tribe, and one to protect the sacred lake in the East Forest.

It was mid-afternoon; Asemota and Aharu busied themselves working together once again, removing provisions from the stockade and preparing weapons for the warriors who were to protect the area around the East Forest, poignantly near to where the Pit lay. The village people, although relentless with their work, felt an unease, and many of the tribe had become unsettled, wondering why the village had been struck at all.

Nadie was unsettled at not having enough time to explain more to her son, and when he was next at the stockade, she shouted for him, beckoning him to return to their longhouse as quick as he might.

Asemota ran into the house, sweating and panting, carrying a bow and a sack of arrows over his shoulder. He placed them near to the entrance, noticing that his mother was standing at the back of the building, holding a familiar looking scroll, one he felt sure he had seen very briefly when they were last at the Pit.

'Akima has us working so hard, he was obviously receptive to our talk with him the other night, he trusts you implicitly Anna, look how the village has responded.'

'I had warned him enough about the approaching evil but he is very wise, he will trust his instinct…although I fear nothing will prepare the people for what is to come,' said Nadie.

'You must guide us then Anna, you must help us, tell me what to do.'

'I need to speak to Father Bertrand urgently…alone, and I need you understand more of what lies ahead. I have something for you to see, you must learn from it and quickly.'

'The scroll?' said Asemota.

'Yes, you saw me with it in the Pit, but you do not know of its significance. Here, take possession of it and observe intently. You must watch it closely and know its every detail, it holds many secrets, and for you its power will be hard to imagine. It is an ancient Parchment and it will be yours to guard.'

Unsure of what he was holding, the young man felt a surge of mysticism with the strange object in his hands. It was indeed a Parchment, made out of animal skin, an animal his mother knew not of which type or from which time, only that it had been passed from generation to generation over many hundreds, or even thousands of moons. The person beholden to keep 'The Parchment' never questioned from whence it came, it was the duty bestowed upon such a person to carry out its bidding, nothing more. It was the solemn duty of the Pottery Maker.

'Look upon The Parchment Asemota, know it, feel it, absorb it - as it will absorb you, you must open your mind to it,' said Nadie, seeing Asemota's gaping face.

'I am going to leave you with it for a while, I must make haste and find Father Bertrand. Hide yourself in your bunk, do not let anyone see you with it,' Nadie commanded.

Asemota did as he was instructed and retreated to the bottom layer of the house where his bunkbed lay. The texture of The Parchment felt soft, as if it had been made very recently, its unusual pliability baffling the young man. Whichever angle he looked at the image on the surface, the perspective never changed, it was equal in prominence however he viewed it. The image was most eerie, depicting every detail of the Pit and hearth he had seen for real previously; it was if he had actually been transported back to that moment.

Most astonishing of all was seeing an exact pictorial representation of the chequered board and its figurines placed upon it, with the wolf and the bear facing each other, and the other figurines in their rows, aligned in the same order as the real board. On the edges of the pictorial board, just like the real board again, there were shiny gold symbols, which seemed to fluctuate and flutter in movement as he glanced at them, unnerving him. Because of this, he looked away from the image, only to look back quickly, convinced that through his peripheral vision he had seen the bear and the wolf turn to look at him. He stared back, but neither of them moved. W*hat trickery is this?* he thought.

∗

Nadie found Father Bertrand near to the Chief's house, he was trying to converse humorously with Etchemin and Askuwhetau, who although were keeping busy by the stockade, seemed enthralled at the priest's antics, playing along with him for their own amusement.

'Look at the stranger Nadie, he mimics the animals. His big bushy beard moves when he makes the sounds, it is so funny, I think my father will die of lack of air, he has been laughing just like the priest.'

'It is good to see you laugh Askuwhetau,' said Nadie. 'The priest is certainly making himself at home, I think he is a good intentioned man – but have you seen Brother Martel anywhere?'

'No I have not. Him I do not trust,' said

Askuwhetau, suddenly retorting, showing his familiar scowl.

Nadie nodded in half agreement, catching Father Bertrand's attention at the same time. The smile diminished from the priest's face as he saw her anxious expression, it was clear she wanted to speak with him.

'Walk with me,' said Nadie. 'I wish to speak with you alone.'

Her intent was undoubtedly serious, none less the same was the bellow of Akima shouting at his warriors to make haste. The village men and women quickly dispersed from the Plaza, whilst Nadie guided an out of breath Father Bertrand to walk with her towards the river bank.

'Tell me Nadie, I have learned rather quickly that your people have one God you put above all others, one who rules what you call 'The Upper World', am I correct…without offending you of course?'

'You are correct, we call him *Kitchesmanetoa,* which means 'The Spirit Master of Life', he controls all of the spirits in The Upper World which in turn gives us our strength and peace here in The Middle World.'

'I find that interesting, wherever I go on my travels I find that most people believe in a higher God, our Christian teachings show this…'

'I am sorry to interrupt Father Bertrand - but you see, I must tell you that I have a devout lineage which stems from the ancient Mississippian and Cahokian tribes of these lands. My extended family and friends, here in this village, also have ancestors belonging to those ancient tribes. We are now of the Inoca peoples, the Illiniweck as we have told you, and we have fixed religious ideas about the supernatural powers of the world. We are subservient to the rituals which create harmony between our people and the natural forces of the spirit world. It is never just about one God. I can assure you there is a balance...always a balance,' said Nadie, resoundingly.

'I accept your traditions but I would like to invite people to see what our Christian God has to offer. He is the Almighty, the all-powerful...to be righteous under him is to be in his glory.'

'Remember what Akima said Father Bertrand, "If you impose yourself you will be driven out", in any event, you may soon come to realise what our spirit world has to offer. But for now, please, I must ask you, I am a little concerned...where is Brother Martel?'

'Why do you ask?' said Father Bertrand, scratching his perspiring head.

'I am sorry, and I don't mean to be rude, I was just a little curious about him...I am afraid he makes some of us a little uneasy, perhaps because of his size and the way he looks. I just wanted to make myself more acquainted with him,' said Nadie, disguising her intent.

'Well, he has probably gone for a walk into the woods, which I fear seems to be his preference at the moment, that and his wretched book.'

'What book?' said Nadie.

'Oh never mind, I spoke out loud and I shouldn't have - it's just that I am a little concerned about him too – he seems fascinated with other matters besides my teachings and the teachings of our religion.'

The river bank neared and Father Bertrand welcomed the chance to take some water, he was pleased to be conversing with Nadie, she would be a useful ally in his quest to teach the Native Indians about his God. Intuitively he had quickly discovered that Nadie was the spiritual conscience of the tribe, a woman of profound wisdom and one who was so revered.

'What book?' repeated Nadie, clearly showing concern in her voice.

'Oh it's an historical book, a book of findings from different religions, and it's a book of ancient prophecies, one which offers an insight into cultural ideologies and myths. My fear, is that Brother Martel has become incessant with his quest to collect such ideas and writings, filling his head with such nonsense wherever he goes...he has become engrossed with it.'

'Perhaps then, he and I could share some thoughts, I could perhaps teach him some of our spiritual customs - surely he would find this interesting. We could turn his interest to our advantage?' queried Nadie, using the ploy.

*

The Parchment was still in Asemota's hands when his mother returned to the longhouse; he was transfixed, exulted in its presence and hardly able to put it down. Nadie felt comfort with his expression of wonder, recognising a little of herself through his character, remembering fondly when she first laid eyes on the scroll herself.

Yet her heart was pounding, she knew that the

time was drawing ever closer and still more work was needed. She and Father Bertrand had parted somewhat disconcertedly, although he had undertaken to inform her as soon as he had news of Brother Martel. Nadie had a deep sense now and felt resolutely sure that Martel was her adversary, an evil man who would have been plotting this moment for some time.

'Anna, the image on The Parchment, it moves I am sure of it…it shows me things, the wolf and the bear are the same as last night and the writing on the board glistens like a golden fire, I felt as though the figures were staring at me as if they were drawing me to them. But what of the mirror in the image? I am convinced that I saw your reflection, and for that I am fearful, look the tall figure in the picture resembles you.'

Nadie did not answer, she merely placed a gentle hand on her son's shoulder and asked him to roll The Parchment and place it back into the sack. The light would start to fade soon and she felt unprepared. Hurriedly she ushered Asemota out of the house to walk with her, her immediate intention to seek counsel with Akima, before her work really began at the Pit in the East Forest.

Akima was sat in his longhouse, accompanied by his most trusted warriors who were all in their customary places within the circular body, smoking their tobacco pipes, chatting fervently about their plans. Nadie was called to join them, all anxious for her sentiment.

'I am sorry Akima, but from our conversation night before last, I fear the moment has drawn closer.

I feel a terrible presence now. I believe the bad spirit is with us.'

The warriors fell silent, seeing the anguish on her face and feeling the concern. Akima stared hard at Nadie, showing his deep furrowed brow and aging lines around his eyes – he could see the abject fear in her face, he believed in her, he trusted her.

Intuitively, Akima turned and spoke to Asemota. 'Fetch Father Bertrand young man, find him and bring him here at once.'

The task need not have been given, for standing at the entrance to the Chief's longhouse was a distraught, ashen looking priest, profuse sweat pouring down the sides of his face, he was desperate to talk.

'What is it Father Bertrand?' shouted Nadie.

'Martel has gone! I have checked everywhere…he has taken all of his belongings from the longhouse. I saw him last this morning when he said he was going for a walk…he had nothing with him then. He must have crept back when I was out conversing with the warriors - but I am afraid that is not all.'

'What do you mean?' said Nadie.

'He left me a note, torn from that wretched book of prophecies I told you about, I…I don't really understand what it says, but perhaps you will,' said Father Bertrand, handing the note to Nadie.

'Tell me Nadie, what do you have in your hand, what symbols are they?' said Akima.

'I fear Martel is the evil one, I have sensed it and I am sure he is the evil who will scour our people and our land - but he will be after me, I am the one he has travelled for…he knows who I am - these are his words,' said Nadie.

"My time has come, for in this place I have found the Maker, and the hour draws near for me to shape the future of the prophecy, I shall wreak havoc on those who stand in my way, the Maker's time is at an end."

Etchemin cried out, 'but he is just one man, as big as he is – what can he do against us?'

'But what of the *Machk Matchitehew,* he will come, then we will all perish!' cried Asemota, not thinking.

The other warriors broke their silence, muttering insults towards Asemota.

'That is sacrilege!' said Askuwhetau. 'You dare frighten us with mention of the appearance of such spirits, spirits that we can neither see or touch, you are insolent young man and you are a conjurer!'

Akima calmed his men, concentrating his efforts on Nadie; now was not the time for squabbling.

'Dusk is upon us now Nadie, what should I tell my warriors?' said Akima.

'I will take Asemota to my sacred place and I will see more of what is to come, Martel I fear will be waiting and he will be prepared. Akima, prepare your men and women for battle, I do not know what will oppose us but I know it will be a mighty foe, like nothing you or your warriors will have ever seen. If you believe in the gods and the spirits, then believe me now and trust me. You have men and women positioned where they should be, they must be alert now, and we need a signal at the earliest point. I will need a strong guard to stand by me in the East Forest, not too far from the lake,' said Nadie, authority in her voice.

Commands were given and everyone dispersed, some frantic with their thoughts, others curious and disbelieving, yet all following their orders. Father Bertrand hurried to collect his bible before joining Asemota and Nadie to make their way to the sacred Pit in the East Forest. It would be opportune time for Nadie to glean more about Martel from Father Bertrand, as she and Asemota prepared, provided she could wrestle the priest from his nerves.

The warrior troops swept through the forests and meadows to their standpoints like cats stealthily stalking their prey. A detachment of elite warriors stayed near to Akima, although he had released Etchemin and Askuwhetau to command the two separate forest troops, their strong leadership and courage would be needed when it mattered most. The old people and children had already been moved to the far end of the West Forest and Aharu had been dispatched along with a small troop of warriors to look after them. Under no circumstance was he to abandon his post.

The stillness and the eerie silence remained, permeating around the Pit, something which Asemota had become accustomed to, but not so for Father Bertrand. The priest firmly believed his heart had actually risen to his mouth, and he was not sure whether to stand and pray to his Christian God, or run away from bearing witness to the devilry he suspected would unfold before him.

Asemota and Father Bertrand were merely onlookers, watching Nadie enter the Pit to take the stone chequered board and manipulate the figurines, intently reading the image on The Parchment at the same time. The kiln in the hearth started to roar in readiness, as if responding to Nadie's presence and her actions. The terracotta figures were dampened with water before being placed with the board into the top opening of the kiln. She covered the opening with mounds of earth, then watched as the fire at the base of the hearth hissed and thundered, sending an unearthly bright light into the entire Pit.

'What you will witness, will be beyond your comprehension Father Bertrand, and your view on your God may change tonight, but stay with me and trust me,' said Nadie.

'I...I will pray for all of us when the time comes,' stuttered Father Bertrand.

'Father Bertrand, you must know that Martel is evil...he is the evil one whom I have dreaded for so long, and with him will come the *Machk Matchitehew*, an evil bear - a monster,' said Nadie, her attention suddenly diverted to The Parchment.

The image within The Parchment glowed and shimmered; the golden hieroglyphs on the side of the board were dancing, appearing to give a warning. One of the terracotta figures within the image was fluctuating between two positions, to and from its normal standing place and the other nearer to the centre of the board.

This worried Nadie intensely and she hastily brushed away the earth from the top opening of the kiln, removing the real stone board from the fire, hardly daring to cast her eyes upon it and see how the pottery figurines had formed. In astonishment, Father Bertrand gaped at the clay pieces, some of which had morphed entirely differently than when first placed in the kiln. In particular he noticed that the wolf and the bear were now completely entwined in a violent maul.

The demeanour of the wolf and the bear, Nadie expected, but most shocking of all was the terrifying display of one of the evil deities, standing on a row behind the bear, it was the hideous tall grey, antler horned figure of The Piasa. Its head was turned and its arm was outstretched, pointing it seemed, to one of the front row demigod soldiers on its flank. The miniature, armoured clad, sword wielding soldier had moved at least three board spaces nearer to the grappling bear and wolf.

Never before had Nadie seen a soldier step into the playing area of the board, it was clear to be seen by all – and yet, The Parchment did not show permanency, merely a fluctuation of the soldier between one position and the next. The contradiction between the board and The Parchment was all too confusing, making Nadie despair.

'I know not what the prediction is with the soldier, it makes no sense, my reliance is on The Parchment, yet the board does not conform. This can happen when supernatural forces are at play...and what's more I have never seen The Piasa morph in such a way before,' explained Nadie.

'Who, or what on Earth is The Piasa?' said Father Bertrand.

'It is a demon from the underworld – never before have I seen one change its stance on the real board. Only at times have I felt him and the other figurines stare at me from the image on The Parchment, as you have felt Asemota.'

'A demon?!' shouted Father Bertrand.

'A true evil spirit,' said Nadie. 'Not like the Spirit Wolf or the evil Spirit Bear, they are both creations of this Earth, and they are mortal beings of longivety, guided by the spirits to protect those who are destined to be protected. The Piasa is just not of this world.'

'But what of the demigod soldier Anna, what is it doing? Will it appear?' said Asemota, frantically.

Before Nadie could answer, a thunderous roar silenced them, an unearthly noise permeated the entire forest surround, and it seemed so close – it was a beast.

Hearing the profuse, ear penetrating sound, Father Bertrand dropped to his knees and pushed his hands into the leaves and soil of the Pit floor, praying as hard as he could, hoping that his verbal outpouring of the words to a jumbled Latin sermon would discard the feelings of damnable terror coursing through his veins.

Nadie and Asemota alighted the Pit to find Etchemin and five other warriors standing nearby, all looking out towards to where the terrible roar had come from - the top of the knoll by the West Forest. The most fearful dread had adorned the troop, as if the sound of the hideous roar had penetrated their very souls.

'Douse your fire torches,' said Nadie to the gathering. 'Have you made the fire by the lake

Etchemin?' she asked.

No words from his lips, all Etchemin could do was turn and nod his head towards Nadie, a look of resolute fear in his eyes; never before had he heard such a sound, never did he think in his wildest dreams that such a thing could be upon this world.

'Good, that will help to distract the *Machk Matchitehew,*' said Nadie.

The thunderous roar came again, even louder this time.

'By now the bear must be within sight of the warriors in the West Forest...Askuwhetau and his troop of men and women...they may see it at the farthest end of the knoll ridge,' said Nadie.

Nadie ordered Etchemin and his men to stay together and guard the Pit at all cost. Father Bertrand and Asemota were to remain by the Pit and heed to Etchemin's command. She had to find Martel.

'I shall hunt for the giant priest...but if you see him, then maim him, slow him down, do anything you can to stop him getting into the Pit,' said Nadie, authority in her voice now as she readied herself. 'Asemota - get Father Bertrand out of the Pit and keep him by your side, we will need his help soon enough.'

'I will kill Martel on sight...but what of the evil bear, by the power of *Kitchesmanetoa,* what shall we do against such evil?' said Etchemin, breaking his silence.

'You will not be able to kill Martel, if I am right he will be protected by the spirits and I am the only one who knows how to kill him, you will leave that part to me...' said Nadie, stopping short.

'Look over there!' shouted Asemota at the top of his voice.

From the direction of the sacred lake, came the *Manitou Mahweewa,* the Spirit Wolf - crashing through the foliage and the trees, out onto the village meadow, heading out towards the far end of the knoll ridge. Such was her speed that some of the troop could barely see her, although others could, seeing her silver coat shimmering in the moonlight, and her enormous white teeth on display as she headed towards her adversary, the vile *Machk Matchitehew.*

Nadie shouted out, 'Time my beauty! Draw him to the other side of the lake, fight him with all of your courage! Keep him away from this sacred place!'

Hidden in a discreet location near the Pit, Nadie collected her longbow and leather pouch full of arrows. Once armed, she took hold of Etchemin and Asemota by their arms and called upon them to gather strength, to fight for their families, to fight alongside her and defeat the encroaching evil, giving their lives if they had to.

The passion in Nadie's voice could only help to inspire Asemota. Determinedly, he ushered a weeping, pitiful Father Bertrand to where the warriors were taking cover, attempting to allay the priest's fears by keeping him busy - instructing him to help protect the sacred ritual objects of The Parchment and the chequered board.

Hiding in the foliage, Etchemin whispered to Asemota.

'Ceenkweeki...ninkwehsaa.'

'What did Etchemin say Asemota?' said Father

Bertrand.

'He said what we are all thinking – that the roar of the bear has made him very afraid.'

*

Dark had succeeded dusk, and now, save the light of the moon shining intermittently through the gathering clouds, all orientation had become distorted. Nadie had run through to the meadow where the longhouses were, faintly making out a trail of fire torches moving down the knoll ridge towards her direction. Should she wait or should she move on? It was never wise to stand still for long in the dark, and she was desperate to be with Spirit Wolf. Nadie waited.

The torches drew nearer and moments later her hunch came to fruition, Akima and his troop were running nearby and she called to them.

'Akima, the bear with the evil heart is here, he is very close now - but my Spirit Wolf will fight him soon enough, she will fight him to the death, she is the only one that can kill him.'

Disbelief ran through the troop; a frantic murmuring could be heard amongst all of them.

'And what of Martel?' said Akima, trying to calm his warriors at the same time.

'My instinct says he will be near the evil bear, but I know he will be trying to find my sacred place. He cannot be allowed to defeat us, if he succeeds who knows what untold evil will be unleashed on the world. I have left Asemota and Etchemin with the other warriors in hiding by the entrance to the Pit.

There is a fire by the lake to try and distract the pretender…' Nadie stopped talking.

'Shhh,' whispered Akima, placing his hand over Nadie's mouth.

The other warriors had already looked back towards the top of the knoll ridge. At the farthest end, to where the line of the West Forest trees began, a silhouette of an enormous beast could be seen, distinctly bear shaped in the light of the full moon. It was standing with its head stooped, as if it was looking down to where Nadie and the others were positioned, and they could all hear the deep, resonant, underlying growl of the enormous beast as it panted…and waited.

Without warning the giant bear stood up on its hind legs and let out a gruesome, mind bending, deep throated roar, causing sheer dread to fill everybody's heart. The bear dropped its enormous frame to the ground again and started to move off slowly towards the direction of the temporary village. Screams could be heard from the older people and the children as Nadie clasped her hands over her face willing desperately for her Spirit Wolf to appear.

The evil Spirit Bear stalked slowly, grizzling as it moved, and then it stopped in its tracks, still near to the top of the knoll ridge. A thunderous sound could be heard coming from the far side of the river, to the south of the West Forest along the tree line heading towards the ridge. The giant bear turned its head to gaze at the approaching menace, all the time the pace of the sound quickening. The screams of the village people fell silent as the gnarl of the wolf cascaded through the air before she bounded up the ridge and struck the bear on its side with full force.

With an almighty crunch the wolf buried its jaws into the side of the enormous bear. But the bear had reacted quickly, trapping and spinning the wolf's head with its right paw, sending them both plummeting thirty metres down the knoll side and thumping onto the ground of the meadow by the line of trees. The fall made each of the beasts release its grip upon the other, free now to face off from one another as they scrambled to their feet.

The giant bear stood slightly taller than the Spirit Wolf at shoulder height and it was heavier and stronger - but not as nimble. It presented a most daunting, formidable foe – the strongest and most vicious Spirit Wolf had ever encountered.

Her piercing blue eyes, stared hard at the glowing red eyes of the evil black bear as they circled each other, first to the left and then to the right. Cautious of the bear's mighty strength and its powerful claws, Spirit Wolf would have to find a way to wear the bear down, to a point where she could go for the final kill - at the jugular.

The long grass of the meadow swayed in the breeze, the trees in the West Forest rustled and the moon light continued to silhouette the great beasts as they taunted and teased one another into further combat, moving around each other in a fierce demonstration of unbelievable power.

Suddenly, Spirit Wolf took flight towards the river, south of the meadow. Looking behind her as she ran, she slowed a little to see if the bear would take the bait, and sure enough he did. Charging after her, snarling and gnashing his teeth, a furious rage gripped the bear as the wolf bounded over the width of the river in one gigantic leap. The bear crashed through the water, menacingly chasing the wolf through the meadow on the other side before climbing the long, shallow valley ridge.

Hoping to test the resilience of the huge bear, Spirit Wolf sprinted to the top of the valley ridge and arched around, behind a set of large sandstone boulders, placing them between her and her adversary. However, the bear was quicker than the wolf gave credence and the black beast was soon hurtling straight towards her, launching itself from a large rock to take aim at her. Swiftly, Spirit Wolf moved her body out of the way, avoiding the crushing bulk of the bear, before she regained the advantage to strike at him.

The bear thudded to the ground, falling onto his side with his paws facing the wolf. Fearing the clawing of the bear's feet, Spirit Wolf ran around his enormous grotesque head and stood behind him, although now the beast was starting to scramble to his feet again. The powerful wolf lunged for his neck, yet he was able to snap his head back at the same time, the base of his cranium hitting Spirit Wolf sharply on the bridge of her nose, sending her reeling, and thwarting her intention to grip the bear's throat. She yelped loudly, her whole body skidding across the craggy, rocky terrain before she came to rest, thudding hard against an old cotton wood tree - branches and leaves falling everywhere. The debacle could be heard right across the valley terrain, the ensemble of warriors and village people in awe and disbelief at the unfolding drama.

*

Resolutely, Etchemin's party stayed guarding the Pit, even though they could hear the sounds of the enormous beasts fighting and growling ferociously on top of the valley ridge. Despite being unsettled, Etchemin remained determined, ensuring that he had all possibilities of attack and all approaches to the Pit under control, dispersing his warriors accordingly; if Martel appeared now, he and his troop would be ready, and he would be the first to strike him.

Hiding in the thicket was no real comfort for Asemota, and he was desperate for word from his mother, knowing that in trying to track Martel she was putting herself in mortal danger – as perhaps they all were. He turned his attention to Father Bertrand who was, by all accounts, somewhat of a curiosity to him, not least of which was his religious exasperation for all things around him. But the Jesuit Father would know a little something more of Martel.

'You must tell me Father Bertrand, what kind of a man is Martel, what is he likely to do? What are we to face?' said Asemota.

'I…I am confounded Asemota, I am disturbed by my lack of comprehension of what it is I see and hear. I believe now that Martel must be a man possessed of evil spirit, the stories of his great strength will now perhaps ring true. I heard tell of priests and brothers who would show him off to others, getting him to lift ponies and great rocks and such like. My God, I should have fathomed him out then, I should have guessed what his plan may have been all along.'

'Guessed what Father?'

'The Book of Prophecies...how he wrote about his fascination with all things lurid and fantastical, how he revered the strange and mystical oddities in this world. I should have predicted his propensity for evil - his whole demeanour has been an affront, hiding within his core, a demonic essence that I should have seen...this is all my doing, God forgive me - whatever are we to do?'

'We must deal with what we see and act accordingly,' said Asemota, appearing outwardly calm and assured. 'My mother has said that he is not to find the sacred articles and get into the Pit, if he is able to use the power of the kiln and the board, then we will all be sacrificed. Right now, the great spirit creatures fight on the other side of the river along the valley ridge, and I pray by our spirits that the *Manitou Mahweewa*, who is our Protector, will be our saviour. We must not fail her, and yet my greatest fear is a power beyond hers, a power that has tentatively revealed itself, and a power which Martel himself may forebode.'

'The Demon?' questioned Father Bertrand.

'Yes, perhaps the Demon, perhaps The Piasa...although I am not so sure. I did not see the figurine move on the board but it pointed at the sword cleaved demigod soldier, an unearthly being that my mother said has never shown itself in the centre of the board before. If this ungodly creature appears, I do not know how it would be defeated.'

'Perhaps through his prophetic discoveries - Martel would know how to make it appear?' said

Father Bertrand.

'We cannot assume or discount anything…but I do know Martel has to be stopped,' said Asemota.

*

Warriors lay dying and injured in an around the West Forest, ravaged from a previous attack by the evil bear, who shortly before Spirit Wolf had managed to engage him, took advantage of those warriors isolated on open ground, unable to escape his menace. After Akima had parted from Nadie he had made his way to find Askuwhetau, only to see the incomprehensible devastation of his fallen comrades. Akima was grief stricken but tried to console the others by rallying them and inspiring them to avenge the hideous attack by the bear.

People from the temporary village were tending to their beaten brethren, moving them to shelter wherever they could. One of the injured warriors was Aharu who, against his orders, had bravely left his post at the village to go and fight with Askuwhetau's troop, only to fall to the mercy of the mighty beast. It would be a miracle if Aharu survived.

Akima ordered Askuwhetau to split his remaining men and women, sending some of them to guard the temporary village and others to reinforce Etchemin and his troop by the sacred Pit. The Chief decided that he would double back again with his small band of warriors, to find Nadie once more, and join her in the hunt for Martel.

Anxious and in a dilemma, Nadie stood and pondered by the riverside, not far from the sacred lake, yet there was no time to ponder. She could see the fire torches of Akima's troop once again, although this time there were more warriors, and they were heading towards the Pit.

There was little sign of Spirit Wolf beyond the valley ridge and Nadie dared not go after her. Nadie did not want to be too far away should Martel all of a sudden reveal himself within the East Forest; no, the wolf must fend for herself, the Spirit Beast must be trusted and reach the sacred lake where the fire burns.

Nadie turned and ran, sprinting across the meadow in great bounds to meet up with the gathering of people by her sacred Pit, her fear now that Martel would have seen the activity and he would be somewhere near, secreted and ready to wreak havoc.

*

Quickly regaining her composure from the fall against the cotton-wood tree, Spirit Wolf scrambled to her feet in just enough time to blight the ominous full on attack from the bear. Forcing the explosive release of every sinew in her body, she bolted – turning away from the near clutches of her adversary, to head along the top of the valley ridge, keeping the East Forest and sacred lake in sight. She could see the fire in the distance and now she knew the time had come to head towards it, using as much of her mighty speed and power as she could muster.

The clash with the bear and the blow against the tree had slowed her a little, but instinct drove her on, and she would have to summon all her strength to prevent the black bear snapping venomously at her heels. The Great Wolf turned sharply away from the valley ridge and charged as fast as her legs would allow, downhill towards the firelight. Only then, when she turned, did she realise that the pain inflicted by the vile bear had lingered in her body - her nose was bleeding and her ribs were hurting, but she had to make the lakeside, for it was there she would make her final stand against the monstrous creature.

A dull haze of clouds surrounded the moon, dimming the light across the land. For the second time, the disbelieving warriors, standing or kneeling at their points near to the sacred lake and sacred Pit, caught sight of the unearthly spirit beasts - this time charging ever closer towards them.

A sixth sense enveloped Nadie as Spirit Wolf and the bear approached, she could feel the plight of her Protector, and instinctively changed direction, running at great speed over towards the lakeside fire before she even had chance to reach the Pit. Through the last line of forest trees before the lake, she could see that the wolf was injured and had slowed - the bear was so close and Nadie felt helpless.

Straining her lungs and desperate for an end, Spirit Wolf neared the bottom of the river valley, the part which bordered the sacred lake. She felt the hot foul breath of the bear on her neck, and felt the earth shake as he pounded the ground just behind her. Then, taking her by surprise, the giant bear ran up the hill for a short distance before gaining further momentum and charging back down with more speed.

It happened in a split second; Spirit Wolf tried to dodge the attack but the bear clipped her back legs with his front claws, sending her sprawling over the lake embankment and into the lake waters. The bear followed, leaping to put his full weight on the wolf and crush her in the water. About to take the full force of his weight, Spirit Wolf quickly flipped onto her back and used the power of her legs to deflect the bear's huge mass sideways, sending him thudding into the mud and silt across the embankment. The bear flailed, roaring violently and gnarling its gigantic teeth, his furious rage all too plain to see and hear. Spirit Wolf prepared herself for the final assault.

*

'Martel! Martel is here!' screamed Asemota, his telling voice reverberating around the forest.

Nadie reacted and left the lakeside, running instinctively towards the cry, shouting at the warriors by the lake to fight for their lives and fight for Spirit Wolf.

Two of the three warriors guarding the rear of the Pit had retreated from the huge menacing figure of Martel, the third lay slumped on the ground having been caught by a casting net thrown by the giant man, who had pierced the poor warrior with his purpose built Roman spear.

The two surviving warriors ran towards the remaining troop, forming a line with Etchemin and the rest of the men and women who had all purposefully drawn their bows and arrows.

'He has made his own weapons - they are the ancient weapons of Rome!' shouted Father Bertrand. 'Look see, he has an Iaculum, the weighted casting net and it has caught that poor warrior…he would not have stood any chance.'

Martel stood angrily at the rear of the Pit, pumping his enormous chest and arms in an evil rage. The top half of his priestly robe had been torn, exposing his torso, of which he had covered himself in thick black peat. In his left hand he was dragging the casting net in which lay the tangled, contorted dead body of a village warrior. In his right hand he was holding a formidable Roman spear, a Venabulum, over two metres in length, augmented with an iron winged head and point which he had so diligently made.

'Only the very strongest of men can fight with those heavy spears,' said Father Bertrand. 'I have never seen a Venabulum of that size, he will cut the warriors down with such a weapon.'

'Get behind the line of warriors,' shouted Asemota, grabbing Father Bertrand by the cord of his robe.

No more than a second later, feeling confident with increased numbers by his side, Etchemin ordered the troop to fire a volley of arrows towards Martel, and then a further salvo in an effort to slow the hideous man down. It had no effect, Martel merely deflected the arrows at will with his spear and speed of foot, laughing in the face of the warrior's intent. He stood ever menacingly, defiant in their presence, fueling the belief in some of them that they were not dealing with any normal mortal human being. Infuriated, Etchemin ordered a third volley, only to be met with the same defiant reaction.

Martel circled around the Pit heading towards the line of warriors, grimacing and displaying his physical prowess. Father Bertrand broke through the ranks and headed towards the giant man, falling to his knees only a few metres from him.

'Brother Martel, I beg of you – stop, in the name of God stop!'

'Your God will not help you today little man,' shouted Martel as he raised the long spear to strike Father Bertrand.

In an effort to save the priest, Asemota ran out of the line and smothered Father Bertrand with his body, ready to shield him from the blow of the spear, as futile as this might have been. Martel raised the fearsome Venabulum in the air, both men sprawled across the ground at his mercy, waiting for the death blow. It never came.

To everyone's astonishment, Nadie appeared through the forest, her tall athletic, muscular body travelling at great speed through the thicket as she charged towards Martel. In one giant stride, she leapt clear over the entire Pit before striking the giant man on the side of his head with her fist, sending him sprawling to the ground and releasing the grip on his spear. Such was the blow, that for a moment he lost all of his senses and had to shake his head vigorously to regain his composure. He looked up in a daze and stared at Nadie.

'Finally…Maker…you have revealed yourself, now we fight, prepare to be defeated!' shouted Martel.

Martel stood up, taking hold of the spear, only to see Nadie charge at him again, snapping the spear rod with a powerful kick. He managed to retain the spear head and lashed out at her, missing her torso by millimetres.

Etchemin could not stand and do nothing; he ran from his position in the thicket, wielding his canoe axe, trying to take advantage of Martel being distracted. The false priest saw the old warrior in his peripheral vision and quickly snapped out a kick, hitting Etchemin in the body, sending him falling to the ground, only to lie motionless with his face buried within the dirt and leaves.

Screaming in a rage at the sight of her old friend having fallen, Nadie unleashed her ferocity, raining further hammer blows upon Martel, making him retreat. Asemota, and Father Bertrand rushed to where Etchemin lay and dragged his body away from the impending fighting carnage between Nadie and her adversary.

*

Spirit Wolf had weakened, and such was the inextricable link between her and Nadie she was afraid that Nadie may have sensed this, and in turn Nadie's worry would, conversely, weaken her own fight against Martel.

The evil bear had now cleared itself of the mud and silt and was wading after the wolf through the lake waters. Spirit Wolf gulped as much air as her lungs would allow, oxygenating her body to swim through the lake as hard as she could to reach the far embankment, nearer to the Pit, where a line of huge, aged Cypress trees unfurled their roots at the water's edge. The bear was a better swimmer and Spirit Wolf could sense that if he caught her again, she may not have the strength to stop him from drowning her.

Additional warriors arrived by the wooded embankment, headed by Akima, and Askuwhetau who, unable to settle, had run from his post in the

West Forest to join his Chief and do battle. An incomprehensible sight greeted them, yet they rose to the challenge, heeding Akima's orders as he bellowed at them to fire their arrows towards the *Machk Matchitehew.*

The lakeside fire burned ever brightly, and the warriors remained high on the water bank, repeatedly firing at the evil bear to try and slow it down – but there was no effect.

Although quickly weakening, Nadie had managed to draw Martel into a small clearing near to the line of Cypress trees by the lake embankment, closer now to where her Spirit Wolf was about to make her last stand. In part, the fire had worked; both Martel and the bear had been drawn to it, and it was here that they would have to be slain.

Asemota and Father Bertrand had been keen to follow Nadie through the forest as the fight unfolded, stalking their every move, shouting at the warriors to fire on Martel every time they had an opportunity. Now they were in sight of Akima and his troop, and the Chief quickly turned his attention towards his Princess.

'Release yourself from him Nadie, let us take aim at the imposter,' yelled Akima.

'It doesn't matter how many warriors you have Pottery Maker, you and they will soon perish – look at your spirit beast, she is beaten, she has no more to give, my Protector is all powerful and he will strike her down,' growled Martel.

'*Manitou Mahweewa!*' shouted Nadie. 'Remember my beloved wolf, you must strike at the right time – this imposter and his evil bear are connected by the same evil spirit and they must be killed at the same time!'

As she weakened even further, her heightened desperation was compounded by the thoughts of her son, Asemota; Nadie could hear his voice but she could not comprehend what was being said as blow after mighty blow rained down upon her. Any resistance was faltering and the only way she could bring about the final strike was to cause a distraction, for that she would need Asemota and the sacred possessions.

The young man rallied to his mother's cry for help, comprehending her plan immediately. He ran into the clearing only to see Nadie at Martel's mercy, she was down on one knee, blood pouring from her mouth, with dark heavy bruising to her legs and rib cage, she looked so forlorn.

Martel turned to see Asemota, casting his eyes on the chequered board and The Parchment being held aloft. An evil laugh sprang forth from his throat and he tipped his head back in utter defiance.

'Come, watch your mother die now, child,' said Martel. 'Those possessions will be mine very soon, then you will all suffer.'

Succumbed as she was, Nadie managed to signal Spirit Wolf, willing her Protector to make the kill; timing was everything now and the bear would have to be in a death throe before Nadie could make her final strike.

The warriors were furiously hollering and goading the bear, firing arrows relentlessly in an effort to distract it, but it was no use, the mighty beast charged.

Spirit Wolf raised her chest, let out the most fearsome growl, willing the bear to strike her where she stood on the embankment. With one almighty leap from the waterline near the fire, the bear launched itself towards her, claws ready to strike a ferocious blow. Cleverly, and at great speed, Spirit Wolf dropped once more onto her back, avoiding the bear's lethal paws, and piercing the bears throat with her huge powerful teeth as she flipped her body on top of him. There she held, pinning the bear down as it thrashed around in sheer carnage, trying to release itself from the death grip.

Martel removed his mind from the distraction and lunged once more at Nadie, striking her to the ground; this being too much for Asemota to bear. He handed the chequered board and The Parchment to Father Bertrand, picked up a large stone and ran for Martel as the giant man stood over his mother. Martel stared at Nadie, losing himself in a brief moment of evil indignation, enough for Asemota to land a blow to his head with the stone. The false Jesuit did not flinch, turning to hit Asemota with the back of his hand, sending him flailing back towards the direction of Father Bertrand. They collided heavily, both falling to the floor, nearly unconscious.

Nadie took advantage and raised herself, pulling from her pocket sheath, an ancient bone handled Cahokian dagger. She struck Martel with all of her strength, forcing the dagger deep into his chest.

'Now *Manitou Mahweewa*......now my Protector!' shouted Nadie at the top of her voice. 'Now is the time!'

The wolf heard the cry. Her deep blue canine eyes

widened as she impaled the bears throat deeper with her enormous teeth, and with one final powerful twist, she tore the muscle and sinew away from the bear's neck.

Falling to his knees, Martel looked down at the dagger pressed into his chest, clasping his hands on the bone handle. Nadie too had fallen to her knees again, and her body felt so weak it was as if she was bleeding everywhere inside. With one last surge of strength she pushed the dagger further into Martel's huge chest, piercing his heart. He let out a huge cry, yet before his final breath, he rained a double fisted blow to the base of Nadie's neck, instantly crushing her spine, sending her to the ground once more. She could not move.

Martel fell to his death at exactly the same moment the evil bear gasped its last breath, and Nadie's prophecy had been fulfilled – but at such a great cost. She lay badly injured, a disheveled Asemota by her side, holding her body, comforting her head as the light from her eyes started to fade.

Akima was bereft with silence as he and his warriors watched the great Spirit Wolf rise slowly from its kill; the carcass of the giant evil bear was motionless, the lake waters lapping against its body as it lay across the roots of the Cypress trees by the embankment. The moon became brighter again, with any remnant of cloud finally dispersing over the valley ridges. People from the village flocked to the lakeside, hearing the news of their savior and that of the terrible beast which had been slain.

Sadness and despair filled Spirit Wolf's heart as she turned to walk towards the small clearing, and she whimpered, her deep blue eyes glistening, sensing that Nadie would not recover.

Nadie awoke momentarily, her head in Asemota's arms and her eyes fixed upon her son and her beloved Protector who had knelt by her side, softly and mournfully nuzzling her snout against Nadie's dying, broken body - Nadie could scarcely breathe.

Full of grief, Akima too came nearer, beckoning the entire village to bow and kneel to their beloved Nadie, the Princess of Cahokia, their forever saviour and conqueror of evil.

Asemota begged for her life and cried relentlessly as he held his mother in his arms.

'Anna...Anna, please Anna...please my Anna...,' Asemota cried as his mother's breathing started to fail.

An instantaneous reaction from the villagers reverberated around the forest and the clearing as they started to chant for their Princess, Akima unable to respond himself through emotion, but encouraging others to do so, and they sang with their hearts;

'Kitelile...kinakasi...neekalaaci...iisinaakwahki'

'Kitelile...kinakasi...neekalaaci...iisinaakwahki'

'I say to you...you leave me...I am abandoned...it is so'

Nadie spoke quietly for one last time. 'You are my soul Asemota...*nincihciikama* - Asemota. There is something you must hear before I die my child,' she said.

'You cannot die Anna, you are my mother, you are our saviour...you cannot die,' Asemota said, desperately.

The chanting continued as Nadie signaled Asemota to place his head by her lips. A secret he was told, a sacred passing that could only be given from the old Pottery Maker to the new, a solemn duty now beholden to Asemota, one that he must never reveal. Asemota pulled his head back, his mother's head still in his hands as she passed, breathing her last as she smiled at him. He laid her head softly on the ground and cried her name - Akima sat beside him and cried her name too.

Spirit Wolf howled and whimpered in utter sorrow, her heart completely broken – her beloved Princess Nadie was no more.

Chapter 10

Aftermath

A cold wind blew around Asemota's body as he sat amongst the rugged stones coursing the top of the knoll ridge. He stared out towards the valley where his mother had first seen the priests appear, tears rolling down his cheeks as he thought of her - her innate courage, her display of selflessness as she had defended the village against such evil – she died for everyone.

Akima had climbed the knoll ridge, stopping short to observe Asemota, pausing, not really wanting to disturb the young man in his time of sorrow and mourning. The aging Chief looked over the village in the meadow, watching curiously as the strong cold wind rustled the trees in the nearby forests; it was as if the spirits were trying to tell him something, or the spirits were merely disturbed – he couldn't quite be sure. His people busied themselves making their final preparations to break for winter camp - except this time, it would be different, there would be no return to their beloved meadow, this would be sacred ground now. The village people continued to work hard, trying to keep their minds free of the events which had unfolded just five days before, some blanking it from memory, others unable to fathom what had happened, with many acquiescing to a perpetual turmoil of disbelief.

A deep concern caused Akima's familiar furrowed brow to broaden; he folded his arms and stood rigidly, wondering how his people would ever recover. Asemota saw him staring at the people below and felt obliged to join him out of respect.

'Forgive me my Chief, I did not hear you or see you until just now.'

'Your conversation in our tongue is getting stronger now boy,' said Akima.

'Yes, it is as if I have been blessed with new knowledge, everything seems clearer…I do wonder if it is a gift perhaps?'

'I did not intend to disturb you Asemota, you must have time to grieve, as we all must. Nadie, your mother, was our saviour. I had known her most of my life, I know she was the protected one, a spiritual human being - she was a woman of profound knowledge and purpose, and she had a special place in this world as I believe you now have.'

A moment of silence as they both looked upon the meadow, provisions being collected from every corner of the village, most notably the food – the squash, the pumpkins, the corn seed and the abundant *shikaakwa* – the wild onion.

'We can never return to this place Asemota – you

know that. It has become a sacred place now…so many deaths. The people know that too. When the camp has broken we will head out to the West and there we will remain, never to return.'

Asemota agreed, clutching the deer hide sack that his mother had given him. Inside was The Parchment. He had not let go of the sack and its precious content since Nadie's passing. A sacred task had been passed to him, a task so indefinable it was hard to contemplate. Others may go on to speculate, but only he knew of its secrets. The dawning of his time had come, yet there was nothing Asemota could share with anyone.

Akima and the young Pottery Maker returned to the village, only to be met by Father Bertrand standing outside the Chief's longhouse – the priest appeared to have aged ten years, he was thinner, paler and quite solemn. The Jesuit thanked Akima and prayed that the village would be protected. He explained that he would be returning to his homeland as soon as he could, although the journey would take many months. Akima ensured Father Bertrand had enough provisions for a few days and bode him farewell, leaving him in the company of Asemota one last time.

'I sense the events which have unfolded here are never to be spoken about,' said Father Bertrand. 'Any doubts of the spiritual world not existing have been eroded…I shall pray to God everyday - all day.'

'You return to the French?' queried Asemota.

'To France I will return, across the large ocean, then I must seek an audience with my great Holy leader…The Pope.'

'He is your Chief?'

'He is the head of my church, and leader of my religion, he is the anointed Holy one that gives wisdom to our faith. I must talk with him on urgent matters.'

'He will not believe what has happened here, surely you will not reveal so?' pressed Asemota.

'I will not mention the events of which I have witnessed, but I must show him Martel's book - this confounded Book of Prophecies that led Brother Martel down such an evil path, attempting to discover the secrets of the Pottery Maker. This book has been used by those who are overly ambitious or evil and I fear it will be used again unless the Jesuit Order protects it. I will take it to Rome and ask the Pope to keep it safe and locked away.'

Asemota said no more. The two men hugged and Father Bertrand turned towards the knoll path, pulling the pack horses with him. The priest feared he would have to guard the book with his life, he could not destroy it, it was too valuable – too much knowledge resided within it and it would need deciphering, the Pope's wisdom was needed.

The village people stood and waved to Father Bertrand as he reached the top of the knoll ridge, himself returning one final wave before he disappeared over into the next valley. Asemota was sad to see him go, the priest had become his friend and he wished him safe travel.

*

Later that night, returning to the sacred Pit in the East Forest, Asemota could see that the kiln fire in the hearth was still glowing and would be ready for the chequered board and its newly made figurines. He followed his mother's last instructions and placed the board into the top opening, checking one last time with The Parchment to ensure the loose figurines were aligned correctly – and they were. All the miniature clay figurines were arranged exactly as per the image, ordered in two opposing rows – as if a balance to the spirit world had been restored. Into the furnace the board and the figurines went.

His final instruction was to keep watch on the mystical Parchment, something which was hard to do. Asemota stared in wonder at the change process within The Parchment image, and wonder turned to absolute disbelief as his own prophecy came true, the absorbing transformation occurring before his very eyes - the formidable secret of 'The Cloth' had now been revealed.

PART TWO

PROPHECIES

Prelude II

In this fast paced modern world, sometimes the old ways still serve a definable purpose, they serve a tradition which resolutely manifests itself over countless generations, a tradition which is deemed unbreakable. For centuries the Pottery Maker had recovered and sifted natural deposits of earthen clay from the lake waters, ready to be hand crafted and forged into miniature, baked earth structures. The ancient art of kneading and shaping, wedging and turning, cutting and re-joining, was the only way to remove the trapped air and spread the moisture evenly throughout the little terracotta bodies – and make them strong. Manipulated in the finest detail, the Pottery Maker carefully and deftly carved the figurines, such was his sleight of hand, using a skill which he had mastered through what had seemed to be an infinite age.

He had discarded the old pieces from the chequered board and replaced them with the new, keeping an eye on the spell-binding metamorphosis of The Parchment image, taking care to read the hieroglyphs and position the new figurines - exactly as instructed.

Opposing forces faced each other, impeccably lined up on the chequered squares as if vying for supremacy, as if to the observer a mesmeric power struggle was about to unfold.

Once again the Pottery Maker had deciphered the intricate instructions, he had done as he was told, rejuvenating the menagerie of spirit beasts, demons and demigods – he had availed their transformation, but for what final end he could not tell.

Yet, forlornly, he knew the time of change was drawing near.

Chapter 11

A Demon

Sam stared at Anippe, not quite sure whether the smile appearing on her face was genuine or slightly wry. Shrugging his shoulders, like a little boy lost, he gestured aimlessly towards Joyce, expecting a little sympathy.

'Please come out of the room Sam,' said Anippe.

'Forgive me Anippe, my policing instincts and curiosity got the better of me, you can imagine my interest and intrigue with the room of books, I just thought I would be nosy…and incidentally, I have stumbled across a reference to a painting called 'The Pottery Maker'. I wondered then, if you were going to tell us more?'

'Well now, you have seen it haven't you? But I don't take kindly to you snooping around,' said

Anippe, willing Sam to leave the small room.

'Again forgive me but I am stuck out here in Egypt, trying to fathom out the truth and what my next move should be. Instinct tells me I have got to track down a brute of a man called Krell who, I am pretty sure, has killed one of my police officers, and quite possibly another - a man who stole a painting which you know more about than you have been letting on. I am absolutely certain that we need a frank conversation.'

It was agreed, upon Joyce's clever suggestion, that they should all reconvene, civilly, at the Semiramis Hotel. Anippe was a little relieved at the temporary respite and breathed freely again when the pair left; yet underneath she was still deeply concerned – a second, more urgent call to her contact was needed.

Closing her office door with a hard push, she grabbed for her phone on the desk and slumped quite readily into her black leather chair, feeling uneasy and desperate for wisdom as she stared at the Book of the Stele. Anippe pondered on how to start the telephone conversation, dubious as to whether she and her contact should now tell more to the enquiring couple.

'I am going to meet them at the hotel, I'll probably reveal a little more about the Book of the Stele…Sam is relentless, so inquisitive and headstrong…and Joyce is so clever. Surely we can't keep much more of this from them, I need to know that Sam is able to be prepared?'

There was a moment of silence as the person on the other end of the phone appeared to ponder and consider.

'I fear Taraka and Krell will gain the initiative if we do not act quickly. Taraka is an unknown quantity and I also fear that he will have gained an insight into the prophecies, we do not know what he knows about the secrets of the Pottery Maker,' said the voice.

'Whatever knowledge either of them possess, nothing can be done without The Parchment, even if they do gain further knowledge and discover the nature of the making,' said Anippe.

'Sam must track Krell to see where he has gone and what his intentions are, but if Sam or anyone else faces Taraka now it could be too dangerous. Our readings have taught us that the Temple of the Devi Patan could hold secrets, particularly within the Atharva-Veda; the ancient Vedic Script that lies hidden in a vault somewhere. I would guess, perhaps, that Taraka and Krell will be near to the Temple…in Tulsipur,' said the voice.

Anippe wished her contact was with her in person, guiding her, informing her on what to do step by step - but he wasn't and couldn't be; yet time was of the essence and thorough preparation was now paramount.

*

An hour had passed and the three gathered in the private lounge of the impressive, refurbished Semiramis Hotel; they sat next to the large sun-screened windows, observing the prominence of the Nile River, captivated by the busy waterway and its endless stream of boats and ferries.

Sam apologised to Anippe for his actions, quoting his frustrations, wanting to reassure her that much would be done to try and solve this mystery. Joyce watched the relationship between the two unfold, not feeling threatened in any way, just curious with their interaction.

'My Bureau Chief has informed me that Krell took a flight from the U.S. to England and then more than likely to India. There was a man purporting to be an Orthodox Jew on one of the flights, possibly carrying a false passport. CCTV from Heathrow and the New Delhi Airports reveal sightings of a huge man, undoubtedly similar to the description of Krell. According to local police in India, a very large gentleman has been spotted several times on a train journey through the Uttar Pradesh region…heading towards the border with Nepal, I believe,' said Sam.

'Any idea where he is now, exactly?' asked Anippe.

'I have been asked to make contact with a Police Superintendent in the Balrampur District, I presume that must be within the Uttar Pradesh State. Joyce and I need to think about getting out there as soon as we can,' said Sam, closely analysing Anippe's reaction.

'He may have gone to Tulsipur,' said Anippe, pervading her knowledge.

'Why there?' said Joyce. 'Or perhaps is it the Temple there he seeks…the Devi Patan perhaps?' she responded, taking Anippe a little by surprise.

'How do you know this?' Anippe questioned. 'My guess would have been, yes…perhaps he would make his way there.'

Sam interrupted, 'You have both lost me – what is the Devi Patan?'

'An ancient Hindu temple in the town of Tulsipur,' said Joyce. 'It is supposed to have one of the important Hindu Vedas Mantras. The Mantras are said to be capable of creating mystical transformations and one of them - called the Atharva-Veda - is believed to be able to cast spells and charms. You'll have to forgive me Anippe, I saw a note on your desk with the words "Atharva-Veda" on it, and it got me thinking.'

'Even so Joyce, your knowledge of such things is profound,' said Anippe, caught off guard.

'But how have you deduced that Krell would make his way there?' questioned Joyce.

'I cannot say, perhaps just a hunch, Sam mentioned the Balrampur District. Well, Tulsipur forms part of that District – and the Devi Patan Temple may indeed house the Atharva-Veda. It is one of the four Canonical Vedas that could hold answers,' said Anippe.

'Or an instruction for someone? You mentioned that there would be a person behind Krell, I think you know who that is,' said Joyce.

Anippe remained silent for a while, staring deeper into the waters of the Nile, finding herself inadvertently counting the bow waves formed from the vessels as they passed by. Perhaps she had revealed more than she had wanted to, and exposed herself with her comments. Nevertheless, Joyce in particular had intuitively steered the conversation.

'Did you know that the Hindu word for how the Vedas are viewed or looked upon is 'Apauruseya' - meaning 'not of human ageing.' The oldest scripts are nearly four thousand years old,' Anippe then paused.

'His name is Taraka.'

'Who?' said Sam.

'Taraka,' said Anippe. 'Krell will meet Taraka in Tulsipur, I am certain of that.'

'Who the hell is Taraka?' said Sam.

'You must go to India but beware of what you do and see, there will be no quarter given, you must have all your wits about you,' said Anippe, with emotion.

'Krell, I believe is the protégé of Taraka, of course Taraka is then by definition Krell's Mentor. They will both be very dangerous,' said Anippe, giving as much as she dared.

The Egyptian lady promptly stood up and adjusted her white hijab, using the motion as a distraction, trying to hide her concern. She cleared her throat and wiped away a small tear, Sam and Joyce feeling some reverence for her; clearly she was emotional and her portrayal of events was far more heart felt than Sam could have imagined when earlier they met.

He did wonder from this why it was also difficult to shake off his obscure feelings of familiarity towards her, feelings that he felt sure would only become more profound the more he got to know her, if indeed they were to meet again.

'My intuition tells me that the painting and the Vedas Scripts have some connection, along with your Book of the Stele and the Book of Prophecies – do they all tell the same story? And if so what is that story?' said Joyce.

'Some of the extracts in the Book of the Stele tell

of a human story, a story of human kind, of suffering, of wonder, of magic, and of spiritual significance. I cannot hope to make you understand all of it, although you have made the connections very well Joyce. I believe the Atharva-Veda and the Book of Prophecies give reference but may not have all the answers, and that can be dangerous for those with little knowledge who go looking for such things,' said Anippe.

'You believe Krell and Taraka have access to those other readings?' said Sam.

'Yes - but I don't know what they know, I...'

Sam gently interrupted. 'And do you know who Taraka is?'

'I believe Taraka is a man who is shrouded in mystery, legend befalls him - the locals are afraid of him and say that he is demonic. He is rarely seen, but what little I know is that he lives near the Devi Patan, possibly disguising himself as a Hindu worshiper. Stories tell of a strange looking giant that lives in a cave near to the water's edge not far from the Temple. What could be certain is that wherever Taraka is, Krell is sure to follow,' said Anippe, relieved now that she was embellishing her knowledge.

'Curious name,' said Joyce.

'Why?' said Sam.

'According to Hindu mythology, Taraka is the name of a powerful Hindu Demon who posed a threat to all living existence. His power was, or is, depending on your belief, said to be so great that only the almighty Hindu God Shiva could defeat him. Shiva had entrusted his champion named Karttikeya to do battle with Taraka. It is alleged that Karttikeya is the only one capable of destroying the demon,' explained Joyce.

'Again, you astonish me,' said Anippe. 'But of course, so much of what is written in the Mantras is folklore.'

'Nevertheless, a curious name,' repeated Joyce.

'Perhaps a little too much hokum for me,' said Sam. 'Whatever the circumstance, I need to catch a murderer and a thief,' he re-iterated.

Time was pressing, and the policeman and his companion would have to fly out soon enough, perhaps in the middle of the night if they could.

'I bid you well, the both of you......rely on your contact out there in India, make sure you understand what you are getting into and ensure you have protection at all times,' said Anippe, placing her hand on Sam's arm.

Anippe's eyes warned of danger and although a little intrigued with her demeanour, it made Sam edgy, slightly uneasy at the prospect of hunting down Krell and his Mentor – this so called Taraka. India beckoned.

Chapter 12

Three Wise Men

Mike Tremble sat in one of the scruffy wooden chairs, a number of which were strewn across the log cabin porch; he was perusing the surroundings of the Campbell homestead and, impressive as it was, it was alien to him. He preferred the rugged open air terrain of his village, basking in some of the traditions of his ancestors. Sleeping in his ancient style longhouse or beneath the stars would be his karma, and an everlasting promise to his father and grandfathers before him.

Albeit, he admired James Campbell and what he stood for; James was part of the evolution of America, a man who stood up to prejudice, and a man who faced adversity to be where he was today. They had faced the same prejudices and had common ground and Mike believed that this was the basis of their lasting friendship, despite the long years since they had seen one another.

The huge door to the front of the cabin was open, warm air sifting from the impressive brick stack fire place, enveloping Mike as he relaxed, contemplating why he had perhaps left it so long since making contact with James. Yet now here he was, grateful that the friendship could be rekindled.

Mike had helped James chop the last of the available timber, placing the logs on the smoldering cabin fire, a fascinating central stack design with a small grate beneath a miniature oven door, built within the brick work over the fire -rather like a small kiln.

The logs soon blazed within the base fire, causing embers to cough and splutter onto the fire-guarded red carpet protecting the oak floor of the main cabin room. James stood by his old friend, taking great pleasure in stoking the fire, before casually sauntering off to the little cabin annex to fetch two cold beers from the cooler.

'Do you think Walters will come?' said Mike, slowly relishing the cool beer.

'Yes, he will, he did promise and I believed him, even if he is a little late, he's got a busy job in the City I guess. I was pretty insistent though. My son is half way around the world chasing some maniac criminal and I want to know what the hell is going on.'

'That is if you trust Walters to tell you the truth…how long have you known him?' said Mike.

'Perhaps thirty…thirty-five years, I remember him early on in the force, I was Editor in Chief by then and amazingly he doesn't look much different now than from the first day I saw him,' said James.

'How old do you reckon he is?'

'Difficult to say, I would put him at just over sixty.'

'Positively young then?' said Mike, smiling broadly.

The cragginess of Mike's face became accentuated as he continued to smile, and James had a fleeting moment, thinking of the wise old Native American embracing his tribal culture, telling stories and performing rituals embellished by Mike's people through the ages.

'What is it old man, are you jealous of my youthful looks?' laughed Mike.

'What a mixed bag we all are,' said James. 'Here's you, a Native American, 'an injun' - if you excuse the phrase – you are a descendant from a long line of Illinois Chiefs, sat here next to the great grandson of a 'negro slave' who both live in the middle of America…forged, rightly or wrongly, by the hand of the English, the French, the Spanish and finally the Colonials. Did you ever stop to think about this?'

Mike stared at James, the smile never leaving his face before the smile turned into a chuckle.

'Less of the 'injun',' said Mike.

Both elderly men were still laughing uncontrollably when they heard the sound of the silver Range Rover crunching its wheels along the gravel drive.

Walters stepped out of the car wearing a black leather jacket over the white shirt of his uniform, a small paunch was evident against his otherwise broad muscular frame. He waved across to the smiling elder gentlemen who seemed very content sitting on the cabin porch, and he relished the prospect of meeting with them. As far as he could remember, although he knew them both quite well, this was the first time all three had gathered together. Walters had worked with James, predominantly as a media officer in the CPD press liaison office, his job to link in with the editorial staff of the City newspapers. His fascination with Mike and the Native American community had grown over time, beguiled by the ancient stories and traditions Mike and his people would tell. Walters was also sad at the plight of the Illinois tribes who had endured such historical legacies – although, like many, the aging policeman was quietly enthused by the tribe's recent resurgence.

As he stepped closer to his friends, Walters could see the smile on James' face change to a frown of concern, and intuitively the Police Chief took a deep breath, preparing to face the inquisition; the old newspaper man's guile would not be missing, even after all these years and he couldn't blame him for the concern about his son.

James greeted the policeman with a warm hand shake, and couldn't help thinking that Walters had indeed aged a little, perhaps the top job was causing a little strain, his dark skin looked somewhat gaunt. The offering by Mike of a cold beer was most welcome, helping Walters to settle a little as he sat alongside the other men.

They chatted with small talk for a while, reminiscing over old times, recognising, perhaps oddly, that they had never come together informally before, and it puzzled them without being able to discover why they hadn't. It wasn't long before Walters felt compelled to change the conversation.

'Perhaps I could pre-empt your thoughts James, and my apologies for doing so, I am sending Sam to India,' said Walters, glad that he had broached the topic first. 'I've made contact with the Police Chief in the region where Sam and Joyce are going – they should be looked after quite well.'

'Your colleague has died?' said James. 'I am sorry for that. This man Krell must be a brute of a man, I don't understand…,' said James, tailing off.

Walters gauged his answer. 'I am still trying to get the accounts of all those who were at the scene. Much of it is hard to believe. One thing I do know, is that my people were caught off guard. Whatever was executed by Krell was well planned, he knew what he was after and he knew how to strike.'

Walters bowed his head, staring at the cold bottle of beer in his hand. His large frame changed posture, slumping further into the wooden chair as James and Mike looked upon him in anticipation.

'I suppose I don't need to tell you how concerned I am about Sam going after Krell, and I know you will want to look after him - but why don't you just leave it to the police over in India to get the fugitive, surely we have a treaty with them?' said James.

'Yes we do, but it's never that easy, you invariably need someone on the ground in such a country, they like to hear and see face to face what they are dealing with, and Sam is best placed to do that,' said Walters, sounding official.

'I find the whole thing fascinating,' said Mike. 'From the little I have gleaned it seems quite an adventure, quite mysterious… respect to your colleagues of course, and if I was Sam, I would want to get out there and catch my man.'

James smiled. 'You are supposed to be on my side Mike!' he said, and they all laughed.

'Talking about mysteries,' said James as he stood up to go into the cabin. 'I have one of my own that I should perhaps share with you.'

Walters and Mike were slightly baffled with the sentiment from James, especially during mid-conversation about Sam's inquiry abroad.

Returning, with a well-used, tattered looking journal in his hand, James started to flick through the pages until he came to a marker, one which he had placed in the journal many years before.

'Forgive me for a moment,' said James, eager to reveal his story. 'I have kept many old journals, for posterity if nothing else – but this one is special. It recounts a bizarre event that I bore witness to, one I have never spoken about to anyone, not even my son. I don't know why I feel compelled to tell you now, other than perhaps the coincidence that Sam is in Egypt and he too seems to be on a bizarre quest.'

'I have never published this story, nor would I, it's a story no-one would have ever believed - so I ask you to keep it to yourselves in complete confidence.'

The other two men agreed.

James stared at the open pages for a few seconds, then closed the book, before taking a deep breath and placing the book on the cabin floor beside him. He recounted the events of his journey through Egypt during the Suez Crisis, explaining that he had been diverted on a surreal quest, eventually finding his way to the Dahshur Pyramids south of Cairo. He told of his meeting with the beautiful female Professor, Bektamun Ayoubi and how they had both visited the ancient Pyramid of King Snefru, there finding in its vaults an historic Egyptian tablet, a Stele. This particular Stele was so significant to the archaeologists that all those who were present at the find were sworn to secrecy, James himself swearing that he would not reveal of its secret.

'What is its secret?' said Mike, curiously.

'I can't say fully, that part seems a little cloudy these days but I do know it was a moment of wonder, a moment of revelation.'

'You can't keep us hanging on like that James,' stated Walters, pushing himself upright from his slumped position.

The focus of the story remained with the interaction James had had with Bektamun Ayoubi, eluding to the 'magical' moment when all those gathered in the hidden tomb started to understand what it was they saw before them. A deeper sense of things found James stalling from saying much more, perhaps it was only *he* that felt an uncanny resemblance between his own quest all those years ago and what Sam was perhaps embarking on now.

'Intriguing, I sense a kindling with you and the Professor you mentioned. Did you ever see her again?' said Mike.

'Yes I did, some years later. We had kept in touch by letter, never really having the opportunity to ever meet, even though I travelled all over the world. It was by chance that she came to America one time, during the late sixties, I remember I had not long got back from reporting in Vietnam…she was visiting the Chicago Institute…but I'll leave it there!' said James, a little embarrassed.

They all laughed.

The evening was drawing in, a brilliant sunset started to dip under the row of trees in the small forest at the far end of the land. Although still warm enough to sit outside, all three men were drawn closer to the log fire still glowing in the centre of the cabin. Mike remained by the fire, whilst James asked Walters to walk with him to the house and help prepare some food.

'Carl, please tell me more of what you know and I'll mention to you what I am trying to understand…if that makes sense,' said James as they walked.

'I know you are afraid, I am a little too, but I have told Sam to be guarded. I don't want him confronting Krell unnecessarily and in any event not without all the support he needs from the local police.'

'Yes, but what is this about…really?' asked James. 'Why would Krell steal this painting and use such extreme violence? Sam has talked to me on the phone and mentioned that he and Joyce have been with Anippe Khu, the lady from the Cairo Museum, talking about ancient texts and stelae, not unlike the story I uncovered all those years ago with Bektamun Ayoubi. I have not had chance to tell Sam of this - but I feel I ought to.'

The two men collected the food, already prepared

for cooking on the fire grate back at the cabin. Walters appeared a little perplexed, James had the uncanny knack of making him feel as if he was under investigation, not something he was used to.

'From what you have said then, I am not now convinced that any treaty will work out there in India, I don't believe the Indian Government will just allow Krell to be extradited so easily, and what about any of his contacts, he can't be working alone?' queried James.

'It's complicated, but I have made contact through Interpol and the Indian Ministry of External Affairs. The extradition process can be agreed when I have issued a Red Corner Notice, which is like an international alert for an arrest. Sam is going to meet the Superintendent in Balrampur who will be the link for the process. There is a court house in Delhi, called Patiala House, where we hope to get a warrant from the Chief Metropolitan Magistrate,' explained Walters.

'Very detailed, well…I did ask,' said James smiling. 'There is still something else though, I can see it in you Carl?'

It was at that point that they returned to the cabin to see Mike, in his element, pummeling some extra logs he had inadvertently found nearby for the fire – the other two men watching in awe at his sublime skill with the axe.

Walters took a while to answer James' last intrusive question.

'We think Krell has a contact and it must be something to do with the painting, I guess. We don't know where and how they are going to meet, but the hunch is that it will be somewhere out in Balrampur, in the North India territories, some mysterious fellow named Taraka…yes, Taraka, I think,' said Walters.

Mike was immediately distracted and swung the axe wildly, sheering the wood well away from the centre of the block; he turned to stare at Walters when the name "Taraka" was mentioned. He fully expected more to be said by one of them and looked at them inquisitively.

Before any further conversation, James opened the small iron grate at the base of the small oven door to the cabin chimney stack and placed the prepared meat on a steel grill. 'If you get the fire right, you can even bake clay in here,' he said, nonchalantly.

It wasn't long before the food was cooked, with all three men falling silent as they consumed the beef and chicken with vigour. Mike contemplated heavily, and he felt compelled to open the talk about the name he had heard; the mention of the name Taraka had disturbed him.

'You know there are stories going way back with my ancestors. I have my roots in the ancient tribe of Cahokia, who ruled most of the lands around here, you may have heard of the Cahokian Mounds in South Illinois, near St. Louis. Such stories have been passed down from generation to generation at formal gatherings, where I meet with my people and re-enact ancient tales. We use the old language as much as we can, and talk of the ancient religious ideals of the Cahokian and the later Illiniweck peoples - something we Illinois Native Americans are proud to share today,' said Mike, profoundly.

'I have never heard you say much about your past or the plight of your people, you have our attention it seems,' said James, nodding across to Walters.

'But my point is this,' said Mike taking a deep breath. 'We of the Illiniweck believe in a supreme being, like most religions. We have a spirit who is the 'Master of all Life', we call him *'Kitchesmanetoa'*, and he is for my people the ruler of the Upper World, he is Master of the Sun and Thunder. At our gatherings we perform ceremonies for him, so that he can guide us and create harmony with the natural forces of this world and human kind. Many people, within their religious ideals, would do the same thing. I know people practicing the Hindu religion have similar ceremonies and religious festivals celebrating their higher God, Shiva,' said Mike, continuing to hold attention.

'Why mention the Hindu religion? I am fascinated by what you are saying, but you could have picked any other religion, surely?' queried Walters.

'Most religions have adversaries to their higher gods, there is evil in this world and I know this, I feel this,' said Mike, shuffling in his chair. *'Kitchesmanetoa* has a spiritual adversary called 'The Piasa'. The Piasa is a terrifying evil demon who rules the 'Lower World', and he is a gruesome creature, with deer horns, orange fiery eyes, a lion's body, and has a hideous bearded human face and a long fearsome tail. We have a belief that the supreme being, *Kitchesmanetoa* brings balance to such evil and has the power to create the Manitou's or spirit animals in the form of birds, wolves and other creatures…who in turn protect the tribal warriors in times of battle and great tragedy.'

'This is rather profound,' said James. 'I have never heard you speak of such things before, and the point is?'

'I heard Walters mention a name, just before I missed the centre of that last block of wood. It's a name I heard once - in a conversation I had with an acquaintance who was a practicing Hindu living in Chicago. We had made comparisons with our beliefs…and I remember a name which I found quite poignant at the time.'

'You mean Taraka?' said Walters.

'Yes…Taraka, a demonic name if I remember, equivalent in some aspects to the Demon in my culture - The Piasa,' said Mike.

'You talk as if you believe in such things Mike, surely such ideals are merely folk tales and suspicion,' remarked James. 'I am sorry to offend you, but I struggle with such things. Omnipotence is not my forte, I would rather deal with facts - no disrespect meant to your ancestral beliefs.'

'No offence taken James, but you believe in your God, do you not? I can understand how it seems, but never mock the Spirits, you just never know what lies in store,' replied Mike.

The two elder looking gentlemen continued to converse vibrantly, not realising that Walters had sidled further into the cabin to stand and warm himself by the fire. The policeman stood looking at the flames, admiring the craftsmanship of the ornate fire surround, neatly placed within the brick stack structure so that all four sides of the grating could be seen. Small iron railings encompassed three of the sides, whilst the fourth led the eye to the small iron door and grate openings in the brick stack.

The fire roared along the cladded brick chimney, smoke billowing out through the contrasting, modern aluminium flu placed cleverly in the roof of the cabin. Walters turned his gaze away from the fire, sensing that the conversation between the other two had stopped, he had been noticed by James.

'Have you ever made any pottery James?' queried Walters, changing the subject completely.

'Bits and bobs, mostly some little figures or small pots, the turn table is right through there in the annex - before you get to the cabin tool shed. I haven't made any in a while though. Sam used to love me making little pottery toy soldiers when he was a boy…in fact he still asks me if I have made any from time to time,' said James, smiling.

'I like the art of pottery making,' said Walters. 'I had a dabble myself once, I even joined an art class to see if I could turn my hand to it, that never lasted though. After joining the Police Department, I lost touch with it…it takes skill, time and patience to get proficient I would imagine.'

'Does that small grate at the bottom actually work as a kiln?' said Mike, joining in.

'Yes, just like I said before, but only for small pieces,' said James. 'You have to get the temperature right to get the water out from the clay. You know it's all in the kneading.'

'Yes, making sure that the moisture is even throughout the body and the trapped air is removed,' said Mike, following on.

'Enlightening, we have a common interest between the three of us,' James remarked.

'It is culturally embedded with my people,' said Mike. 'The pottery making within the Native American tribes is notorious. As a child I learnt from my mother who, herself, had learnt from her grandmother. Pots and jewelry, trinkets and clay dolls, these are still made for our use as well as being used for simple trade.'

'We should all perhaps compare notes on our pottery making expertise next time,' said Walters. 'Any way gentlemen, I must be leaving, I'll let you know if I hear any more from Sam, that's if you don't hear from him yourself James.'

'I'll be off too,' said Mike. 'It's a bit of a trek back to my village and I need to see my family before they turn in. It has been an interesting end to the evening gentlemen, I will say that for sure - until the next time?'

Further pleasantries were exchanged and the three men parted company, leaving James a little bewildered. He didn't seem to be any further forward with knowing much of Sam's endeavours, despite some of the coincidences from his own experience that played on his mind. *Curious though about the pottery making,* he thought – a common interest indeed, and perhaps a way that may bring all three of them back together again soon.

The Devi Patan Temple.
Tulsipur, India.

Chapter 13

The Devi Patan

The Delhi air was hot and humid, a stark contrast to the dry heat of Cairo, as Sam and Joyce were greeted by the erstwhile Senior Superintendent, Raju Kumar of the Uttar Pradesh State Police. Fortunately for the pair, the rest of the journey from Delhi to Balrampur, across the North India Territories, would be by helicopter, sparing the travellers from a long hot journey by road and rail.

With a slim frame and long limbs for his body, Raju Kumar appeared taller than he actually was. He was an impressive, smart man - being 32 years of age (young for a senior officer in his position), sporting a renowned handle bar moustache, making him look slightly older. Raju was an undoubted character; authoritative but at the same time charming, and very welcoming as the two visitors discovered immediately.

Speaking perfect English, Raju motioned for the two arrivers to make haste towards the pristine

Augusta-Westland 'Grand' helicopter, its rotor blades turning at full speed on the helipad. All three scrambled into the rear seats as the smartly dressed State Police pilot and navigator, wearing khaki suits and blue berets, shouted at them to fasten their seat belts. The doors to the aircraft were slammed shut, and as the occupants grappled with their belts, the twin turbine machine lurched into a stomach wrenching vertical lift, catching them all a little by surprise.

A spectacular view greeted the passengers' eyes as the helicopter sped across the expanse of the huge North India Uttar Pradesh Territory. With its twisting rivers, colourful fields, expansive terrain and the majestic sight of the giant Himalayan Mountains on the horizon - a moment of silence befell the visitors. Raju noticed them and smiled. Weighing them up, he was curious to know how this matter had all unfolded. The mere fact that he was utilising an exclusive State helicopter said something of the priority his superiors had given to this enquiry. Raju was normally calm and robust, using his intelligence to read situations carefully, yet he couldn't help but feel a little perturbed at the emergent, fast paced events.

'It's quite a long journey to Balrampur, over 600 kilometres. We will land near to the Police Headquarters this evening and we can have a short briefing there before you get to your hotel in the town. I suggest you try and get some rest now for a while,' said Raju, not least wanting to put himself at ease.

Raju had many questions to ask of them and wanted to be sure they understood the potential threat they were about to face. He stared out of the helicopter window, looking away from the Himalayan skyline, his thoughts steering towards the potential predicament. The strange stories and legend of a deformed hermetical giant living around the Devi Patan Temple in Tulsipur had not surfaced for many years, the giant had hardly been seen recently, and any sighting would normally be thought of as merely rumour or conjecture.

If indeed the Englishman, Krell, was in any way connected to the 'hermit', then real danger may lurk for them. It appeared to Raju that Krell himself would be extremely dangerous and difficult to catch, but if Taraka revealed himself, that was a different ball game. One thing Raju was convinced of, was the draw of the Temple. Whatever was being planned, Raju considered that Krell would be the one who would have to carry out the dirty work, especially if the Temple was to be targeted. Taraka would not step inside the Temple, especially during this time of the forthcoming 'Mela', the famous Hindu festival.

Three hours passed and the executive helicopter landed on a disused hockey field just outside the main town of Balrampur. The party barely had time to place their feet on the ground before the aircraft soared into the air once more, making haste to return to Delhi.

*

The blissful coolness of Raju's air conditioned office was only surpassed by the glorious sight of the magnificent, white tipped Himalayan Mountains, which, due to their size, seemed ever closer through the large office window; *simply majestic*, the onlookers thought.

'We are close to Nepal here, if you didn't know, the flat fields are a total contrast to the mountains, idyllic wouldn't you say,' said Raju.

'Yes,' said Sam and Joyce in unison, both gaping through the window.

'I will get to the point,' said Raju turning to business. 'There is a festival tomorrow in Tulsipur, one which marks the fifth day of the 'Chaitra-Navrati', part of the rituals that hail the start of the Hindu calendar. We call it the 'Mela' and it is a very important religious festival...people will come from miles around. If your man Krell is going to do anything, tomorrow may be a good day because of all the distractions.'

'I know of this ritual,' said Joyce. 'The people of Dang in Nepal bring an Idol to the Temple of the Devi Patan. I believe the Idol is the Avatar of Shiva who led the Guru Gorakshnath towards Nathism.'

'You are well informed Joyce and very wise to the events, although there are many versions of the story,' said Raju.

'Indeed most Hindus believe that the Ratannath Baba Idol is the Avatar of Shiva that led our beloved Guru to his righteous path. That is why the Temple of the Devi Patan was founded by him - giving birth to the Nath Sampradaya – the oldest seat of the Nath Sect in Northern India. But again it depends on how religious you are, you can imagine how stories mix with legend and how legend mixes with facts. I can tell you that most people in Northern India would not know the full extent of the Hindu Scriptures,' said Raju further.

'The Nath Sect or Cult has been mentioned to us before,' said Sam. 'This Taraka fellow is one of those I believe?'

'The Nath Sect are a devoted group of people dedicated to the religious knowledge of Hinduism. I have to tell you that the hermit Taraka has not been seen in these parts for many years. If he is here, he is well hidden…and he is not a Nath, even though he may purport to be. Some say he is inherently evil and therefore cannot be classed as Hindu,' said Raju, firmly.

Raju continued to talk as Sam contemplated Krell's capture. Joyce, on the other hand, was resplendent in the discussion about the Hindu rituals, and she was relishing the opportunity to enhance her knowledge.

'Tomorrow's festival indeed commemorates that our beloved Guru Gorakshnath is the incarnation of Lord Shiva. Gorakshnath is the Yoga form of Lord Shiva. You know this term 'Yoga' of course Joyce?'

'Yes of course, where Yoga is the supreme power which stabilises the universe and which, some believe, is itself the whole universe,' she said smiling.

'More so that Gorakshnath is the Yoga power of Lord Shiva, who himself is the whole universe,' said Raju.

'Is Shiva your main God?' said Sam, in all innocence.

'He is one of the principal deities of Hinduism, Mr. Campbell, one who brings a balance to creation by first destroying it, allowing for the other Gods to create it.'

'I find it all a little confusing, your conversation is losing me I am afraid,' said Sam.

'Not to worry, let us talk about what should happen tomorrow,' said Raju, knowing that his next comments would not make the detail any simpler. 'The Idol, or Avatar as we like to call it, will be worshipped tomorrow alongside the 'Devi', or Goddess. There will be thousands of people milling around trying to get a glimpse of this very profound ceremony going on inside the Devi Patan Temple. Only a select few will be allowed inside the Temple initially.'

'But what do you think Krell is here for?' said Sam. 'He must be after something inside that Temple, something that the stolen painting may have led him to. Our friend in Egypt, Anippe, suggested there might be an ancient script held there?'

Raju paused for a moment, not answering, preferring to deliberate over his dual concerns of how he was going to police the festival, and keep one eye on any plot he envisaged Krell and Taraka may be scheming to get inside the Temple. Of real concern though, was the scant detail about a supposed hidden vault within the Temple. Legend had it that the vault housed the very script Sam was hinting at, a fact which Raju had not eluded to yet.

*

Krell had been exposed to very little sleep over the last couple of days, he had been harangued by Taraka constantly, and he felt weary as he sat on the edge of his four poster bed in the enclosed stone walled room within Taraka's lair. Only a dim electric lamp was available for company, and sanity. Time and time again he had gone through the Book of Prophecies to see if there was any further clue as to what his approach would be with his assigned task tomorrow - although much of it was a blur now, his mind slowly becoming addled by the perpetual bullying and innate ferocity of his Mentor. Krell knew he was in the presence of twisted evil, the brutal attack he had suffered previously was testament to that.

He stared at the lamp and started to drift to sleep, but it wasn't to be; moments later, a loud thumping noise on the bedroom door startled him.

'Jeremiah!' bellowed the inhuman voice of Taraka. 'Your adversaries have arrived in Balrampur. You will speak with me now.'

The voice was from a nightmare it seemed, taking time to register in Krell's over tired mind. He scrambled to his feet and opened the door, being confronted immediately by Taraka, who ordered him into the main chamber. The large, grotesque fire was still roaring as if having a life of its own, its light overpowering the dim light of the wall lamps. An evil smile spread across Taraka's face as he paced back and forth around the room, and he appeared full of glee. His ornate robed attire had gone, only to be replaced with a soiled hessian robe with a large pointed hood that reached half way down his enormous frame.

A befitting disguise, Krell thought, seeing that Taraka's huge oily looking belly was still exposed, reflecting the style of the Nath Sadhu worshippers. Strangely, it was also noticeable that Taraka's black beard looked longer and more prominent, as did the knotted bun of hair on top of his head; although Krell was not at liberty to comment on such things, he merely waited for instructions.

'I shall be near to you tomorrow young Jeremiah, but of course I shall not go into the Temple, that is your job. My presence will be as a Nath, befitting of my lasting legacy…what do you think of my attire?!' said Taraka, uproariously.

Krell smiled politely. 'You mentioned my adversaries?' he queried.

'The woman and the policeman from America are here you fool - they have tracked you down it seems.'

Krell said nothing further, he merely observed Taraka's accentuated behaviour, pondering whether his Mentor's odd demeanour was because they were close now, close to capturing the Atharva-Veda from the hidden vault in the Devi Patan Temple. The capture of the ancient Vedic Script was, after all, why they were here and it would be Krell's dedicated task. If he was successful, perhaps the false Nath would then hold him with some esteem.

A previous reconnoitre of the labyrinth of cave tunnels leading from Taraka's lair, had enabled Krell to work out a route through to the Devi Patan Temple and the Surya Kund, a pond of water so named because of the nearby Surya River. Pilgrims would flock to the pond, and they would bathe in the water to cleanse their souls, and this would be a perfect way for Krell to disguise himself amongst the people, giving him a chance to approach the rear entrance of the Temple.

Taraka shouted again, wrenching Krell out of his thoughts.

'You haven't commented on my robe, quite the hermit, do you not think? People have come to know me as the Nath hermit. Take a good look Jeremiah, take a good look at how people see me, the Nath hermit who lives in a cave!' he cackled, his eerie voice reverberating around the chamber, sending a chill down Krell's spine.

At this the giant Taraka stooped his shoulders, to such a degree the top half of his back became hideously hunched and deformed. Next Taraka seemed to cradle his head to one side, reducing his height even further to that below the height of Krell, and although this was still tall, it was not inconceivable. Taraka's transformation into the Nath Sadhu hermit was complete.

*

The following day, the drive to Tulsipur was busy with people massing along the route, heading for the Devi Patan Temple. Sam had not slept much, his contemplation on how to approach this particular day had consumed him. Joyce, on the other hand had slept well, relishing the prospect of seeing first hand a spectacle such as the 'Mela'. She felt excited and comfortable, even though the morning temperature had already drawn a bead of sweat on her forehead.

Sam and Raju, along with some of Raju's senior officers, had studied the maps and photographs of the Devi Patan complex earlier in the morning. The key thing, Raju had stipulated, was to guard all entrances and exits to the Temple building, which would be a major task considering the thousands of people who would be in and around the area. Raju had expressed that the religious leaders would not sanction a closure or restriction of the Mela inside the Temple grounds, and it was their sacred right to allow the people such freedoms; the police would just have to deal with what they were confronted with at any given moment.

Arriving at the Temple grounds, Raju and his two guests made their way to the Temple entrance. The Mela celebrations were already starting to spill into the wooded village area of Siktihwa and back along the railway line into Tulsipur town itself. Masses of people were gathering, many dressed in traditional colourful Hindu costumes laden with bright orange, yellow and green fabrics. Placards and writings were displayed, mostly in Sanskrit, but some in English – depicting the annual celebration and worship of the forthcoming Avatar.

Quickly the threesome scuttled through an orange awning which led to the Temple itself, rushing passed the array of trinket stalls, where all manner of religious symbols were being sold. The four sided 'coned' tower at the rear of the Temple was most distinguishable, and Raju was anxious to enter and find the room beneath this tower.

Sam was equally restless, leaving Raju and Joyce inside the Temple. He hurried off to the rear of the Temple complex where the Devi Patan Hospital joined the grounds of the Surya Kund, the large water pond situated behind the entire sprawling complex. Intuitively, the American had guessed that the pond could be used as cover – a person could get to it from the Surya River embankment and easily hide amongst the hundreds of people already gathering around the man made water enclosure.

Raju and Joyce followed members of the public,

walking through the wide open plan frontage of the Temple and finding the farthest room below the dome, as Raju had wanted. The ambience of the 'dome' room was enriched with beautiful, decorative and intricately made idols, captivating all who would be able to view them. One particular idol was a sequined doll depicting the Hindu Deity of the 'Maa Devi Patan', centre to the room.

Joyce was struck by her surroundings, engrossed by the Maa Devi Patan on its solid silver circular platform, above which was a circular copper hood, emblazoned with a detailed Sanskrit inscription, looking all the more mysterious by the fiery bronze lamp of Ghee flickering its light onto the writing.

'I can converse reasonably well in Hindi, but this verse on the copper mount is confounding me,' said Joyce.

'There are many aspects to the story,' said Raju. 'Much of which relate to why the Temple is here. The verse you see talks about the 'she' warrior named 'Durga' who was spawned from Devi, the great Goddess of the Hindus.'

'Hence the Devi Patan Temple?' said Joyce.

'Yes, in a way – but confusingly, Devi was the consort of the God, Shiva, and Devi herself had many forms, including that of 'Durga' who was deemed the greatest warrior of them all. Interestingly, Durga could also spawn warriors in the form of 'Bhati', a sword wielding demigod soldier placed on Earth to slay the demonic adversaries of Shiva. A number of the demons were considered invincible and Lord Shiva could not conquer them by himself, he needed the Bhati warriors.'

'Myth suggests that one of those Demons was called Taraka…am I to presume?' said Joyce.

The Superintendent pondered for a while, acknowledging Joyce's last comment, then he looked at his watch and changed his slant. 'I must tell you there is supposed to be a hidden vault in this Temple, legend has it that it is below this very room, although no-one can be sure…and it may hold an ancient Vedic Script, the Atharva-Veda,' said Raju, deciding to share his knowledge.

'You left that part out before – why?' said Joyce.

'I needed to keep that information tight until today, in any event, we would not be sure how to get to the vault from the secret passage.'

'Secret passage?' said Joyce, emphatically.

Raju grimaced, the more he considered, the more he thought of what the consequences might turn out to be. He wasn't sure where the vault was, although like many, he was convinced it existed. The religious leaders had not co-operated, being sworn to secrecy surrounding the myth; they would protect the Atharva-Veda at all cost.

*

Whilst Raju and Joyce pondered in the Temple, Krell had already started on his journey along the cave tunnels within the labyrinth extending from Taraka's Lair. He approached the large iron gate once again, with Taraka urging him on to make haste, impatiently ordering Krell along.

The Englishman had disguised himself by dressing

272

in traditional Hindu religious attire, wearing an orange robe and a sequined orange sleeved over-garment, similar to that of a Hare-Krishna worshipper; his shaven head was befitting of the culture. The Hare Krishna were common in this area, and they would flock in pilgrimage to the Mela, to pay homage to their God, Lord Vishnu. Krell thought he may blend in more readily and had disguised himself further by darkening his skin with a mixture of rape seed oil and peat.

All of this would only deceive for a while, perhaps just long enough to reach inside the passageways of the Temple. After that, once Krell had got his prize, it mattered not.

He carried a brown leather knapsack, in which he placed an iron jimmy and a small lump hammer to be used for opening gates and loosening stones within the walls of the passages to the Temple. The plan was simple enough, once inside the Temple he would find the secret vault and breach it.

The pond of the Surya Kund was his destination and it would take thirty minutes, traveling through the labyrinth, to get there. Now, away from Taraka's Lair, Krell settled into his task, determined to prove his worth. He could not possibly fail, Taraka's instruction was clear – find the Atharva-Veda or don't come back at all.

*

The enormous man-made pool of the Surya Kund was already busy with bathers and worshippers as Sam sat outside on the hospital steps, staring at the full extent of the impressive round structure. It had a two-metre-high circular stone wall surrounding a huge body of water, siphoned from the nearby Surya River. It looked a little like a grand Roman amphitheatre, equal in size and prowess.

Midday came and the main part of the Mela was drawing near. Huge swathes of people were now in every part of the complex, Sam never having seen such colour, such ambience and such anticipation from a crowd. Men, women and children of all ages and sizes adorned the whole area, with hundreds of people in and around the Surya Kund. Sam scanned the crowd incessantly, looking for any sign of Krell and perhaps Taraka for that matter – assuming that even with a disguise they would remain distinctive. His instinct told him that Krell's approach would be imminent, *yet from where?*

A tap on the shoulder from behind startled him, it was Joyce.

'Raju has gone to check on his men, I spent some time in the ante room of the Temple, but thought I must find you,' she said, noticing Sam's tense expression.

'I don't know how well the plan to capture Krell will work,' said Sam. 'There is no guarantee that he will turn up. If he does, he will have his own plan for sure…and God knows what he will do to carry it out.'

'I'll stay with you for now, I would recognise his gait anywhere, I know you have only seen pictures of him…but I assure you, he will stand out,' said Joyce.

'But he'll be aware of that, and presumably he will have thought about his disguise, everyone should be alert to that fact,' said Sam.

At that moment, Sam received a call on his cell phone, it was Raju and he was desperate to talk, shouting that a detachment of his officers had spotted what they thought was 'the giant hermit' seen skulking through the trees near to the banks of the Surya River about half a kilometre from where Sam was. Raju pleaded with Sam to be even more vigilant, so concerned was he that Krell would soon appear.

The sound of the State Police helicopter soaring overhead drowned any response Sam could give to Raju. The robust, blue and grey HAL Dhruv aircraft had been assigned to follow the procession of the Avatar to Tulsipur, from neighbouring Nepal. Raju must have called the aircraft in closer, Sam thought, because of the possible sighting of Taraka.

The helicopter swooped along the tree line embankment of the Surya River, the sunlight catching its distinctive rear aircraft wings, as it twisted sharply to land near the police vehicles south of the Tulsipur railway line. People watched the aircraft, pausing with excitement, merely assuming that the Avatar must be very near. Loud cheers rang high around the complex and people started to surge expectantly towards the Temple.

The noise cleared a little, Raju was still on the phone.

'I presume the helicopter is for you Raju?' said Sam.

'I can see better from the air, besides if this is a sighting of Taraka, I want to see where he goes.'

'But what about the Devi Patan and Krell?' said Sam, slightly concerned.

'I will return at a moment's notice if I have to, but you have enough police on the ground. If you go to the rear entrance of the Temple by the large conical dome you will meet an Inspector Natesh Choudhury and his men, they are part of the Specialist Unit, his team are excellent and he is a great leader, you'll be in good hands Sam.'

Sam and Joyce walked briskly through the crowd and into the main hall way of the hospital. Bustling through the visitors and staff, they reached the main Temple concourse before hurriedly making their way towards where Inspector Choudhury would be. They found him standing near the Temple dome with his squad of four officers, all armed to the teeth, with side pistols and carbine rifles, *an overt display of weaponry in anyone's book*, thought Sam, although no one else around seemed too perplexed.

Inspector Choudhury was from the local Municipal Police Force, being dressed slightly differently than the State Police. The Khaki uniform was not too dissimilar, but the head gear was different, all officers present wearing blue and gold military styled caps, as opposed to berets. Inspector Choudhury was an older man, near 50 years of age, and was quite short but looked very muscular and tough. His full black beard was impressive yet it did little to hide his graveled, dark skinned, stern looking face, which had the effect upon the visitors that they should adhere to his commands - one of which was to follow the erstwhile Inspector quickly down the spiral steps at the rear of the main Temple, below the conical dome.

To Sam's surprise the steps went further down

than he anticipated, some ten metres, before Inspector Choudhury steered the team through a large wooden door and into a long, man-made tunnel; effectively, a secret passageway between the Temple and the Surya Kund. The passageway had only enough room for the group to walk along in single file. It was dank and wet, with a nauseating smell of damp plaster and stale dirt, a place obviously not frequented at all regularly.

Sam did not like being out of sight from the main area, although he recognised that what they were doing in the secret passageway served good purpose; and if the hunch was right about Krell making his way to the Temple to steal the Vedic script - then surely the imposter, and his Mentor Taraka, would know of such a passageway.

'What is this passageway used for?' said Joyce.

'I assume it is never used now, but it was used for getting people in and out of the Temple secretly, in times of desecration and war. At one time, it led all the way down to the Surya River but since the building of the Surya Kund and the Temple Hospital, the older part has been sealed off.'

'Can you get to any section of the old part via the pond now?' said Sam, concerned they may be in the wrong part of the tunnel.

'At the base of the Surya Kund, there is an inlet where water is pumped in for the hospital. The other part of the old passageway is near there I think, but it is entirely blocked off I can assure you, there would be no access there, not unless you possessed some explosives or some unnatural strength to break through,' said Inspector Choudhury.

*

By now, the end of the of the underground cave labyrinth leading to the Surya River, was near, and Krell had sensed the gradual ascent of the cave over the last few hundred metres. He stopped and shone his torch light on a large round stone blocking his way, one similar to that which he had encountered before, when entering Taraka's Lair. He pulled at an iron lever on the wall, the adjacent spring releasing a double metal lock pressed against the stone. The stone was set on rails as before and Krell had to use all of his mighty strength to move the solid granite block, it weighed tonnes. He forced the circular stone into a space on the opposite stone wall ensuring it locked into its brace and metal clasps. Such was the strain in moving the colossal object, Krell had to take a moment to gather breath. He stared at the stone and having used all of his strength, he knew no man alive (save Taraka) could have accomplished such a feat.

A short distance further on, he reached a small enclave, which had a makeshift wooden lattice roof, allowing a glimmer of sunlight to filter through. Using the iron jimmy in his knapsack, Krell prodded the roof before jamming the tool between the lattice frame and the surface. The roof opened readily and he hauled himself through a gap just wide enough for his enormous body, finding himself in a small clump of distinctive round bodied Shisham trees near to the Surya Kund. In complete contrast to the cave tunnel, the air was hot and muggy, yet there was no time for him to linger.

*

Stuck down in the secret passage, between the Temple and the hospital, was not a good place for Sam to be, he was fighting against his better judgement. His clothes were now damp and soiled from scraping along the surface of the passageway walls, making him feel quite uncomfortable. He had reached the end of the narrow passageway on his own, which, as had been described, was blocked by a purpose built brick wall.

Behind the brick wall he could hear the noise of what sounded like a turbine engine, and Sam assumed that he would be near a pond inlet. He remembered that there was an inlet near to where he was sitting on the hospital steps earlier, the turbine noise was therefore perhaps an interior water pump, filtering water through to the main hospital.

He had to get back outside again, he felt sure that there must be another passageway which had been missed, one perhaps leading from the inlet. He headed back quickly to where Joyce and Inspector Choudhury were waiting.

'There is a turbine near to the inlet, my guess is that it must be pumping water…how does it get maintained?' said Sam, turning his attention to Inspector Choudhury.

'Hospital engineers - although I am not too sure where they would be right now. There is bound to be access via the hospital basement at a guess,' said the Inspector, looking a little perplexed.

Sam said no more but continued to run through the tunnel making his way at speed to the rear entrance of the Temple, anxious to return to the hospital premises. Inspector Choudhury, Joyce and the armed officers followed. Outside it seemed that thousands of more people had arrived, it was almost impossible to surge through the crowd. All Sam could think about was getting to the turbine room at the hospital and pleaded with Inspector Choudhury and his men to help him make haste through the revellers. If his hunch was right, Krell would be making for that inlet.

Chapter 14

The Vedic Script

The Hare Krishna attire was making Krell perspire intensely and, concerned that the disguise of the peat on his skin would dissipate in the sweltering heat, he considered he would have to work faster than he had originally intended.

The small coppice of Shisham trees and their natural discarded foliage near to the river bank, provided good cover for a short while, allowing Krell to pick a suitable moment to move towards the Surya Kund. Almost ready to set off, he was stopped in his tracks, slightly startled, and had to stoop down under cover even more so, watching intently at the police activity. A police helicopter swooped down, skimming the near dry water bed of the river; it was followed by an all- terrain vehicle speeding along the river bank, with its compliment of specialist firearms officers looking decidedly uncomfortable riding in the back.

It could only be Taraka, Krell assumed; his Mentor

was making a diversionary move as he had promised
– *time to move now*, Krell thought. Luckily, people were
walking along the river bank from all directions
heading towards an entry point to the pond. Special
wooden ramps had been placed from the river's sandy
bank, reaching over the Surya Kund wall, and onto
the poolside allowing people easy access to the rest of
the complex. Police and security were everywhere,
and Krell felt himself hunching his large frame ever
further to try and blend into the crowd more. As he
reached the top of the wooden ramp, bustling along
with the mass of people, he was able to see the true
expanse of the Surya Kund, the vital water source for
the Devi Patan Hospital.

Serious looking police guards greeted the
disguised Krell and he winced as they peered at him
curiously, yet the guards eventually appeared to
respect his attire and his outward humbleness. He
went over the wooden bridge without compromise
and quickly turned to his right, walking speedily along
the stone concourse towards the main water inlet near
the hospital.

People were bathing, many fully clothed - all
enjoying the unusual freedom of the Surya Kund
waters during this festive time. The crowd in and
around the Temple area was now vast and furtive,
excited that the Ratannath Baba idol was now about
to arrive within the Temple walls, the idol having
travelled along its famous annual route from the sister
town of Dang in Nepal.

It was time for Krell to go to work. After a few
steps he stopped on the concourse and lowered
himself into the water, practically unnoticed as so

many others were doing the same. Slowly he waded through the water to a point no more than five metres away from his first objective - the large inlet. The water poured into a basement funnel, across which was a lattice iron gate, partially submerged with its lock fully under water at its base. Removing his outer sleeved garment, Krell tied it around his waist, then slowly and discreetly, submerged his bulk into the water, guiding himself to the lattice. Quickly he removed the jimmy from his knapsack and prized the lock, almost taking the gate off its hinges as he did so. Hastily, he looked up out of the water, breathing a sigh of relief when noticing that just about everybody had become pre-occupied with the prospect of seeing the Ratannath Baba. Those hundreds that were previously bathing, were now either clambering out of the water or surging towards the east side of the pond as they saw the procession walking south along the Temple road. Men, women and children of all ages were rushing to catch sight, climbing on top of the Surya Kund wall to gain a vantage point.

Krell submerged again and forced the lattice gate open against the flow of water, closing it behind as he swam through. The inlet led to some steps and he could see a large green door embedded into a wall adjacent to the hospital structure. Smashing his way through the door, he found himself standing in a small room, dominated by a pristine, Pelton machine turbine, blue in colour – the cover of the machine looking like a snail shell and the noise of which drowned all the senses as it pumped the life giving water into the hospital water tanks.

A short series of steps, in front of the Pelton

machine, led to a door which Krell presumed must be access to the main hospital basement, and would be an entry point for the engineers. It would also be an access point for his adversaries, if they had guessed his movements.

He was now singularly focused on the next part of the plan, searching anxiously for a trap door underneath the turbine. The machine was raised on a steel framed platform, with removable steel panels along all four sides. All the panels were padlocked and using his jimmy for the umpteenth time, Krell smashed the lock to the panel nearest to him, revealing a gap underneath the turbine of just over half a metre wide.

A concrete base, flush with the stone floor, was the next obstacle. Furiously, Krell attacked the concrete covering at the corner edges with the lump hammer, making the concrete crumble into holes big enough for his hands to grasp and dislodge the entire base, pulling it completely free from the frame. Looking into the hole, he saw a wooden trap door, which he hoped would be the entrance to the true secret passageway he and Taraka had surmised, and ultimately the route to his prize, the ancient Vedic Script – the Atharva-Veda.

Forcing his huge body through the gap, Krell clambered into the hole, profuse sweat pouring over his face making the oily peat disguise on his skin start to coagulate. The wooden trap door at the base of the hole was easily opened, leading him to a passageway, which by all accounts would steer him to the actual vault where the Vedic Script lay hidden.

*

At a snail's pace the elderly hospital caretaker (whom Inspector Choudhury had managed to find through cajoling the head nurse) led the party down into the basement of the hospital. The caretaker was at pains to point out that he wasn't sure which of the keys he had with him, fitted the door to the turbine room; the normal on site engineers, he explained, were out somewhere enjoying the festivities of the Ratannath Baba.

At the basement entry to the turbine room, Sam watched in mental anguish as the caretaker fumbled the keys, trying to fathom, time and time again, which of the keys would unlock the door. Staring incessantly at the bunch, Joyce tried desperately to note which keys had failed, fighting the urge to snatch the keys from the elderly gentleman as he was close to trying some of them again.

Overhead, in and around the Temple, the Mela was reaching its climax. The large crowd were now in a frenzy as the celebrations blossomed into full swing - with the idol circling the Temple numerous times before it was due to enter. Adorned in multi coloured satin robes, the idol rested on a wooden handled palate, and was being carried by its many followers with hundreds of people surging, trying to get a glimpse and touch the holy object. Further processions and idols followed behind, all of the carriers dressed in beautiful sequined costumes in an effort to pay homage and revere their idol; the incarnation of the Ratannath Baba, the man who had established the Devi Patan Temple in his grandfather's (the Great Gorakshnath) name. Now the people's Avatar had once again come home to its natural place, a place where the Nath Sect would be its guardians.

The entry into the turbine room was finally opened, Sam and Joyce both impatient to get through first, with Inspector Choudhury wincing a little, wishing to place his officers ahead of the erstwhile couple. In any event, all were anxious to discover what lay within. The debris in and around the Pelton turbine was plain to see, and it wasn't long before they worked out where Krell must have disappeared to.

'This has just happened, it must be Krell, we need to go in,' said Joyce.

'He will have nowhere to go and must return this way I would presume,' said Inspector Choudhury. 'There can't be anywhere else out of here.'

'If there is a hidden vault, then perhaps this new found passage must lead the way, or why else would Krell be in there?' said Joyce. 'It is the Vedic Script, the Atharva-Veda, he will be after; I am sure of it – Raju is sure of it too.'

Despite knowing the mortal danger that he would face ahead, nothing could prevent Sam's instinct from taking over, and without any further hesitation he clambered through the gap between the platform and the turbine, straddling the walls of the hole with his feet, before dropping down into the passageway.

'The ground is about four metres down, and I can confirm, there is another passageway here. Inspector Choudhury throw me your torch,' shouted Sam.

'No', came the stubborn reply. 'I am coming with you.'

Forever the leader and not wanting to seem cowardly in front of his men, the Inspector climbed down to where Sam stood, telling his officers to remain in the room with Joyce. Their orders were strict, if anything should happen to him or Sam, and Krell was to escape, they must shoot Krell on sight.

The smell of the newly found passageway was rank, the air thick with dust and the stone walls were obtusely cold to the touch. There was no system of lighting and the policemen had to rely on the only torch, dutifully handed to Sam who now took the lead – holding a borrowed nine-millimetre pistol in one hand, the torch in his other. The Inspector, meanwhile, trained his carbine rifle along the tunnel - following the torch light, being careful to avoid pointing the weapon at Sam.

Both pensive, their muscles tight, and both breathing heavily, the two men slowly made their way, gauging every step as they headed ominously towards the vault.

*

Krell had reached the vault, which lay some fifteen metres below the Temple foundations. He stooped through a narrow stone archway, squeezing his large bulk against either side of the bricks before stumbling into the small dank room. He shone his torch in circular motions, catching sight of a small wooden table and chair in the far corner. On top of the table was a wooden box with a lid bearing indecipherable markings, written in ancient Sanskrit.

There was no lock fixed to the box and Krell was able to lift the lid to reveal its contents. Almost consumed with glee and trying not to gloat heavily, he was in awe at his and Taraka's plan coming to fruition. Abundant thoughts entered his mind as he postulated being one step closer to revealing the secrets of the Pottery Maker, for there inside the box was quite possibly the ancient clue they had been looking for. The box protected an ancient copy of the Verses and Hymns of the Atharva-Veda, the fourth of the sacred Vedas, a testimony to the most ancient of writings within the Hindu Vedic Scripts. Taraka had explained that the collection of papyrus bound verses would be nearly three thousand years old but that the set of papers would seem as if they had hardly withered. Taraka was right.

Krell's heart was pounding as he stared at the book, exhilarated at the thought of the contents, which would be riddled with incantations, charms, and curious metaphysical texts of space and time. He was after a particular forgotten line within a prayer verse, one which had never been revealed in any modern copy of the Script – yet his instruction was clear, he was not to bring back the entire book, he must find the right prayer and tear it out.

Opening the leaves of the Vedic Script, he looked at the sequence of prayers marked in Sanskrit alongside its numerical counterpart called the 'Devanagari' which Krell could see utilised a methodical structure of chapters, verses and lines, visible in each section. He reached the 53rd verse of the sixteenth chapter, marked tri-pancasat ३, understanding that from Taraka's instructions he was reading the 'Prayer to Kâla', meaning 'Prayer to Time'. Krell quivered at its meaning, recognising that this prayer was signified by its primordial power, it was a prayer with a power so strong it was meant to be defined by immortality, one which was emblazoned by the power of the universe itself.

From the work of many people through the centuries, the key to that unspeakable power was believed to be locked within the translation of an ancient Egyptian stele, an Egyptian tablet veiled in secrecy at an unknown location. Now before him was the Prayer of Kâla, the very part of the original sacred text of the Atharva-Veda they had sought, and it was this prayer that would ultimately guide he and Taraka to the sacred Prophecy Stele.

Frantically Krell counted the lines within the prayer, noting that it had three more lines than the thirteen lines written in any modern interpretation. Those extra lines were the key.

About to tear the page from the book, he heard the ominous sound of echoing footsteps stemming from the passageway, and assumed that there must be at least two people heading his way, one of them undoubtedly with a torch, as shimmering light started to catch the entrance to the vault. *No time now to read or check,* he thought - grab the Vedic Script, put it in the sack and escape; woe betide any imposters in his way.

Sam was still slightly ahead of Inspector Choudhury, holding the pistol in his right hand, his arm extended, with the grip of the gun firmly clasped in his palm. He held the torch in his left hand, shining it directly ahead, revealing a small opening five metres in front. The Inspector had his carbine pointing over Sam's right shoulder, trained on the gap.

On hearing the noise, Krell switched his own torch light off and waited in the far corner of the vault, just behind the table. He took a deep breath and held it, remaining motionless. Furious that he hadn't been able to tear the verse from the Vedic Script, he was ready to make his move and face-off whoever came through the doorway.

Agonisingly, both policemen tried to move slowly and stealthily forward, attempting to breathe shallow, profuse sweat rolling down their foreheads. Sam arrived at the small doorway first, shining his torch rapidly inside the vault, quickly catching Krell crouching behind the wooden table. Inspector Choudhury trained his weapon on the giant man and inadvertently screamed a profanity. The Inspector's shout put Sam off, causing the torch light to fall away from Krell's position.

A split second is all it took for Krell to palm the table up in the air towards the two men, making them reel as their arms and weapons flailed in an effort to protect themselves. The table hit them both hard, sending the Inspector flying backwards and falling into the passageway. Sam fell against the nearest wall to the entrance of the vault, dropping his pistol and his hand held torch in the process. He fought to regain his composure but there was no time, Krell was upon him and grabbed Sam's torso with his enormous hands, picking him up off the ground with ease before slamming him with hideous force onto the cold, hard stone floor. Now powerless, hardly able to move, Sam felt the excruciating pain of a dislocated left shoulder and broken left arm. Disorientated, in complete agony and close to passing out, the

American could all but wait for the final blow.

The giant man placed his right hand around Sam's throat but just as he was about to squeeze, a shot was fired, the sonic compression of the gunfire ringing violently around the small room. Krell dropped to one knee feeling pain in his side, and instinctively, like a wounded animal, he charged at Inspector Choudhury smashing him to the ground in an evil rage. The poor Inspector was helpless as Krell proceeded to pummel him, hitting every part of the little man's body before there was no breath left in him.

After such forbidding, Krell charged down the narrow dark tunnel, heading back towards the turbine room, ignoring his wound. To him the wound was insignificant, his task was almost complete and he would not be thwarted now.

Sam was in incredible pain, yet forced himself to stand, trying to shake off the gunshot sound still ringing violently in his ears. Hardly able to move the left side of his body, somehow he managed to scramble around the vault and retrieve the pistol and his torch from the ground. He staggered to the doorway only to see Inspector Choudhury lying on the floor, cradled in a foetal position, his head and face completely unrecognisable. Sam did not have to deduce the Inspector's demise; he had seen enough dead bodies in his time, such a brave soul and he had saved his life.

From the turbine room, the dim sound of the gunshot could just be heard above the whirring of the machine. Joyce and the two constables braced themselves, with the officers pointing their machine guns at the narrow entrance hole to the tunnel. The thump, thump of heavy feet echoed along the passageway, coming ever closer, intuition telling the others that it was probably Krell fast approaching. Joyce gulped and tried to compose herself, praying and hoping that Sam and the Inspector were alright, all the time fearful that something had gone awfully wrong.

A fearsome, blooded Krell reached the shaft at the end of the passageway; he moved swiftly, catching the police officers by surprise, climbing the walls with such speed and ferocity, they became too startled to react. He pushed them away from the opening with such power and menace that they fell unconscious before hitting the ground. Joyce reeled at the sight of the evil man, stumbling backwards towards the green door leading to the inlet.

'Why are you doing this Jeremiah?' she shouted. 'And why are you stealing the Script? You can't get away with this.'

'You have no idea what you are meddling with, you interfering nobodies, move out of the way or I will kill you.'

'Taraka has made you do this, he has poisoned you, come to your senses man, you will surely lose in the end.'

'Intuitive little lady, I must say, but you won't stop me, now get out of the way,' Krell said menacingly, his fierce, evil face glaring back at Joyce, rocking her very soul.

She was indeed terrified, Krell didn't seem at all natural, and he didn't seem in any way perturbed by the fact he was wounded. Joyce thought that she would barely be able to move but she managed to side-step slowly away from the green door, seeing that Krell had given her half a chance. Her courage afforded that she would live and fight again.

Krell kicked the green door open and dived into the waters of the inlet. He tore open the lattice gate and moved quickly through the water before leaping up onto the concrete wall of the Surya Kund, his intention to head back out along the river bed. By now his shaved head was showing parts of his fair skin, blotched by smothering's of the oily peat, and his orange Hare Krishna clothing was filthy and torn with blood spattered on the sleeves, chest and legs.

Joyce went to the aid of the two officers, one of whom was beginning to regain consciousness, although the other appeared mortally wounded having smashed his head against the metal turbine as Krell had charged out of the gap beneath it. She cradled the injured officer, trembling at her own near demise. The other officer regained full composure, got to his feet and went for help within the hospital. Moments later Joyce heard the sound of a cry coming from the tunnel entrance. It was Sam.

'God Sam, you are alive...can you get up?'

'No, I can't move my left arm or shoulder, you'll have to find a ladder – Where is Krell?'

'He's gone, smashed his way through the room and out into the pond. One of the officers is very badly injured, the other has gone for help...'

'Inspector Choudhury is dead', said Sam, struggling for breath. 'We have got to see where that beast Krell goes,' he shouted.

The second officer returned with medical staff who rushed to the injured officer's aid. Joyce clambered up the stairs into the main basement to retrieve a metal ladder, before lowering it into the tunnel entrance.

With his outstretched good arm, Sam was just able to grab the base of the ladder, and despite his excruciating pain, he managed to hold on as hospital staff pulled him up, mauling him into the turbine room.

The blare of the radio belonging to the able bodied officer could be heard, the familiar sound of Raju's voice reverberating around the room as the Superintendent bellowed instruction after instruction, such was the alert.

Not relenting, refusing any treatment, Sam signaled Joyce to go with him and get after the monster, Krell. They raced through the hospital corridors and headed out of the rear entrance before clambering down the familiar steps and through the gateway onto the concourse of the Surya Kund.

The alert had just reached the officers on the bridge leading down to the river bank when they spotted Krell's gruesome, disheveled figure striding over the wooden frame. Three officers tried to draw their firearms, but exasperation ensured that two of them did not succeed, the third drew hastily and misfired. The shot was heard and a cry of disbelief rang out from the few remaining members of the public nearby. One or two began to panic and run in all directions, and those near the bridge scattered, jumping down onto the concourse or down onto the dried part of the river bed, injuring themselves as they did so.

The officer who had fired his weapon and missed, turned and fled at the sight of the giant man surging towards him. The other two held their ground on top of the bridge, but it was no use. Failing to draw their weapons was to their detriment and Krell ploughed into their feeble bodies, using his enormous fists to strike them both into their chests. He then scooped them up with his huge arms, pushing their bodies against each other, before he flung them both, entwined, towards the river base, some three metres below. They hit the ground hard, both writhing about in tremendous pain amongst the mud and stones.

*

In the distance the chop, chop of the Dhruv helicopter rotor blades could be heard. The machine was close to the ground, churning up dust and sand from the dry parts of the river bed as it scurried along, skimming the surface at full speed. Raju had spent the last twenty minutes trying to track the giant hermit, Taraka, who had given them the run around. The pilot and the four heavily armed officers in the back of the helicopter were silent as Raju barked orders over the radio, furious at hearing of the death of his good friend Natesh Choudhury. Two further officers from the specialist group on the ground had gone missing, chasing Taraka through the surrounding woods. Raju had now abandoned that search, ordering his remaining officers to intercept Krell at whatever cost.

Taraka's diversion had worked, and Raju was beginning to realise this; his chasing team of specialist officers had been purposely and cleverly baited away from Krell. Through a series of secret tunnels and hides, not to mention his speed and guile, Taraka had managed to evade capture; more importantly Raju realised that Taraka had shown just enough of himself to keep cajoling the police into continuing the chase.

Raju and his team had lost sight of Taraka near one of the contours of the river bed, nearly a kilometre from the Surya Kund. The news of Krell's escapade and the demise of Inspector Choudhury re-focused Raju's attention, the pretend Nath would have to wait, Krell would be the target now.

The pilot of the helicopter shouted at Raju that he had spotted Krell jumping down to the river bank from the man-made wooden bridge. The helicopter was seconds away from the giant man's position. Swooping very close to the Surya Kund, hovering just one metre from the ground, the rear doors of the helicopter opened. Four men dressed in beige and black Kevlar protected fatigues, leapt out. The officers deployed in pairs, one kneeling, one standing, both teams deploying either side of the helicopter. Heckler and Koch rifles pointed at Krell, red dotting his torso and head, stopping him from moving any further.

It was not long before Sam and Joyce had seen the activity and made their way towards the mayhem as quickly as the debilitated Sam could move. They arrived at the wooden bridge just as Raju was alighting the helicopter, seeing him shout commands at the pilot to keep the helicopter on the ground but with the rotor blades turning. The Police Commander then drew his pistol and trained it angrily towards Krell, screaming at him to raise his hands.

Krell stood perfectly still on the dry river bed near to the base of the wooden framed bridge, slowly raising his arms with his palms facing outwards, half way up his body. The wry smile on his face became even more accentuated, as if it had become a permanent fixture - designed to taunt the officers in front of him.

Raju noticed the knapsack on Krell's shoulder, just making out what appeared to be a book of scripts jutting out from the top; this had to be retrieved, and Krell had to be captured at all cost. The Commander beckoned to the giant man, gesturing for him to kneel down. Krell stayed put.

'On your knees,' Raju shouted at the top of his voice. 'Get on your knees or we will fire upon you.'

Raju sub-consciously started to walk further forward, coming close to within Krell's striking range. The other officers became nervous with their Commander's actions, waving at him to step back.

'Give me the Vedic Script,' said Raju moving his left hand away from the grip of his gun, motioning for Krell to put the knapsack and Script on the ground.

Krell stared at Raju, the smile never leaving his face as he goaded the Police Commander to react; he would never comply with the policeman's instructions, he would simply wait.

At this point Raju became distracted, catching sight of Sam and Joyce on top of the wooden bridge, with Sam pointing his pistol at Krell's head. Joyce spotted the anxious look on Raju's face, instantly recognising that Sam's incensed action was causing confusion and posed a real threat.

Krell caught Raju's glance and turned to see Sam

pointing the pistol at him, a little surprised at Sam's courage. Sam gathered his thoughts and stooped down on the bridge, Joyce helping him to move further back, away from the line of fire.

The police helicopter still roared by the river bed, the noise and dust testing concentration as the officers tried to remain focused, training their weapons on Krell. Raju desperately wanted to see him restrained and couldn't afford to prolong the spectacle any longer. Krell started to become furtive again, looking anxiously around him, searching from left to right. He looked across the river bed and to his right he noticed the small clump of Shisham trees near to the entrance of the tunnel he had exited earlier. *Could he run for it?* Perhaps not. If he charged at the policemen he could destroy them for sure, but would he be quick enough? The volley of fire might bring him down…and he was not immortal…not quite yet anyway. *And where was Taraka?*

Sam lay prone on the bridge, turning his nauseatingly painful body to rest on his right side, exasperated at the sight of this hideous man called Krell. Nothing Sam had ever encountered was akin to this bizarre circumstance – *who was Krell? What was his real goal? And where on Earth had he come from?*

An order for his men to fire was on the tip of Raju's tongue, although it was not his way, and yet the prospect of being able to restrain Krell with any number of officers was going to be impossible.

A decision either way was abruptly taken out of the Police Commander's hands.

First to spot the strange movement coming from

the north, along the edge of the dry river bed, was Joyce. She screamed at Sam, who despite being in agony, managed to prop himself up and cast his eyes on the approaching absurdity. He and Joyce waved frantically at Raju who was still absorbed in confronting Krell.

'What the hell is that?!' screamed Joyce.

'Raju! Raju! For God's sake look, look over there!' shouted Sam, waving even more furiously.

Eventually Raju turned his head to the left, staring in utter disbelief at what appeared to be a swirling dust cloud heading towards them at great speed. Even Krell was distracted, although he knew what it would be. At first many thought that it might be the police officers travelling in the all-terrain vehicle, but as the image moved ever closer, something different, something profoundly horrific started to emerge.

No-one was able to comprehend the approaching, fearsome sight, yet Krell did – and *it was about time*, he thought. Others started to lose all sense of reason, the police officers unable to keep their weapons trained on Krell.

The dust settled from around the approaching vision, revealing the colossal, grotesque figure of Taraka. He was still adorned in the hessian robe, which was now heavily soiled in dust, yet he was not stooped anymore – rather bolt upright, taller than ever, running in great strides at the speed of a horse it seemed. A horrific supernatural being was in their midst, terror and panic gripping everyone.

A cumbersome volley of gunfire rained upon Taraka, having no affect either on his speed or his countenance, and this fact alone made the two officers near him try to flee – but they were caught with one swoop of the monster's hand, sending them both crashing to the ground, heads buried into the mud and dirt. Krell was now invigorated and stood proud, relishing the presence of his Mentor, in awe of his evil prowess and unequalled power.

Although fearing for his own life, Raju had kept his firearm pointed at Krell, and in an instinctive reaction he fired four shots towards him, two of the bullets thudding into Krell's chest causing him to fall heavily onto the dusty ground. As he fell, the Atharva-Veda Script loosened from his knapsack, falling not more than a metre away from his torso.

The pilot of the helicopter screamed as he saw the near three-metre tall monster grab the tail of the aircraft, preventing it from yawing from side to side. In an effort to climb, the pilot pulled back the joy stick, but it was no use; the front of the helicopter reared up out of control before arcing away from the bridge as Taraka held the tail, pinning it down. Everyone watched in absolute terror as the machine hit the river bed on its side causing the rotor blades to churn into the muddy earth sending sand, rock and water scattering everywhere.

Managing to stand, Sam precariously stepped down the wooden framed bridge towards Krell, unsuspecting that Joyce would rush past him to jump down onto the sandy part of the river bed and grab the Vedic Script. Krell had started to stir and was attempting to get to his feet, the impact of the bullets wearing off as if he had been miraculously cured.

In a futile attempt, Raju and the other officers

continued to fire at Taraka; all of them unable to compute the monster's unnatural height and bulk as he wrapped his gigantic arms and hands around the tail of the helicopter. Taraka's snarling evil face, with his hooked nose, protruding teeth and sunken black eyes, made Raju think he was in the very bowels of Hell. Worst of all was the noise that the monster made, a hideous grinding, nauseating sound which seemed to emanate from Taraka's whole body as he turned the helicopter further onto its side, pushing it deeper into the river bed – it was the sound of a beast, a beast from a most hideous nightmare.

Taraka impaled the helicopter deeper into the ground, the blades buckling and breaking as they churned, causing the engine to finally shudder to a halt. The pilot's screams could no longer be heard.

Joyce had put herself in danger and although she had reached the Vedic Script first, she had narrowly missed a swipe from Krell's fist as he saw, out of the corner of his eye, what she was doing. The Script was lying open, its layers of bound papyrus flapping in the mild breeze. Without a moment's hesitation Joyce picked up the Script and moved closer towards Taraka, displaying it above her head in the direction of the monster, intending for him to see what she was doing. The beast let go of the helicopter tail and turned to Joyce with such demonic ferocity, she near ran for her life.

Yet, she had sensed something with the Vedic Script and she was not going to let go, after all - *why hadn't Taraka charged at them?* she thought. *The same reason the monster had sent Krell to steal the Script*, she further surmised.

The test was all too plain to see; the others, including Krell, remained motionless, trapped in a vortex of time as the scene seemed to play out in slow motion. To everyone's incredulity, Joyce walked even closer towards Taraka, all the while keeping the Script aloft. The effect was astonishing, the creature reeled backwards snarling and bellowing, his evil face contorted and grimacing even more so as the challenge presented itself.

'I will crush you all, you pathetic, futile beings, you know nothing, you think you are all so clever, my time has come and you will all suffer!' growled Taraka, his voice sounding anything but human.

'That's far enough, Joyce,' shouted Sam. 'No further! Whatever you are doing seems to be working.'

'Look! He is afraid of the Script,' said Raju in disbelief.

'Yes, that's why he has used Krell to steal it, he dared not enter the Temple vault himself or touch the Script,' Joyce shouted.

Taraka was enraged at the revelation and without hesitation, catching all off guard, the beast buried his fists forcibly into the ground, sending huge chunks of broken earth, mud and silt in all directions. Joyce fell to the ground, releasing the Vedic Script as she tried to protect herself, and Sam fell on his back hitting the wooden slats of the bridge - whilst Raju and his remaining standing officers also stumbled heavily, losing control of their weapons.

Krell saw his opportunity and pounced on the fallen Script, noting that it had opened on the very page he had been after, the 53rd verse. He grabbed the text and ripped out the individual papyrus sheet before sprinting away, heading back north along the line of trees.

Taraka roared and snarled at those around him before bounding off at great speed, surging ahead of Krell and making towards the clump of Shisham trees where one of the entrances to his labyrinth lay.

Sam lay almost motionless on his back, breathing regularly but in searing pain, he had fallen on his dislocated shoulder and had almost passed out. Joyce quickly went to him, cradling him, holding his hand as he lay on the bridge.

'We'll get you sorted Sam,' she said with affection. 'It's not as if there isn't a hospital close by,' she smiled.

'How did you know what to do?' said Sam.

'It just made sense. Why would Taraka not fetch it himself? No-one would have been able to stop him. Diverting some of the police whilst Krell stole the Vedic Script from the vault was very clever, but I suspect that the Atharva- Veda is a spiritual Hindu Mantra and may have a power or spell over Taraka's evil,' said Joyce.

Raju meanwhile was very solemn; the two officers who had been struck by Taraka had been killed and the two officers who had been crushed by Krell were still alive but needed attention quickly. The commotion would have been seen by others, despite so many watching the ceremony of the Ratannath Baba Avatar, and the Police Superintendent would have to gather his wits, first gathering medical staff and other officers to the scene before contemplating how to explain what had just happened.

The Atharva-Veda was picked from the ground, Raju dusting off the sand, grateful at least that it had been recovered - but what of the stolen page? Answers were needed and there was only one person he could seek who would provide such knowledge, the resident Guru-Nath.

Chapter 15

Too Much for the Eye

It wasn't that Sam could not comprehend what he had seen, his feelings were directed more, upon reflection, to an absurd notion that he had revelled in the supernatural debacle. It was as if, deep down in his soul, an expectancy had come to fruition, one which had coiled around his belief, and one which had given him an answer to many of his self-perpetuating questions. Although he would give the impression to others that all such manner of supernatural things was hokum, his hidden conscience told him something else.

As he lay on his bed in the crowded Devi Patan Temple Hospital, he drifted in and out of consciousness, his thoughts constantly shifting from what he perceived would be an inevitable police inquisition to that of him attempting to philosophise what he had seen.

Incomprehensible would have been the sight of Taraka for most people, but somehow not for Sam, not if he reflected and thought deeply enough. *Was it confirmation that there is a world outside of our own?* he thought, *a world of gods and spirits who roamed within and beyond the realm of the Earth?* he further considered. He could not suppose what kind of being Taraka was, nor could he suppose who or what Krell was either. If, as Sam thought, there was an evil spiritual domain, then there had to be a good one too – surely there would have to be a balance, a natural order of things?

It was the afternoon on the day after the arrival of the Ratannath Baba Avatar, the ancient doll representing the founding Priest of the Devi Patan Temple. People were still milling around and celebrating, with much hustle and bustle throughout the complex. Sam had been operated on, his left forearm and his left shoulder needed re-setting under anaesthetic, such was the force used by Krell when slamming Sam onto the floor of the vault.

His conscious periods were becoming longer; on occasion he managed to sit up in bed listening to the reports on TV about the extraordinary events occurring just outside of the Surya Kund. Many witnesses were unsure of what they had actually seen, whilst others had supposed it may have been a Bollywood movie set, which had gone disastrously wrong. Some people even reported that one of the Mela procession elephants had run amok, causing the helicopter to be destroyed in the process – but all that was said was assumed, no-one could have imagined the truth.

A minority talked about the myth of the giant hermit, a beast who had almost passed into folklore, a creature who had not been seen or spoken of for many years; something which the police played down. Sam watched Raju strain with the official police statement on the local TV channel, deflecting any questions on terror, mad men and beasts – preferring instead to rest with 'an open mind' on the investigation.

Afternoon passed into early evening and the Mela celebrations became a little noisier again, people remaining a little curious about the helicopter crash, whilst most were still trying to get a glimpse of the Avatar in the Temple. Sam awoke from a short sleep, feeling someone gently holding his unbroken arm. It was Joyce, and she was smiling warmly; he smiled back, relieved to see her.

'You were so brave,' said Sam croaking his voice. 'How we came out of that, I do not know.'

'You were brave too Sam,' said Joyce, staring into his dark brown eyes.

Sam looked gaunt and tired; the hint of grey hair on the sides of his head seemed to be more pronounced, and although Joyce felt sorry for him at that moment, she had started to feel a deeper affection for him. Sam had started to feel the same for her; not only was she beautiful but she was so intelligent and unbelievably courageous - his admiration for her was immeasurable.

Doctors and nurses were busy everywhere and Sam felt at ease in the clean, fresh surroundings of the ward, with fresh linen on the bed together with the clean cast on his arm and the clean bandages around his torso, the staff had done their utmost to make him comfortable. He caught sight of a cleaner polishing the ward floor next to the beds of the injured police officers, and he felt a wave of pity.

'What now?' he said.

'We need to think,' said Joyce. 'We must presume Krell and Taraka have what they came for, their next action may decide what we do.'

'Why did they leave the main part of the Script, why didn't Krell just take it all?'

'I can only surmise that Krell tore out part of the Atharva-Veda that relates to a certain verse which they needed, that together with Taraka's fear of the whole Script. The main Script has now been given back to the Guru-Nath by Raju. The Guru-Nath is the religious leader of the Nath Sect, and he is only one of a few who have the knowledge on how to decipher the true meanings of the verses within the Script.'

'We need to obtain that knowledge, we need to speak to such a leader, and fast.'

'Someone has already done that,' said Joyce.

'What do you mean?' said Sam.

Joyce said nothing; she just smiled and turned her head around to face the ward entrance. Walking along the ward corridor, towards Sam's bed, was a figure he recognised. A woman dressed in an orange sari with her beautiful face shrouded in a brilliant white hijab, it could only be one person. His heart leapt for a moment, pleased at who he saw, but feeling entirely confused; he could only lie on his bed in disbelief as the person stood beside him.

'Anippe?' Sam whispered. 'You came to us, why are you here?'

'Joyce contacted me,' said Anippe, tears welling, as she cast her eyes over his battered body. 'She phoned me straight away, as soon as you had been brought here to the hospital. I got a flight from Cairo to Delhi in almost no time, then I chartered out to Balrampur, it cost me a little,' she laughed.

Once again, Sam was endeared by Anippe's wonderful broad smile as she spoke. It was infectious, and both he and Joyce couldn't help but be enamoured by her presence once again.

'We haven't much time Sam,' said Anippe. 'Joyce introduced me to Raju who then arranged for Joyce and I to meet the Sri Guru-Nath, the leader of the Nath Sampradaya Sect, they are the people who protect the Vedic Scripts contained within the Devi Patan Temple.'

'The sub-sect of the Nath, they live and work in tunnels and caves, that bit I do remember,' said Sam, still relishing Anippe's presence.

'The Guru-Nath is from a long line of Nath spiritual leaders. He is a descendant of the Ratannath Baba whose Avatar has been celebrated during the Mela. I spoke to the Guru in his Temple chamber.'

Joyce became agitated and had to speak.

'The Guru was a miniature version of Taraka. He had the same dark oily skin, exposing his upper torso - and his hair was the same, sporting a long grey beard and head hair wrapped and coiled on top of his head, he was a nice man but his similar appearance was a little disturbing.'

'And the Atharva-Veda Script?' asked Sam.

'He spent time looking at it in front of us. I informed him who I was and what was at stake. In the end he was forthcoming with his knowledge,' said Anippe.

'And what of the stolen page?'

'It contains a special text from the 53rd verse of the sixteenth chapter, a charm which, ordinarily, would be ten lines in length. Yet the Guru-Nath stated that the stolen verse is unique, unlike any other copy, and has an extra three lines. I have no doubt these were the lines sought after by Taraka and Krell,' said Anippe.

'I wonder - how did the Priest know of this?' said Sam.

'The Guru-Nath has spent a lifetime studying it, he knew exactly what was on the missing page,' said Joyce.

Anippe collected her notes. The Guru-Nath had verbally given them the three verse lines, reciting them in the original Sanskrit. Joyce was a little unsure of the verse context, but Anippe had managed to grasp it all, deciphering its meaning. Her devout studies over the years had proven useful.

'The whole verse is about time,' said Anippe. 'Where time is designated as the primordial power. The verse or charm gives time the aspect of immortality, telling everyone that our world and all other worlds, are merely wheels for its use. The verse goes onto say that time created the Earth and the Sun and that all creatures in Heaven and on Earth should be spiritually balanced.'

'I am intrigued, but what is the point to it all?' said Sam, eager for Anippe to continue.

'Well, this is the interesting part,' she said. 'The Vedic Scripts were written three thousand years ago, which I know was a very long time after the Egyptian King Snefru Stele was made, or certainly placed in its pyramid. You know of the Stele Sam, I told you about it.'

'I understand, but what of the connection?'

'The three missing lines seem to give an instruction, and I am sure now that they are a proclamation of the inscription on the Stele; The form of words is similar to those in the Book of the Stele…and are interpreted as such.'

"Time will allow man to travel across the drinking waters and great oceans, settling in spiritual lands across the being.

Time will honour he that shall control the spirits, giving enduring life, letting the spiritual maker endure the sight set before him.

The maker has a gift from Time, set in the Temple of Snofru in the lands of Misr – to guide the maker with the sight set before him."

Silence befell the three for a short while, each of them processing the information differently. Sam was a little bewildered, not fathoming much of it, and was relieved when Joyce spoke.

'Being means 'World',' she said. 'Snofru is another version of Snefru, the ancient Egyptian Pharaoh…and Misr is Arabic for Egypt.'

Anippe smiled, glad for Joyce to be such an ally.

'I get the feeling this is not just a man hunt,' said Sam. 'I did say I needed some more answers before we left Egypt, that is why I pressed you Anippe.'

'I know Sam - I am sorry - my worst fears have come to fruition. That's why I am here now; we will all have to work together from now on.'

'Taraka and Krell now have the details of the prophecy from the verse, and I have no doubt that they will have decoded the meaning and make for the Snefru Pyramid. That's where the Stele still rests,' said Joyce.

Anippe contemplated many things, not least of which she realised how close Sam and Joyce had come to serious harm and even death. Her deepest concern was what Taraka and Krell would do from now; she had to accept that they would know where the Snefru Stele was, and she hoped to God that the instructions she had given to her staff to have it moved were carried out.

'Get some rest Sam, I'll go for a walk with Joyce, there is much we need to plan, and besides…I want to see the Surya Kund,' said Anippe.

Walking onto the concourse, Anippe looked upon the Surya Kund with admiration, gaping at its voluminous presence, before catching a glimpse of the carnage over at the west wall where the helicopter was still strewn across the river bed, being examined by all manner of officials. Security personnel quickly halted the two women, guiding them to another part of the pond where they could sit and talk.

'I am glad we have the chance to talk, I am deeply worried about what will happen next. I have spoken to Raju and he said there is a national alert for Taraka and Krell. You know he said to me that he felt powerless and extremely remorseful that he couldn't prevent them from escaping, he feels so responsible for all the deaths,' said Joyce.

'He will do, but he should not take the blame, the issues at stake are much more than any of us could have dared to imagine. We must act now – I only hope my instructions to have the ancient Snefru Stele moved were carried out. I haven't heard anything from my team, there will be such a forbidding if Taraka and Krell place their hands on it,' said Anippe, her eyes staring into the stillness of the pond water.

'Anippe, can I ask, what is really at stake here?'

'It is something which I have set my life's work upon, something that is so powerful and mystical that I find it all difficult to comprehend at times. I feel very vulnerable now, and I should have dealt with it differently...I did not calculate the risk properly.'

'Remember what the Guru-Nath said about Taraka,' said Joyce. 'And how Taraka was supposed to have terrorised the local people for decades with his hideous deportment. He would surface from time to time, disguising himself as one of the Nath Sadhu, dressing like them and adopting their physiognomy, whilst living in the surrounding caves – all perfect conditions for Taraka to fit in with the Nath and plot his attack,' said Joyce.

'No wonder the Guru-Nath felt so ashamed, the Atharva-Veda Script had been guarded by Naths in this region for centuries, the Guru and the other Naths believing that it would always be safe. They probably knew Taraka could not touch it himself, but they were caught off guard by the arrival of Krell. The Guru-Nath should have listened to Raju and done more to protect the Atharva-Veda.'

The conversation was making Joyce turn cold, yet the discussion over the Atharva-Veda was not the worst part. Standing previously in front of the Guru-Nath in the Temple chamber, Joyce recalled the most frightening of moments when Anippe asked the old man what he thought Taraka was.

'A vile, putrid and despicable demon of the underworld, capable of all manner of atrocities,' came the reply, without hesitation.

Snapping out of her recollection, Joyce quickly changed tack.

'You are fond of Sam, are you not?' said Joyce.

Anippe turned and smiled graciously.

'I think he likes you Joyce, and you have eyes for him, I can tell.'

'I don't know...I see the way you both connect...it is wonderful to see.'

Anippe did not reply instantly, instead she was trying to think pragmatically and formulate a plan on what to do next, as forlorn as she was about the whole situation. She would suggest that Joyce and Sam should go home - to Chicago and that she would go back to Egypt to make further preparations for the Stele. Then she would come to America and join them.

'I am sorry to have said anything to you about Sam,' said Joyce.

'I don't particularly want to hide anything

anymore,' said Anippe. 'Too much has already not been said. You and Sam could have died and that would have been my fault, and it would have been a burden that I could not have coped with. There is a tumultuous test ahead, one I can hardly bring myself to comprehend. You will know soon enough Joyce. There is something important that I must tell you, but you must be sworn to secrecy. I cannot let this matter be revealed to anyone else just now, but if anything should happen to me, you alone I trust to tell the secret…do you understand? Do you promise me?'

The emotion was clear in Anippe's voice and once again the tears welled in her eyes. Her bottom lip started to quiver slightly as she moved closer to whisper in Joyce's ear.

The comments were passed and there seemed to be a delayed reaction as the enormity of the revelation sank in. Joyce reeled back in shock, placing her hands over her mouth. She shook her head in total disbelief before clutching Anippe's hands firmly and reassuringly, portraying the utmost trust.

Chapter 16

Cahokia

A cool breeze washed over Mike Tremble's face as he closed his eyes and absorbed the atmosphere of the evening. He could hear the rustle of the Red Cedar and Bald Cypress trees clumped together in their hundreds throughout the small forests, surrounding him from every direction. The swaying of the trees seemed to accentuate the air whipping around his body, making him feel alive, but at the same time enthusing a calmness and a peacefulness deep within him. Here in this sacred place he was at one with nature; in his mind he was home, standing amongst the ghosts of his ancestors in the glorious ancient city of Cahokia.

Mike stood on top of the archaic pyramidal mound, opening his eyes to look down nearly forty metres towards its tiered earthen base, which spanned a fourteen-acre perimeter and could be seen from miles around, visible even from the nearby industrial town of St. Louis lying only a few kilometres away on the banks of the broad and winding Mississippi River.

He closed his eyes again and imagined the Cahokian City to be alive as it would have been at the height of its power over eight centuries ago, attracting thousands of his brethren to live and work amongst the bustling streets, the high-rise homes and the trade centres. Men, women and children would be busy at the markets buying trinkets, exchanging food, trading animal skins and generally socialising within the dazzling plazas, perhaps gossiping about who was in the know. A hierarchal order had existed, where people would have lived in lavish thatched roofed long houses on top of their own purpose built mound of earth, with palisade walls and long steep steps leading to the uppermost tier; the bigger the house, the bigger the mound, the more you were up the social ladder.

All around him were the remnants of a once great city, with the expanse of the plazas still visible together with smaller earthen mounds that could be seen dotted all over the vastness of this now protected site. The Cedar trees and Cypress trees formed many foliage enclaves, which covered archaic mounds that had not yet been excavated, and caused Mike to wonder what further ancestral treasures and artefacts would be found. He returned to reality, casting his eyes towards the modern Visitor Centre which lay half a kilometre to the south of the giant 'Monks' Mound on which he was standing. A curious name for the Mound, he always thought, so called by a group of travelling monks in the 1800's, and who were people that had no clue of its historical significance, no clue that it was a prophetical beacon for its once proud citizens; a spiritual centre piece so revered that it would have been blessed as sacred ground.

Tonight that significance would be played out and Mike was nervous. He was nervous, excited and all together bursting with pride at the thought of the ancient ceremony that was about to take place on the very spot he was standing. Time was pressing now, and soon he would have to greet his guests.

He walked back along the Mound plateau, stopping for a moment to glance at the Sun which was dipping below the horizon, its diffracted orange light streaming across the St. Louis City skyline and shimmering across the waters of the nearby Horseshoe Lake. The night was set to be clear with the stars already starting to show their glittering prowess – *perfect*, Mike thought.

A special re-enactment of an ancient ceremony was to take place on Monk's Mound and importantly, for the very first time, Mike's son, Huritt, would recite the main story. There would be many tales and myths spoken on this night but Huritt would perform centre stage, with his incantation of a legend so revered within the Native American community, it would make everyone stop and listen, and be in awe.

From all around, people from the living embodiment of the Illiniweck and Mississippian Tribes would come to hear the story; people who lived and worked in places where their ancestors sought refuge after the demise of Cahokia, displaced within Southern Illinois, in the ridges and valleys of the forest creeks – near to Eagle Creek and Wolf Creek in the modern day counties of Shelby and Moultrie. They would come forward tonight and listen to the rituals of the Calumet.

The Calumet ceremony would define Mike and his family on this most prestigious of evenings and he had accordingly dressed in his traditional Native American costume, as he would be expecting most people. He wore leggings and a shawl made out of bison skin, both garments covering a breech cloth, woven from deer hair. He wore a traditional headdress of the Cahokian Tribe, which would later, he thought proudly, become adopted by the Kaskasian and Preiora Tribes of middle Illinois. The headdress was in the form of a quilled, black head band, full of multi coloured feathers and bison hair tassels knitted into his own hair, which had been cut in the traditional archaic Illinois style – spiky and short on top with very long strands either side of his head. A neatly cut feather fringe adorned his forehead, and although his hair was very grey, he had not thinned - much to his continual delight.

Once back at the impressive Visitor Centre, Mike stood in the lobby, looking around at the auditorium, bumping into acquaintances and rekindling old friendships. He waited impatiently trying to catch sight of his children, many other people coming up to him and wanting to talk with him, knowing how special this night was for his children's ascendancy into the tribal hierarchy. He found it difficult to concentrate on much of what was being said, being far too excited in the desire to find his kin. Then he saw his children, walking away from the life sized, magnificently crafted Cahokian model village at the rear of the auditorium. He shouted and they turned, walking as quickly as they could towards him, embracing him, kissing him and smiling with tumultuous excitement.

Huritt, the eldest son, shook Mike's hand firmly after their embrace, whilst Chogan and his twin sister Kimi had trouble letting go of their father, such was their affection and endearment on this proud night. All three were young and athletic, the two young men looking very similar, both being tall with handsome faces and sporting long, jet black flowing hair, very much in the beaded style of their father. Kimi was also tall and extremely athletic; she was a brilliant runner with the stamina to match any of the men. She was dressed similar to Huritt and Chogan but was wearing her matriarchal pendants made out of conch shells taken from snails collected from the river banks and lakes nearby. She also wore a braded deer skin skirt over her bison skin leggings - as a mark of traditional femininity, something for which she was a little uncomfortable about but recognised how important the garment was for such an occasion.

'I am so proud of you all, you have always retained your tribal names and for that I am eternally grateful. Tonight you will give your names to the brethren and you will recite your stories under the ceremony of the Calumet, and then all three of you will ascend into the hierarchy of the Illinois and Mississippian Tribes…and like me you will be Akima, you will be Chiefs…' said Mike, emotionally.

'What about you father, will you recite your true name or will you keep your western name in the proceedings?' said Huritt, anxiously.

'Mike is the name my western employers coined for me so long ago, and as you know Tremble is the

English version of my true name because as a small child my hands used to tremble when I tried to pull the string of the bow,' Mike said, making the others laugh. 'And I guess Mike has stuck with me…but I am the Akima of this entire region and I will honour my status with that name before I pass that privilege to you Huritt, through the Calumet recital.'

'Chogan and I are so proud of you Huritt, you will receive the Calumet tonight and then you will be the Akima elect…I may even shed a tear when this happens!' said Kimi smiling.

'I cannot imagine you shedding a tear,' said Chogan jokingly.

'Do you have the Calumet father?' said Huritt.

'Yes I have it here in my deer skin sack, I can never believe that this small feathered tobacco pipe represents such a symbol of power…it represents both the God of Peace and of War, although most believe it is the true bringer of peace.'

'I hope so - are you ready for the dance of the Calumet Huritt?' shouted Chogan enthusiastically.

'He will have to be, but don't forget, my reign of the Calumet ritual being handed over applies to all three of you, you will all have to dance tonight.'

'And will you dance too father?' said Kimi.

They all laughed nervously.

Everyone bid their temporary farewell as Huritt and his two siblings went off to make final preparations for their recitals. Huritt in particular had the most important test, and his story would have to be chanted in a gracious voice to honour the most revered legend in Illinois tribal history.

Mike felt a little lost seeing his kin depart but soon spotted the face he had been wishing to see. James Campbell was standing by a gallery of drawings and paintings, right next to the book shop on the opposite side of the auditorium. Mike's elderly friend was staring at a particular painting and seemed unable to cast his eyes away from it, even at the point when Mike tapped him on the shoulder and greeted him, James was hardly able to turn his head.

'This painting is morosely captivating,' said James. 'I don't think I have ever seen a portrayal of a beast that looks so human in one instance, yet so demonic in another…I presume you are able to tell me what it is?'

Mike felt uneasy, finding himself momentarily transported to a different place, away from the hubbub of the Visitor Centre, to a place which frightened him, finding it difficult to talk about.

'I am glad you came James, this means a lot to me, you are one of my most trusted friends and tonight's celebration with my children, I think you will find both fascinating and exhilarating. You should see the gathering of my kinsmen and women on the top of Monk's Mound already, I shall be so proud later on,' said Mike deflecting the conversation.

'The name on the base of the picture frame…it says, 'The Piasa'. Wasn't that the name of the folklore beast you mentioned at my house?' said James, engrossed.

Mike sighed. 'It is a gruesome picture, that I must say. And yes, it is a modern depiction of the beast we call 'The Piasa'. Many stories abound of it James…it found its way into Illinois tribal folklore hundreds, perhaps even thousands of years ago, although down the years I fear its mystical presence has been somewhat contorted. My ancestors would have drawn and carved similar images on cave and rock walls, but as I recall, history notes that the Jesuits introduced the depiction of the Piasa to the New World colonialists in the 1600's. They discovered a painting on a rock wall just outside the homestead of one of the local tribes, and within a short space of time they aligned it to a portrayal of their own demons, perhaps the Devil himself.'

'Well you could see why at the time. The Christian religious fervor was reaching a peak and I am sure the Jesuits would have used this image to put the fear of God in people,' said James.

'I can only presume so. What I do know is that it still remains an important part of my ancestral history and beliefs. We believe in the supernatural, it is what binds us and makes us grateful for what we have - but we do believe that there is also a darker side, a demonic world that can haunt our very existence. I stare at this painting with you and I feel that fear, which to you must sound a little crazy,' said Mike, wishing to walk away and return his mind to the forthcoming ritual.

'You are steeped in fine traditions and beliefs, it is not my place to say anything other than you must be so proud of your lineage and your customs, as I am of mine. I would never question anyone's beliefs…I will always remain open minded about what higher powers may exist.'

'Let us go James, the ceremony is imminent and I must find my place, please stay with me on this most sacred of nights.'

*

The two men climbed the long wooden steps across the gigantic two-tiered grass covered Monk's Mound. All around people passed them, to and fro, excited at the prospect of being at such an auspicious occasion. Children ran on ahead climbing the steps as fast as they could, leaving frustrated parents behind trying to calm them. Revered elders acknowledged Mike's presence and James lost count of the times his old friend was referred to as Akima.

Out of breath, the two elder men reached the top of the Mound, which looked huge, the plateau expanding over two hundred metres in length. There were masses of people, mostly dressed in Native American costume, with an array of animal skin clothes, coloured shawls, elaborate beaded necklaces and finely threaded garments, the likes of which James had never seen before. People were gathered in circular rows around a centre piece of which James couldn't quite see just yet, and many men and women were already chanting prior to the actual ceremony, causing James to wonder if he had actually stepped back in time. The night was very clear and James felt a little out of place with his raincoat and canvass trousers, not to mention his trusty old desert boots – although he had not wanted to take a chance with the cool April air.

'You are wise to wear your coat James. You must think of me and my sons when we have to remove our upper garments to reveal our bear chests for the ceremony, my aged body will not be a good sight,' laughed Mike.

'This is truly fascinating, tell me more of what happens here Mike.'

'Well it is our story, it defines who we are as a people, and although the tale has passed into legend, it is still one that embodies and enriches the existence of all the surrounding tribes. Most of us can trace our ancestral roots to the time and place you will hear of tonight.'

'What happens to you, and what of your sons and daughter?'

'You may have caught a glimpse of the centre piece in the middle of the Mound, you will see it more clearly in a moment. That is where I will present the sacred Calumet pipe to my eldest son Huritt and he will recite the story by heart. Then all three of my children will be accepted into the hierarchy of the tribes, with each taking their place as an Akima in their own right.'

'But the story?' said James.

'You will hear more of it soon. It is our most sacred story, a story of epic heroinism. There was once a beautiful Cahokian Princess who saved our people, she was called the wise or beautiful woman... her name was Nadie, and she was 'The Maker'.'

*

A concerned Carl Walters was desperately trying to finish writing his notes from the conversation he had had with Sam on the telephone, forgetting to ask whether Sam had informed his father, James, of his plight whilst in India; Walters was not in favour of informing James of Sam's demise himself, and now he was late for the Native American ceremony, which Mike Tremble had insistently asked him to attend.

He clambered hastily into his Range Rover and set off along the Saint Louis Highway, a journey to Monks Mound just short of three kilometres from his home in Collinsville. Hearing Sam's voice on the phone had pleased him, although the portrayal of what had happened sounded horrific. Sam and the others had most definitely had a near death experience, and Walters could not have coped with another police officer death. A second CPD officer, Elaine Marston, had died of her injuries just twenty-four hours ago. The fact that Krell was still on the loose, along with the purported man beast Taraka, sounded incomprehensible and he felt unsure on how to prepare next.

Walters could only hope that Sam and Joyce would return home as quickly as possible; their experience would be vital in any preparation over the next day or so, depending on where and when Krell and Taraka would reveal themselves.

*

Five minutes to go before the ritual, Mike placed himself in the line of people within the inner circle, who were all stood around a huge animal hide mural, the mural itself placed on the ground central to the proceedings. Directly opposite Mike stood Huritt, and either side of Huritt were Chogan and Kimi, all poised for the ritual. James stood next to Mike, excited for them but at the same time implicitly curious at Mike's previous comments about 'The

Maker'. James wasn't sure if the comments were inadvertent and were not meant to be said; however, the coincidence of such a term and the connection to a name he had heard so many years before, when standing in the secret vault of the Snefru Pyramid, seemed too uncanny. For now, he would say nothing, he would watch, listen and learn and support his old friend in this glorious moment.

An extraordinary pictorial representation adorned the mural, which looked alive with its detailed drawings of a wolf and a bear in a calamitous battle, surrounded by tribal warriors with their spears and bows pointing towards the fighting beasts. A village scene, looking rather like the mounds and longhouses of Cahokia, was set in the background, whilst central to the depiction was a painting of a tall female warrior, dressed in flamboyant regalia and jewelry, her long black hair flowing across her back. She was pointing her bow and arrow at the gigantic, petrifying black bear, gesturing towards her warriors to stand defiantly against the onslaught of such evil.

'The figure of the tall lady is our beloved Princess Nadie, the saviour I told you about James. She was a warrior Princess, believed to be a descendant of one of the great Cahokian Chiefs. We honour her tonight in the ceremony of the Calumet.'

'You called her 'The Maker', I am curious as to why she was referred to by that name,' said James.

'She was the maker and giver of all things, she was believed to have power beyond all imagination…' Mike stopped short.

Three Native American men dressed in the

traditional Illinois tribal attire, sat cross legged with a small conical drum in each of their laps. The leader of the three nodded to Mike and shouted, 'Time now Akima!'

Mike removed his shawl and placed it neatly on the ground next to James. He removed the Calumet pipe from his knapsack and stepped onto the large circular mat, opening his arms out wide, holding the pipe in his right hand as he turned 360 degrees to catch the eye of all the people surrounding him. He composed himself, drew breath and spoke as voluminous as he could.

'My brethren, my friends, my family, honoured guests and all visitors…welcome to Cahokia. Welcome to our most reverent of ancient Native American sites. Tonight is the ritual of the Calumet, the pipe of peace, here in my right hand. The drums will play and we will chant, as my son Huritt - so named because he is 'Handsome' - recites the story of our ancestral Princess, the beloved and most revered Nadie. She gives us strength and power, and she gives us peace, peace to all men and women, and to the sacred creatures of this land. And my son Chogan – so named because he is like the 'Blackbird' – together with my daughter Kimi – so named because she is our 'Secret', will pay homage with Huritt. Tonight through this ritual we are one family, *Mihtohseeniaki* - my people…let us begin!'

Huritt stepped onto the mural, his muscular torso on display along with his intricate tribal tattoos. He was visibly pumped and eager for the ritual to begin; Mike walked towards his son and passed the feather lined smoking pipe to him, shouting the command.

'*Ninkwihsa*…my Son - take the Calumet, be all knowing and powerful…do honour to our beloved heroine, Princess Nadie.'

They bowed to each other and Mike walked slowly backwards away from the mural, returning to the line from which he came, shouting to all those gathered and pointing to Huritt - '*Iiliniwita…Iiliniwita…*he is a man!'

The drums started to play and the crowd chanted in low, mellow voices so that the high chant of Huritt could be heard. The story of the great illustrious Princess Nadie unfolded as Huritt conversed in the old Miami-Illinois Native American language, dancing around the mural display as he sang the recital.

After a short while, Chogan and Kimi joined Huritt and chanted parts of the story in support of their elder brother, as the Calumet was passed between them in a symbolic gesture of friendship and peace.

Relieved that the ceremony had started, Mike was a little startled when he turned to James and saw Walters standing there right beside him. The policeman was out of breath, having forced himself through to the front of the crowd.

'At least I won't have to translate the story twice,' said Mike catching their attention. 'I am glad you made it Carl, I was beginning to wonder.'

'I do apologise Mike…how do you do James? Good to see you both so soon, how is the ceremony going?' said Walters.

'Huritt has not long started…he chants now about the heroic Princess Nadie and how she saved our ancestral village from evil, and how before she saved the village she had found love with an African Prince who, like her, had become a slave in the Eastern colonies. They had a child called Asemota, given such a name from the African Benin shores meaning 'God has answered my case'. Asemota too became a slave, but Nadie escaped back to her people in the far-away lands of the Illini, only to return many years later to rescue Asemota when he had come of age. Not long after her final return to the ancestral village with her son, there was a great battle with the Manitous, the great spirit beasts.'

'It is a proud tale and an emotional one it seems,' said James.

Walters watched and listened, yet seemed to be mesmerised and fixated on one particular part of the mural image. Worried about being noticed, he quickly shifted his gaze towards Huritt and the dancing spectacle.

Then his cell phone rang and he answered it nervously, moving away from the crowd.

'Nadie died in that battle, bringing peace to the land. Then the Akima made the land sacred in Nadie's honour and moved his people further west, away from the colonialists. After Nadie's death, Asemota left the village, some say he later died of grief for his mother, some say he took on his mother's spirit, others say he was destined to travel the wilderness in eternal strife - but no one really knows...' said Mike, noticing Walters sloping away.

'He seems distracted - I wonder if it is about Sam?' said James.

'Go and see him. The main chant has almost finished, we will catch up shortly I am sure,' said Mike.

The crowd bustled with excitement as the drums seemed to play ever louder, and Huritt, along with his brother and sister, recited the final chants to their story of Nadie and Asemota. The people around the mural, whooped and hollered and started to join in with the chanting.

James belied his 82 years, scurrying after the policeman with sure foot, catching him before Walters had chance to descend the Mound.

'Do you have news from Sam, I have not heard from him, nor can I get hold of him,' James shouted.

'He is fine, he and Joyce are making their way to Delhi Airport to come home. Sam has been injured, but he is walking ok,' said Walters pensively.

James was unsure on how hard to press for information, although it was his son he was enquiring about and his eagerness could only be thwarted to a certain degree. The retired reporter detected an air of unease with the Police Chief, similar to that which he had witnessed the other day at James' home. Although grateful for the shared concern, James detected something more underlying; there was a reddening in Carl Walters' eyes and the policeman's face appeared gaunter than ever before.

'But what about Krell, did Sam and the Police in India manage to catch him?'

'No', said Walters. 'That's what I am afraid of…and the fact that Krell has someone with him, someone just as evil and powerful.'

'Taraka?' said James, intuitively.

Walters said nothing further and placed his cell phone in his jacket pocket, looking nervously over James' shoulder and back towards where Mike Tremble was standing. A bewildering nod between the two other men made James curious, and his curiosity was further fueled when Walters abruptly brushed passed him to make a beeline for the old Native American Chief.

A raucous ceremony now ensued as the new Chiefs were inaugurated, large groups of people gathering around Huritt, Chogan and Kimi, praising them and respecting their new privilege. Mike had watched on with pride, yet his attention was now drawn to Walters; he would leave his children to relish the night - more pressing matters were now at hand.

Walters and Mike walked away from the crowd and quickly traversed the steps heading out to the vast Plaza at the base of the Mound. They were spotted, James not relenting in his pursuit after them – perhaps they had forgotten he was there, or their intention was to ignore him and lose him from their sight, either way, James had to see what they were up to.

It was hard to keep up, the older man just making out that Mike and Walters were heading out towards a dark wooded area on the south side of the open Plaza. James kept his distance, trying not to lose sight of his friends, concerned as he watched them disappear behind a small mound nearly a kilometre away from Monks Mound.

A large expanse of small trees and thicket coiled around what appeared to be a rusty old barbed wire fence at the rear of the smaller mound, preventing James from venturing further. Instead he doubled back a little and hid behind a large Red Cedar tree in a small expanse of open land; he felt sure that the other two would reappear, and then he would confront them.

As he stooped behind the tree, his mind raced, trying to fathom the sudden turn of events. It was as if Mike and Walters had become totally oblivious to the Calumet ceremony, and now in this secret of places, James had no idea what they may be up to - *and why wouldn't they tell him what they were doing?* He did not have to wait long before they re-emerged.

The two figures stepped out from the shadow of the small mound, clambering through a gap in the barbed wire and foliage. Mike was carrying something, a holdall of some sort, although at first glance it appeared to be made of animal hide, James wasn't sure. They approached his position and James automatically leapt out from behind the tree, shouting for them to stop. They were clearly startled, mouths wide open at first, either unable to speak or not knowing what to say, perhaps shocked that James had had the guile and tenacity to follow them.

'I take it you were going to explain to me what you are doing, or is it none of my business? You will have to forgive me but my concern for my son is paramount and I would like some answers. I get a sense that something more is going on and the confusion is fueling my concern…pray tell gentlemen?!' said James, forcibly.

The other two men looked at each other, both appearing disheveled, covered in earthen thicket and soil. Walters was the least out of breath and it was he who was the most capable of speaking.

'James, I apologise for our behavior, but I need a favour – a favour that is out of the ordinary and one which I know will seem quite obscure.'

'If you would endeavour to give me some answers and ensure that my son is to return home safely, then I may consider it.'

'I need you to take Mike to your home and allow him to stay there for a day or two. I will join you some time tomorrow. Sam should be home by then, along with Joyce Marsh too. The Egyptian lady, Anippe Khu, is flying out from Egypt, she has asked to be collected from Chicago Airport mid-morning, tomorrow – I will have to ensure that this is done. Please will you help, for all our sakes?'

The last plea from Walters was startling and James believed him. The look in the eyes of both Mike and Walters was fearful, full of dread, instilling a similar feeling within James. The old reporter was perplexed but considered that he would have to go along with what was being asked of him, after all he had no real reason to mistrust them.

Walters ran off towards the Visitor Centre, disappearing out of sight very quickly; Mike stayed with James, a deep furrow on the old Native American's brow - *the prophecy had returned*, Mike thought, and his people must be prepared. *The Piasa will come and he will know the secret of 'The Maker'!*

Chapter 17

Darkness Falling

Krell felt mightily powerful, as if he had been given the key to roam the world at will, conquering and devouring all before him. Taraka, the Beast, had lain a path for him, one which Krell would change the destiny of the world forever, if he was to become the Pottery Maker. Finally, the elusive sought after secret of *'The Maker'* had been revealed by the Snefru Stele, and it was now in their hands, as was the hidden legacy of The Cloth.

Thousands of years had passed for this chance to be beholden, a chance revealed by the appearance of Taraka, a true demon conjured by the forces of evil – and now Krell knew who Taraka really was. For the Demon was *'The Piasa'*; Taraka was the very same vile creature, vomited upon this world by the opposing dark forces of nature.

Jeremiah Krell had witnessed Taraka basking in all of his own grotesque glory, and Krell had been in awe of the hideous spectacle the Beast had displayed. The incident at the Devi Patan had only been a foretaste of what was to come at the Snefru Pyramid.

The Jesuit pretender had been taken under Taraka's wing, flying aloft with the Beast in the stratosphere as if the Demon was some strange mystical dragon, bending time and space it seemed, before arriving at Dahshur amongst the ancient Egyptian pyramids. Night had fallen and no-one would have seen or comprehended the presence of the supernatural being, with its prodigy astride, as they descended from upon high to land in the desert at the speed of a shooting star.

The power and might of the Demon had smashed the walls of the Snefru Pyramid before Krell had entered the secret chamber and taken the sacred Stele. Military guards had been mercilessly killed during the attack, suffering the full exorbitant rage of Taraka as he roared and ravaged to gain the spoil.

In a defiant stance, Taraka had evilly embraced the enlightened secrets of The Maker, exuberantly cradling the Stele to his chest in a ghoulish gesture of defiance. Then he had soared to the edge of space in a furious rage, crushing the prophetic stone to dust in his giant claws, letting it scatter in the high winds of the Earth.

It seemed nothing could stop them now.

The confrontation with The Pottery Maker would be their next goal, to finally steal the one true 'Parchment' and claim the sacred right to the prophecy.

Soon they would travel once again from Taraka's Lair, flying high to the ancient Cahokian lands, where they would do battle – fighting beyond redemption to capture the prize. Then, and only then, could the forbidding power of The Piasa be unleashed and wreak havoc amongst mortal men and women.

Chapter 18

All Things Considered

Sunday morning arrived, Balrampur time, ten days after the brutal attack and subsequent deaths of what was now two Chicago Police Department officers. Once again the swish Augusta Westland helicopter swept across the clear skies of the North India territories. Sam remained in pain, ever more so as the helicopter buffeted and bounced through its long flight towards Delhi Airport, his arm and shoulder heavily strapped to try and stop any unnecessary movement. He kept his mind occupied by observing all those around him, watching a very tired Raju sitting in the front navigator's seat, making further copious notes for his full police report on the Devi Patan incident. Sat next to Sam, with her head resting on a pillow against the seat window, was Joyce, furtive of mind and restless; she too was making notes, more so to take things off her mind, as she scribbled facts and observations from the preceding events. *She'll make sense of it all somehow*, Sam thought.

His fondness of Joyce was growing daily and he smiled at her. She caught him looking and smiled back, before quickly returning to her notes, although the fondness was reciprocated, she had been reticent of her feelings because of the closeness she had seen between Sam and Anippe. She forced herself to concentrate on the matters in hand and her notes were revealing many threads to the catastrophic events, as she tried desperately to apply an element of logic to it all. She was fascinated, if not a little disturbed, by trying to decipher the obscure facts. Restraint was a virtue though; Joyce was very conscious not to reveal what Anippe had told her on the concourse of the Surya Kund. This was a startling revelation, one which she could not, and must not articulate until it was appropriate. Her main angst, shared with everyone else, was the thought of Anippe having to cope with the aftermath of the brutal and devastating circumstances of the Snefru Stele being taken. Joyce deduced that Krell and Taraka must have left for the Egyptian pyramids in Dahshur immediately after the incident at the Surya Kund - but how they had travelled so quickly to reach such a destination, she could only assume it was through some supernatural means.

Anippe had arrived at the Devi Patan and had shown real concern for Sam in particular, and Joyce sensed that this must have caused Anippe to underestimate, or not grasp, what was likely to happen in Dahshur.

Emotion can be a strange thing.

Perhaps no-one could have second guessed that the ancient Vedic Script would reveal the location of the pre-historic prophetic Stele, which was still contained within the bowels of the Snefru Pyramid. As Joyce processed these thoughts, she noticed Raju had stopped writing and was staring out of the side cockpit window. He looked solemn and full of disbelief. So many of his officers had been lost and he had so much to consider; he was indeed exhausted, beginning to wonder what fate lay in store for everyone.

Raju contemplated the difficult conversation he had had with the Guru-Nath whilst Sam was lying in a hospital bed. He was furious with the Guru for not having revealed the location of the Vedic Script – Raju could have done so much more to protect people if he had known; he would have had the Script removed. Officers may not have died, and Sam and Joyce would not have been put in mortal danger. Raju also tried to rationalise the nature of the supernatural power that he and everyone had witnessed – there was nothing anyone could have done to prepare for that. It was clear, he thought, that the Guru-Nath had true knowledge of Taraka's whereabouts and what he was capable of, and had therefore lived in intrepid fear of him. But then again Raju guessed that the Guru would have known that the Vedic Script probably protected everyone from Taraka, so perhaps the Guru was right to keep it a secret – it was all a little confusing.

For the rest of the journey silence reigned in the helicopter cabin, contemplation changing to abject tiredness, although they all wondered, fearfully, what was to come.

Delhi Airport approached and the helicopter slowed dramatically as the pilot prepared the rotor blades for hovering mode, altering the pitch through the joysticks as it descended onto the helipad, landing with a slight bump. There would be no time for pleasantries, a chartered flight out to Chicago was already waiting for Sam and Joyce, and they had only minutes to reach the plane.

'I will walk with you to the airplane,' shouted Raju at the top of his voice, guiding the two away from the incessant noise of the helicopter. He carried on shouting.

'Sorry I have not said much to you both, I have so much to think about…so many fallen comrades, it is very difficult for me. But I wanted to say thank you, you have both been so brave and I am sorry we could not capture Krell, I fear it may take much more than what we tried to do at the time.'

The Gulfstream Executive aircraft awaited, ready to take the two visitors home, quickly and safely, as Walters had ordered. Raju remained shouting, standing by the aircraft door as the attendant was trying to shut it.

'Sam you saw what we are dealing with, there is no telling what evil power Taraka could unleash, you must be careful my friends,' said Raju in exasperation.

'Anippe may hold the key to all of this and I believe she will come through for us, she will join us in Chicago as soon as she can, there is only so much she can do now after the terrible events in Dahshur. She will need to bring the Book of the Stele, that may be our saving grace…that and of course the Atharva-Veda…we need that Raju!' shouted Joyce.

Raju bowed his head in despair, 'I know, but I am

afraid the Guru-Nath has the final say on the Vedic Script, I have tried to get it from him. Understandably he and the other Nath are living in abject fear for their own and everyone else's life!'

A prompt from the aircraft crew told Raju his time was up and they were to embark. He looked forlornly at his comrades and waved as the cabin door was about to close.

'But we need the Vedic Script desperately, please Raju!' shouted Joyce once more.

The plea was heartfelt, leaving Raju with a feeling of solemnness he could not bear; he had tried so hard to keep the Atharva-Veda but for now neither his superiors or the Guru-Nath would allow it, they were far too afraid.

*

Arriving in Dahshur, Anippe walked into indefinable chaos. The King Snefru Pyramid had been attacked through the west entrance causing devastation to the tunnels and the tombs. The secret tomb, where the Prophecy Stele had been kept, was also obliterated. The Stele had been removed and discarded in a manner no one could fathom, most presumed that the precious pre-historic artefact had been annihilated in some way. Taraka and Krell must have gleaned what they had wanted, and now, terrifyingly, they would hold the secrets of the Pottery Maker.

Anippe told herself that she had failed, in so many ways – but she knew she was dealing with the forces of evil. For a person to guess that a clue to the location of the Snefru Stele might be written within the most ancient version of the Atharva Veda, was perhaps a reasonable one after all – Anippe had been searching for the clue nearly all her life, in order to protect it. Yet she had never been in a position to know exactly where the Vedic Script was hidden – and now it was too late.

Her judgement in retaining the Stele in its original place of discovery she had stood by, and those knowing of its whereabouts were sworn to secrecy – she had trusted her colleagues, although many of whom were now dead, slain at the hands of the brutal monsters whilst trying to save a legacy.

As for Krell, she presumed that he was but another Jesuit pretender, the holder of the Book of Prophecies - yet another false Jesuit who had managed to get his hands on that cursed book. Over centuries, each clue (no matter how small) when pieced together, had eventually led to this moment, helping Krell to discover what he needed, to become The Maker. To ponder over her failure to retrieve the Book of Prophecies was undoubtedly futile, nevertheless it weighed heavy on her mind.

And what of the painting stolen by Krell?

A decoy had been used – the story of the painting was just a concoction, a ruse – designed to flush out the key players, drawing Krell and Taraka out into the open and into action. Yet too many sacrifices had been made, and that is why, in her mind, Anippe thought she had failed and would fail again unless she could devise a more scrupulous approach – and she could not bear the fact that Sam had nearly died, that was never supposed to happen.

Now airborne on her very own chartered flight from Cairo to Chicago, her only thought was to prepare everyone for what was to come. In her luggage she had packed the leather bound Book of the Stele which had a full translation of the entire prophecy; she would read it again until she could no longer open her eyes if she had to.

Before boarding the airplane, the very last telephone conversation with her contact had been distraught, and now she was rushing head long into a desperate situation, one which she had no idea of the outcome. The most disturbing part of the conversation was the recognition that the Snefru Stele was the only scripture in the world which revealed the secret of The Cloth, and not even the Book of the Stele had anything transcribed within it that would reveal such a clue – this had been done for a reason.

Now, held in the palms of their evil hands, Krell and Taraka had the secret of The Cloth, the very secret that would unlock the powerful legacy of how The Pottery Maker comes to be.

Chapter 19

The Gathering

The flames flickered and danced, casting shadows across the log cabin floor, illuminating a small table adorned with clay figurines, recently having been blasted in the kiln at the base of the fire before being painted by an experienced hand. Sam stared at the fire, looking through it, as if in a trance, imagining the figurines coming to life in the background. Childhood memories surged through his mind as he fondly remembered his father's teachings on how to make such fine pottery miniatures.

Disorientated by time, not comprehending that it was still only early Sunday evening in Illinois, Sam was starting to feel very weary – the pain in his arm and shoulder fluctuating with bouts of nausea, and yet, what kept him going was the prospect of meeting the important people about to gather at his father's homestead.

Mike Tremble was already here, staying at the

behest of his father and at the specific request of Carl Walters. Mike's son's and daughter were about to arrive, as was Carl Walters himself.

A voice shouted across the tiered lawn, distracting Sam away from his gaze into the orange flame.

'Sam...Sam, Anippe has landed in Chicago, she has made it here!'

Joyce was waving frantically at him from the porch, standing on the nearest side of the old white house, facing the cabin - it was as if her comments had wrenched the very thought of Anippe out of his mind, how uncanny. He found it difficult to leave the sorcery of the flame but he was distracted further when he heard the sound of a vehicle crunching the stones along the gravel drive. Another hail came from Joyce to let Sam know Mike's kin had arrived. A black and white Ford pickup truck ground to a halt and out stepped two magnificent looking Native American men, practically identical in size and shape, both showing their muscular prowess through tight fitting grey T-shirts and blue jeans. A tall athletic young woman, beautiful in features, with dark skin and long black hair, stepped alongside the men, linking arms with them, all of them busily chatting as they stepped onto the house veranda.

The newly arrived vehicle captured Sam's attention. To the rear, covering the entire trunk space, was a taught, green tarpaulin. On closer inspection, keeping one eye on the house in case anyone returned, he gingerly lifted the tarpaulin, gaping at the sight of at least thirty or more precision made wooden bows, accompanied by hundreds of lethal looking metal tipped wooden arrows.

The bows and arrows lay neatly stacked, looking pristine and newly made. Sam touched and smelled the wood, recognising the grain and feel to be cotton wood. The craftsmanship of the bows was immaculate, with a thick centre grip and beautifully sculptured narrow ends, double spliced to give maximum flexibility and prevent cracking under the strain of the pull. The arrows were also made out of cotton wood, long and thin with a deadly sharpened iron tip spliced into the end of the shaft which was bound by woven animal hair.

Not able to inspect the find further, Sam hurriedly replaced the tarpaulin, hearing the sound of another vehicle moving slowly along the gravel drive. He turned away from the pickup truck, troubled by what he had seen; clearly the weapons had been made for a specific reason, and this was not for sport he surmised.

Walters parked his silver Range Rover very close to the truck and Sam smiled nervously in his direction. A tentative smile was returned, the look of anxiety on the face of Walters was clear to be seen, far worse than when Sam last saw him, and this was deeply concerning. A deep frown dominated Walters' face, gone completely was any sign of the gregarious nature he quite frequently displayed; it was as if a resonant fear or overwhelming burden had gripped him.

'Sorry you had to go through what you did Sam.'

'No matter, we will all soon be together, I suppose I just need a bit of honesty now, I need to get to the truth – perhaps you can help me with that. Joyce and I feel as though we may have been lambs to the slaughter…this is all a bit more than a stolen painting, and Krell, well, he was the lesser of our worries.'

'All will be revealed Sam - but we need to act quickly. Is Anippe here?'

'You are well acquainted with her then?'

'Yes, I am,' said Walters, not making any attempt to deflect the question.

'She should not be long, let me take you in,' said Sam, slightly perturbed.

The large living room to the white house could easily accommodate the gathering of people. James had adjusted the old oak furniture to allow all of those present to be seated comfortably. Daylight poured into the room from three large windows, one of those windows was facing the elaborate Japanese garden and long gravel drive.

A well-used oak bureau had its frame open, upon which was a large canvass scroll draped over the edges, paperweights preventing the scroll from rolling up again.

Huritt, Kimi and Chogan entered the room with a gleeful looking Joyce, and they were greeted warmly by both Mike and James. As ever, Mike was proud and full of joy to see his kin, his emotion difficult to hide. Joyce chatted away, trying to keep everyone distracted, before others entered the room. Sam and Walters appeared, nervously greeting everyone before their attention was drawn to other matters.

'Have you got them?' Mike said, directing his question to Huritt.

'Yes, forty of them newly made, each with twenty arrows, all in the back of the truck. There are more arrows at the site in different locations. We have spare bows too, near to the Pit.'

'What of the tribes?'

'So far thirty-five hand-picked men and women, our best archers,' said Chogan. 'Most of them are from the Cahokian and Kaskaskian groups, they are to arrive at the designated point as suggested.'

'All three of you will need to join them as soon as you can, you are their leaders and they will need strength from you tonight,' said Mike, authoritatively.

Joyce stepped back for a while, curious with the interactions. She had a view similar to James and was harbouring questions, trying to fathom everyone's intriguing role and how they were all connected. James didn't know whether or not there was a connection between his work all those years ago in Egypt and what was happening now, although he wanted answers like everyone else – he sensed only coincidences.

At the point of asking questions and satisfying his curiosity, James was drawn to the window facing the drive. A black limousine crawled slowly along the gravel, parking right next to the silver Range Rover. A slender, dark skinned lady alighted from the back seat; she was wearing very smart dark blue trousers and jacket, and a striking white hijab neatly furled around her head. Sizeable sun glasses covered her eyes but the distinctive scarring to the right side of her face could still be seen.

The old reporter's heart started to pound, it was as if he had seen a ghost; he became almost breathless, frozen in time it seemed, so much so that he did not notice Sam and Joyce leave the room to run out and greet the new visitor. They had rushed to Anippe's side, embracing her and showing her heartfelt emotion, the others all watching intently as she stepped towards the house. To James, the poise seemed so familiar and the likeness so uncanny.

*

Anippe entered the lounge and for the first time all the relevant people she had imagined were in the room, a thought shared by her and Walters with whom she tried to avoid eye contact, rather preferring to say hello to everyone else. James was transfixed and offered to show Anippe to her room so that she could freshen herself before they got started; she agreed but appeared pensive as she, quite modestly, removed her sunglasses and lowered the hijab from her hairline.

The others remained busy, analysing the scroll and chatting excitedly – all apart from Sam. He had detected his father's reaction at seeing Anippe and keen to understand more, he kept within earshot, remaining at the base of the stairs near to his father's study. James scuttled nervously up the stairs leading from the main hallway, tentatively troubled by what might be said next as Anippe followed.

The resemblance to Bektamun Ayoubi was startling, despite the scarring to Anippe's face – perhaps she was Bektamun's daughter and had followed in her mother's footsteps working for the Cairo Museum. Or was it actually her? *How ludicrous?* James thought - Bektamun would be nearly ninety years of age, being a few years older than he, a fact he remembered distinctly when they had first met. Although it was the eyes and the cheek bones, the same inherent beauty he could not disassociate from his mind.

At the top of the stairs, James opened the door to her guest room, pausing to turn around as he slowly pressed the door open. He saw her standing, shaking, unable to look him in the eye, her face lowered, looking at the carpet – he stepped closer and lifted her chin, staring intently into her large brown eyes.

'You are she, are you not?'

'My name is Anippe.'

'But you are trembling…it is you…it is you Bektamun, surely…but how can this be?' said James, his voice starting to quiver.

Anippe said nothing for a moment, she merely stared at James, barely able to contain her tears. James placed his arms gently on her waist, a gesture that was more of a plea than comfort, he was overwrought.

'There is so much you don't understand James, so much I have never said or ever had the chance to say…you see I had to protect everyone, right up until this moment. This moment, right here, right now, will define us all.'

'And Bektamun, who is she?'

'My name is Anippe Khu…...but I am her – to you James I am her, I am Bektamun.'

'My God I knew it…I could feel it when you got out of the car. How can this be, how can you be the way you are? I have not seen you for over forty-five years, I…I am lost for words.'

Sam had remained at the bottom of the stairs, unnoticed by either of them, listening intently, catching their conversation – his curiosity morphing into disbelief.

'I owe you an explanation James, but we have so much to do, there is little time and there is more I must reveal – to everyone, and I have to do it in the right way – the others will be waiting.'

'You must tell me, please – surely you can tell me how you come to be as you are, your youth? I was right to think all of this mystery was connected to those events all those years ago, when you showed me the sacred stone.'

Anippe did not answer the question, she paused. 'What of Sam?' she asked.

'He does not know, I have never told him, God knows I have tried, but I couldn't find the strength.'

'And what of your dear wife Georgia?'

'She died with some sorrow having never told him, although she begged me to tell him before she passed…she loved him so dearly, as much as any real mother would have done.'

'Now he must know, in this hour of need, he will have to know, he must know who I am and what faces him,' said Anippe, concertedly.

Gritting his teeth, Sam could barely contain his emotions at what was being said, he could only surmise at the consequences, his brain was not interpreting the facts too well, and he had no idea whether he should confront them both now; it was all just too profound.

His father had tried to tell him of an adventure in Egypt, that much he did remember but never in his wildest dreams could he have comprehended the connection with Anippe – how could he now face the others?

*

The room fell silent momentarily, an air of expectancy reverberated around the walls as Anippe poised to talk. Clearly her emotions were heightened although only some in the room may have guessed what had gone on; a tell-tale nod to Walters and a knowing smile towards Joyce were enough for those two people in particular to understand.

Sam sat away from his father, disparate emotions raging - he felt betrayed, lonely and embittered with his plight. He had fought for his very life, only now to discover he wasn't really who he thought he was. No wonder Cuba was so indifferent, no wonder his mother's family appeared so cold - they knew, they must have known all along. So if Georgia was not his mother, then who was? It could not be Anippe she was too young…surely?

'This scroll you see before you, is a smaller representation of last night's Calumet ritual, it tells the story of our beloved princess Nadie and her fight with evil. Anippe, you have the book, perhaps you can tell us all how this came to be,' said Mike, breaking the ice.

The old leather covering creaked and groaned as the Book of the Stele was opened, Anippe carefully turning the pages to the place where she wanted to start; she was grateful to Mike for having spoken first.

'Around twenty-five thousand years ago, we believe Proto-Mongolians walked from the lands of

China and Russia across The Bering Strait - bridged by the ice age - to the lands of the Americas. They brought with them the wonderful rituals and spiritual traditions that last even to this day. There are things we cannot possibly comprehend but the scroll you see and this book I have here, tell the stories of an ancient world bestowed by this spiritual aura,' said Anippe, moving through the pages of her book.

She had their attention.

'This Book of the Stele, which I have here, was written with the exact detail taken from an Egyptian Stele found within the bowels of the Snefru Pyramid in Dahshur. The hieroglyphs were painstakingly deciphered until we were sure of its most probable meaning…'

'Are you talking about the Stele I saw all those years ago? Then how old is the Stone?' said James, catching everyone by surprise.

'We believe it to be around fifty thousand years old, give or take a couple of thousand years,' said Anippe.

'That's impossible, nothing has ever been found to contain any form of writing that old…Hieroglyphs did not emerge until around six thousand years ago,' said Joyce.

Sam said nothing, only listened intently, furious and desperate for answers. Walters stayed focused on Anippe, no-one noticing a slight tear welling in his eye.

'Search your intuition Joyce, is the world the same for you as it was a week or so ago? We are in a different realm now - and all intuitive, common sense thoughts have to be discarded…what you think is impossible, may just be true,' said Anippe.

'You have said 'we' a few times…did you write the book you have?' said Sam, breaking his silence.

Annipe was taken aback and tried not to show it. That question meant only one thing…surely he must know, he must have heard the conversation between her and James. She carried on, trying to compose herself.

'All of you must understand that the prophecy contained within this book is somehow linked to the legacy of humankind…it is inextricably linked to the journey of the human race throughout the ages. The prophecy was written on the Stele and tells of an archaic ritual embedded deep within human culture as we, as a species, have travelled through time. This strange mystical ritual must have been a burden placed upon the Ice Age Proto-Mongolians and subsequently the Native Americans…'

'And what is the ritual?' said Joyce interrupting.

Anippe looked across the room. Mike and his brethren had said nothing further, and she hadn't really expected them to, it was as if they wanted the proceedings to end. Walters had also remained quiet, not taking his eyes off her, his gaunt, pale expression had not left him since his arrival – she was concerned about him but she had to stay focused.

'It is a ritual that is hard to explain, but it is one bestowed on a select lineage who are empowered by the spiritual world, to ward off evil and preserve our way of life. My father and I…' Anippe paused as the others looked on curiously. 'My father and I have researched so much through the years, so much that is connected to the Snefru Stele. Other people have been trying to track it down, predominantly those people who purport to be connected to the Jesuit Order in some way, certainly those who use the Order under false pretence. There is a book called the Book of Prophecies and it is this book that my father and I believe has passed through various generations of priests. The scroll you see shows the legend of Princess Nadie who herself met a devout priest by the name of Father Bertrand. After the death of Father Bertrand's evil companion, Brother Martel, the Book of Prophecies was taken to the Pope and kept in the vaults of the Vatican. Many years later the book fell into the hands of another Jesuit priest by the name of Father Ballard – he was a man who found another Egyptian Stele describing the existence of the Snefru Stele. Of course Father Ballard never found the Snefru Stele but he wrote about the finding of his famous 'Ballard Stele' in the Book of Prophecies. Father Ballard also discovered that one of the Vedic scripts, The Atharva-Veda, may have also described the existence of the Snefru Stele…and of course this what we now know, having seen it with our own eyes.'

'Then Krell and Taraka must have the Book of Prophecies,' said Sam.

'That doesn't matter now,' said Walters, abruptly. 'Through the clues of the Book of Prophecies and their discovery of the Atharva-Veda, they have found the secrets contained in the Snefru Stele. Now they have the secrets of The Pottery Maker!'

Anippe and Mike did not flinch at the last comment - but to the astonishment of the others, clearly Walters was far more informed than he may have led them to believe.

Mike stood up sharply and his kin reacted, following his lead.

'Anippe, we must go – night will draw in soon and my sons and daughter must prepare my people for what is to come. The rest of what you need to say is for these good people,' said Mike, receiving an obvious acceptance from Walters.

Anger and reverence combined was not an easy state of mind for Sam to cope with. He found the dynamics of the group a little absurd, yet synonymous with what had taken place before and what was perhaps to come. Each of them, whether it was Joyce with her innate fascination, or James with his miscomprehension, or Mike and his kin with their sense of urgency – all of them, Sam felt, would yet have a part to play, including he.

The connections between the generations around the table were uncanny, yet real. James was trying to fathom the sense of it all; he looked at Anippe, a woman whom he had not seen for over forty-five years, and who hardly looked a day older. She was indeed the real mother of his son and she was the Professor he had known as Bektamun Ayoubi for a period of nearly ten years. He recalled the day when she fell pregnant after her prolonged stay in 1967 when she had visited Chicago - they had spent a number of weeks together. James had promised to look after the child after Bektamun had begged him to find a wife and for them to take care of their son as their own. How on Earth, and by whichever of God's gifts, did he ever think he would find such a devoted woman as his beloved Georgia, he would never know

– but he did. James and Georgia married soon after the birth of Sam and he would become their child; Sam would never be the wiser.

'My father has spent an extended lifetime keeping track of all the rituals and the prophecies linked to the Snefru Stele, and I started to help him when I was able. Some of you have seen our life's work…'

'The room of books! The ones with the gold leaf spines,' James remarked.

'I have seen that room as well father!' shouted Sam.

'There are so many coincidences here I would presume – and what of the Maker? What of the Pottery Maker?' questioned James, staring at Anippe.

'My Book of the Stele records the transcript taken from the stone where the prophecy of the Pottery Maker was engraved. The prophecy talks of a sacred Parchment and a chequered board, which are the tools of the Pottery Maker's craft. Whoever becomes the Maker, they must learn the art of being able to create the spiritual figurines, those same figurines which mimic the Gods and animal Manitou's described within the religions, myths and legends of our world. It is the Pottery Maker who is interned to the prophecies and revelations of The Parchment, it is they alone who must create order out of the chaos…'

'Then who is the Maker, one of you in this room must be he…or she? Who is it then? Who is the Maker? Is it you Anippe? Is it you Mike? Or is it you father? You have certainly kept enough from me, time now to reveal,' said Sam, intently.

Walters stood up, the look on his face was now

stern and resolute. He looked at Mike, who had not yet left the room. Mike stared back.

'I have to go, we have to go, you know this…time is not on our side now. She will be waiting, you must have felt her presence, she is nearby…we need her,' said Mike.

'Wait,' said Walters. 'I can feel her, and she is weakened slightly, you will have to come with me Mike.'

As she scanned the room and watched the interaction, Joyce's intuition got the better of her. She stared at Walters. 'Your father is still alive Anippe, is he not? And he must be the Pottery Maker?'

'And who is "She" that you mention? Make some sense please,' said Sam.

Anippe could not react, she waited for the response she felt sure would come.

Walters bowed his head and sighed, muttering under his breath, then he made an announcement - 'I am the Maker, I am he who is called the Pottery Maker, and 'She' whom you heard referred to is my Protector, the Great Manitou. She is the Spirit Wolf, The *Manitou Mahweewa* and she is near to us now…'

'All these years I have known you, who are you?' reacted Sam.

'You are Anippe's father are you not – you must be?' said Joyce.

James was open mouthed, his heart pounding in anticipation.

Walters raised his head and stared at Anippe, receiving the appropriate acknowledgement. It wasn't that he thought his moment to speak had been ill timed, nor was he concerned about the impact he would have; it was more the sheer dread of what was to become of himself and the people gathered before him.

'My father was an African Benin Prince and he was given the name Osawaru, which means 'God is able'. He was from the Ahigbe tribe of the Fon people, and their name was synonymous with being indestructible. My mother was the beautiful Cahokian Princess - Princess Nadie - who saved her people from such terror and evil. The name of my true self is Asemota Ahigbe...I am Asemota, born of a union between a Prince and Princess from different lands so long ago. And I am over 350 years old...'

Chapter 20

War Clouds

The emergent full moon cast its brilliant light through the small rain clouds gathering in the darkening sky. The tall cotton wood trees swayed and rustled as if they were trying to talk to their audience, the swirling breeze whipping around the bodies of the three men who stood staring into the blackness of the dense forest.

Smoke still billowed from the top of the cabin chimney, the light from the moon accentuating the shadow of the plume across the tiered lawn and towards the white house. Sam stood next to Walters – a man who called himself Asemota, a man who he now knew was the father of Anippe, Anippe the woman who was revealed as his true birth mother. Such revelations would have been inconceivable only hours ago - but now, surreally, he was standing next to his maternal grandfather and his grandfather's trusted friend Mike, who himself had the honour of being called the Akima – the Chief of the Illinois tribes.

A lineage and connection which Sam could never have imagined had been uncovered, and now it seemed that a terrifying destiny awaited him, a destiny that would be steered by a man who was nearly four centuries old.

It was the cracking sound of branches and thicket being torn away from its roots that Sam first heard. Surely his heart could not pound any louder or beat any faster as he stared into the dark spaces between the trees. Even through the rustle of the leaves and the strengthening wind, the cracking noise could be heard resonating between the tree trunks.

Asemota stepped forward nearer to the tree line, turning his head in an effort to hear further. A deep, inhuman breathing sound permeated the wood, penetrating their very souls, making the three men stand perfectly still.

Sam willed his eyes to adjust more to the dark, making every effort to catch a glimpse of whatever it was that was emerging. A section of tree tops started to sway more violently than the rest, and at first Sam thought a whirlpool of wind was churning the branches, until he realised it was something else.

A silhouette, then the outline of a huge creature came into view, its silvery coat occasionally catching the moonlight as it moved slowly out of the dark forest. Disbelieving, Sam watched the enormous beast gracefully push past the remaining thicket before showing its giant head beyond the tree line. Its piercing blue, human like eyes were so entrancing that Sam thought he would be hypnotised, and he had to work hard to rationalise what he was seeing in front of him. The rest of the creature's body started to emerge and only then did Sam grasp the true measure of the awesome beast. Standing near five metres at the head and displaying a formidable muscular frame, the Great Wolf showed off its supernatural presence.

'My Protector,' cried Asemota. 'My Spirit Wolf - *Manitou Mahweewa* - you are home, thank the Lord!'

The Great Wolf bowed her head and knelt down on her front legs, Asemota rushing towards her to embrace her cheek and caress her enormous snout. The huge beast smiled at the attention, her lips curled in the corner of her mouth, her eyes narrowed with enjoyment as Asemota poured exaggerated fuss upon her.

Spirit Wolf opened one eye, catching Sam's eye as he stared at her emphatically, not knowing quite what to do. The creature stood up and started to sniff the air, moving ever closer to where Sam stood, much to his initial dismay. He didn't know whether to run off, although he knew this would be futile – *best stay put instead*, he thought, and let the Giant Wolf's natural curiosity unfold. Sam bowed his head in utter submission.

'She greets you Sam,' said Asemota. 'Walk through and stroke her chest and belly.'

Sam did so, able to walk under the wolf's chest bone without touching his head, stroking the underside of her gigantic silver haired body before walking back around her hind legs. He noticed the smile had returned upon her face as she watched him intently with her brilliant blue eyes – eyes brighter than the moonlight.

'What mystical being is this?' Sam asked. 'Truly

magnificent, where does she come from, how can she be?'

'She is the Great Spirit Wolf, Sam. She is over one thousand years old, and has been the Protector of the Pottery Maker during all the centuries she has been alive. She protected my mother Nadie, and she protected Nadie's father before that…now she will protect us.'

'Taraka?'

'Yes, she will fight The Piasa,' said Mike.

'He will be her most formidable foe, she will not be able to fight him alone for long, and she knows that. We will have to pool our strengths to defeat him and Krell,' said Asemota.

'And what of Krell? He must be your adversary…and I assume he will be mine now as well?'

'Intuitive of you Sam. You will need to learn my ways…and quickly,' said Asemota.

'I sense she is weakened slightly,' said Mike.

'I feel it to, perhaps she is tired, she will have been prowling for days now, waiting in anticipation – fearing what is to come, but she will be ready,' said Asemota.

'Perhaps she caught herself on something,' said Sam. 'I noticed a small smattering of dried blood on her hind legs as I walked through, perhaps she is injured?'

Spirit Wolf stood proud and raised her head, bracing her body as if to distract the men from their conversation. She moved further away from the coppice, lifting her snout into the air, a low growl emanating from her throat.

'What is it my beauty? What do you sense?' said Asemota.

The wolf turned her head briefly back towards the small forest, causing the men to follow her gaze, before she distracted them again through her rigid deportment.

'She may have caught herself, although I can't tell – it matters not now, she is preparing herself and we must be ready to go with her,' said Asemota.

The wolf's mighty body was now completely rigid, her head not moving as she looked skyward to the northwest. Her tail was now extended and the low growl had turned into a deep unearthly sound that sent chills down the spines of the three men.

'Calm my Spirit, I know they come,' said Asemota stroking the wolf's side.

The wolf looked at Asemota momentarily and nodded.

'This is our time!' said Mike. 'Run and tell the others Sam, tell Anippe, Joyce and your father to make for Cahokia, as fast as they can – we will meet them there!'

There had been no need for Sam to have made contact – Anippe had already rallied the others, organising them to the point of distraction. James had readied his trusty Jeep and gave a signal to Sam that he should return to the other men.

Clambering onto the Great Wolf, as she lowered herself for him, Sam was able to perch himself alongside Asemota and Mike, the Akima. Bracing themselves, all three men grabbed a loop of the wolf's thick silvery hair, coiling their feet in the same manner, knowing that they would soon be hanging on for dear life.

'Cahokia is a long way, surely we cannot make good time this way?' said Sam.

The other two said nothing as the Great Wolf stood on her gigantic legs, facing her body to the south - she prepared to run.

'Hang on Sam, lean forward,' shouted Mike.

The force of the creature powering her legs as she charged forward was something Sam could hardly comprehend. She sprinted away over hedges and fields, across rivers and valleys, and along wooded paths at the speed of an express train. The three men watched the ground rush before them and after what seemed only a few minutes, they were miles away, diminishing any concern Sam had of not reaching their goal in time. *Such supernatural power, surely she would be an equal match for Taraka?* Sam couldn't imagine anything being able to overpower her – but the wolf knew otherwise.

*

With barely enough room for three people to sit, the Jeep had been laden with knapsacks, boots, maps, books and even James' trusted rifles, all of which were products of a hasty contingency. Once all aboard, churning stones from the gravel drive, the Jeep screeched onto the highway, reaching top speed as fast as James could drive, straining his strong eighty-two year old body and mind as much as he would dare

Tension was a little high, with Joyce and Anippe arguing over who was to blame for not better convincing Raju that he should have followed them with the Vedic Script. The Atharva-Veda remained the central topic of conversation, along with the Book of the Stele, and the only thing the women agreed upon – was that without the Vedic Script, how on Earth would they be able to defeat Taraka? For James, he was confounded, yet acutely aware that something terrifying was about to happen, and he was desperate to understand – but his instinct to protect Sam was overwhelming, quite ready to give his life for his son if he had to.

*

Thirty-five tribal warriors, hand-picked from the Illinois tribes, had assembled awaiting the arrival of Chogan, Kimi and Huritt. Dimly lit and sprawling elegantly within the central grounds of Cahokia, the Visitor Centre was perfect for the gathering, where the expert bow men and women had travelled to - from far and wide. A night for which they had trained most of their lives was now upon them, and they were ready to sacrifice themselves, they would do whatever was necessary to repel the evil and save humanity; it would be a night of glory or sorrow, of destruction or triumph but they would do all they could to defeat the terrible Piasa.

By now there was no sign of the setting sun, the brilliant full moon dominated the sky and the wind roared through the trees surrounding the Cahokian fields and mounds from every direction, the trees swirling like an angry circle of people. Red and white war paint, intricately blended into tribal tattoos, donned the faces and torsos of the warriors. Bows strapped to their backs, with a casement of lethal arrows blessed by their Gods, the warriors dispersed around the ancient site, commanded by Akima's kin. Chogan and his warriors covered the South Forest, which ran from the Visitor Centre all the way to the edge of the great Mississippi River. Huritt commanded the warriors in the Northern Forest, which network of small coppices spread across to the east towards the impressive Horseshoe Lake, and lay near to the sacred Monk's Mound. Kimi took charge of her elite squad, which would roam the perimeter, hunting and searching for the threat, reacting at speed to where she and her warriors were needed the most.

Men and women stepped out onto the ground, scurrying across the Plaza and fields as if ghosts from the ancient Cahokian City had appeared, once more controlling the mounds and walkways of this most sacred place.

And there was no doubt who would take his place in overall charge once he arrived, there would be no dissent or obstruction to his authority and wisdom. Mike, the Akima would fulfil his destiny, his job to ensure the protection of the Pottery Maker at all costs.

*

The Great Spirit Wolf stopped short of entering the Cahokian City, instead she set down the exhilarated party of men, just to the east of the modern Visitor Centre, out of sight in a dense thicket, near to a small innocuous lake. Whilst the contingent of warriors dispersed, Huritt waited for his father and the other two men near one of the many mounds, he was anxious to see them, yet equally anxious to join his troops.

'Welcome my Akima…and to you Asemota and Sam. Everything is arranged, the warriors are assigned to their positions, including by your Pit Asemota. Kimi will protect the Pit and the surrounding area, the rest of the tribe will be spread through both forests, I await your instructions father.'

'I will stay near Monks Mound with you, we will hide in the forest to the north side. No doubt you will make for the Pit Asemota, and you would be wise to go with him Sam. May our heavenly spirit *Kitchesmanetoa* be with us all tonight, and may The Piasa be slain and go back to hell,' said Mike, stirringly.

'The Parchment must be in my possession at all times now, I cannot risk missing an instruction. Sam, come with me,' said Asemota.

'The Parchment?' Then it truly exists?' said Sam.

'It does exist. Not much time to explain, but you will see soon how the Pottery Maker does their work, and you must learn - quickly.'

A chill went down Sam's spine, it was as if he had been prodded by some unknown force, taunting him, playing with him, laying bare his future – the significance of what Asemota was saying could only mean one thing…

*

It would normally take four hours to drive to the Cahokian Mounds from his home along Route 55, but that would have been too long. At the risk of being caught by the police, James notched the speed of the Jeep to over 160 kilometres an hour, unnoticed by the two women who were still frantically exchanging notes and thoughts.

'The Cloth...the Book of the Stele keeps referring to the Cloth,' said Joyce.

'The Cloth provides the secret,' said Anippe.

'And now Taraka and Krell have acquired that secret - from the Stele itself?'

'Yes, the Stele was the only place the actual secret of The Cloth was written, I left the exact part out of the book, I told you that Joyce.'

'But you have not told me the secret.'

'The Cloth provides the power- it transforms the Pottery Maker.'

'You mean whatever The Cloth is, it forms a new Maker?'

'In a sense, and if the time is right, yes.'

'And what of tonight then?'

'Krell wants to be the Maker and Taraka will help him. It is the time of change and we must stop them,' said Anippe.

'But what of Sam and your father?'

Anippe did not reply immediately, she simply stared through the front window of the Jeep, scanning the wide open road, watching numerous car headlights approaching, contemplating whether she should answer fully.

'Strangely, I should not know the secret of The

Cloth, but I do. I found the Stele all those years ago…you were there James. My father and I had been searching for the Snefru Stele for years. I transcribed everything, apart from the secret of The Cloth, into the Book of the Stele. My father already knew the secret, it had been passed down to him by his mother, Nadie. He wasn't to know it would be recorded on the ancient stone, I saw it and told him. We swore we would never write it down anywhere.'

'I never thought for one minute any of this would come to fruition,' said James breaking his silence. 'All those years ago I thought it was something fantastical and since then I had buried such a concept in my mind, the only reminder being my tattered old diary. But Sam's quest resurrected a curiosity in me, and now I know the tablet I saw was not a fallacy, it was not some superstitious nonsense – and The Parchment – it exists, heaven knows it exists!'

*

Narrow wooden steps led to a large basement within the confines of the sprawling Visitor Centre and Sam found it difficult to hide the pain in his shoulder as he trundled behind Asemota into the dark room; Asemota – a man who had purported to be a Police Chief, and God knows how many other people in his life, a man who was leading him towards a destiny he could scarcely contemplate.

All around Sam, people were preparing for battle, a battle that would change the world and, for what he could only suppose, would change the realm beyond this world. Sam wished desperately for time to think, although he knew he had none, instead he would have to carry on inexorably - deciphering and processing information from Asemota as fast as he could.

Ceiling lights flickered and a small extractor fan started to whirr as Asemota headed towards an annex room, populated only by an aluminium wash basin, which was just partly visible to anyone standing in the main basement area. From behind the basin, Asemota removed a brick from the wall, pulling out what appeared to be an animal hide sack, brown and white in colour, with a piece of heavily woven string attached to it for the purpose of carry.

'Open the sack Sam, take out the item and tell me what you see.'

Sam took a moment, first peering inside the distinctive sack, then closing it again, he was almost too afraid to look. He closed his eyes and took a long deep breath, placing his hand on what he thought was some form of scroll, although it was heavy - much heavier than he expected, forming the bulk of the weight. Having pulled it out of the sack, Sam rolled the scroll out onto a nearby wooden trestle table.

'It is the same as the painting...the very painting that caused me to embark on a chase half way around the world,' Sam remarked. 'So this is the Parchment, then the painting was merely a ruse?'

'Yes and I know you must have known that. It was a ruse, one designed to flush Krell out and make him react, and importantly reveal the whereabouts of Taraka. I am sorry for what you had to go through Sam, truly. We wondered whether Krell would actually subject himself to the ploy, but he did – through his incessant desire, idiotically, he accepted the ruse.'

'But it hasn't stopped him and Taraka finding out all they need to know and finding us!' said Sam, exasperated.

'We have control of The Parchment, therefore we must dictate the events from now on, at all costs.'

'What will it reveal?'

'You will only know once it has spoken to you properly.'

'But why me?' said Sam, dread surging through his body.

There was no answer. Sam continued to unravel the scroll making sure the heavy animal skin Parchment was flattened on the table, having to use any paperweight he could find to compress the edges. Indeed then, before him lay the ancient Parchment, a picture woven into an animal skin which was tens of thousands of years old, a picture which seemed alive and freshly painted - it was the same in every small detail as the picture he saw on the computer screen in Egypt, except one.

'A mirror, there is a mirror on the back wall within The Parchment image, I can see the outline of your face Asemota – this was not in the painting I saw on the computer screen in Egypt. The mirror must be significant, not something you wanted Krell or Taraka to see, yet my guess is none of that matters anymore. And…I can't quite believe it…the picture of the chequered board in The Parchment seems to be alive! I felt sure I saw it move, or at least the gold writing symbols move…they appeared to chatter,' said Sam.

'Come the hour, the mirror will be the most important thing for you to remember and act upon

Sam. Now you must study The Parchment in as much detail as you can, what do you see?'

'I can't take my eyes off the chequered board, and the figurines…I could have sworn they moved too, they seemed to stare at me then look away again! I see what looks like the Spirit Wolf in one of the rows on the board.'

'And what else – look closer?' instructed Asemota.

'Taraka, I see Taraka…his depiction is placed on one of the back rows, opposite to Spirit Wolf, standing proud, larger than the others on his side. Now it seems that the gold writing on the edge of the board is shimmering, the writing symbols are changing,' said Sam in disbelief, having to look away from The Parchment, momentarily in fear.

Returning his gaze to the representation of the board within the Parchment, Sam noticed something even more significant, something horrifying.

'In a moments glance from me to you, Taraka has moved, and he has changed! He has morphed!' Sam backing away from The Parchment as he spoke.

Reverently, with closer inspection, Asemota scoured the picture, then he also stared intently at the picture of the chequered board, examining the gold hieroglyphics and figurines with a face that emanated beguiling wisdom. Taraka had indeed morphed into a larger being, easily the most dominant figure in his row. Spirit Wolf's figurine showed itself centre stage, its mouth wide open, bearing snarling teeth towards the Demon, and this Asemota expected.

Unexpectedly, something else caught Asemota's eye. Only once had he seen this particular depiction before – a Demigod had broken ranks and it was clearly positioned on a flank, in a central square facing inward, although not aligned to any particular side. Not since the battle all those years ago involving his mother, Nadie, had he seen such movement, only this time it was more real, there was no fluctuation on the pictorial chequered board, the image of the Demigod remained steadfast.

'We must get to the Pit, that is where the real board is,' said Asemota. 'I have no idea whether the Demigod is good or evil, whether it is with us or for Taraka – The Parchment is telling me to make it, so I must, I cannot contradict anything The Parchment portrays – do you understand?'

Sam remained silent.

'We must create the scene you see in The Parchment Sam and we must do it quickly, Taraka will soon be upon us, although I fear creating the Demigod is a terrible risk to take.'

Sam rolled The Parchment and placed it back into the deer hide sack. He and Asemota scurried out of the basement, all the while Sam feeling a new found fear, praying that the others would arrive soon and that everyone would be able to gather strength in numbers.

And why such a warrior Demigod? Surely conjuring up more demons was not the answer?

His longing for the others was quickly rewarded, he and Asemota were greeted by an exasperated trio in the Visitor Centre lobby, Sam realising that his father must have travelled at break neck speed, pushing the trusty old Jeep to its limit to get to Cahokia in time.

*

To the north of the Visitor Centre, in a cluster of trees near to Monk's Mound, Spirit Wolf cleverly lay her immense bulk, immersing herself out of sight in the thicket of the wood. She gazed skyward looking intently at the stars and in particular at the full moon, watching for any shadow they may show itself across it, scanning for the hideous form of Taraka.

Not too far away, on the highest point of Monk's Mound, stood Mike Tremble – The Akima, and his eldest son Huritt, both surveying the land and the forests. They were aware of Spirit Wolf's presence, hoping that she would give a signal at the right time. Akima was prepared for battle and he was prepared to die, as were all of his warriors, and he knew that his sons and daughter were anxious, but he also knew that they were highly trained, having trained them himself for this very moment over many years. Like his forefather Akima, centuries before him, the sacrifice would be inevitable, he would not be able to save all of his warriors; the significance of Nadie's death over 350 years ago was testament to the extent of that sacrifice.

The rally cry from Spirit Wolf would be unmistakable; it would be the signal for all around her to brace themselves and prepare for the battle of their lives, for no one could be under any illusion. The ancient tales of The Piasa passed down by so many generations were foremost in Akima's mind – a fearsome creature that had not revealed itself in over two millennia – why it would reveal itself now to his people he could not fathom, only that it must be ordained as his destiny to confront such evil.

*

The Pit was hidden within a small Cahokian mound, the mound itself situated deep inside the confines of the extremely dense southern-most forest, with mature Cyprus trees and thick vegetation surrounding the Pit exterior. Asemota opened a wooden trap door, lifting it by a metal handle, revealing purpose built wooden steps, which led to an underground concrete chamber. The chamber lay directly below the centre of the ancient mound and was dank, with cracks appearing in the walls and mould prominent in the corners of the room, filling the air with a damp earthy smell. A brick and earthen hearth dominated the centre of the rear wall, protruding a metre or so into the room; it was a replica of the Pit hearth created by Asemota's mother, Nadie, all those years ago.

A chequered board lay on a tri-legged wooden table, its figurines neatly placed in rows facing each other, and a small potter's wheel stood against the steps, a pot of sodden clay resting against its feet. The fire in the hearth was glowing, a distinct roar starting to bellow from its interior as the light glistened through the symmetrical oblong gap near the top of its structure.

'Pass me The Parchment Sam, I need your help to make the figurines, you can grab the wet clay in the pot near to the wheel…and start turning, I assume you have been taught by your father?'

'Yes, fortuitously it seems…but it has been a while!'

'No time to ponder, we have to take a chance –

Taraka will be upon us soon in all his might and I am sure Spirit Wolf will not be able to fight him on her own for long...besides which she is a little weakened and I can't fathom why. I hope to God that whatever we do here will help her,' said Asemota, nervously.

The small potter's wheel grinded and squeaked as Sam pressed the cantilever pedal at the base of the stool. A clump of wet earthen clay, gathered from The Mississippi River water's edge, was slapped hurriedly onto the stone circle, and Sam started to manipulate the sodden doughy material. He focused on The Parchment, in awe of its spiritual mystique, trying to copy the shapes as best he could from the pictorial design. It was hard, very hard to do.

'I cannot rush this, they are intricate in detail, how am I supposed to do it in time?' queried Sam.

'It will come to you, focus,' said Asemota. 'Use the knowledge you have and let your hands loose...shape the outline of the figurines, concentrate on Spirit Wolf, Taraka and the Demigod as you see in The Parchment, the rest you will not need to reform, merely douse them with water – they will be rejuvenated by the ancient fire.'

Quickly and delicately, Sam made the figurines, forging the earthen clay, first into the spectacularly looking Demigod and then the Spirit Wolf in its poised, menacing fighting stance. Last, and begrudgingly, he molded the hideous morphed shape of Taraka, its pictorial resemblance appearing to stare at him with such evil prowess - Sam felt utterly perturbed.

Once made and into the fire, he, nor Asemota,

would have any idea of the final outcome, the furnace would forge the figurines – The Parchment in the meantime may possibly change again and the interchange in the furnace would align itself accordingly, until finally, when the light started to fade, the board could be drawn from the fire.

'Surely this is too much of a gamble to perform such an action,' said Sam, as his strong fingers manipulated the clay.

'We have to gamble,' said Asemota, concern in his voice.

'When they are fired, what happens then, what happened the last time you created the Demon and the Demigod?' asked Sam.

'I have never had to do this before!' came the reply.

Chapter 21

Battle the Second

Akima felt tense and ill at ease as the gusts of wind suddenly stopped, the eerie silence penetrating his nerves as he looked skywards from the top of Monks Mound, searching - scanning the moon lit sky for something he knew not of what form it would appear, his only understanding was that the form would be of such terrifying evil.

The rumbling growl of Spirit Wolf nearby alerted Akima and he dashed down the side of the Mound as fast as his aging body could carry him, heading for the North Forest where Huritt and his warriors lay hidden in the dense thicket.

'Spirit Wolf has sensed the evil Piasa, he comes, what should we do father?' said Huritt anxiously.

'We must wait and continue to hide here and we must let Spirit Wolf tackle the mighty Demon, we will know when to help, but it is her fight now, she was supernaturally born upon this Earth to fight this day.'

Nervously, with hearts beating faster and breath drawing shorter, they looked skywards once again. Suddenly they caught a glimpse of a hideous monstrous shape forming a silhouette across the light of the moon, it was a creature of such size and prowess, and one of such contorted evil form, Akima and his brethren hardly dared to look. A murmur of abject fear ran through the tribe and Akima was concerned as to how he would contain such despair; despite their earlier signs of courage, some of his people now seemed ready to flee.

Within seconds the shape had gone, appearing to vanish into thin air. Akima felt sick, bowing his head in exasperation, the time had come to face the putrid Piasa but neither he or any of his warriors would have known what perplexing evil they were about to face.

A mighty beast, the size of a four storey house, thudded its grotesque demonic body onto the top of Monk's Mound, making the very ground shake and deform, tearing earth and stones from their foundation and sending such debris at bullet speed towards the entire surround.

For an eerie moment, a swirling cloud of dust morphed and wrapped around the gigantic figure, molding to the creature's frame, before the cloud slowly started to dissipate. Gasps and cries could be heard from the tribe as the evilest eyes of fire started to emerge, piercing the very souls of those who would dare to look.

The Piasa had come, the ancient evil being had arrived, a creature who was woven into tribal folklore, a creature so terrifying the very thought of such a beast struck resolute fear and horror into the hearts of the strongest men and women.

Now stood before them, the Demon started to unfurl its coarse, bat like wings, showing its long haired lion shaped torso, and, as it slowly lifted its monstrous face, layers of spiked antlers could be seen protruding from its head. Its face appeared scarily humanoid, covered in thick black hair, with a huge hooked nose and elongated saw like teeth illuminated by the creature's fearsome eyes. Most frightening of all was its thick black tail, a tail that extended longer than the height of the creature itself, and one which had, at the very tip, a formidable pincer shaped club, capable of ripping through bone and flesh.

The metamorphosis of the vile Demon Taraka had truly taken shape, he was now indeed The Piasa, a beast from the underworld - forsaken to wreak havoc upon the Earth.

Without any warning to the others, Huritt shouted out, his eye had caught the movement of a human form scampering away from the Demon, heading in the direction of the Pit, towards the South Forest. It was Krell.

*

'Krell is upon us,' said Asemota. 'I can sense him. He has travelled with the Beast, The Piasa is here. I must leave you, and trust that you will fulfil what needs to be done. Remember what I told you about The Cloth. You must carry out the prophecy when the time comes. It does not matter what is happening around you, it does not matter who may be hurt or dying, you must secure your fate.'

Sam acknowledged the words but he did not

respond, he was mesmerised by the foibles of The Parchment and the trance like features of the fire blazing in the earthen kiln, knowing soon enough that his burdensome task would have to be carried out, one which had no guarantee. In his deep deliberation, Sam never noticed Asemota leave quickly, and ominously, out through the trap door of the Pit.

Outside in the forest, Kimi patrolled with her troop; she spotted Asemota and cried out.

'Asemota, he is upon us, Krell is here…but now I have lost sight of him!'

'Ready your warriors and stay hidden in the forest nearby, you must protect Anippe and the others wherever you can. Krell will come to me, it's me he is after…'

Asemota had barely moved from the Pit entrance when suddenly, from behind the Pit Mound and through the dense thicket, Krell appeared, leaping towards him. With a blow that would have killed any mere mortal, Krell smashed his fist into Asemota's jaw, but the Pottery Maker did not fall, instead he stood his ground, deriding his evil attacker. Then they clashed, like two enormous buffalo locking their horns, the supernatural men became embroiled in a violent struggle.

Paralysing fear nearly overcame Kimi as she saw the fight unfold, trying to command her small group of warriors to come to Asemota's aide, contrary to his orders.

As the scene played out by the Pit, Anippe had already dragged her two trusty companions nearby, only to find the milieu between Asemota and Krell taking place, and Kimi bellowing orders.

Seeing her father, a distraught Anippe followed Kimi's lead, both women instinctively drawing their bows aiming arrows towards Krell's torso. Yet, composure was needed, one false move and they would hit Asemota.

Kimi had not heeded Asemota's instructions and continued to scream, begging him to break free from Krell's grasp so that she could have a clear shot at the evil beast of a man. Asemota was acting on pure instinct, grappling with his foe, punching with all of his might and wrestling with Krell's inhuman strength, tormented as to how he would ever be able to overpower him.

*

A tired and distraught James followed Joyce as quickly as he could, both managing to reach the Pit entrance away from the scene in the forest. In unison the pair lifted the heavy trap door and descended down the wooden steps, catching the glow of the fiery kiln within the hearth. They noticed the potter's wheel standing in the corner of the room behind the door, and a small tri-legged table supporting the chequered board with its strange looking figurines. But there was no sign of Sam.

'Where can he be? Where could he have gone?' shouted James.

'I did not see any movement out of the Pit…but we all lost focus when Krell revealed himself, Asemota must have tasked Sam with something, he would never have left him otherwise. The board – I must examine the board,' said Joyce.

'What can that tell you?' said James, his stomach writhing in anguish.

'I studied the meaning of the board in the Book of the Stele, enough to know that it takes its instruction from The Parchment through the ancient hieroglyphs you can see on the sides. The Pottery Maker makes the figurines according to this instruction, then places them on the board for firing in the earthen kiln, in this very hearth before us. As far as I can comprehend the board and its figurines then morph according to the representation described in The Parchment - in a disturbing supernatural enactment, as the powers of good and evil play out their ruse.'

'Like the pieces in a game of chess? And what of the 'pawns' in the front row?' said James.

'Those, I believe, are warriors…they are Demigods and are called the Bhati – an ancient race of foot soldiers, not unlike the terracotta warriors of old. They can be summoned by The Pottery Maker, and this I wonder if Sam and Asemota had been planning?'

'But what does the board say?'

'Well it's difficult to understand, but there is a figurine missing, it must be one of the Bhati. What a risk it would be, even making a choice and thinking that one of the Bhati creatures could be conjured up in our favour!'

'We cannot fathom that here and we are running out of time,' said James. 'Asemota must have given Sam some instruction and now whatever the risk, I must get to my son.'

*

Taraka, stood motionless on the top of Monk's Mound having coiled his wings around his enormous hairy torso once again. His head remained bowed, yet none of the tribe still dared to move from the forest, such was the intrepid fear they felt.

Suddenly, the forest awakened to the sound of a deafening growl; Spirit Wolf had emerged and was ready for battle. Taraka raised his head slowly from the embrace of his wings, his orange fiery eyes blazing brighter, penetrating the surround whilst scanning for his adversary.

Spirit Wolf was poised and started to move slowly, circling around the Mound, her head motionless whilst the rest of her body swaggered. She would not venture up the hill for fear of the obvious disadvantage, she wanted to draw Taraka away, but her timing would have to be impeccable and she knew Taraka would not be such a fool to her tactics.

Taraka tracked her movements as she paced back and forth, and then started to slowly move his gigantic frame as if he was charging his body with energy, shuffling the ground like a bull preparing to fight. He then arched his back and he roared furiously, whipping and cracking his tail at the same time, the sound and sight of which even made Spirit Wolf wince and cower.

The Wolf spotted her moment and changed tack, charging at Taraka, taking advantage of his self-glorification. Such was her speed; this took him by surprise as she aimed for his throat. At the last second, he was able to deflect her powerful lunge away from his neck, but could not prevent her from sinking her razor sharp teeth hard into his body.

Infuriated at letting his guard down, Taraka punched at the Wolf, sending her sprawling down the side of the Mound, yet she was able to recover and charge again, feigning one way then the next, intent on attacking Taraka at the base of his tail.

The Demon was wise to this and had already whipped up his vile tail ready to strike. It whirled around and cracked like gun fire as the clubbed tip passed through the air at such speed. Through her feigning, Spirit Wolf narrowly missed the tip of the tail, but her plan was now foiled. The tail whipped around again and the speed of the second recoil startled her, giving her no time to think. The tip missed her, but the coarse edge of the tail caught her legs, pulling her onto her back, and it was only the angle of the mound and her momentum that enabled her to scramble free from the coiling grip. The Giant Wolf sprinted away into the forest for cover, she would have to revert to her original plan and try to lure the Demon away from the open ground - but she needed help.

*

The narrow muddy path leading from the Pit was not easy going as Sam stumbled through the thicket. The path was worse now, the start of heavy rain slowing him down as he tried in desperate haste to reach the area where the earthen clay could be found. The Horseshoe Lake, although nearby, had initially seemed distant as the light from the moon appeared to diminish completely amongst the emerging black clouds. Suddenly, hardly comprehending, Sam found his way onto the Lakeside shore, his feet starting to sink slightly into the silty clay.

He fumbled around inside the sack he was carrying, removing the figurine he had created under Asemota's instruction, and then buried it into the sodden clay. Next he took The Parchment out of the sack and tried to clear his mind and decipher the sequence of hieroglyphs shining from the chequered board depiction.

Asemota had repeatedly explained what Sam must say as the hieroglyphs formed, yet now Sam was unsure, and he found himself, anxiously, starting to recite the sentences in different ways.

'From the Earth the Bhati will rise, to claim or protect the ancient prize. Whosoever creates such a creature this day, must do so with the utmost allay. For it is written......For it is written...What is written?!' shouted Sam, furious with himself.

The last part of the recital escaped him and no amount of staring at the golden hieroglyphs would help him remember. The small figurine remained buried in the damp silty clay, unmoving, waiting, as if suspended in time. Sam turned around, looking away from the lake shore and over the tree tops towards Monk's Mound. He pondered over how matters might be transpiring, but felt so forlorn at the prospect of Spirit Wolf's insurmountable task, and that of his grandfather. Nothing he was able to do at this moment could help them.

In the pouring rain, Sam tried to calm himself, harking back to the moment when Asemota explained what he must do once the figurine had been taken from the chequered board.

'The Bhati Warrior is an ancient breed of fighting Demigod, spawned from many cultures, and they can only be removed from the board once they have shown themselves in the centre of it,' Asemota had said. 'You must take the one that shows itself to the shore of the Horseshoe Lake, following the narrow path through the densest part of the wood which then leads to a small inlet near to the clay ridden shore. Take the Parchment and read the hieroglyphs as they appear in sequence. There will be four phases of words and they will repeat in a continual cycle until the Bhati reveals itself – but you will have to interpret the meaning exactly, and you must learn this quickly…'

The mental block remained and Sam tried desperately not to let his anxiety turn into absolute panic. As he fought to regain his thoughts, he heard a pattering noise behind him. Turning and struggling to see through the dark and the rain, he could make out the outline of two human figures, one running fast, the other jogging slowly behind.

'Thank all!' Sam shouted. 'Joyce…and father!'

Joyce sprinted towards him, barely containing her emotion, embracing him hard as soon as she reached him, her squeeze was so tight he could hardly breathe. A mixture of new found euphoria and existing despair filled his body as he clamoured to explain his plight.

Cleverly, Joyce quickly grasped the essence of what he was saying and soon realised that they would have to work together to help Sam remember the sequence of words.

'I have read such a prophecy in the Book of the Stele, the creation of the Bhati is an ancient ritual. Try and remember what Asemota said to you Sam and I will read the signs on the Parchment at the same time,' said Joyce.

'I just can't remember the last sequence…and we haven't got much time.'

'I know, let me look and I'll try and jog your memory.'

Once again Sam retrieved The Parchment from the sack, all of them squinting their eyes at the glowing light of the hieroglyphs in the rain filled dark. Joyce waited for her vision to adjust before she read the sacred symbols, disbelieving the supernatural splendour before her.

'From the earth the Bhati will rise, to claim or protect the ancient prize. Whosoever creates such a creature this day, must do so with the utmost allay. For it is written upon the stone - stone or board? I am not sure,' said Joyce.

'Stone, Asemota said stone.'

'For it is written upon the stone, when the sacred…or ancient, can't quite work out… power foretold should atone…'

'Sacred! He said sacred.'

'When the sacred power foretold should atone, there will be no reprieve or time to preconceive, a destiny will unfold for ancient glory you will behold…'

'That's it Joyce, those are the words, I've got it now!'

Slowly and deliberately Sam read the hieroglyph sequence as it appeared, the others holding onto him as he spoke.

'From the damp Earth the Bhati will rise,

To claim or protect the most ancient prize.

Whosoever creates such a creature this day,

Must do so with the utmost allay.

For it is written upon the stone,

When the sacred power foretold should atone,

There will be no reprieve or time to preconceive,

A destiny will unfold for ancient glory you will behold'

*

Neither Anippe nor Kimi had lost their vigilance in keeping watch over Asemota as he battled with the evil Krell, for what now seemed like an age. Every step of the way had been tracked and Anippe had not faltered with the training of her weapon. Krell continued to rain blows on Asemota, who continued to defend himself against the false Jesuit, occasionally landing his own blows and kicks to send the pretender sprawling across the rain soaked ground. Momentarily this would allow Asemota to part from his adversary, enabling the warriors to fire a volley of arrows towards the mighty Krell, although mostly this was ineffective, such were the giant man's reflexes and skill.

Deep within the Southern Forest, some five hundred metres away from the Pit, Asemota started to tire, feeling sure that he would have to use all of his power and experience to thwart his enemy. Anippe could sense this from her father, and she desperately tried to find a weakness in Krell, concentrating on firing her arrows at the same point on his body. Kimi followed suit, both managing, intermittently, to hit Krell on the same spot underneath his left arm, close to his heart. For the first time they saw him wince and muffle in obvious pain.

In a fearful rage, a mighty blow struck Asemota on his head, disorientating him, Krell using his full might to hit him and break away. Krell charged at the band of warriors, screaming obscenities at them as he did so, and Asemota could only look on in horror as he tried to recover from the blow. Before Asemota could react, Krell tore violently into members of the tribe, some of them scattering further into the forest in a desperate attempt to get away. Anippe was in that group, she was one of those people close by, and Asemota could not tell if she had been hit.

Chogan had joined Kimi, and watching the commotion unfold, instinctively he charged at Krell, wielding a long knife, fully intending to lunge at the beast and save his people from such a demise. However, it was too late to avoid Krell's wrath. Swiftly and powerfully, with supernatural strength, Krell charged again at the tribal group, grabbing their torsos and crushing their bodies against the hard tree trunks. Chogan stalled and reeled at the horrific scene, fearful now that they were all at Krell's mercy.

Anippe tried to fire an arrow, but it was to no avail – Krell had targeted her first and had struck her with the back of his hand, hitting her head, sending her falling hard towards the thicket covered ground.

Gleefully, Krell smiled and stood gloating over her body, ready to strike a further heavy blow. Through his distraction, he did not notice Asemota rise and charge. Asemota pelted towards him at great speed and using the full leverage of his body, leapt up and directed a savage blow, striking Krell's temple, almost burying Krell into the surrounding earth. The evil man was heavily dazed, although not unconscious, and he writhed around the foliage like a wounded animal.

Seeing his beloved daughter stricken on the ground was not something Asemota was able to cope with and he filled with utter despair, snatching Anippe from the thicket and carrying her towards the Visitor Centre, hoping desperately that he could save her.

*

Taraka hovered then moved slowly through the air near to where Spirit Wolf had hidden in the forests surrounding the Horseshoe Lake. The great *Manitou Mahweewa* steadied herself, watching the evil Piasa as he drew near, tensing her muscles ready to strike at him as soon as he would land. Intrepidly, Akima's warriors lay alongside her not knowing what to do or how to really prepare themselves, only to fire upon the Piasa at any given moment.

The Demon drew near and the Wolf could feel his breath billowing through the thicket where she lay; her eyes did not move from him. Suddenly, Taraka turned his head sharply, looking over the line of trees and towards the lakeside shore.

'He has seen something, something quite profound

I fear...what can it be?' whispered Huritt to his father.

'I am not sure, it is something over on the far side of the lake shore, we must gather our forces and send word to Chogan and Kimi – let them know the Demon may be headed their way.' said Akima.

Taraka moved through the air at speed, shifting his gigantic beastly body over the dense forest towards the lake waters. Spirit Wolf scrambled through the thicket after him, similarly distracted by a new emerging presence, but she knew not whether it was friend or foe.

*

The earth started to shift and tremor as Sam shouted the very last word of the recital. He had the presence of mind to usher his companions quickly into the tree line beyond the shore, away from the morphing clay. Once under cover they looked back and stood in awe as the silty clay twisted and turned, writhed and formed – stretching this way and that, bringing the prophecy to life. The Bhati was emerging.

The sound of the vast mold of clay lashing and groaning into form was accentuated by the compact swirls of air getting trapped in its body; the three companions felt sure that the high pitch noise would bend and crack the very trees they were standing amongst.

Watching on in oblique curiosity, James clung onto Sam and Joyce, seeing the mighty figure emerge out of the silt and clay, and it cut a terrifying presence. A warrior creature, akin to so many of the world's cultures - for Hindu's they would name it the Bhati, for the Native Americans they would call it the Kachina Warrior and for the Mongol and Chinese cultures they would name such a monster as the Terracotta Soldier – and now beholden, it was here.

'Protector or slayer?!' shouted Sam.

'What have we done?' said Joyce, despairingly.

'I suggest we move further back into the forest, out of sight completely,' said James, already letting go of his companions as he started to scramble up a muddy bank.

As they fell back deeper into the forest, they all found it difficult to withdraw their gaze from the supernatural Bhati as it completed its metamorphosis and started to show its emerging features. It had a definable permanent grimace on its wide face, and although most of the top part of its head was covered with a rounded clay helmet, the grimace of its mouth could clearly be seen. Standing over six metres tall, the colossal new born soldier carried a long spear in its right hand, and its left arm seemed to be moulded into the shape of a mighty curved sword, that reached ground level when the warrior stood upright. Body armour surrounded the creature, stretching and blending into its defined torso as it started to slowly move its feet.

*

The rush to track and keep pace with Taraka and Spirit Wolf had distracted Akima intently, yet something gnawed away at him. In the heat of battle there was always confusion and someone had to be calm and wise enough to make sense of it. Akima had stayed with Huritt, and like the others in the party, had instinctively headed to where the carnage of the beasts would likely unfold – but he slowed – something was desperately wrong, the strength of which overwhelmed him.

'You go on ahead Huritt, I will take two of your warriors and head to the Southern Forest, near to the Pit…you must stay with Spirit Wolf and stay as near to her as you can, I fear a new beast may have joined the fight…Asemota talked of conjuring the Kachina Warrior, or the 'Bhati' as he called it. We must pray that his gamble has paid off,' said Akima, placing his hand affectionately on Huritt's shoulder.

'Chogan? And Kimi?' said Huritt.

'You sense it too? I must go to them.'

Huritt bid farewell to his father and turned to command his troops to follow, all diligently obeying and placing themselves into neat formation behind him, their long bows and arrows at the ready. He tried not to think of his brother's and his sister's fate, it petrified him not knowing what had become of them, but he had to leave that to his father now. As the eldest son, it was his duty to confront the supernatural beast Taraka, the ancient Piasa with whom no one, as legend would have it, had done battle with for nearly two millennia. With men and women from the Illiniweck tribes he had the finest people under his command, and they would follow him to the death, although he was not about to sacrifice them lightly.

Moving deftly in formation, along the trail to the Horseshoe Lake, Huritt and his warriors soon arrived at the tree line against the lake shore. With their arrows poised within the tension of their bow strings, beads of sweat upon their brows, they were confined to watching the grotesque spectacle before them.

Taraka had swooped over the forest and landed square in front of the fearsome Bhati. The two beasts stood tense and motionless for a moment until both, in unison it seemed, let out ear shattering, ungodly roars – then they clashed. The Demon lashed his lethal tail towards the head of the Bhati warrior - who easily blocked the hideous weapon with his mighty sword arm. In return, and at blinding speed, the Bhati kicked Taraka mid torso sending him sprawling across the silt and dirt of the shore.

In retaliation Taraka charged menacingly at the Bhati, the Demon's contorted evil face all too plain to see, even by Huritt and his troop nearby. The Bhati became trapped in Taraka's giant antlers as they locked around his torso, allowing Taraka to thrash wildly, shaking the giant warrior violently in the mud and the sand.

Spirit Wolf emerged from nowhere, spotting her opportunity, charging out of the forest - sending branches, leaves, dust and thicket out into the air. At speed she cut across the wide shore line like a missile, her one focus to capitalise on Taraka's distraction and aim for the base of his tail. With all of her mighty power and force, she leapt high and descended to sink her enormous razor sharp teeth into the fleshiest part of the Demon's tail, preparing herself to hang on for dear life. Taraka reacted instantly and stood away from the Bhati, leaving the ancient warrior to flail in the silt. A bone crunching evil cry poured from Taraka's throat as he felt the base of his tail being torn from his body, his futile attempt to gain height thwarted by Spirit Wolf's weight and momentum helping her to keep her footing. Enough time was made for the Bhati to gather himself again and charge with his huge curved sword arm, cutting a swathe through the air before it lashed at Taraka's wings, tearing into the tough folded skin between the Demon's arms and torso. Wings and tail now potentially disabled, the onlookers all hoped that the Demon would now face his demise.

*

Panic stricken, hoping beyond hope that help would come, Asemota comforted his beloved Anippe in his arms as he lay her gently on a couch in the lobby of the Visitor Centre. She was not only his daughter, she had been his working companion for so long, his right arm, his conscience, he could not comprehend her demise – after all he had caused this. He cradled her head, blood seeping from her nose and her ears, her breathing so shallow. All sense of the encounter with Krell had diminished and his mind was now insensitive to the horrors being unleashed by Taraka.

Anippe regained a little consciousness and tried to whisper something to him. Asemota held her head and caressed her brow, trying to calm her, trying to reassure her, tears welling in his eyes.

'You must make sure Sam knows of The Cloth…he must use the it at the right time, Joyce will help him, she is very clever…she has learned so much…you must save Sam…' Anippe said, falling unconscious again.

Asemota tried to console her.

'Rest your mind daughter, we will prevail…I will get help…I must get help, I can't lose you,' he whispered.

He cradled her further, willing her to stay alive, but even with all of his powers and her strong will, he feared the worst. She had suffered a terrible blow from Krell and despite her mental and physical courage, Asemota didn't know how she could be saved.

*

Krell had vanished and the scene of carnage greeting Akima in the woods by the Pit was heart breaking; a scene of slaughter greeted his eyes, with many of his warriors laying slain on the ground. Only a handful of Chogan's warriors remained, but where was his son – and where was Kimi? He shouted at the top of his voice, a call of distress bellowing from his dry throat until he heard a cry from deeper within the wood. He raced to where the noise had come from, stumbling over ground laden branches and thicket before he saw the disheveled sight of his kin. Kimi was crying, lying next to a limp figure of a man who had been forced, it seemed, against the base of a tree – it was Akima's beloved youngest son, Chogan, and he had perished.

Akima dropped to his knees, embracing his child and crying out in sheer anguish, the rain smattering his head as he tried to clear the war paint from streaming into his eyes. Woefully, Kimi explained how Chogan had died heroically, how he had valiantly defended the other warriors, and how in the end he had thrown his body in front of her to protect her before Krell grabbed him and pummeled him against the tree with one hand, the very tree which Chogan now rested against.

Whether Akima heard all of what Kimi had said, it was not certain – but something clicked inside him, and his heart filled with a mighty rage.

'Follow me Kimi, and the rest of you - now!' shouted Akima. 'Move quickly to the Centre, Krell will be there I am sure of it, he will be hunting Asemota and Anippe!'

Nobody hesitated, not even Kimi who was distraught at seeing the demise of her twin brother, yet she knew she would have to gather strength and join her father in an attempt to defeat the vile Krell.

*

Slowly and deliberately, Krell opened the main glass door to the lobby of the Visitor Centre, gloating at having caught up with his adversary once again. An evil power coursed through his veins, and he couldn't help the wry smile emerge from his contorted smug face.

Asemota sensed Krell enter the lobby but did not take his eyes or move his arms away from the lifeless Anippe. She had passed just moments ago and Asemota's grief was insurmountable; he held her head tight to his chest and prayed to God that her soul would be protected, and that on this night good would prevail over evil, for her and everyone's sake.

'You cannot win Pottery Maker, your people are defeated and soon Taraka will slay the Spirit Wolf - accept your defeat and hand me The Parchment... and The Cloth,' said Krell, evilly.

The deep resonance in Krell's voice perturbed Asemota; clearly the evil man was growing in stature and power, driven by an evil force that was becoming more difficult to contain. His thought's raced as he turned to stare at the giant, the grief for Anippe was all consuming, but now it was a matter of survival – and of protecting Sam.

Quietly and assuredly, Kimi and Akima had entered the Visitor Centre through a side entrance, allowing them to stalk unseen towards the rear of the lobby area, near to the side of the auditorium. Asemota braced himself to resume his battle with Krell, oblivious to his comrades who were hidden out of sight. He was unaware that Kimi had taken an accurate aim with one of her arrows so that it was now sighted on the weak spot under Krell's left arm. As he was about to lunge towards Krell, Asemota hurriedly stopped in his tracks, watching the arrow hit the imposter, and for the first time seeing how such an arrow had been able to penetrate his enemies flesh.

Krell let out a terrifying yelp and roared at Asemota, ripping the arrow out of his own body before discarding it disparagingly across the tiled floor.

A chance to exact revenge, Akima thought, whilst Krell was distracted he would charge and drive his hunting knife into the open wound and slay him.

Akima could not move quickly enough and Asemota could not react in time to stop Krell deflecting the blow from the knife intended for the gaping wound. The brave Akima had aimed for the spot but had fooled himself into thinking he could overcome the speed and power of the giant. Krell grabbed Akima's wrist and smashed the bone handled hunting knife out of his hand, placing Akima at his mercy. The inflicted blow was violent and final, leaving the lifeless warrior crumpled on the lobby floor. Mike Tremble, the Akima, Chief of the Illiniweck tribe was dead, a forlorn hero to the last.

The subsequent charge of rage by Asemota lifted Krell clean off the floor as he drove his shoulder hard into Krell's chest sending him crashing through the entrance doors, pieces of glass and wooden paneling flying everywhere. Once more into the driving rain and sodden ground, the two men fought, raining blows and kicks upon each other, each of them with the ardent intent to destroy the other man.

*

Inexplicable was the loss to Kimi of her father and her twin brother, as was the loss of Anippe to Asemota, yet so committed were they in the struggle for the soul of every being on Earth, that they would not (and could not) allow their individual grief to overcome them. The battle between Spirit Wolf, the Bhati and Taraka raged on, the creatures having circled the entirety of the Horseshoe Lake shore in their tumultuous carnage. Asemota continued his struggle with the gruesome Krell, all the while thinking that he must get back to the Pit and to Sam.

Gallant troops of Illiniweck warriors chased and harried through the two unfolding events, taking opportunity to fire the occasional volley of arrows to distract the enemy. Huritt ordered his troop to keep pace with the beasts as best they could; he did not know that his father had been killed and he was not sure if his brother Chogan was still alive, he assumed the worst. He would fight on with his men and women and hope above all else that Sam and Asemota could find a way to end this horror and bring peace.

∗

The warmth of the Pit was a temporary, albeit welcome relief for the three tired souls as they clambered to get near the glowing hearth and dry themselves. A little respite and time to think was much needed.

'What should we do now Sam? How on earth is this going to end?' said Joyce, helping a very tired James to sit down closer to the kiln.

'I need The Cloth desperately – but Asemota has it, we kept The Parchment and The Cloth separate on purpose, the reasons will become obvious. I will need it for the time of the change, I only hope that he can make it here. The change depends on so many things, I have no idea if it will all come to fruition,' said Sam, troubled.

'I take it Krell has not yet been defeated?' said James, anxiously.

'We can assume not…at least not yet, I'd hoped with the combined strength of the tribe they would have slowed Krell down, allowing Asemota a chance to break free and join us here at the Pit. Confront Krell he must, yet Asemota knows he must return to me…he has The Cloth…and it can only be passed to me at the right time,' said Sam.

'What do you mean?' said Joyce.

'We will see. The ritual of The Cloth is a

dangerous one according to Asemota. If Krell gets his hands on it, we will all be in peril.'

'What about the board and The Parchment?' said James.

'I am guessing that Krell and Taraka know that The Parchment is needed for The Cloth to work,' said Sam.

Silence fell within the small room of the Pit, all three staring at the hearth and the glow of the kiln opening, watching the shadows flicker and dance across the chequered board and the little cotton wood table it rested upon. From time to time anxious looks turned around to glance at the trap door entrance, waiting, hoping…praying for Asemota to return quickly.

*

Despite the resurging battle with Krell, returning to the Pit was never far from Asemota's mind and logic suggested that if the plan with the Bhati had worked, Sam and the others would already be there. In any event he had The Cloth sewn into his pocket, and he could not succumb and allow Krell to take it from him; at the earliest opportunity he would have to break free from the giant man's grapples.

Away from the Visitor Centre, as if by instinct, they had found themselves further towards the Pit, in a place by a number of burial mounds adjacent to the expanse of the ancient Plaza. Krell's exuberant strength was starting to weaken Asemota even more so, and he was goading him.

'You are weakening Pottery Maker, I know of your secrets and I shall claim them…where is the sacred

Cloth old man? I know you have it, The Maker always has it, give it to me - you vile bastard!' Krell said, despicably.

Asemota became enraged, which momentarily gave him new found strength, allowing him to break free from his menacing attacker and dash at full speed the remaining short distance to the Pit.

*

A weary Spirit Wolf gazed at Taraka, instinctively perplexed at how the Demon seemed to have regained his strength after the attack from her and the Bhati, when ripping at Taraka's tail and wings. The Wolf could only attack sporadically now, and only when Taraka was distracted by the giant clay warrior. Higher and dryer ground was needed and for that Spirit Wolf would have to cajole Taraka away from the lake, back towards Monk's Mound, exploiting the effect of her apparent weakness.

Taraka was enraged and was hell bent on tearing both Spirit Wolf and the giant soldier apart. On the water's edge he grappled with the Bhati, still trying to use his deformed tail to lash out and behead the sword wielding adversary. The Bhati was able to fend off the weakened tail lashing about its head, yet was finding it difficult to move its feet in the sodden ground. Spirit Wolf, herself dodging the whipping tail for a countless time, charged at Taraka's rear, knocking the Demon forward and off balance towards the warrior. In an instant the mighty Bhati kicked Taraka against his hips sending the Demon flailing into the lake waters. Opportune time for Spirit Wolf to nod her head and beckon the Bhati to move and seek refuge on dry ground.

*

Standing near to the Pit entrance, Joyce was first to hear Asemota's shrill, and she quickly prized open the heavy wooden framed trap door, ushering the others out and up the steps to greet the cold rain once more. Before they could take cover in the trees Asemota was upon them, waving his hand furiously at the trio to keep moving, but they would not. Sam could see the perilous contorted face of his grandfather as the old man lunged for the Pit entrance.

The trio froze as they saw Krell come into view, and with one almighty leap the giant man crashed into Asemota, making them both fall through the trap door and roll in a violent tussle into the Pit itself. Krell's strength seemed to have doubled, and Asemota tried desperately to remove The Cloth stitched to his own trousers, hoping that one of his companions might see it and take it from him. Sam and Joyce had already reacted by following Asemota, yet they could not approach the grappling men, only being able to watch the milieu in sheer angst.

In the confined space of the Pit, furious fighting between Krell and Asemota intensified as the battle for supremacy continued. The earthen kiln fire appeared to react and its glow became brighter, roaring at the two adversaries, casting larger than life shadows of the men across the room.

'Look The Cloth - Krell has wrestled it from Asemota's hand and he is trying to put it on his own face, I must help!' cried Sam.

Emphatically, Sam stepped further into the room towards them, and at the right moment, when Krell had his back to the entrance, Sam leapt quickly onto Krell's torso, placing his strong arm around Krell's neck in an attempt to distract him. For a split second it worked and Asemota was able to snatch The Cloth out of Krell's hand, only then to see it fall onto the dirt ridden Pit floor.

By now James had reached the bottom of the steps, and in a futile attempt, he tried to retrieve The Cloth, placing himself in mortal danger. Within moments Krell had thrown Sam off his back and sent him flying to the ground, at the same time bowling over the cotton wood table where the chequered board and figurines rested. Inevitably, James got caught in the action and suffered a glancing blow from Krell's flailing hands, he too sent careering and into the wall adjacent to the Pit opening, knocking him out cold.

Joyce watched on in horror, feeling helpless, trying not to lose her nerve – Krell seemed unstoppable. Asemota gathered as much strength as he could and charged at Krell once again, pressing him up against the roaring hearth.

Almost completely out of breath, The Pottery Maker screamed.

'Grab The Cloth Joyce - give it to Sam…now!'

*

Kimi had finally appraised Huritt of the tragedy and he had asked her to send all the remaining warriors to his position near Monk's Mound, sensing that the battle would soon enter its final stage. He had asked her to accompany him too, but she knew her place was to return to the Pit as quickly as she could and help protect Asemota once again.

She doubled back around the forest perimeter, placing herself out of sight, as she watched her fellow braves running at pace in the opposite direction across the Plaza towards Huritt, and to await his orders. Kimi strained her athletic body to its limit, drawing her bow and arrow as she moved closer to the Pit; the commotion inside could be heard all too clearly.

A scene of carnage greeted Kimi's eyes; James lay unconscious, slumped against a wall, the impact causing rotten plaster to fall around him, and Sam was disorientated, writhing around the floor holding onto The Cloth with his hands. Krell and Asemota were tangled in a brutal wrestling hold that neither seemed to be able to break free from. Joyce was shouting at the top of her voice.

'I have given you The Cloth Sam, place it on your face before it's too late – do it now!'

Sam finally did so and instantly felt the coarse texture of the weave envelop his face, as if a strong hand had grasped every nerve on his head forcing him closer to the ground. Surprisingly, he felt a surge of sudden energy and all the pain of his injuries seemed to subside as The Cloth wrapped itself even tighter around his face and skull.

Out of the corner of his eye, Krell saw this happening, and, roaring with evil rage, managed to force Asemota away from him, landing a terrifying blow to Asemota's head, sending the unconscious Pottery Maker crashing against the gaping hole of the kiln fire. Immediately, Krell turned his attention to Sam, grappling The Cloth on Sam's head, before eventually tearing it from his face.

With an arrow drawn, Kimi capitalised on Krell's distraction with The Cloth and aimed at the wound under Krell's arm again. A horrifying shrill shook the very walls of the Pit as the arrow found its mark, Krell screaming in agony and falling to the ground.

'Take this Kimi,' said Sam, passing her the deer hide sack with The Parchment inside. 'Run with all your strength to Huritt and the other warriors and stay protected. Joyce go with her, help her, I will join you as soon as I can – now go, both of you!'

*

Out of sight, two kilometres to the east of the Cahokian Monk's Mound, an Illinois State Police helicopter, carrying a young Police Superintendent from India, swept down from the sky, arriving in whisper mode to land deftly on a small clearing within a coppice of misshapen Cyprus trees.

Raju Kumar stepped hurriedly out of the aircraft, instinctively bending his body to avoid the rotor blades, before he waved the pilot farewell and started to sprint along the pebbled track which would lead him to Cahokia. He was clutching the leather bound papyrus papers of the Atharva-Veda, the sacred Hindu text which had been protected for centuries by the Nath Sampradaya of Balrampur and Tulsipur. The Guru-Nath had realised the grave consequences and had changed his mind, convinced that the Atharva-Veda was the only thing that could condemn the vile Taraka back to Hell.

Raju's lean, fit body did not fail him as he ran at full stretch, heading towards a rendezvous point that only moments before he had been able to arrange with Joyce. She had been jubilant in the knowledge of his arrival, although she had managed to tell him how desperate the situation was, fueling his drive to make contact as soon as he could.

*

The clouds appeared to become darker and the driving rain remained relentless as Spirit Wolf enacted her ploy with Taraka. She hid once again in the Northern Forest, near to the base of the colossal Monk's Mound, only this time she felt sure the trees would betray her position as branches and leaves were torn away by the arduous wind. The menacing Bhati warrior was out on open ground, parading across the base of the Mound like a prowling animal, walking this way and that, waiting for the Demon to appear. Spirit Wolf watched him and felt some comfort with his presence; but she had never felt so tired and weak and she wondered if she could find the spiritual strength she needed to continue on and belie Taraka of his quest, yet she simply had to try.

Even with faltering wings, Taraka had managed to hover his great bulk over the extended line of tree coppices, extending from the Horseshoe Lake. Luridly and defiantly, the Demon landed once again on the top of Monk's Mound, his evil roar and hideous fiery orange eyes directed towards the Bhati, who simply glared back at him, not fazed at all by Taraka's goading and grimacing.

Taraka sensed Spirit Wolf nearby, detecting her deliberation and smelling her fear; she was indeed weak, and once he had defeated the Bhati, the Demon surmised she would become easy prey.

Without any further hesitation, the Bhati warrior sprang to the top of the Mound in two giant leaps, facing off the evil beast. Spirit Wolf reacted and moved out of the thicket, slowly stalking up the northern face of the Mound - the opposite side to her companion - putting Taraka between her and the clay warrior.

A ferocious, ancient war cry bellowed eerily from the Bhati's chest, and with his mighty sword arm raised, the terracotta warrior charged, intending to leap and bring his sword down on the Demon's head. Taraka was ready and had anticipated the attack, stooping his enormous body to the ground, before spinning out of the way of the sword and lashing his tail towards the Bhati, who was still in mid-flight. Taraka's tail wrapped around the Bhati's torso, pulverising the warrior's pelvis, before the crushing effect tore the Bhati in half, sending his legs flailing and the remainder of his body falling onto the sodden ground, where he lay on his back, his sword arm still outstretched.

*

Krell gathered his wits and left the carnage within the Pit behind, smashing his way through the trap door and out into the forest nearby. He had become incensed at Kimi for injuring him again and this fueled his rage, notwithstanding that she now had The Parchment. *Yet that would soon be his*, he thought; *his quest would be relentless, he had The Cloth - how could he fail now? He would hunt Kimi down, claim The Parchment and end this debacle.*

*

The deer hide sack containing The Parchment was drenched, and Kimi grasped it tightly, so afraid she might lose it. She and Joyce ran as hard as they could, never daring to look back as they made their way to a small burial mound, very near, but out of sight from Monk's Mound, praying that Raju would appear at any moment. To their relief they did not have to wait long, Raju had made a point of diverting away from the track, preferring instead to skirmish the coppices to avoid detection, before he reached where he thought he should be.

'You have the Script?' said Joyce, gasping for air, yet utterly relieved to see the policeman.

'Of course, but we must act now. As I approached I am sure I witnessed the terrible demise of a clay warrior at the hands of the monstrous Taraka, such evil I could not have imagined. We must have courage and climb the steps to confront the Demon with the Atharva-Veda. God help us, he must be destroyed!' shouted Raju.

'I will move to the base of the steps and wait for any sign of Krell, I feel sure he will make his presence known there - he must have taken the bait,' said Kimi.

'But what of Sam?' said Raju.

'He has Asemota to protect him, he has the Pottery Maker, and they will chase Krell and harry him, mark my words,' said Joyce.

'The Maker? So the prophecy is true, everything we see before us is unfolding as we had imagined,' said Raju, clutching the Vedic Script passionately.

'You will have to keep The Parchment and protect it with your life, if it falls into the hands of Taraka and

Krell, all will be lost – I know you know that Kimi,'
said Joyce.

*

Huritt and the remaining warriors had seen the
Bhati fall. They marched quickly and stealthily,
ascending the west face of the Mound, firing volley
after volley of arrows towards Taraka. The Demon
swatted the arrows like flies, not bothering or paying
attention to the presence of the tribe, his sole focus
was now with Spirit Wolf.

The Demon stood astride the fallen Bhati, gloating
over his victory, and now he was ready to end the
Spirit Beast. Yet something stopped him
momentarily, he could sense that the Vedic Script was
near and in defiance he let out a screeching, unearthly
roar, his fiery eyes glowing brighter and his face
becoming more contorted with evil as he did so.

Spirit Wolf stood on the northern most tip of the
Mound, two hundred metres or so from where
Taraka was standing over the Bhati. She was ready for
one final assault, ready to give her all, her fear
subsiding as she and Taraka faced each other, both
poised, snarling and growling.

Shouting at the top of her voice, Kimi yelled
towards Raju and Joyce, who by now had already
reached the half way point of the ascent, where the
first tier of the Mound joined with the second. Joyce
and the Superintendent turned around anxiously trying
to catch Kimi's words, seeing her look at them but at
the same time point out towards the expanse of the
Plaza.

'Krell, I can see Krell fast approaching…and I can

see Asemota and Sam, but they are far behind!' shouted Kimi.

'Run to us Kimi – gain higher ground, you cannot fight him on your own!' Joyce screamed.

'We must reach the top,' Raju interrupted. 'We cannot get involved in this fight, Kimi will have to defend her position and pray Asemota and Sam get there in time, our job is to distract Taraka.'

Holding her arm persuasively, Raju raced with Joyce up the remaining steps shouting at her to place the Vedic Script above her head. Taraka had already been disturbed by its presence and now the sacred spiritual aura of the Script unsettled the Demon even more so, making him writhe and grimace, edging him away from the fallen Bhati.

Her deeper senses sharpening, Spirit Wolf detected that Asemota and Sam were near, and so the time had come. Any fears of the Maker and his protégé's demise had to be assuaged, her part was to destroy the Demon, laying her life on the line if she had to. The Wolf charged.

*

The whip of the Demon's tail came out of the dark, unseen, and its strength was miscalculated by the Great Wolf. The hardened tip of the tail obliterated her front legs, breaking them both at the femur and she fell in diabolical pain. This was too much to bear for Huritt and his warriors, and they charged to the top of the Mound firing repeatedly at the torso of the putrid Piasa. Taraka covered his torso with his wings, some of the arrows notably starting to penetrate previous glances on his body, yet the injuries were still not to his detriment and he remained powerful, defiant, unrelenting.

*

Her arrow poised, Kimi steadied her nerves as she climbed a few steps to higher ground, watching Krell reach the base of the Mound. She fired once and quickly placed another arrow in her bow, the first arrow serving only as a distraction with Krell swatting it away. The closer he came, she thought, the more chance she would have of hitting the wound. He slowed his pace and started to walk up the steps to where Kimi was standing on the small plateau at the top of the first tier.

Kimi backed up a little further and fired a second arrow, but this time she stumbled, falling over a wooden plinth adjacent to the steps, making her lose the sack containing The Parchment. Krell saw his chance and frantically grasped at the sack, trying to remove The Parchment from it.

Asemota had gained ground, not slowing for a second, and before Krell could retrieve the sacred article, Asemota leapt onto Krell's body, placing him in a bear hug to prevent him from pulling The Parchment away.

Sam was not far behind and once again he joined the milieu, trying to wrestle The Cloth from Krell's hand. Yet the same fate befell Sam as before - one sweeping blow from Krell was all it took to send him crashing down a number of steps where he lay unable to move, pain searing through his body once again.

The fighting had really started to take its toll on Asemota, his injuries were now making him suffer badly, and he was almost passing out with acute pain. It was a matter of survival now; his despair was difficult to hide as the monstrous Krell was getting the better of him. Yet through it all, Asemota knew he would have to act accordingly, it was for him to create the defining moment, which if not carried out would plunge the world into a putrid eternal darkness.

The presence of mind from both Raju and Joyce, in their efforts to contain the Demon, would be paramount. Near to the top of the wooden steps they stood, staring at the mighty stature of Taraka; he was marveling at his fallen foe, the Great *Manitou Mahweewa*, the Great Spirit Wolf, who had been maimed irrevocably. And the Bhati, who was lying on his back, completely motionless without his legs, still with his sword arm in a prominent upright position facing skyward. Joyce cried out at the demise of the Wolf, the Spirit Beast was lying on her side, seemingly barely able to move, her front legs having been crushed by the whipping of the Demon's tail. Raju calmed his companion and gently took hold of the Atharva-Veda. As he did so, Taraka slowly turned to face them.

'Joyce, the Atharva-Veda is key now, we must not overreact, let me show you which part we must recite. This is a sacred book of charms and within it are certain hymns that can ward off and even contain evil, the Guru-Nath told me which verse to recite...and we must do it together...Taraka must see us and he must hear us!' shouted Raju.

'But the book worked on its own last time, without any recital,' said Joyce.

'I know, but this time we have to perform the

recital; he will be wise to the book and he will either move away or simply stand his ground in defiance...but he is turning towards us - look, he sees us now!'

'The words are in ancient Hindi; can you speak the words Joyce?'

'Yes I think I can.'

'Part of Hymn Sixteen, the prayer and charm against demons...' said Raju, resolutely.

Together they chanted the words of the charm, and by now Taraka had turned to face them fully, scowling and grimacing, the epitome of evil - yet he was unable to step forward, thwarted by the power of the Vedic Script.

There could be no compromise now, the duo had to be prepared for any outcome, never wavering from their task.

'May the potent Gods who destroy the Demons, bless us and shelter us, and may Taraka be overcome, as he is a voracious fiend that must be driven away!

We pierce thee with this sacred Script so that our men and women you will not slay.'

The chant was repeated over and over again, and Taraka edged back. It started to work, and the pair shouted louder and more vehemently. The Demon stopped a few metres away from the end of what remained of the Bhati's torso, Taraka's rear still facing the forlorn figure of Spirit Wolf, his despicable eyes of fire fixed on Joyce and Raju, it was if - for a moment - they had actually contained him. The Piasa roared, bellowed and cursed all manner of foul things but he could not move forward, and so too was he finding it difficult to retreat. Come what may this would be a last defiant stand for him, he refused to be defeated, confident that Krell would conquer soon enough.

*

Hardly able to speak or breathe, Asemota clung onto Krell for dear life, grasping the giant man's torso as tightly as he could to suppress him, but Asemota felt his own supernatural strength start to ebb, fear almost overwhelming him. Krell had already managed to wrench The Parchment out of the deer hide sack and he had placed The Cloth on his own face, The Cloth now enveloping and shaping around his evil head. It was impossible for Asemota to rip The Cloth from Krell's face and try to contain him at the same time, Asemota's only hope was to hang on long enough for help to arrive.

Krell's body surged with the new found power The Cloth had given him; Asemota thought that every sinew in his own body would snap and that all would be lost. The Cloth fell away from Krell's head revealing his evil facial imprint, indelibly marked on the woven material. If Krell was able to merge The Cloth and The Parchment, it would truly be the end. With one almighty last effort, Asemota screamed at Kimi, who was trying with all her courage to get to her feet.

'Pass me your hunting knife Kimi!' shouted Asemota at the top of his voice.

Kimi registered the words and rallied to the call. She hurriedly unhooked her bone handled, long bladed hunting knife from her leather belt and placed it as best she could in Asemota's hand, avoiding the thrashing of Krell's head and body.

The Cloth and The Parchment lay apart from each other on the steps and with Asemota losing more of his strength, Krell was able to twist himself away and grab at the sacred items. Kimi was horrified at seeing Krell on his feet and was at a loss seeing Asemota's demise.

Krell had only one focus. He picked up the sacred Cloth, admiring his own emblazoned image upon it, and moved to set it within The Parchment in the place which he and his vile Mentor had discovered when deciphering the Snefru Stele. *Soon I will have the power, the very essence of which will enshrine me as The Pottery Maker*, Krell thought.

Most bravely, Kimi reacted; seeing what Krell was about to do, she started to wrestle The Parchment away from him, making it difficult for him to place The Cloth within The Parchment properly, but it was only short lived, Krell pushed her away and she fell against the steps once again, only this time harder. She lay unconscious.

*

A supernatural roar of defiance emanated from the Demon as he sensed that Krell was about to triumph. No more would he bend to the Vedic Script; he would now see his protégé become The Maker. He tilted his grotesque giant head back and raised his wings, his voice roaring ominously towards the heavens. Yet through all this he did not see or sense Spirit Wolf behind him, who had courageously managed to twist herself onto her back before springing onto her hind legs.

In tremendous agony and in a death throe, she charged at Taraka, covering the ground as fast as she could, running solely on her rear quarters before she pounded Taraka from behind with all her might and spiritual power. She leapt onto the Demon's torso, sinking her teeth into his neck, and with such force being used, Taraka fell forward uncontrollably, instantly falling onto the upright sword of the Bhati. The sword ominously penetrated The Piasa's evil heart, severing it completely in two.

At exactly the moment the Demon's heart was pierced, by some act of extraordinary inner sense, Asemota fell upon the giant Krell just as he was about to finally merge the Cloth with the Parchment. The Pottery Maker plunged the hunting knife into Krell's open wound, this time piercing his heart fully.

The evil Mentor and protégé fell to their deaths in unison, each crying out as if the very bowels of Hell had opened up and consumed them, such were their high pitched screams. Krell slumped, The Cloth in his hand falling away from the Parchment, never the twain to meet.

The monstrous demonic body of Taraka slowly but surely dissipated into the cold, damp air, his evil entity crumbling into oblivion – his very dark soul separating out from his vile torso before neither existed in the real world. Shortly after Taraka's demise, the remaining part of the Bhati's torso did the same, dissolving into a tornado of golden dust, which reached for the heavens before the warrior's essence was finally lost amongst the stars.

Spirit Wolf lay alone on the grass covered mound, her shiny silver coat slowly moving up and down as she breathed ever more shallow. She had sacrificed herself, knowing that the blow from the sword would not only penetrate the Demon but that it would penetrate her own heart too. Huritt and his warriors started to move towards her forlornly, she had saved them, the brave and mighty Spirit Wolf had given her life to save them all.

Sam lay on the ground in mental and physical shock, unable to comprehend what had befallen upon him and his comrades on this night. He could see people starting to rally and he could hear the sound of feint joyous raptures, knowing that Krell and the Demon Taraka had been defeated. Although desperate to get to his father, Sam heard the commands from Huritt - who had dispatched a number of warriors to rescue James from the Pit and make sure he was safe and well. Yet where was Asemota, his grandfather? The man who he had known as Walters, a man who had acted as a mentor to him most of his adult life, where was he in this victorious hour? Sam feared the worst…and then he heard the subtle cry.

'Take me to my *Manitou Mahweewa* – I must be with my beloved Spirit Wolf,' cried Asemota .

Kimi had managed to gather her senses and called upon Huritt to help her carry Asemota up the remaining steps and along the Mound to where Spirit Wolf lay. Other warriors helped, carrying the heroic Asemota in a human cradle before placing him by the side of his Spirit Beast, so that he could be with her to the last.

The embrace from Raju was one of sheer joy and utter relief as he held Joyce, having the utmost respect for her bravery. She handed Raju the Vedic Script and thanked him for his tenacity, hailing him as a saviour amongst men and women. She quickly turned her attention to Sam, clambering down the steps to reach him, handing him the sacred Parchment and Cloth she had collected on the way – he would know what to do with them now.

The Illiniweck warriors laid their spiritual leader in the bosom of the great Spirit Wolf and she coiled her head towards her chest, nuzzling Asemota closer towards her as he too lay mortally wounded, each breath of his becoming harder to manage. They smiled at each other, Asemota grasping at her fur, tears running down his cheeks as he gazed into her fading blue eyes, she was losing her grip on life. For a thousand years had she had roamed the Earth protecting the Pottery Maker's against evil, now it was time for her to pass, time to pass in peace knowing that her greatest foe of all had been defeated – the mighty Piasa, Taraka, had been conquered.

A solemn prayer chant murmured from the warriors, Huritt and Kimi standing side by side, encouraging their brethren to make their voices ring out. The enchantment did indeed ring out and Asemota and his beautiful Spirit Wolf took their last breath together, their souls passing to another place, their very existence on this Earth transcending into folklore.

Asemota lay still. Spirit Wolf, mesmerisingly and

assuredly turned to a white earthen clay before she slowly dissolved into the Mound, spreading her essence and her being across the sacred, hallowed ground.

A gentle caress by Joyce's hand was enough to help Sam get to his feet. He clutched The Cloth and The Parchment, staring at them intently.

'The time is yours now Sam, the battle has been won. Great sacrifices have been made, but it's your time, you must embrace it...do what is right,' Joyce smiled as she spoke, loving eyes greeting him as Sam smiled back, adoring her...she was his hero and he was hers.

Chapter 22

Transition

Dawn was near. The rising sun was just below the eastern horizon and no one had noticed that the rain had stopped and the sky was clearing. The partial brilliance of the full moon was giving way to the bright orange reflection, which by now had embraced the remnant wisps of clouds.

The chanting of the ancient verse had subsided, the warriors standing in silence over the forlorn figure of Asemota; he would be buried in a spiritual place within the sacred grounds of Cahokia, in a place known only to the guarding clan of the Illiniweck tribe.

The tribe were consumed by the passing of Asemota and Spirit Wolf, and all who had survived were gathering on top of Monk's Mound to pay homage. Huritt and Kimi had embraced each other within the crowd, not letting go of one another, consoling each other in desperate grief. Trying to cope with the loss of their father and brother would be so profound over the forthcoming weeks and months.

Two tribal warriors had returned from the Pit, walking with a tired, disheveled James, who was heavily bandaged around his head and was carrying a long stick to help him cope with a slight limp. The sight of his son sat next to Joyce on the base step of the Mound made James smile, his pain subsiding, copious relief and joy filling his heart.

A moment of hesitation hung in the air as Sam contemplated his happenstance; such predestination could not be taken lightly. The Cloth in one hand and The Parchment in the other – to perform this act now would ensure decades or even centuries of uncertainty, a destiny hard to comprehend, yet one deep down he felt he must endure.

A temporary reprieve as Joyce nudged Sam for him to clasp his eyes on his father coming towards them across the Plaza. In a brief moment Sam looked away from his predicament, catching his father's beaming smile and wave, filling Sam with unmitigated joy, making him tremble.

As James stepped closer, the two accompanying warriors clambered up the wooden steps of the Mound, rushing to join their brethren in this time of mourning and reprieve, leaving the three erstwhile companions alone together.

No one else seemed to be around the base of the Mound now, and Sam returned to his undertaking, embracing the presence of his father and the courageous Joyce.

The horrid image of Krell scorched on The Cloth was disconcerting, yet facing such adversity, Sam placed The Cloth on his face. He felt the tautness return as the woven fabric wrapped itself around his head, forcing itself onto his cheekbones and his eyes, making him arch backwards and lean his body against a higher step.

The burning sensation returned and his breathing became rapid and shallow, fueling his anxiety to remove The Cloth, although accepting that this time it could not be forced and that it should fall naturally from his face. Minutes passed and finally The Cloth gently loosened, Sam sitting upright to catch it as it fell calmly into his hand.

The Cloth had transformed once again from his aura, and there he saw upon it, a startling emblazoned image of himself, an uncanny real life resemblance of his facial features, almost photographic in nature.

The pictorial image in The Parchment was shimmering and fluctuating in every part; the hieroglyphs on the side of the chequered board representation were flickering violently, and the images of the figurines were in a state of flux – shifting in and out of view. Most notable was the image of the mirror, its golden frame seemed to be holographic, prompting something, inviting Sam to perform an act.

The depicted image of Asemota within the mirror was fading, as too was the tall figure of The Pottery Maker stood next to the representation of the earthen kiln. Sam placed The Cloth perfectly over the image of the golden framed mirror and watched in complete awe at the transition. His own emblazoned image on The Cloth seemed to rise and then descend slowly and deliberately into the mirror, bright light shining momentarily as the image metamorphosed. Not a word was said, nor any action taken as James and Joyce remained perplexed, their captivation insurmountable.

The Parchment continued to shimmer and fluctuate until finally it settled, Sam's mirror reflection all too plain to see, with his deep brown eyes, grey tint in his hair and perfectly shaped nose revealed. The tall, dark figure standing against the kiln had also morphed, the unmistakable gait of Sam in the picture being clear to any observer.

The Cloth had morphed with The Parchment and now he, Samuel Campbell, a descendant from an ancient lineage, was now truly The Pottery Maker.

*

An eerie silence between the three was broken as Sam started to speak; at first it seemed like a garbled interpretation of what had just happened, but then slowly, the other two recognised he was recounting what Asemota had explained to him, about the enormity of the responsibility now cast upon him. Joyce held Sam's hand and James placed his arm around his son in a small gesture of reassurance, not beginning to understand what lay ahead for the younger man.

'I must continue my mother's work, and my grandfather's for that matter. Certainly he must have worked for centuries to better understand his plight…now I know why there are such books in the Room of Books in the Cairo Museum, they must be his life's work, and that of Anippe's,' said Sam, quietly.

'Now it is all starting to fit,' said James. 'My time in Egypt was not so ill spent as I had thought all those years ago. Anippe showed me the Sacred Snefru Stele and I saw with my own eyes the nature of the prophecy now befallen to you Sam, although I had no idea what it meant at the time. From that day on Anippe must have hatched a plan which meant, I suppose, that I would have a part to play!'

'My belief is that Anippe and Asemota did not have time to reveal much of what they knew, and it is for us to try and find out. We have no idea how this inexplicable prophecy came to be, nor of the legacies that surround it,' said Joyce.

'I have so many questions…we will have so many questions. This world has a supernatural essence; of that we can be sure – but where does that come from? How can it be that The Parchment in my hand exists in such a form…how old is this sacred article? And who on Earth, or from elsewhere for that matter, created it? You spoke of the tablet you saw Dad, reputedly tens of thousands of years old, the transcriptions of which now lie in the Book of the Stele. I will have to learn this and you will have to help me…both of you,' said Sam, staring at his father.

'And what of the chequered board?' said James. 'Most terrifyingly, the clay figurines seem to have a spiritual misdemeanor, as if the little clay representations actually become possessed by the spirits they are meant to look like – how do they jostle so within the kiln? And what about the kiln? It seems to be a law unto itself, a mystery within a mystery.'

'My assumption is that Asemota and Anippe would have had the same questions, their prior research - and now our research - will be paramount. Clearly there must be a supernatural tripartite arrangement between The Parchment, the earthen kiln, and the chequered board with its figurines – my sense tells me that they feed off each other somehow, with one of them perhaps being the dominant essence,' said Joyce.

'The Parchment?' said Sam.

'One can assume nothing, it certainly may control the workings of The Pottery Maker, but what power does it actually hold?' said Joyce.

Raju had departed from the gathering on top of Monk's Mound, humbled by what he had seen and felt from the Illinois tribal people, revelling in their rituals and beguiled by their reverence to such heroism. Clutching the Vedic Script, the young Police Superintendent from India descended to where his new found friends were seated, anxious to have dialogue with them, desirous of wanting to understand more.

'Lest we forget The Atharva-Veda holds so much knowledge and power – it is a Vedic Script that must have been passed through the ages, a Script that would have perhaps been written by so many, although we may never be sure…but my mind hurts to think how it is linked to the prophecy of the Snefru Stele and who, or what, made this come to be?' said Joyce, acknowledging Raju as he sat beside them.

Sam's contemplation of such things was bewitching him and he remained deeply pensive about what the future entailed. The future it seemed was firmly in his hands, literally, and it would be a journey through which he would endeavor to find out the truths of his calling.

He pinched the skin on the back of his hand, seeing a marked difference as the skin returned to normal much more quickly than it had done recently, and he noticed that the pain from his arm and shoulder seemed to be dissipating quickly, as extraordinary power and strength surged through his body.

His deeper sense became overwhelming, every part of his mind reflecting and processing his inner thoughts and consciousness. His grandfather, Asemota, and his mother Anippe had spent a lifetime trying to understand the prophecy beholden to the lineage of which Sam was now part of. A lifetime of discovery written intricately into the revered books everyone had mentioned. Sam wondered if Asemota had sworn after the death of *his* mother, Nadie, that he would try and understand more of which had befallen to the lineage – and, indeed, who was the first person in pre-historic times to be burdened with such a legacy?

Sam hoped for his own sake and those around him, that he would learn quickly and thoroughly, continuing the quest laid down by Asemota and Anippe, to one day honour them with his discoveries.

'Such a legacy has befallen me, and I have no idea how much immortalised I am, I have no sense of how long I will or should now live. How do I prepare for such a forbidding?' said Sam.

'The Vedic Script I have in my hand encapsulates the essence of 'Time' through its spells and charms, and it is a Script I feel sure you must get to know Sam

– its inextricable link to all things said and done here is profound,' said Raju.

'That and so much more,' said Sam. 'I heard mention of the Book of Prophecies, which we assume Krell must have had, a book we must also assume has been dispatched elsewhere, perhaps to a new and unsuspecting evil creature who may wish to delve into its mysteries.'

The last sentiment made Sam shudder, the enormity of his undertaking was enough for him to try and comprehend, but to think of such a legacy of evil, which may strike again, was inconceivable at this moment.

Such vile evil *had* been displayed. The supernatural Piasa had come forth in the shape of the Demon Taraka, a powerful being from another realm or dimension, of that no-one really knew, least those who now survived. Through Taraka's despicable acts, and those of Krell, knowledge of The Pottery Maker's skills and tools of his trade had been revealed and may now be recorded in some form within the Book of the Prophecies. *Damn! That book had to be traced*, thought Sam.

So much work to do, and so much to fathom and learn.

For now, though, there would be a reality. In days to come, the outside world would merely be led to believe that a crazed man named Krell had wreaked havoc upon this night - killing and maiming so many brave people trying to trap him, the same man who had killed the police officers in Chicago, the same man who was now dead.

From the aftermath, strewn bodies, slain by the hand of Krell, now lay scattered across the Mounds of Cahokia, and more time for reflection and prayers would be needed from the Illiniweck people who would pass the night of battle into tribal folklore, to be recounted for all days.

The deaths of his real mother and newly discovered grandfather, a man who had purported to be so many other people for such a long time, would not be comprehended, they would not seem real and this aspect would haunt Sam considerably, he felt. His rational thought was to believe that they had existed to become the most courageous saviours the world was ever likely to see, and they were such people whose plight and sacrifice would live in his memory for an eternity.

Now it was he, Samuel Campbell, who was interned as the saviour, it was he who would be responsible for the very soul of every being on Earth, and it was he who would be the one to carry on such a legacy into a new era, no matter what that era may foretell.

Chapter 23

Manitou

Deep within the coppice, a lone creature walked without falling for the first time, moving away from her warm, nesting surround. For over thirty hours she had lain and stumbled in her prepared den, a den dutifully made for her, with copious amounts of leaves and thick bracken folds, which had embraced her body like a protective warm blanket.

Now that she felt able to walk more robustly, the creature raised her nose fervently and sniffed excitedly at the damp air, her sharp eyes flitting here and flitting there, looking furtively for an opening in the thicket. She had cleaned most of the dried blood from her head and torso, revealing a beautiful shiny silver coat.

The creature walked slowly, continuing to sniff and look around intently at her surroundings. The moon shone bright and could be seen low in the sky through a small gap in the forest, fixing the creatures gaze. As she crept a little awkwardly towards the opening, she slowed further, checking and re-checking all the noises and smells in her vicinity. She moved tentatively out of the small forest and there stood still, gazing across the wind swept grassy meadow towards a log cabin which was billowing heavy smoke from its chimney stack. Further along the meadow was a white house with a veranda surrounding the entire building, the lights from the house shining dimly across the swaying lawn.

Noises could be heard with voices resonating from the log cabin, and worried that she may be seen, the creature stooped in the grass, fixing her attention on the sound of the people. Already the size of an ordinary fully grown wolf, she was keen to hide her bulk as best she could, yet, come what may, her brilliant blue eyes and glistening silver coat would catch the moonlight in such an open space.

Three human figures appeared out of the cabin and walked through the grass towards the white house, two tall dark haired men and a woman with lighter hair were holding each other and talking in low muffled voices. The elder of the two men started to walk briskly towards the entrance of the white house; the woman chased after him, and placed her arm through his. Then she turned around towards the younger man and the wolf stooped lower still.

'Come on Sam!' the woman shouted.

And the woman and the older man disappeared into the house.

The younger man pensively slowed his walk, before nervously coming to a complete halt, preferring to stand momentarily in the grass, midway between the log cabin and the white house. The young man purposefully raised his head as if aware of a presence. Seeing the man's motion, the creature tentatively raised her head too, alerting herself to the man's poise. Slowly but surely the man turned around, fixing his gaze on her brilliant blue eyes. The man's jaw lowered, and he gasped, trying to take a sharp intake of breath.

He rubbed his eyes in disbelief, and stared again…and the wolf smiled.

Printed in Poland
by Amazon Fulfillment
Poland Sp. z o.o., Wrocław

49062507R00251